Way Back

Also by Sara Cox

Till The Cows Come Home (2019)
Thrown (2022)

Way Back

SARA COX

CORONET

First published in Great Britain in 2024 by Coronet
An imprint of Hodder & Stoughton Limited
An Hachette UK company

1

Copyright © Sara Cox 2024

A CIP catalogue record for this title is available from the British Library

Hardback ISBN 9781529392500
Trade Paperback ISBN 9781529392517
ebook ISBN 9781529392524

Typeset in Swift LT STD by Manipal Technologies Limited

Printed and bound in Great Britain by Clays Ltd, Elcograf S.p.A.

Hodder & Stoughton policy is to use papers that are natural, renewable
and recyclable products and made from wood grown in sustainable forests.
The logging and manufacturing processes are expected to conform
to the environmental regulations of the country of origin.

Hodder & Stoughton Limited
Carmelite House
50 Victoria Embankment
London EC4Y 0DZ

www.hodder.co.uk

This book is dedicated to British farmers.

'My grandfather used to say that once in your life you need a doctor, a lawyer, a policeman and a preacher. But every day, three times a day, you need a farmer.'

Brenda Schoepp

She likes the way it's pulling while we're tillin' up her land
She's even kinda crazy 'bout my farmer's tan
She's the only one who really understands what gets me
She thinks my tractor's sexy

Kenny Chesney,
'She Thinks My Tractor's Sexy'

Part One

1

The thing is I can't quite take my eyes off James. And not in a good way. He's still licking the fork.

Twenty-three years and twenty days we've been married and still it astounds me how he licks his cutlery like a burglar wiping a door handle free of fingerprints.

James' tongue has always looked slightly too big for his mouth; it lolls out when he sleeps or concentrates, as if sunbathing, grabbing the chance to dry out from the wetness of his mouth.

The tongue makes him lisp, which I used to find kinda sexy. I used to find most things about him kinda sexy, even his plummy accent and penchant for fast cars and nice watches. But not any more. I pick up his plate before he can lick that too.

'You'll take the pattern off,' Mum would say, back in the eighties when the whole world was garishly patterned and I inexplicably felt hungrier at the end of meals. She wouldn't eat with me, preferring instead a drink.

'Spoilsport.'

'Sorry. Was it nice?'

'Nah.' He shrugs, reaching to put the fork on the retreating plate with a clank. 'Wasn't keen.'

Classic. One of his regular little jokes that. James has a few in his repertoire. There's that one and the one where he chats away on his phone for minutes at a time then hangs up and says, 'Wrong number.'

Quipmaster General is old James. I used to chuckle but these days a grimace will slide across my mouth before I can catch it.

Funny that the things that drew me to James all those years ago now repel me. I say funny, though it's anything but. I used to be fascinated and charmed in equal measure by our differences in upbringing and family, but a small pit of doubt about our compatibility formed a decade ago and has widened into a chasm.

I chuck the plates in the sink and return to be met with the full beam of James' cheekiest smile that stretches across his mush like a glistening hammock strung up between his ears and earned him the nickname Cheshire after the cat. 'That smile could power half of Lancashire, James,' Mum always says, to which he always replies, 'Oh I didn't know you had electricity up North now, Sandra.'

Mum always thought he was such a catch given how well-to-do he was compared to us. She laughs as he spouts snobbish stereotypes about the North. I used to as well, though I'd feel a low rumble of shame for my disloyalty to the place I was raised.

'What?' I ask him. He's still occasionally cute, to be fair. A good guy and a great dad.

'Sorry. My jokes are cheesy. They're getting cheesier, I think… it's worrying.'

I think he looks a bit sad for a second. Then he brightens. 'The pasta was delicious, as was the appetiser.'

Despite the years of marriage I feel suddenly coquettish. 'Yeah. Who'd have thought we'd still have it in us?'

Quick as a shot he replies, 'Well, you definitely had it in you.'

I scowl but can't help laughing.

We'd shagged before lunch, a quickie in the downstairs loo – the only room in the whole house with a lock. We forsook the comfort of our marital bed for old times' sake; clandestine clinches aplenty had happened in there when Chloe was little – muted groans and gasps while CBeebies babysat. James unwittingly (or maybe wittingly) adding an extra frisson by clamping a hand over my mouth to muffle my cries of 'Fuck!' as I came.

Our giggles afterwards were drowned out by the telly: 'What's the story, Ballamory? Wouldn't you like to know... you pervert.'

Today I tried my best to be in the moment and not to be distracted by the cracked tile near the hot tap that gathers grime like a dirty thumbnail – concentrate on the sex, Josie – but then I noticed the jojoba handwash is running low. I fleetingly wonder if there's any person in existence with the name Jo Joba – there must be. Anyway, god, right – sex is happening. Focus, Josie.

We rocked together, me leaning on the sink, him pulling my hair a little as he swept it to one side to kiss the back of my neck. We know the mechanics of each other's bodies so well after so many years that the sex, when it happens, is always very good.

Ironic really as James has popped round to chat about our divorce.

'One last hurrah,' I say now, getting up to make coffee. Every time I peruse my collection of medium grinds from Uganda, Peru and Myanmar I think of how my teenage self would scoff into her Mellow Birds at how poncey I'd become. My working-class roots seem closer to the surface these days, poking through the cracked surface of my privileged middle-class life like weeds between paving stones.

'Hurrah?' says James, shouting slightly to be heard over the tap as I fill the water tank. 'More like three encores and a standing ovation.'

I turn off the tap and he lowers his voice almost as if talking to himself and I tip the coffee into the filter paper and switch the machine on.

'I was half expecting an audience to appear tossing armfuls of roses at me,' James mutters, then he chuckles. He's always been able to entertain himself like a baby playing with its own feet during a nappy change.

I sit down opposite him at the dining table, a vast wooden thing that seemed to me the size of a cricket pitch when it was first delivered. I glance out of the kitchen window and notice the bruised sky. I know we're doing the right thing in divorcing, but still, I feel waterlogged by sadness.

If James is feeling the same he hides it with a stiff upper lip and some joshing – years boarding at one of the country's top schools will do that to you. Any feelings of vulnerability or abandonment given a bloody good thrashing with a game of rugby and twelve pints.

He sips the scalding coffee and yelps – he has no patience to wait.

'You'd better take your vitamins,' he says, stretching his tanned arms up into a Y-shape, fists clenched. 'Today could be the first in a flurry of daytime sexual gymnastics while we sort everything out – splitting up clearly gives us the horn.'

'I don't think that's a real concern to be fair.' His face falls a little so I go on, 'Though it *was* very good, James, well done.'

He does a mini fist pump.

'Which brings me rather awkwardly, in a not so smooth gear change, to Friday, the big day? How are you feeling?' I ask.

'Fine.' He grins, though his eyes betray him.

I know we've been married for twenty-three years and twenty days because it was at our twenty-third anniversary dinner nearly three weeks ago over sushi that we decided to break up. Since then we'd barely seen each other and we needed to talk. For the last fifteen years or so James worked late into the night because of his dealings with the New York office of the bank. Today he's taken a long lunch break to cycle from his vertiginous glass office in the City to our house in leafy Hampstead, north London where, as my best mate Fay puts it, 'the streets are paved with knobheads'.

I'd put it much more delicately: it's beautiful round here, the wisteria-clad houses, the winding lanes. The street where I live, in a neat curve of white Georgian townhouses, is a world away from the red-brick council houses of my teenage years. No mattresses on the front lawns here.

So James had cycled along the high street, no doubt past the crowds of cockapoos and hoards of lunching ladies wielding handbags that cost more than my first car, their frozen foreheads masking their dismay as they pick at another rocket salad whilst dreaming of chips.

And here we are, post coital, post penne, working out how to best put our marriage out of its misery.

Though it's not in misery so much as... a plateau. A lonely nothingness. A forgotten sample floating in formaldehyde in an abandoned lab, our marriage is just suspended in one place, bobbing on the spot.

'Marry Your Best Friend' is a headline I saw in *Elle* a thousand years ago and I did – a best friend who was funny and posh and kind. Who used to shag me a lot and who loved all the things in life that I grew to love once I could afford them. I'd pulled myself up from nothing to get to uni, get my degree and forge a career in finance in New York and James seemed like the perfect Prince Charming to complete my rags-to-riches tale.

We married in a whirlwind and I threw myself into being a wife and then a mum. But I forgot how to be just Josie. Bit by bit the foundations of our marriage – the fun, the regular sex, time together – eroded away until the whole thing seemed to slump off a cliff and into the sea.

Over the past few years, whenever we discussed trying to rekindle, reignite, reconnect (all the re's), we managed only to exhaust even the most determined marriage counsellor.

Agreeing to split up was a relief, like getting home and taking off your bra. We had at least put on the brakes before we skidded and smashed into bitterness, so hopefully we still had time to find happiness and a sense of self without each other. But, it is sad. It is not the happy ever after I wanted, or my mum expects.

As if reading my mind James says, 'What are you going to tell your mum?'

Ah, my mum. On cue there is a deep rumble of thunder that makes us both jump then eyeball each other dramatically, as though we've summoned up Sandra in weather form. We just need a flash of lightning for her pantomime baddie arrival on stage. In fact, that's not fair, she's not a baddie, not any more. She's just... a lot.

The rain that has been threatening all day breaks through, hammering on the skylight and I'm back in our cold little council terrace, Mum drunk and weeping over an unexpected downpour soaking the washing on the line. Bedsheets haphazardly pegged and trailing on the dirty cobbles, my school jumper clinging on to the line for dear life. We were barely clinging on back then, caught in the storm of Mum's mood swings.

'I'll use Fay's "old dog" analogy,' I tell him now.

'I'm intrigued,' he says, taking a swig of his coffee.

'When she heard we'd finally gone, as she put it, totally tits up, she said it was like a much loved decrepit family dog who was limping a lot and whose tail was falling off.'

'Can I just check she's not a qualified vet?'

'Affirmative. Anyway, she said kinder to put it to sleep now before the dog/marriage starts rabidly biting everyone and while we still remember the happy times. So, I'll say that to Mum.'

James doesn't look convinced. In fact, he couldn't look more sceptical if I'd just told him that if he squeezes his nipples hard enough Vimto will come out.

'OK...' he says, then rubs his eyes, looking weary like a toddler after a day out. The doubt in his eyes is contagious. There it is again. The thud in my chest, the rising feeling of hot panic that floods up from my ribs, circles my neck and bursts in my ears with a thump-ing heartbeat. A dread of all the rubble we'll have to pick over in the coming months – the explaining, the paperwork, the organ-ising. Even though things are amicable the path ahead is strewn with emotional debris, and the biggest victim stumbling splutter-ing through the smoke of the aftermath will of course be Sandra, my mum.

I know I'm going to have to comfort Mum through my divorce, which she will no doubt make all about her. She loves James so much that a casual observer might presume she is *his* mother and my mother-in-law; during minor squabbles she's always leapt to James' defence and turned on me. James could say on a Wednesday it was definitely a Tuesday and Mum would loyally concur. She's from a modest background, is impressed by wealth and sees James as our saviour and her long-term security. 'I'm going to let James choose my care home,' she'd say, twinkling at him. She's implied on numerous occasions that I'm not good enough for James. News of our divorce will also strip her of her bragging rights to her friends about her wealthy banker son-in-law.

What I wouldn't do to be able to wave a wand, say 'Divorce-aramus!', and be two years down the line, decree absolute in one hand, glass of Laurent-Perrier in the other.

'You OK?' James is watching me and I realise I'm nibbling the skin around my thumb, a stress habit he knows well.

'Get that out your mouth, you don't know where it's been,' Mum used to say, which I found a bizarre comment seeing as it was my thumb.

'God, it's going to be exhausting isn't it?' I say and my voice cracks a little.

'We'll be OK. We'll get through it.' That stiff upper lip again.

We chat some more. James is planning to take Thursday off to pack up most of his gear and move to the temporary place he's renting near work. The bigger stuff – bikes, rowing machine, vinyl, skis – will go into storage until he finds a permanent abode.

'How's that going?' I ask. His face lights up.

'Well, actually, I've seen a great place on the water near work.'

If he's trying to keep the excitement from his voice he's failing. 'Nice. A bachelor pad on the river.' I try to stop a snark rippling through my words and I'm not sure I succeed. 'You'll have to learn to swim properly in case you tumble off your balcony after too many Aperol spritzes.'

James has always hated swimming, another legacy of boarding school, being towel-whipped by his pals in the mouldy changing rooms as their creepy housemaster watched on a little too keenly. On our holidays abroad together he had loitered in the shallow end of the hotel pool, as out of place as a sheep in a spin class.

He leans back in his chair, hands behind his head like he's sunbathing. 'Whatever,' he says. 'The challenge still stands – you learn to ski and I'll get into swimming... it's never too late.'

'Nah, you're all right. I'll leave the romper suits and braying over après-ski to you poshos. Besides...' I pause. 'Swimming is a life skill. No need to be jealous because I could heroically pluck a stranger from a watery grave and you, well, couldn't.'

'Pfff,' he snorts. 'Here we go. "I have the moral high ground because I spent my teenage years saving a weight from the bottom of a piss-filled pool whilst wearing my pyjamas."'

'Yeah, well. You may have spent your teens jetting to Courchevel, getting wasted and trying to finger chalet girls but it never saved anyone's life.'

'Fair point.' He pauses. 'Bloody good fun though.'

I sip the last bit of my coffee to hide my smile. He's always been able to make me laugh. I'll miss that about him. *Stay strong, Josie, you're doing the right thing.*

'I'll be taking this on Thursday.' He nods at his Ducati mug, a father's day gift from Chloe.

'Course,' I say.

Over salmon rolls at the anniversary/divorce dinner James had made it clear that he was in no rush to sell the house. He'd always been able to talk about money with the confidence of someone who's never had to worry about the damn stuff. To him money was like the sky or the ground underfoot – it was and would always just be there. I'm different. To me money drips from a tap that could be turned off indiscriminately by the fickle hand of fate. I love and fear its power in equal measure.

James has always been in charge of our finances. I was busy raising Chloe so he brought home the bacon and I rustled up the butties. Now though... well, I feel a bit rudderless. I can't be a stay-at-home mum when our only child is no longer at home. It's bad enough I blamed her for my muffin top until her twelfth birthday.

If I'm not a mum at the school gates or a wife organising the home then who the hell am I? Where's the woman who took herself off to uni, who bagged a great job in New York, who worked hard and played harder?

What next?

At least I'm not at the mercy of a dickhead husband out to hurt or deceive me.

James had waved his chopsticks in the air at dinner, flicking a tiny grain of rice over his shoulder and said, of course I could stay in the house for the foreseeable, he was in no hurry for the money and besides it was Chloe's childhood home. She'd still have her old bedroom to crash in after uni.

For the time being the house will still be our home. Its walls are sodden with our memories: going into labour standing at the kitchen sink; Chloe's first steps along the hallway gripping a spoon in each hand; James spinning me round the lounge in his arms after each promotion at work. I still pinch myself that I get to live in such a beautiful home, the dark wooden floors echoing with all of our happy and sad times.

The rain subsides and now watery sunshine breaks through. I stand at the kitchen window and automatically scan the brightening skies.

'Still looking?' James asks softly.

I have a habit of looking for rainbows, a legacy left behind by my dad's death.

'Always will.'

I'd read somewhere that when children lose a parent they look for signs that their loved one is still close by. For me, it is rainbows. My early childhood memories on the farm when I still had two parents, are candy-striped, broad swathes of colour arcing over the fields most days. Once Dad left us, the world was a much darker place.

I'm in my bedroom at the farm on the night of Dad's crash. It is lashing down outside and I hear screaming coming from downstairs. I hear a thud and the slam of a door. An engine starts. I'm not curious about what's going on, instead I have a heavy sense of foreboding and climb under my duvet to muffle the conflict.

I shiver. James comes and flops his arm over my shoulder. I let myself lean into him, the familiar curve of his collarbone. We stand for a moment looking at the clouds.

I kiss his cheek gently and he strokes my hair. It's a nice peaceful moment, we let the matey joshing pause. My sadness about the split deepens as I think about Dad.

I let the melancholy wash over me, the slow wave of sadness that comes whenever I think about my father. I've learned over the years to let it envelop me, not to fight it.

My phone buzzes, breaking the spell. Mum. Her profile picture is one that Chloe took years ago, a deep sea diver snapchat filter that had Mum gawping out bemused from inside a huge underwater helmet.

'Uh oh,' says James. 'Sandra in the hizzy house. I'm off whilst the rain's stopped. Send her my love. Call me later if you need me.'

He heads for the door, grabbing his cycle helmet and keys from the ledge in the hallway.

I pick up before Mum rings off and presumes I'm lying dead in a skip or worse, ignoring her.

'Hiya, Mum, give me one second.' I cup the phone in my hand and hiss 'James,' hoping Mum's hearing aid isn't cranked up to nosy. 'We need to discuss Chloe – are we going to tell her together?'

James pops his head back round the door from the hall. 'Nah,' he whispers. 'Don't worry about Chloe, I don't think she'll be that shocked, she keeps asking if she'll have a nice room at mine when we finally "uncouple". I'll talk to her, and you –' he pauses then stage whispers – 'can tell your mum. Good luck!' He gives a cheery thumbs up and disappears.

2

'Hi, Mum.'

There's a silence, just a slight crackle on the line before, 'Oh hello. Sorry, am I disturbing you?'

Mum loves pinning the word 'sorry' randomly through her conversation. She has never apologised for any of her behaviour – and there's been a lot of behaviour over the years – but says 'sorry' more than any other word.

'Just wanted a teeny tiny catch-up, sorry. Do you have a minute, my favourite daughter?' I am an only child.

'Course. For you I have many minutes, hours, a lifetime if you need, o-mother of mine.' In recent years as she's mellowed I've become bolder with her, less afraid of the fragility of her feelings. It nonetheless still feels rebellious to show her I'm no longer as afraid of her.

'Very poetic. You sure? If you've got visitors...' I can hear Mum's nose twitching down the phone, like a giant rabbit. She's always on the scent for any scraps of gossip and in that respect, I've been a disappointment. Until now. Careful what you wish for, Sandra – is a divorce juicy enough for you? That bombshell can wait for now though.

'No, it's fine, I'm alone.'

I don't add any embellishments. 'You have to have a good memory to be a liar,' she always said. Mum makes a noise like a cow pining for its weaned calf.

'Maaaaw... On your lonesome rattling round that big house. I'm sorry but you must be so bored. By the way, have you spoken to Chlo recently? I sent her a package but not heard a peep.'

During her time at Brighton studying textiles and business Chloe had received parcels of 'essentials and treats' from Mum. Chloe thought it was cute at first but that had worn thin about eight packages ago. 'Please can you speak to Nan? She's sent more M&S knickers and bath bombs – I've told her we don't actually have a bath. Also she sent condoms again! Even if I was getting the chance to use them – which I'm not – it's so weird she sends them, can you imagine – "Here, let's be sensible, pop this on, it's from my nan."'

'No, Mum.' I sigh now, picking at a loose thread on my jeans, 'but I'll give her a nudge to call you.'

She clears her throat like she has an announcement. 'Thing is, I'm sorry' – was that the fourth 'sorry'? A new record surely – 'but I need to know for sure if you're actually coming up this weekend? I can't live my life on tenterhooks waiting for your next move.'

The irony isn't lost on me here. I spent most of my teenage years at the mercy of her temper and drinking, trying to predict the next catastrophe. Only in recent years have I realised I was a carer for her. That this mother-child role reversal wasn't normal. No wonder I ran away to New York and then married the first man who offered me security and a future so distant to my past. See, the marriage counselling did work – it didn't save my marriage but it made it make more sense.

'So?' Mum says.

The wellness weekend at Shearness Manor was a Christmas gift from Fay. The hotel is about an hour from Mum's and I'd promised we'd stop off en route.

'Yes, it's still on unfortunately. Not unfortunate that I'll see you, obviously. It just seems a long way to go to meditate with a bunch of strangers.'

Mum ignores my ruminating and rumbles on. 'Thing is, I'm thinking about maybe renting out the spare room to a lodger. Melody from the village, you know her – very large nose and rake thin. In fact, it's a good job she's got that hooter or she'd fall down a grid. Anyway, she has an overseas student staying with her, Malaysian he is, very polite and no trouble. If you're definitely coming I can hang fire with the mini refurb before I take someone in myself.'

'OK, but why? You're not really into... people staying though are you, Mum? I only had one sleepover at ours, when Anneka came for my fourteenth birthday and you nearly had a breakdown.'

'Shhhh, my baby,' Mum purrs.

'What?' Then I realise she's talking to her dog.

'Sorry, Mouse gets anxious when I'm on the phone. He's very troubled recently – the vet has given me some valium suppositories for when he gets in a state, but popping a tiny drug torpedo up a whippet's bottom is not high up on my bucket list, so I've been putting my CBD oil in his breakfast.' She takes a breath 'Where were we?'

'Anneka?'

'Ah yes – well, I'm sorry but Anneka was not "no trouble". I seem to remember her drinking a whole bottle of vodka and vomiting behind your headboard?'

'Ah yes, I forgot about that.' Neither of us mention it was Mum's vodka.

'Anyway, I *do* like people, I'm just better with dogs – less complicated, that's what Clive always said.'

Clive was Mum's late husband, my stepdad during my twenties and thirties, although I never introduced him as such, he was Mum's husband. There was only ever one father figure in my life, albeit briefly.

Clive was a man so still it was like having a mannequin around the house. He was older than Mum, an accountant with a penchant for whippets who looked after Mum until he passed away as he'd lived – with little fuss, not wanting to be a bother. Sometimes it feels as if I've dreamt Clive, until Mum mentions him.

'Since Clive's passing, the house has been so quiet.'

Ironic really as the man barely uttered a word, but I guess it's quieter because Mum's got no one to talk at. I don't share this observation. Instead I say, 'Yeah, I bet.'

She sighs. 'Well, I'm sorry but I for one am pleased you're going on a wellness weekend – it means I'll get to see you and it'll do you good to get away. Help you focus on your next chapter.'

Mum is big on 'next chapters' – always focusing on what's coming up, on moving on. Her speciality is not looking back, ever. Even if sometimes that is what I've needed her to do the most, especially when it comes to my dad.

As a teenager I was all but barred from mentioning Dad's death. It was too painful for her. Mum made it clear that to talk about Dad, even the happy times, was an act of brutality against her. She preferred to 'look forward, not back. He's gone and it's pointless to dwell. We can't bring him back, as much as I'd like to, and I can't cope with trying to keep him alive with useless chat.'

I didn't process his passing, I wasn't really allowed to grieve or show emotion. So now, where a sadness should lie there is instead a void. An incomplete part of me. I am not a woman whose father died when she was little. I am a woman whose father was erased from her life. I have so many questions unanswered and still to this day, Mum refuses to open up. From silly things – what did he have for breakfast on the day he died? – to bigger things, like how did he propose to her, what did he say to her before he left on that fateful final journey?

The doorbell trills, followed by a familiar voice shouting, 'NELSON! NO!'

SARA COX | 18

'I've got to go, Mum, sorry – I'll text and let you know what time to expect us on Friday! Good luck with Mouse.'

I can see through the frosted glass of the front door the unmistakable outline of Ruth. She is a lumpen figure hunched over, draped in her trusty green waxed jacket, so that through the glass it looks like a small hillock has appeared on my doorstep.

I swing open the door and see she is wrestling a miniature dachshund into submission.

'Nelson SIT,' she shouts, trying to flatten him with her large hands, which only makes him wriggle more, his glossy black body bending and flexing like a comedy rubber truncheon.

'Tea?' I say and she looks up then, rosy cheeks giving way to a big smile.

'Go on then.'

Ruth is owner, CEO and sole employee of Hound Stretcher dog walking services. Only the middle classes would get a dog then pay someone to walk it. I know I'm being unfair. I have a cleaner don't I? I can't whip out my working-class credentials like Columbo showing his tattered ID, then discreetly slip them back into my pocket when my floors need mopping.

I've known Ruth for about twelve years. I'd watched her dropping off various dogs for a few weeks before we met properly. I wasn't spying as such, I just loved watching the organised chaos that ensued whenever she returned the dogs from their early morning or afternoon sessions. I'd hear her first – the rattle of her van's engine blended with a chorus of woofs of all pitches.

Ruth would pull up, hop out and slide open the side of the van, the excited cacophony no longer muffled by the door. 'OK, team! Enough!' she'd shout.

Bruno the Airedale is always first out, bounding up the steps to No. 12 with the ivy-framed maroon door, Ruth's little legs only just keeping up. The door key was located in a huge jangling clump attached to a bungee cord on her belt. Each house was the same. Unoccupied: door key, alarm beep, dog in, alarm beep, door slam. Occupied: door key, 'Helloooo we're back!', release dog, door slam.

After Bruno there's the King Charles spaniels Boo and Radley, sweeping the checked tiles of the path of No. 10 with their feathered tails; Jeremy the chocolate Lab who gallops up the stone steps of No. 7; and finally rescue Jack Russell-cross Muffin heads at a no nonsense trot into the loving arms of my next door neighbours, the two Chrises. The routine is the same every day and by the time Muffin is home, Ruth is ready for a cup of tea.

The only shifting factor is when Ruth is dog-sitting an extra pooch, hence Nelson the wriggly dachshund who appears to be joining us this morning. I enjoy having a dog in the house again. It's been just over a year since we were left broken-hearted by Sammi's departure – our Lakeland terrier claimed by old age. 'A good innings,' people kept saying, though nothing felt good that day – the trip home from the vet's with his lead and collar dangling redundant from my hand, calling Chloe to break the news to her.

The first time Ruth and I spoke all those years ago I'd been watching her drop off a large orange and white Pointer called Prue who used to live opposite us at No 1. Prue had spotted Joan's cat from next door on my wall and pulled free from Ruth, careering after the ginger feline into my front garden, and in the melee that followed Prue smashed a couple of my plant pots, whose long dead inhabitants were awaiting their final journey to the green waste bin.

I'd swung open my front door perhaps a little too enthusiastically and as Ruth offered her flustered apologies, while Prue barked furiously at the retreating cat's arse, I offered her coffee.

'No thanks, but a tea would be magnificent please,' she'd replied.

And with that a new friend entered my life. Before Ruth, I'd been feeling lonely on Oak Walk. But now I had a local friend who was on a similar wavelength to me and who didn't make me feel like some common oik when I was chatting to them. With most of my neighbours I'd talk in what my mum would call my 'telephone voice' – affecting a slight poshness. I hated that some self-conscious nugget of me would make me do that. My accent is definitely Lancashire that's been dulled by decades in London, so my voice sounds odd in both places. Up North I'm accused of sounding posh and in London cabbies often gurn, 'Aye up, you from Yorkshire then?' With Ruth I could be myself.

'Nelson, bless him, is a gold-plated twat.' Ruth smiles as she heaves herself onto a stool at the breakfast bar. Nelson looks up momentarily from the Croc he's trying to shag by the back door.

'I have him for another few weeks then he's gone, thank god. His farts smell like I've dug up the dead and he's too excitable around all my female clients.' She calls all the dogs her clients. 'I swear if he grows a mullet I'll know for sure Peter Stringfellow has been reincarnated as a dachshund. Biscuits?'

'Absolutely.' I grab the tin from the cupboard and prise the lid off. There are only three rather sorry looking ginger nuts. 'Don't go wild,' I say. She peers in. 'Of course not, there's only three in there.' Ruth always takes things literally. She selects a biscuit and takes a bite. 'Anyway, how are you? I saw James earlier, whizzing in on his bike as I headed out. Everything go OK with the conference?'

'Yeah, fine,' I say, debating whether or not to mention the sex. I don't need to debate much longer.

'You had sex didn't you?' she says, a fine spray of ginger-nut crumbs landing on the island's marble top. 'You have that whiff about you, like a bitch that's just been rolled in the dust by a big-dicked mastiff.'

'That's disgusting.' I laugh. 'But yes, I was rolled. Long overdue to be honest. I regret nothing.'

'Good for you,' she says, 'though I don't envy you and your sinful yearnings. My fanny closed for business the week after my sixtieth birthday and I don't miss all that panting, not to mention the fluids.' She pops the rest of the biscuit in her mouth.

We both know the reason she's not had sex for five years is because that's when Maud, the love of her life, suddenly passed away and we both also know neither of us will mention it as it's still too painful for her.

'I miss the cuddling, of course,' she ponders now, 'but I always have a dog around for that.' On cue Nelson abandons romancing the Croc and trots over to lie under Ruth's stockinged feet, which are swinging off the stool.

'Will you miss James?' she asks.

I sip my tea. 'Yes and no. I don't know really. I feel I've done so much of the grieving already over the past few years. We both knew our hearts weren't in it. In fact, I feel a bit like we've already sep-arated... like he's no longer mine, just a possession I've sold that's yet to be shipped.'

'Well I guess once he's gone you'll know how you feel. You'll have the space to think about it. Exciting really. The world will be your oyster, Josie. You could sell up and travel the world! I'm sure the two Chrises would approve.'

'Yeah, they'd chip in towards my one-way ticket.'

The two Chrises next door owned various properties and had made it clear over numerous drinks how much they love mine and James' home, and how they'd snap it up in seconds if ever it was put on the market.

'Yeah, especially Crab,' smiled Ruth.

Chris aka Crab was given that nickname by James after our first dinner out as a foursome. Chris had wolfed some soft-shell crab and choked so badly that he coughed up a whole intact pincer from the depths of his gullet like a scene from *Alien*. It was an astonishing spectacle. Chris Crab was the younger of the two men, a successful children's book illustrator with a neat beard and year-round tan. He also fancied himself as an interior designer and property magnate. Other Chris was willowy and quiet but after a bucket of red wine had a wicked sense of humour that could make a fleet's worth of sailors blush.

'We'll see them soon anyway. They're having a barbecue for Other Chris' birthday.'

'Ooh, you could test the water, even for sport just to see Crab's little face light up.'

'You're a very wicked woman, Ruth. But yeah, could be fun. I'll be back from my wellness jaunt with Fay by then. I'll wear a carnation in my lapel so you recognise me as I imagine I'll look like a new woman. I'm presuming you're coming to the barbie?'

Ruth nods. 'Yup. It'll be a double celebration – that's also the day Nelson is pissing off back home to his mother.'

3

I wake early on Friday morning and sleepily mull over the day before. James had eventually left with the very last of his belongings. His intern from the office, a well-spoken foetus called Jacob, was following one van to the storage facility in an Uber and James was heading to his new place on his prized Ducati. As he'd started the engine, Chris Crab was on the way out of the house with Muffin. 'James!' he'd shouted over the throaty growl of the bike. 'Your bike seems to be making a very strange noise – is it OK?'

James had lifted the visor. 'Sorry, what?'

'Your bike,' shouted Crab, pointing a manicured finger at the exhaust. 'I think it's broken. It's making such a racket.'

James raised an eyebrow 'Oh, don't worry, Crab, that's just the sound of my mid-life crisis.' Then he tipped down the visor and roared off.

'Well,' said Crab to me, 'I would make a joke about a throbbing beast between his thighs but it'd be beneath me.'

We'd watched as James' bike turned left out of the street and Crab sighed. 'End of an era. Me, you and our friend Pinot have put the world to rights and talked of little else over the past few years, but are you all right, really? With him going?'

'Yeah,' I'd replied, Crab's sudden tenderness catching me off guard. He'd been a good friend to me. 'It's been a long time coming but I know in my heart of hearts it's the right thing.'

'Well, my door is always open to those with broken hearts and a strong liver function if you need to come for wine and a whine.'

'Talking of wine, what can I get for the birthday boy? Only a few weeks left now of his forties.'

'Nothing – what can you buy a man who has everything?' he'd asked, gesticulating at himself with a flourish. 'Just bring your effervescent self – we have everything else.'

I'd headed back indoors and shut the door with a click, which echoed in the crisp silence of the house.

I ponder all this as I lie in bed: Crab's kindness as we watched the brake lights on James' bike flash then fade at the end of the street.

I pull back the duvet and manoeuvre my legs into the shaft of sunlight peeping through the gap in the curtains, enjoying the warmth on my calves. I glance at the scattering of dark hairs poking through on my shin, not missing James' jokey running commentary on my imperfections. He comes from female stock that are plucked and painted to perfection. Once Chloe started pre-school and my days opened up I too fell into a rota of self-maintenance in an attempt to be a well-turned out woman, but time seemed to creak to a standstill as I waited for my nails to dry. No legs will be entwined with mine for the foreseeable so I might as well let them grow plush. Embrace my inner Sasquatch. Same for the moustache I battle daily and the eyebrows I beat back. Let it grow, let it grow, let it grow.

It dawns on me how much mine and James' marriage, limping along with both of us in its grasp, had held me back from finding me. My life has felt on pause, tethered as it was to James and the cloud that had been looming above us for so long. I'm sure James is waking up feeling just as relieved.

I have commitments still – a daughter who occasionally needs me and bursts of charity work, but otherwise my time is my own.

I'm fifty-one, an almost divorcee and unemployed. Why do I always feel so busy when I don't actually do anything?

Since Chloe started sixth form, I've tried and failed to kick-start a number of part-time careers. The thought of resurrecting the bones of my long deceased banking career was frankly terrifying. Instead, I had embarked on a half-hearted stint as a personal trainer, an online course to become a relationship counsellor (oh the irony), and worked briefly with a company called Wardrobe Warriors who offer a service to slim down peoples' over-stuffed cupboards with the motto, 'Clear your closet, clear your mind'.

Each new venture would be met with an encouraging smile from James – similar to the one a parent gives a child when they announce that they're going to be a pirate. He never held me back but he certainly didn't push me forward. 'We have enough money,' he'd say. 'I love looking after you, why not enjoy our fortunate position instead of putting yourself through all this stress?' James comes from a family where the men earned and the women juggled not careers but au pairs, keeping house and charity work.

One time his mother asked me, 'Really, sweetheart, why do you need a "career"?' as if the whole idea was ludicrous. She may as well have been asking me, 'Why do you need a spaceship?' How to explain that the comfortable life her eldest son funded wasn't enough? 'Well, Barbara, because I can feel my brain frosting over from lack of use and I'm so bored I may pull off my own head and overarm bowl it at the smug mums clustered around Gail's just for something to do.' That would've sufficed but instead I smiled and said, 'I think Wardrobe Warriors is an exciting new challenge. I could even do yours?' She'd laughed.

James was always there when the latest scheme faded into an embarrassing silence to be swept under the heated wooden floor. I'd made a second career of petering out. It sounds ungrateful but in the end James' support just undermined my attempts to do something with my life. I got a pat on the head from him when what I needed was a kick up the arse.

A global pandemic had made it easier to put any thoughts of re-entering the workforce on the back burner. But now I have no more excuses. I have to do something, start again.

My phone buzzes.

A WhatsApp from Chloe.

> Dad says he's rly moved out then? It's good I think, you both have been sick of each other for a minute. What are you going to do?

What I'm going to do is make some coffee and maybe have a shower, I type back a little tersely.

> Encouraging that your sarcasm is still functioning. Srsly tho, you OK, mamakin? Need me 2 come home?

I reply, *I'm fine, thank you, sweetheart,* though I can't help feeling a little maudlin. Now that Chloe knows it's really over it feels more final.

There's a pause, with a little buffering symbol on the screen. She's trying to find the right words bless her. Her message comes through with another buzz.

> OK good – Coco throwing an Agatha Christie bday party and I'm going as Poirot. Gtg. Love you.

Who was I kidding?

First things first, before I embark on the first day of the rest of my life I'm going to need coffee.

The kitchen is calm, bathed in a golden light. I pad across the floor in my bare feet and notice with satisfaction that it is exactly as I left it the night before. Neat, clean. No keys or jacket on the table. No crumbs strewn across the worktop from James' post-work snack, no un-rinsed mug. Maybe I'm going to enjoy being alone for the first time in twenty-five years.

We first lived together in his flat in Camden. He called it an apartment but that was an exaggeration. It was like the storeroom of a sports shop with tall stalagmites of trainer boxes lining the hallway. His bedroom contained only a bed, and his fridge was empty apart from a bottle of Smirnoff and some breaded chicken.

I knew him from university when Fay had introduced us so wasn't surprised by his flat – he'd never been particularly organised. A toff torn from the home comforts of his upper-middle-class life and flung into adulthood.

Our relationship at uni was booze-soaked and sweetened with pills at the weekend as we raved together and came down together through the second summer of love. Any hopes of it continuing were doused post graduation when I took a job in New York. It was for the best – we needed space to grow up. And, y'know, New York.

On my return a few years later we bumped into each other in Covent Garden. He told me later over our fourth drink that he'd watched me for a few minutes, enjoying spying as I stood browsing one of the stalls, 'working a curl of hair around your fingers,' he'd said. I told him that was the creepiest thing I'd ever heard but I was secretly thrilled.

Our wedding day was on Valentine's Day 1998, an unseasonably mild Saturday. 'As soon as I hired an interpreter I realised she was the smartest, funniest woman I'd ever met,' James said in his speech, a gag at the expense of my broad northern accent.

*

The coffee machine gurgles away as I put a bagel in the toaster and dig around in the fridge to excavate the smoked salmon. Two days past the eat-by date. I hear Mum's voice: 'Trust your nose.' I'm no stranger to the game of fridge roulette, one day I may be felled by a prawn but it's worth the risk to never ever waste food; another legacy from childhood.

Mum had once thrown a dish of soggy Frosties at me in a hungover rage. She'd accused me of using too much milk. I'd explained the milk was nearly off anyway, but she was furious I'd answered back.

Mum never really hit me but she was a keen thrower of things, with a devilish aim. I had ducked left as she threw the bowl at me, its plastic rim skimming my ear, the trailing curtain of milk splashing the shoulder of my one good school shirt. The look on my face and the sorry sight of me standing there must have snapped her to her senses. She would never apologise, instead she made some lame joke about not crying over spilt milk as she helped to pick the bits of cereal from my hair. I wiped the shirt as best I could with the dishcloth, but all day I could smell stale milk.

At university I was particularly gung-ho with use-by dates. 'You must have a stomach of steel.' My housemates would grimace as I scratched off mouldy bits from my food with my nails, like a teenager picking at zits. 'It's fine,' I'd proclaim as they turned green.

'It's her northern hardiness,' Fay would chime in. 'It's one of the many reasons I love her.'

'Plus,' James would add, 'in a post-zombie apocalypse world I'd stick with these two commoners – Josie could forage for any old nosh and Fay here could then rustle up one of her many delightful dishes.'

'Oh yeah,' Fay had said. 'And what use would you be Tory boy?'

'Simple. I'd use my wit and natural charm to negotiate a deal with the zombies, ultimately becoming their ruler. All lower classes, from zombies to northerners just need strong leadership.' He'd earned a playful whack for that.

*

I look at my reflection now in the black-glass tiles above the hob, the only dark square in the white-marbled landscape of my kitchen. I'm turning into my dad. I have no siblings and like to imagine an undiluted concentration of him has been glugged into my DNA. Memories of Dad play like grainy footage through my mind – I know I stand like him, arms folded, head tipped slightly to one side as I appraise myself. I remember he always stood like this when he was talking to people, his arms a barrier, his head at an angle as if confused by folks and their ways.

I'm slender like him, with a neat nose, wide mouth and grey eyes glaring back at me from the paleness of my face. On a very good day I've had Cate Blanchett, on a bad day Audrey from *Corrie*.

I see his square jaw, his wavy hair, though mine is longer, chopped bluntly below the ears where I tuck it when nervous and blonder, from a bottle to hide the greys. I see his frown. Beyond that the memory of my father softens and fades.

The crinkles around my eyes hint at my fifty-one years but I celebrate getting older, I embrace it, I am grateful. My dad didn't even get to his thirty-ninth year.

The bagel pops up from the toaster and makes me jump. I'll have breakfast then pack for the wellness weekend. I make a mental note never to agree to anything Fay suggests again. I've no idea where my sports bra is, and Fay has been threatening to buy us matching yoga gear. The woman herself is collecting me at midday.

I pour a large mug of coffee and sip it as I make my sandwich – salmon, black pepper, squeeze of lemon left over from last night's G&T. I plonk it on a plate, licking a smudge of butter from my thumb, and sit at the kitchen table. I open up Notes in my phone as I chew. I'm suddenly ravenous.

Title? I write simply 'Next' – I can't bear to add 'chapter'.

SARA COX | 30

'Come on then? What IS next, smart arse?' I say out loud. Oh god, it's started already – I'm gonna grow into one of those women who chat out loud to themselves, the radio, her hanging baskets.

I've no appetite for returning to banking, the only reason I followed that path in the nineties was because I needed to earn, I needed to shrug off poverty, empty cupboards and cold nights. I craved distance from my upbringing and I was scared of becoming too reliant on Fay or James – the scaffolding that held me up when I was down. I worried if I let them look after me much more I'd collapse without them.

They'd fulfilled the role that should've been Mum's during our years at university. They gave me the confidence to be myself, nurtured me, encouraged my ambitions and in return what had I done? When stoned I would become maudlin and ask what they saw in me and they would gasp and cluck at the outrageous question. They would sandwich me in a smoky hug and tell me I was the strongest person they knew. They saw my childhood not as a failure but as a tale of triumph over adversity, that I'd come out in one piece despite the odds. They told me I was resilient and badass; funny, loyal and kind. I tried my best to believe them.

When I got the job with the bank, they threw a party at the flat and waved me off at Heathrow when I left for the States. I loved the work and being in New York, the independence it gave me. I didn't have to answer to anyone and I could reinvent myself.

Even if I wanted to get back into banking things will have changed beyond all recognition. When I was last a banking hot shot Rachel had yet to discover Ross was in love with her, I used to fax my London clients and Bill Clinton was busy not having sexual relations with that woman. It was an age ago. I'd be a dinosaur. A menopaurus wreck.

I type 'Travel?' underneath 'Next'. This sparks a flurry of ideas. I've always fancied New Zealand, so I add it to the list, or a stay on a working ranch – I type 'Arizona/Texas?'. I could relive the magic of my pony-obsessed childhood. I see myself rounding up cattle by day, drinking whisky by the campfire at night.

Apart from Ruth and the Chrises, I wouldn't be missed much around here.

Fay would be outraged if I buggered off but she'd get over it.

My feet are not remotely itchy but isn't that what people do? Pack up after a trauma and go and find themselves on a Goan hillside?

I add 'India' to the list and pour more coffee.

4

'Fuck's sake.'

I'm jolted awake from a glorious snooze, Fay has her forehead resting on the steering wheel.

She's chunnering as if in private prayer. The god she's speaking to seems to be in charge of traffic and doesn't mind the F-word.

I stretch as much as the low roof above and the bag of snacks below in the footwell allows.

'Sorry, did I wake you?' she says to the pedals, unmoving. She speaks in the low monotone of a death-row prisoner in a documentary, resigned to their impending doom. 'We've literally not moved for twenty minutes.'

'What a load of bollards,' I say.

'One hundred and nine. I counted them.'

'Really?'

'Nope.' She sighs towards her knees. 'It's just I don't really know why everyone seems to be on some grand excursion to the North. Is Jesus actually from Blackburn and this is pilgrimage traffic? Or is there a two for one on flat caps or something?'

'That's northernist,' I say.

'Well I'm allowed, I'm the most northernist in the car. You're northern-*ish* these days. You mislaid your roots when you started sourcing olive oil from a Greek website.'

'Bollocks,' I say. Then cringe as it comes out a bit posh sounding.

'See,' she says. I can see her teeth as she smiles in the gloom of the car. 'Can't even say bollocks properly. You'd better start practising your earthy northern tones before we get over the border.'

The lorry in front lurches forward a metre and I nudge her. She lifts her head from the wheel revealing an indentation stripe of pink above her eyebrows. 'The steering wheel has certainly left an impression on you,' I say, pleased with my quip.

She catches up with the lorry then glances at her face in the rear-view mirror and rubs at the mark with her fingertips.

The lorry in front slowly pulls away again then grinds to a halt.

It's dusk and all the car lights start blinking on, sensors recognising the approaching darkness. Not this car though, because we're in Fay's car, which definitely predates automated headlamp systems, heated seats and cruise control. It's barely got attached doors. I imagine airbags so old that on impact they'd flop out like a dusty old ball sack escaping a pair of Y-fronts. It's a Vauxhall Astra, though after being rear-ended by a Range the back badge has cracked – the 'tra' clung on for a few weeks but then fell off leaving just 'As' on there. 'We can't go all the way to Manchester in the Vauxhall As,' I'd protested in vain. 'It'll be like being dragged up the M1 on a spade.'

'Come on, it'll be fun – me, you and the Astra, off on an Easter adventure. We'll make Good Friday Great Friday.'

How could I resist that smile? 'It'll be another Easter miracle if it gets us beyond Watford, that car is older than God's dog,' I huffed.

'Excuse me – it's not old, it's borderline vintage.'

'Pfft,' I'd said. 'Yeah, like I'm a borderline supermodel.'

She'd laughed but remained resolute. The car was her pride and joy, her silver dream machine gifted to her from her dad at the start of the millennium, so here we were. I try not to think about the massage settings on the plush seats of my hybrid Volvo. I try but fail to find an old skool charm in the grey plastic interior of the rust bucket we are in and instead peer out into darkness. We start to roll along at an arthritic snail's pace and eventually see a sign for Loben Woods. This is where Mum now lives, just west of Manchester and a good thirty miles of winding roads from our final destination.

'Next junction,' I say, trepidation creeping into my voice. I still feel my tummy tighten on seeing these familiar signs in starkly floodlit letters. It's a sense of coming home, but it's complicated. For many years I never knew which Mum I'd arrive home to, what stage of inebriation, depression or drama I'd find her in. In recent decades this feeling of dread has mostly dissipated; it helps that where Mum lives now is very different to the area where I grew up.

Mum finally made it to Loben Woods thanks to Clive and his successful accounting business. The house he once shared with his late wife became his and Mum's, then when he passed away just Mum's.

As the name suggests, Loben Woods nestles in acres of forest and it is beautiful. It was here that we'd drive on a Sunday sometimes when I was around thirteen, just to look at the posh houses. Mum would insist I join her, bribing me with jam butties she'd made for our breakfast and we'd drive around the winding roads that curled up through the dense woodland. Mum always wore her best headscarf and would say we were going for some fresh air but we both knew the real reason – we were there to ogle at the houses from our car. We both had our favourites. Mine was a huge white Spanish-style villa, built in the fifties, with a terracotta roof and white shutters over the cathedral windows that in summer would be folded back against the whitewashed walls. One side was covered with wisteria like a beautiful lilac scar across its cheek. I'd stare out of the window of the passenger side, mouth gaping at the house, trying to will myself in there. If I concentrated hard enough maybe I could teleport myself through the walls and I'd suddenly be inside, lying on my four-poster bed in my fantasy bedroom, which would definitely be entirely blue gingham.

We'd have the radio on in the car and Ed Stewart would be playing requests on *Junior Choice* and we'd sing along. Mum always turned the radio down whenever we pulled up outside a house, which made the experience all the more intense, as if we were staking the place out. I think she was nervous about being spotted. One time a woman came out of the front door of the Spanish house and saw us parked up there. A girl and her mother eating jam butties in their tatty car on a Sunday morning. We must've looked peculiar. Mum had started the engine and slowly pulled away and for some reason I waved at the woman. I think to my young mind she was my other mother, the one from my dream. She looked confused but waved back politely, frowning to try to recognise us. Mum had laughed when we got round the corner but then her mood turned sour; like she was embarrassed. Humiliated that her secret entertainment had been exposed. We didn't go back again. In fact the next time I went to Loben Woods I was visiting Mum and Clive at their house there.

Finally we reach our junction and, liberated from the grip of the congestion, we speed along into the night, one tiny car flying solo like a rogue starling peeling away from its murmuration. Fay winds her window down and rummages for her vape. The car fills with plumes of vanilla smoke. She looks at me from the corner of her eye. The street lights illuminate her features every couple of seconds like a slow strobe. 'Uh oh,' she says.

'What?' I reply.

'You're doing your thinking face.'

'How can you tell? It's dark.'

She snorts. 'I don't need to look at you. I can feel it. I can almost hear the cogs of your mind crunching round.'

We watch the road for a few minutes more.

'Go on then,' she says eventually, 'the suspense is killing me here. Is it my vaping?'

'Nooooo,' I reply. I feel silly now. 'Did you mean what you said? About me losing my northern roots?'

She pauses mid-puff. 'Not in a bad way, it was a joke and... people are allowed to change, Jose. I've changed. You scarpered from the north at eighteen, which was...'

'Centuries ago?'

'Exactly. You're bound to have grown into a different person. Fair play – you had a lot to get away from.'

'Yeah, maybe. I still feel like the same little girl though, I still feel working class, still northern. Maybe you're right. Maybe I need to come back, return to my roots.'

'It's all very well saying that but what? You're telling me you'd give up your lovely life in London? I can't imagine you being able to survive being more than a hundred metres from a Paul's; not sure how many French patisseries there are on the Pennines.'

'Ha-ha. Yeah, you're right. Jesus, I'd need their macarons airlifted to me. It'd be like when the Red Cross drop food parcels after an earthquake.'

'I can see you now,' she laughs, 'all windswept as the chopper hovers above you with your deli delivery: "Here's your gazpacho!"'

The headlights sweep across the darkness, revealing huge trees lining the road.

'I don't know – I do feel like I'm just treading water but can I be arsed to do anything about it? Is that bad? James has buggered off and everyone keeps asking me "what next?" But why can't my "next" be more of the same?'

Fay stays quiet. Ever since uni she's let me think out loud like this, given me space to work out stuff by myself.

'Maybe a change of scene would do it, at least if I left for a bit everyone would be happy that I've got away and I'm not just sitting around in leisure wear counting down the days to my first botox.'

'You missed your window for that years ago, babe,' she snorts. 'Women are starting in their mid-twenties these days. You'd need a harpoon full of the stuff to make any difference now. I'm the same – we'll just have to have faces "full of character" now.'

'I could move, temporarily. I mean, really, what's actually keeping me in London?'

'Charming,' she says.

'Apart from you obviously. But apart from you, my house is empty and my closest friend on the street doesn't even live there. I've more in common with the street's dog walker than with any of my actual neighbours. Maybe I'm ready for a change.'

'Are you convincing me now or yourself?'

'All I'm saying is maybe I need a new challenge.'

'Well, not long till your first challenge – we're about to see your mother.'

5

Mum's house is one of the smaller ones in Loben Woods but it's still very pretty. Grey limestone with a neat square of lawn out the front. White pillars entwined with ivy stand either side of the wide red door. It reminds me of the houses you see in a Christmas rom-com when the main character brings back their new squeeze to meet the extended family with hilarious consequences.

But it's not Christmas and behind the front door awaits not a bunch of quirky aunts and uncles but Sandra, all alone apart from her anxious whippet, Mouse.

I notice Fay is standing up straight as if waiting outside the head-teacher's office. I ring the bell and smile tightly at her.

She mouths, 'Good luck.'

No sign of Mum. I ring again. I told her we'd be with her for six p.m. and it's only quarter past. Immediately I catastrophise – an old habit of imagining the worst has happened, a rush of guilt that I wasn't here to prevent whatever has felled her. She's slipped making dinner and is surrounded by a halo of cauliflower florets like a bridesmaid's hairband. I'll have to climb through a window or...

The door opens and I breathe again.

'Oh there you are. Better late than never,' tuts Mum, pulling me in for a brief hug. She's wearing ski pants and I see Fay clock them with satisfaction.

Mum is seventy-six and still enjoys showing off her figure. Today she's sporting a halter-neck vest top in the green of an under-ripe banana. She's attempted to apply fake tan but I can see the bits she's missed as she releases me and holds her arms out for Fay, her underarms a saggy patchwork quilt. Her hair is auburn and falls in thick coils down her back, dusting her exposed shoulder blades. At first glance an impressive head of hair for a woman of her vintage but these glossy locks were harvested from the scalp of a younger woman from a faraway continent – Mum is wearing one of her wigs. The hair on her face is fake too, eyebrows are tattooed on in deep brown and she wears false lashes. She says her lashes going was worse than her hair. 'Alopecia is a spiteful bitch,' she'd say when I was growing up. I hated when she swore. She spoke about alopecia as if it was a girl she knew who'd ruined her life, saving the worst of her vitriol for her drunken days. 'Taken everything from me, now wants every last strand of my hair. Wants to humiliate me even more by taking what beauty and dignity I have left.'

'Fay!' Mum squeals girlishly now. 'I'm sorry but look at you! Always so pretty. Pretty AND successful.' Mum looks at me and says, 'Don't ya just hate her?' from the side of her mouth with a comical accent and eyeroll like a Brooklyn stand-up.

Mum's smashing her own personal bests. She's already managed to shade me through praise for Fay and we're not yet over the threshold. Maybe I'm being paranoid or maybe it's just what five decades of weathering Storm Sandra does to you.

'Well, I wouldn't go that far but I'm doing OK thanks, Sandra, how are you?'

'Lonely. Lonely and unloved but surviving.' Mum pouts.

'Mum,' I protest, 'you're not unloved.' She looks up at me. 'Mouse loves you.' I point at the whippet, cowering behind her legs.

'Oh I thought for one moment you were going to say something nice there,' she huffs. 'Come on, come in, no use hanging outside like a couple of overgrown carol singers.'

We take off our shoes and leave them neatly on the beige hallway carpet. 'Go through, go through,' she trills. We do but I can't resist glancing back to see Mum move each of our shoes a centimetre so both pairs are placed perfectly parallel. Mum's obsessive tidiness is always there, but the shoe shuffle is a sure sign she's stressed. I think again about her plan to have a lodger – one or both of them would be driven to a nervous breakdown by her demand for perfection.

The three of us go into the kitchen, Mouse trotting lightly at Mum's side, the knobbles of his spine visible though his fawn coat.

Without being asked, Fay and I head to the sink and start to wash our hands. Long before a global pandemic made stringent hand-washing all the rage Sandra was a fan. The first time Fay met Mum was on a rare trip home from uni one summer. Mum had recoiled in horror at Fay's outstretched hand when she introduced herself, as if Fay was thrusting the limp carcass of a rat at her.

During my teens Mum would grab me the second I came in from school and march me to the kitchen sink to scrub away the threat of dirt and disease from every inch of my hands, rubbing carbolic soap – the deep pink of a processed pudding – between my fingers. They became chapped and sore depending on Mum's mood – the more stressed she was, the more her germ paranoia grew, the hotter the water. I'd sometimes yelp and try to snatch my hands away from the shock of the scalding water and my protest would jolt her to her senses; she'd hold me, sobbing with remorse, which was almost worse. This wasn't always my mum. There had been a different time, a happier time on the farm before Dad died, but there's no hiding that my teenage years were tough. Mum is split into two in my memory, like identical twins, one good one bad. Before and after the farm and the events that meant we had to leave.

Mum makes a pot of tea. She is fascinated by everything that is going on at the British Library where Fay works as a curator, and it soon becomes clear that Mum has told various friends about Fay and her brilliant career like she's the daughter she never had.

'So,' she says at last, turning to me. Mouse's big black eyes watch me nervously as though even the whippet can sense I'm in danger. 'What's new with you, Josie?'

'Not much,' I say, avoiding looking at Fay. 'Chloe's enjoying her final year. She loved her last package, she's fully stocked up now thanks to you.'

'Well, that's good to know. And James? How's his work?'

'Great, he's busy as usual, off to New York again in a couple of weeks, just for a few days this time.'

Mum nods then looks at me, head cocked like a kestrel looking at an injured sparrow. 'Sorry but you look cream crackered, Josie. Have you been sleeping OK?'

'I'm fine,' I say but I can't stop a slight wobble in my voice and Fay leaps in to save me.

'I was saying the same about myself – I look like something dis-covered in an Egyptian crypt most mornings. I blame the London air – that's why it's so nice to escape up here. Think this Wellness Weekend will do us both the world of good.'

The oven makes a beeping noise and Mum gets up. 'Well, I hope you're both hungry, I've made a cottage pie.'

'Lovely,' says Fay. 'Need any help?'

'There's elderflower cordial in the fridge and a jug over by the sink if you could do that please, Fay love, while Josie sets the table.'

I stand and shuffle over to the cutlery drawer. My bones feel heavy like I've spooled back in time to my teenage self – sullen, resentful of any minor task Mum asks of me.

We eat the pie and Mum and Fay chat. Mum asks her if there's 'any romance on the horizon?' as if men are an oasis in a desert, something mystical to hope for. Fay dishes up her usual quip about how she's too busy with work and the only men she has time for are Churchill, Anthony Eden and Hitler, which shuts Mum up for a couple of forkfuls.

I'm desperate for a glass of red but Mum's is a dry house, kept so since Clive's death lest she slip back to her booze-sodden days.

Mum dabs delicately at the corners of her mouth with a paper napkin. 'Right.' She stands up and her chair scrapes. 'Josie, I have something for you. You remember I mentioned to you about a lodger?'

'Yes?' I reply warily.

'Don't look so suspicious. Sorry but what's that face for?'

'It's just...'

'Your face, I know. That's what you always say, "It's just my face".' She imitates me with a whiny voice. Fay sits back a little in her seat.

'Well, it IS my face. I can't help the way it is.'

Mum has been sidetracked by the squabble and I can tell she's trying to remember what we were talking about. I'm not about to help her out. She's always so snarky and her disappointment with me is magnified when she makes such an effort to be nice with Fay. I know it's pathetic feeling this way but I can't help it.

'Lodger!' Mum says. 'That's it. As I was saying, we may be welcoming a lodger, possibly an overseas student and he or she, preferably he, sorry but men are much less complicated –' (Was that a slight on me or just half of the global population?) '– will stay in the spare room. In the spare room is a wardrobe but no drawers. There is however a nice chest of drawers up in the loft – the ones from...'

I know exactly the drawers she means. The drawers that followed us from the farm to the scruffy little two-up two-down terrace. The drawers that were shoved in a corner and ignored but never left behind. A wedding gift from my dad's parents to the happy young couple starting their new life taking over the old family business, Thistlefold Farm. They are oak with a thistle design etched on the top corners.The drawers used to live in the dining room at the farmhouse, where Dad would commandeer one end of the dining table to complete his paperwork – regis-tering calves, paying bills, reading glasses perched on top of his head. I never took much notice of them aside from admiring the pattern on top.

Still Mum can't bring herself to say 'the farm' or 'Thistlefold' and heaven forbid she ever tried to say 'they were Dad's' – she's barely spoken his name since he died.

Mum stumbles over her words 'They're from...'

'The farm?' I ask.

She nods. 'No use them gathering dust up in the loft, so I emptied them out last weekend and gave them a wipe and they've come up lovely.'

This may seem like a normal, reasonable thing to do but Mum is neither of these things. From the unnaturally high pitch of her voice I can tell it's a big deal to her that she's dealt with the draw-ers' contents. I feel my chest tighten. What has she found amongst the bills and paperwork?

Her nerves seem to make the air shimmer like summer heat off tarmac as she babbles on. 'Anyway, Sally from next door lent me her Bob and despite his bypass he's still strong as an ox and he carted them down from the loft. Should've seen the cobwebs on there though – size of a bath towel! Bob said – '

'You've emptied them then?' I interrupt.

Mum pauses. 'What?'

'The drawers?'

'Yes.' She laughs with an impatient flap of her hand. 'That's what I'm trying to tell you. There was lots of useless stuff in there – invoices, that kind of thing – but there was also something I thought you'd like.' She pauses.

My heart beats faster, trying to keep pace with all this information.

Mouse barks suddenly, a sharp yap like a warning and we all jump.

'Mouse! Honestly, for a dog named after such a quiet creature you've got a very big gob.' The dog lays its chin back on its paws as if to say, 'Don't say I didn't try.'

'Photos,' Mum says. 'You can look at them later. They're from... back then. I thought you'd like them.'

6

An hour later Fay and I are sitting by the fire in The Woodsman.

After helping Mum clear away after dinner, Fay faked a headache and I suggested some fresh air. Mum knew this was a ruse but seeing as she'd rather take a mallet to her own toes than talk about the past, she seemed relieved when we left. She waved us off with her jiffy cloth, kitchen spray clenched under her armpit ready to lay siege on the germs we'd smothered her kitchen in. I was right – her tweaking of our shoe placement earlier was a clue to some underlying stress. The cause of her latest anguish is tucked under my arm in an envelope which seems to tremor like it's alive.

The pub lies at the end of a winding footpath through the woods and there's a slight chill in the air, but it feels good to be out of the house and away from Mum. We walk in silence, just the crunch of the forest floor under our feet.

The pub is all hanging baskets outside and polished brass inside. It's quiet despite the long weekend and we settle at a table by the open fire. The flames have died to a glow, their work done taking the edge off the evening nip.

'Right, wine.' Fay looks me up and down 'Large or bottle?' She knows me well.

'Bottle,' I reply.

A young lad takes our order and returns a few minutes later with a couple of glasses and a very nice looking Rioja.

The brown envelope is A4 and feels light; its corners crumpled from being shoved in amongst other paperwork.

Fay pours the wine and it sloshes a red wave up the inside of the glass, the colour tinting the sides before fading. I see Fay is watching me. I realise I'm studying the wine glass like I'm expecting it to perform a card trick.

'Cheers,' she says and takes a sip.

I drink a mouthful and look down at the envelope. My hands feel clammy. I tell myself it's just an envelope of photos. But the truth is this feels like a big deal because it is: once we left the farm all those years ago, I didn't really see any photographs of my dad.

The only images I have are in my head and I'm no longer sure how accurate they are. Over time his face has probably changed in my mind's eye as my recall faltered, my imagination sketching in any blanks – the shape of his chin or the curve of an ear. I have no photograph to check against, to power up the picture I store in my head. In fact the strongest reference point I have for Dad is looking in the mirror. Throughout my childhood people told me I was Dad's double. It was said with a tickle under the chin when I was little, and Dad would ruffle my hair. 'Poor thing,' he'd joke.

After his death it was said less and always out of earshot of Mum so as not to upset her. I think now that Mum struggled with me and my teenage obstinacy because it must've been like having Dad glaring back at her, refusing to give up.

I did have one photo but it was lost. Not long after Dad died I was doing a school project on my family tree. I knew I wouldn't be allowed to take in a photo of their wedding day but I was pretty good at drawing and planned to carefully trace my favourite photo for the opening page of my project. I found their wedding album, a book I knew well from looking at it so often when I was little – its blue velvet cover feeling familiar.

The first page was empty, which was strange, just a yellow shadow around where the print used to be. I turned to the third page, the best one – the photograph of them on the church steps, Dad laughing like he'd won the lottery. Mum smiling shyly in a white A-line lace minidress with long sleeves and white sunhat, all the rage in 1969 thanks to Yoko Ono. That photo was gone too.

In fact none of the photos were in there except a few of older relatives I didn't recognise, dumped in the back pages like day trippers accidentally abandoned by a coach driver. Faded smiles on middle-aged ladies wearing hats that looked liked swirly cupcakes. They were probably in their fifties like I am now, though to my twelve-year-old eyes they were ancient.

What had Mum done with the photos of her and Dad? I had a hollow feeling in my tummy that told me there was a darkness at the centre of the story.

A few days later Mum asked me to throw a pile of papers in the bin and she didn't have to ask me twice. I remember I seemed to be constantly tiptoeing around her bad moods back then like she was an unexploded bomb. That's when I spotted it, stuck on the concrete ground behind the bin. A photo of Dad grinning up at me, his face partly obscured by some spilled potato peelings. I knew it was from the wedding album because I could just about see his tie and white carnation buttonhole, though he'd been sheared diagonally across one shoulder towards his hip in a jagged scissors cut. He was grinning into the camera, looking deliriously happy despite now being a severed half torso stuck behind a bin. Were the rest of the photos in the bin? I didn't find out, a storm was rolling in and big fat raindrops started to fall. I slipped the photo in my pocket and ran back in.

I knew to keep quiet about all this, I wasn't daft. I was twelve and understood that parents sometimes fell out. Tammy Green's mum and dad had divorced and they bought her a puppy. She was lucky, at least she still had a dad.

I kept the photo safe in my purse for months, which I then lost on a school trip to the zoo. The teachers couldn't work out why I was hysterical and my mum became irritated by how inconsolable I was at the loss of a cheap Dorothy Perkins purse and, of course, I couldn't tell them why.

'You OK?'

I snap from my thoughts.

Fay is watching me, her eyes gently scanning my face. She reaches out and squeezes my knee. She knows everything about me, every dark corner of my childhood and my teenage years, nothing was left unexplored during our long stoned chats at university. 'Suck the poison out so healing can begin,' she'd said once, and we'd got the stoner giggles 'cos she said it like some Aussie bush ranger rather than a girl from Blackpool's North Shore.

'Whatever's in there this can only be a good thing, eh? You've always wanted pictures of your dad.'

'I know,' I say. I try to grin but instead I bare my teeth as if getting her to check for spinach.

'Want me to look first?'

'No.' I look down at the envelope. It isn't stuck down, the once sticky strip is dry. I pull out the flap which is tatty from being shoved inside the envelope in haste – today? Forty years ago? Weekly? Had she just been waiting for the right time to give them to me or had she genuinely stumbled across them in the drawers amongst the yellowing paperwork?

I take a deep breath and reach my hand inside the envelope, Fay watching me with round eyes over the rim of her glass. I take out the photos, each the size of a drinks coaster.

The first is of Dad sitting on his tractor. My breath catches at how lovely he looks. The photo is in colour and to see him now, his tanned skin, ruddy cheeks and hair brightened by hours spent working outside under the sun, is like finding he's alive again. He's framed by a bright blue sky and is laughing, as is the little girl on his lap. She's wearing a yellow bonnet and is clapping her podgy hands together. They're like peas in a pod. That little girl is me. It is also my daughter Chloe. My vision swims. I place the photo on the table for Fay to look at.

The next picture is of a huge Hereford bull standing on our lawn. His immaculate mass fills the whole photo. His conker brown coat encasing three quarters of a tonne of rippling muscle shines in the sunlight. He stares into the camera with the self-assured nonchalance of a superstar and is wearing a polished leather head collar with a white rope attached – whoever is at the other end of the rope has stepped out of shot so the viewer isn't distracted from the prize bull's glory. This is his moment. I laugh out loud when I spot myself and look up to see Fay grinning, enjoying my joy.

I'm about three years old I reckon, and have been plonked on the bull's back. I look quite at home there. Herefords are a placid breed and this huge chap clearly didn't mind my presence. I'm in red dungarees and yellow wellies, grinning into the camera, my little fingers gripping the hair on the animal's withers. On the ground in a semicircle is a display of silverware from the season's winnings: trophy cups in silver and gold with red, white and blue 'Best in Show' ribbons tied to the handles, huge silver salvers and wooden presentation shields. The glittering display is festooned with rosettes.

Next is a photo of a birthday party. The farm kitchen is full-on seventies garish orange – the cupboards, the tiles, even the kettle. I'm sitting at our small square kitchen table wearing a pointy party hat, my wavy hair restrained into two pigtails. There is a cake with seven candles before me and standing all around are a couple of school friends (Jenny Crook and Margaret Bradshaw) and a bunch of kids from the village. I recognise some of them – Tammy Green whose parents ran the post office is there with her little twin brothers, Paul and Tommy; Jackie Jones with her bright red hair and then a taller, serious-looking girl hiding behind large blue NHS specs who I don't remember at all. At the edge are two toddlers who've wandered into shot and a younger boy with a lopsided grin and dark curls who I can't place, though he looks familiar. The surrounding farms always had other kids knocking about, mini-mes in mucky overalls keenly following in the welly steps of their parents. I'm about to blow the candles out, patiently holding my smile in place waiting for the photo to be taken so I can get on and make a wish. I don't know what I would be needing to wish for back then.

Photo number four is Mum and Dad at a party. They're in each other's arms on a dance floor. Dad is laughing and pointing at someone out of frame but Mum is blowing a kiss at the camera. She looks stunning in a black minidress with lashings of dark eyeliner.

The next photo is me on a beach with Mum. I'm about two and Mum is sitting on a towel on the sand. I'm standing between her legs, which are bent at the knee providing me some shelter from the elements. The wind is whipping up our hair and I'm clinging to her, my thin little arms around her neck, looking back over my shoulder at the camera. Judging from the dishwater sky and my pale blue legs I think it's Lytham.

The next picture is Dad and me. I can only be a couple of months old and he's holding me in his arms. I don't recognise the room, it must be at a friend's house. Dad is studying my face and looks serious, like he's been snapped unknowingly. His Border collie Jet is sitting at the side of the chair, chin resting on Dad's knee, watching the bundle with fascination. I'm asleep, wrapped in a navy striped blanket, a tuft of wavy brown hair peeping out.

The last photograph is a clearer close-up of Dad and me. I gasp. The jawline, the frown, it's his but it is also mine. Dad looks pensive and I'm wearing his frown on my young face like a reflection. We're at a restaurant and I can tell from my outfit that I'm just twelve; I'm sporting a sky-blue satin blouse with a pussy bow tied at the neck – me and all my friends loved Lady Diana and wanted to dress like her, though I don't know if she shopped at C&A like we did. I wore the blouse to my first secondary school disco and was devastated when it was ruined in an incident involving some cherryade and an imbecile called Jonny.

All these memories come rushing back. The village kids, Jet the dog, our old farmhouse kitchen, even Jonny the imbecile – now all bursting into Technicolor thanks to the seven photos, like the moment sepia-toned Dorothy opens the farmhouse door to find the world of Oz exploding in vibrant lush hues of every shade.

'Wow!' Fay is looking at the last picture.

'I know,' I say, 'we're the spit of each other.'

'Yes, you are,' says Fay, 'though my wow was actually at that blouse.'

I laugh and it brings me back to the present. Fay has always been good at doing that.

'It was 1981. You're lucky my pedal pushers are out of shot.'

'Haaa! I had those. Come on, were yours maroon velvet too?'

'Old ladies' armchair fabric? Course.' I sip at my wine.

'What now?' Fay asks

'More wine? Maybe some nuts?'

'Ha-ha,' she deadpans. 'You know what I mean. Do you want to talk to your mum about these pics, about why she's just decided to give them to you? Why now?'

I shrug. 'The answer to all those questions is a firm "who the fuck knows". I know that back then half of the photos on a roll would be blurred or covered with a thumb or whatever but still... there must be more?'

'You'd think so. Are you going to ask or let the dust settle? This feels like a big deal her giving them to you.'

'Is that your polite way of saying "please can we not have any more drama and instead just stay here in the pub getting gently sozzled"?'

'Absolutely not!' Fay looks outraged then softens. She leans in to me, her breath smells like berries. 'I also think that knowing your mum, she'll do her classic Sandra head-in-the-sand number, leaving you with more questions than answers... Maybe just give yourself time to enjoy these photos for what they are. Just... I dunno... enjoy being with your dad for a bit.'

She's right of course. In the years since he died Mum has never spoken about Dad or his death. At first I was too young to know that was unhealthy. Back then people didn't talk through their grief as much, but even so Mum's reaction wasn't normal. Over the years I've made excuses for her behaviour. Mum is a post-war baby and came from a generation whose parents lived through a time of grinding, unspeakable horror and much was left unspoken. Mum was taught through example that if you didn't want to unravel in times of pain and despair, best to keep everything neatly and tightly tied up. Mum kept her grief packed away and bound with the strings of her own sorrow.

That didn't help me though.

My childish enquiries – 'Did Daddy have to die?' to later on, 'Where was he going when he died?' were never answered. People die in tragic accidents all the time but Mum's refusal to talk me through the last days and hours of Dad's life means for me they feel hidden behind an impenetrable wall. In my early teens I could only paint a sketchy picture of his death from the titbits scattered by careless mouths in whispered conversations.

This is what I picked up: there was a terrible storm with torrential rain and high winds. Dad had set off in the dark to find some lost cattle that had escaped. A flooded section of the road caused Dad's car to slide out of control and smash into a tree. They said he would have died instantly.

I looked for the newspaper story of the night's events when I was home from uni one summer, sitting in the stuffy archive room in the town library as the July sun blazed down outside, feeling like my heart might thump through my T-shirt as I slowly scoured the pages of the *Howlesden Echo*. Eventually I found it – 12 October 1982, reported two days after his death. Tucked away on page fifteen, a small footnote next to a larger story about a proposed new hospital and underneath an advert for Rumbelows. Just the bare details beneath a tiny headline: 'Farmer Dies in Storm'. No whys or whats answered.

> *A farmer has died after being involved in a collision with a tree on Blacksmiths Lane during Monday night's storm. Fred Wylde aged 38, of Howlesdon was believed to have been trying to locate lost cattle that had escaped during the bad weather. He leaves behind a wife and daughter.*

I'd foolishly hoped the article would give me a fresh angle.

In the days after the crash I felt like a sailor lost in fog, hearing voices in the distance, feeling like I was going mad. Carloads of visitors trooped in, hugging me tightly, sobs catching in their throats, balled-up tissues plucked from cardigan sleeves like magicians pulling out silk handkerchiefs.

A quick blow of the nose then on to making themselves useful, talking over the noise of the kettle, brewing tea. 'Well it was his prize cows and calves that had got out,' and people chuckling sadly that he'd always preferred animals to humans. I know he'd taken Mum's little runaround rather than his Land Rover, which even in its battered state would've handled the water and the impact better. If only he'd been in that vehicle, maybe he wouldn't have spun out of control, the four-wheel drive would surely have held the road, pushed through the flood water and safely out the other side? My whole world was knocked off its axis by the car keys he grabbed in his rush.

Over the years I've accepted that you can't live in the land of 'if only', it will send you mad. 'If only there hadn't been a storm/cattle hadn't escaped/the road wasn't flooded'. Rash decisions, weather, animals... all beyond my control and all collectively responsible for altering the course of my life forever. Uprooting us from the familiar lanes and fields of the farm and being thrust out into a harsher, lonelier world.

A loud cheer goes up from a gang of lads playing pool and I watch as they high-five each other, the losers already signalling to the bar staff, getting a round in as penance.

Fay is scrolling through her phone.

'Sorry, I'm not great company tonight,' I say.

'Literally only here for the wine and to watch young men get all alpha over a game of pool. There's something quite alluring about twenty-somethings in grey jogging suits.'

'Oh god, you and your youth detention centre energy.'

'Yup.' She drains her glass. 'That "are they gonna mug me or shag me?" vibe.'

'You pervert.' I risk a glance sideways. The lads are all in leisure wear; they look so young and bouncy.

The photos are in a small pile on the table and I look through them again, the adrenaline from the first viewing subsiding into something more pleasurable – a feeling of connection to my past, to my dad.

'You're right,' I say, 'I've no appetite for a fight. I'm pleased to have them at all.'

7

The next morning I come down to breakfast having had the weirdest dreams about Dad. I'm meeting him in a field at the top of a huge hill but I can't get to him. I'm running up a steep staircase dug into the turf, the steps crumbling under my weight as I slide back down the grassy slope, grasping at the earth, clumps of the stuff coming away with my fingers. I imagine looking at the photos until the early hours caused my dreams. I had studied them like I was to be tested on every detail – the colour of my party hat, the make of Dad's tractor – absorbing every tiny nuance by the glow of my phone.

Mum and Fay are already downstairs at the kitchen table. Mum has done away with her wig and instead is wearing a silk headscarf, cream with cherries on it. It is wired so at the front there is a perfectly constructed bow in the style of a land girl.

Fay is wearing the kind of tortured smile you'd give a steward who's sauntering over to free you from a jammed turnstile while a small crowd looks on.

'Praise the lord for she has risen,' chirrups Mum.

'Morning,' I say, sitting down and helping myself to a slice of toast from the toast rack. Mum's table is a non-ironic nod to a seventies' seaside B&B.

'I do look like I've come back from the dead to be fair. I didn't sleep great.' I groan.

'Nothing some caffeine and your mum's fig jam can't solve,' says Fay.

Mum plonks a coffee down in front of me and studies me. 'I'm sorry but I think you'll need more than one slice if you want to soak up the booze that's sloshing around your innards from last night,' she says.

After Dad's death Mum spent the next thirteen years gently stewing in drink but that doesn't stop her shaming me over half a bottle of Rioja. She's never acknowledged she drank too much, the closest she came to confronting it was when I rang her from New York and she was drunk and weepy.

It was eleven a.m. in Manhattan, the sky from my apartment a clear blue, and only four p.m. at home. I couldn't hide my disgust 'You sound pissed, Mum.'

'I don't have a drink problem,' she'd insisted, 'but I suppose I must admit that my drinking is problematic.'

She was never quite a vodka on the cornflakes drinker, unlike old Roy from the end terrace who was hammered from the moment he woke until the time he fell back onto his unmade bed at night, but since my teenage years she'd drunk every day and way too much.

She's always liked a drink and relied on it once Dad died. Her seven p.m. G&T quickly became her six p.m. treat and crept earlier and earlier until eventually she regarded it as her lunchtime sharpener. By the evening the only thing sharp about her was her tongue.

Then the day before her fiftieth birthday she met Clive in the supermarket. It was, thankfully, late morning – her golden time, when the hangover had cleared and the day's drinking was yet to begin. They chatted at the till and she could tell from his trolley that 'he was lonely. A small pork pie, some easy peelers and a can of Mr Sheen'. A widower was preferable to a divorcee. 'He's sixty-one. I'd worry more if he *didn't* have any baggage.' But a dead wife, no children and a decent pension was a very attractive package. Mum found his fondness for whippets curious but over time she too fell in love with the gentle breed.

She romanticised her boozy past ('Clive knows I've had my struggles') and somehow, she became sober almost overnight. I loved Clive for this. Quiet, calm Clive, the solid dock Mum could fasten herself to.

So Mum was miraculously cured by the love of a good man or, if I was being cynical, the prospect of being loved by a good man in his house in Loben Woods.

Mum lifts the lid on the butter dish and scrapes off curl after curl of butter, slathering her toast with an undercoat of yellow before the top coat of fig jam, an unctuous burgundy paste. She's wearing a towelling robe and teamed with her headscarf and raspberry lipstick she looks like a synchronised swimmer waiting poolside for her squad. She has no lashes on this morning and I can see a version of her own have grown back, half a dozen spidery strands on each eye.

I smear a little of Mum's home-made jam on my triangle of toast and bite into it slowly, savouring the earthy sweetness.

Fay is gazing out of the window at the bird feeder on the back lawn and Mum seems engrossed in her toast. When she's enjoying food she closes her eyes, as if drifting away on a dream, lost in the flavours. She's always done it with any food she likes – a Mr Whippy 99, cockles in vinegar at Lytham.

I think back to a gentler Mum, on a northern beach, us both with ice cream, side by side. I must've been about six or seven. She used to let me bury her feet, though she was very ticklish and would howl and giggle if I touched them as I patted down the sand. After a while she'd wriggle her toes and they'd emerge through cracks in the mound like zombies coming up from the grave. She was softer then, I remember leaning my head in her lap, a beach towel for a blanket as the clouds covered the sun.

I look at her now as she eats, her eyes closed, savouring the jam. Mum has always been able to disappear by simply closing her eyes, like a child hiding its face in the nook of their elbow.

Despite what I said to Fay last night I do want to talk about the photos. My vivid dreams about Dad have left me feeling unsettled. I just want to talk about the most important man in my life with the woman who knew him better than anyone. Is that too much to ask?

'Thanks for the photos,' I begin hesitantly.

'No,' she instantly snaps as if pre-empting my words.

'But—'

'No!' she snaps again, eyes still closed. 'I don't want to talk about them. I don't want you hijacking this perfectly nice breakfast.'

'I'm not, I'm just thanking you for them.'

She inhales deeply then blows out slowly through pursed lips.

'In that case, you're welcome.' Still she doesn't open her eyes.

I glance at Fay who raises her eyebrows.

'And don't look to Fay either,' Mum says.

How the hell does she do that?

'Mum, I'm fifty-one years old, do you have to talk to me like this?'

'I'm perfectly aware of how old you are, thank you, Josie. I was there when you were born and I have the scars to prove it.'

She opens her eyes slowly. 'I'm glad you like the photos but I'm really not in the right head space to talk about them. I know I've never been particularly open about what happened—'

I can't stop a snort escaping and even Fay glares at me.

'— but it's too painful.'

This is a power play, the not talking. It's the one thing she has over me.

'It's painful for me, too. Will you ever be able to talk about it, Mum?' I feel giddy, this is the furthest we've ever got without a sudden storming from the room (Mum), a tearful begging (me), or raised voices (both of us).

'Sally says I need to take baby steps.'

'Sally?'

'Yes. Sally, next door. She's doing an acupuncture course and she's been practising on me. It's helping with my hair too, I'm sure. Last month she popped round and I looked like a human pin cushion but within a week I had two more eyelashes.' She flutters them in demonstration. 'I'm a big job though, she says a lot of my pathways are more congested than the M4 on a Friday. She says I need to heal, take things slowly. I thought this was a good first step, the photos.' She smiles sweetly. 'But it doesn't mean I now want to pick through the past like a seagull at a rubbish dump.'

I finish my toast in silence and go and pack my bag.

By mid-morning we're standing by the car. Mum is now sporting grey checked ski pants and a mint hoodie with 'YOLO' splashed in hot pink across the back. Her wig is swept round into a low side-ponytail.

Fay is in the passenger seat and fiddling with my phone, putting our next destination into Google Maps.

The watery April sun is doing its best to shine. Mum takes hold of my face, her palms feel cool and soft on my cheeks. 'I know you're fifty-one but you'll always be my baby,' she whispers. Such tenderness is rare from my mum. I smell burnt toast on her breath.

'I know,' I say. 'Thanks for having us.'

She's squeezing my face a little now so my lips pout slightly; it must look comical but I don't want to ruin the moment. I nearly add 'and thanks for the photos' but decide not to. Instead I say, 'I love you, Mum,' and she nods. She moves her hands from my face and wraps her arms around me. 'I've done my best you know, it wasn't easy,' she says into my hair. I don't know if she means done her best to be my mum, to raise me, to love me?

She lets me go and I turn to open the car door. 'Stop for coffee if you feel tired, especially after last night's partying.'

And just like that the tenderness is gone, replaced by a dig. A gentle dig between the ribs but a dig all the same. She can't help herself. I turn back to her and shout, 'For god's sake, Mum, I had half a bottle of red, I wasn't injecting crack into my tits whilst noshing off an entire rugby team.'

When I say 'shout' what I mean is I scream it in my own head. What I actually say is, 'Course,' and get in the car.

We're on the M6 northbound and I'm quite enjoying driving a manual car again, I forgot how satisfying it is, listening for the higher pitch of the engine urging me to move up a gear, and ease its strain. I'm grateful for the distraction.

Fay is deep in thought whilst rooting around in a bag of Starburst for a strawberry one for me. She takes off the wrapper and posts it into my waiting mouth.

'Thank you,' I say as I start to chew.

I can see her brows knitting together as she looks out of the window. She'd be a shit poker player, whatever she's thinking is graffitied across her face. Occasionally I've caught her twitching, eyebrows all aquiver, lips pursing and un-pursing and when I've asked if she's OK she's admitted she was reliving an earlier confrontation, playing both parties, her face the stage.

'She's batshit,' she says at last.

'I know,' I sigh. This is well-trodden ground; Fay and I have walked this path many times over the years, going round in circles getting nowhere. Why is Mum so self-absorbed, so self-pitying, so cold towards me?

I sometimes think it hurts Fay more than it hurts me – she basically has survivor's guilt.

'She's a batshit bitch but she's mah batshit bitch,' I say in a sing-song Texan drawl.

'I hate the way she emotionally shuts up shop. She's your mum – it's her job to talk to you about stuff, help you understand all the crap that happened.'

'I know,' I say, checking my mirrors and pulling into the middle lane to overtake a tanker. Come on, Fiesta, don't fail me now. It groans in response. 'The thing is,' I say, 'maybe I should just accept that she's never gonna be that person. I probably need to make peace with the fact that I'll never know how my mum feels about Dad's death, what she went through, 'cos, for whatever reason, she just can't talk about it. I'll always be excluded from her grief. It's pointless expecting something different.'

There's a silence. Fay twists the radio into life and Basement Jaxx are yelling, 'Where's your head at?' Which is ironic and overly energetic all at once.

'You're probably right,' Fay says.

'But having these photos makes me feel like I've got more than Mum now, like Dad's with me too in some way. She's kept schtum for forty years. Maybe I need to follow that prayer thing that's always on tea towels.'

'Yes! I love that. The "know the difference" one?'

'Yes. God grant me the serenity to accept that my mum's a nightmare and I can't change her, the courage to change the things I can and the wisdom to know the difference. Also if you're there, God, please keep the M6 clear and let the wheels of this lil' deathtrap carry us safely to junction twenty-nine.'

'And,' adds Fay, 'if you can chuck a bit of action my way at this wellness weekend that'd be great.'

The roads narrow for the last couple of miles to Shearness Manor, as the fields broaden out on either side.

'We really are in the middle of nowhere,' says Fay.

'You panicking?' I ask. Fay has lived in London since her early twenties like me but unlike me finds being in the wilderness a little unsettling. I find it... settling. As the fields open up so too does my chest, like a weight has been lifted. City life, even nestled amongst the Teslas and tight foreheads in the green of North London, can be suffocating.

'I'm not a country bumpkin like you,' she says, eyeballing a sheep grazing by the side of the road. 'I'm coastal, as you know.'

'I know. Blackpool though, not exactly Miami. How you can find mind-bending expanses of deep black water relaxing compared to some nice green fields, I do not know.'

'Yeah, well that's why we're best friends, opposites attract and all that.'

We drive in silence for a minute.

'It is beautiful, you been here before?'

I smile. 'Yeah, but not for a long time.' I pause because I don't know whether to mention we're close to the farm where I spent the happiest years of my childhood. I know she'll get excited and try to make us go there. I can't resist it though. Fay is my best friend and keeping even the smallest thing from her sits sideways in my stomach like an undigested lump of betrayal. 'We actually went past the turning for Howlesden earlier when you were snoozing,' I say to the windscreen, as nonchalantly as possible.

'No way,' Fay says, sitting up straighter. 'You should've woken me!'

'You couldn't see anything. I didn't even realise we were close till I saw a sign for Lennington. Howlesden is just north of it.'

Her face lights up. 'We should go on the way back!' Her eyes are bright with the possibility of adventure and I hate to disappoint her but I haven't been back in four decades and have no intention of doing so now. I tell myself it's because the place will have changed but I know in my heart it's because I'm scared setting foot up there could unravel me, open up hidden vulnerabilities. I've pulled myself up from the horrors of losing a parent; returning to the farm feels too risky. What if I were to drown in my long-buried sorrow?

'Nooooo… and for what? No way. It's been nearly forty years. There's probably a retail park there now. Our front paddock might be a Sports Direct. It'll be too depressing.'

'I bet it's not, it'd be worth a look. I can't believe you're not curious? Just a bit?'

'I used to be. I was desperate to return for months after we left but there wasn't a chance of Mum taking me and I could hardly hitchhike at twelve. I swore once I could drive I would, but then college, uni, New York, London, life… I just never did.'

'Wouldn't now be a good time? It seems serendipitous now you have the photos?'

'I'm trying to look forwards, not backwards. Concentrate on that new chapter everyone's always banging on about.'

We crawl along, the late morning sun is in my eyes so I go even slower and wind the window down fully, which takes a while because the Fiesta still has handle winders.

Fay notices my efforts. 'Good for the triceps,' she says. 'What with that plus the sticky clutch, stiff gearstick and dodgy sunroof catch, driving this car is basically a whole body workout.'

'That's why you look so fit!' I say and she grins. 'Thanks, Beaut. I might film a DVD – *Fiesta Fitness with Fay*.'

After a minute she remembers something and sits up a little. 'Hey, when are you gonna tell your mum?'

'What about? *Fitness with Fay*?' I deadpan.

'No! About you and James.'

'Oh that. I don't know. Soon I suppose. I'll call her, that way I can drink during the disclosure and flick the V's at the phone while she berates me.'

'Great idea,' she says.

'Also if she's taken in a lodger by then she'll try to react calmly – I imagine she'll do her telephone voice and best manners with him for the first week at least. If not he'll hopefully talk her down from the ceiling.'

We slow to a stop to let a farmer cross with a couple of dozen sheep. He's tall and wears a checked blue shirt, khaki trousers tucked into green wellies. I can see the dark hairs on his forearms and the muscles move in his shoulders as he swings shut the five-bar gate behind him and secures it with a loop of thick rope around the stone gatepost. He pushes round the edge of the animals to stand with his back to us, arms outstretched like a crucifix, his body now a fence. The sheep are clearly used to this trip as is the collie at their heels – they know exactly where they're going. The flock floats over the narrow road en masse like a low cloud and through the open gate on the other side and into the field. The farmer follows, whistles a sharp note and the collie swings around to the left of the flock, sending them right and up the hill. He fastens the second gate with another rope and strides away, looking back to give us a wave of thanks, serious under hair as black as liquorice. We both return the gesture, leaving our palms suspended in mid-air. 'Sweet Lord,' breathes Fay, lowering her hand slowly.

'I know.' I nod, pressing the accelerator and rolling forward. 'Shexy shepherd or what. Nothing hotter than a man in wellies who can whistle.'

'That's pretty niche, Jose. That face though, gorgeous. Is it wrong to hope his sheep escape and end up in my bedroom in the dead of night?'

I laugh lightly but I know already alarm bells have rung in Fay's head.

'Oh god, sorry, bad taste.'

'Don't be daft.' I brush it off. 'It was a long time ago, sweetheart.'

8

After a few miles the drystone wall lowers and seems to sink into the ground at the foot of two stone gateposts. Next to it is a dark green sign saying 'Shearness Manor' in gold lettering. The gravel driveway is lined with beech trees that have connected at the top, creating a canopy of branches and a sun-dappled tunnel.

We emerge into a courtyard, the Fiesta crunching over the gravel as we pull up outside a beautiful large stone building. The grand-looking entrance is in the centre and on either end is a wing jutting outwards towards us, so it feels like the building has arms outstretched to pull us into a hug.

'Nice,' says Fay with a contented sigh.

We sit in the Fiesta for a moment, looking up at the manor, taking in the bicycle rack by the door, the mini trees in stone pots and the huge grey cat on a ground-floor windowsill washing itself.

'Think this is actually the back,' I say, glancing at the cars parked around us.

'Wow, if the back is this impressive the front must be gorgeous,' Fay breathes.

I unfold myself from the driver's seat and stretch, enjoying the sensation of pulling my spine upwards and side to side, creating space between the bones.

Fay unlocks the boot, which yawns open, and we grab our stuff, swinging bags onto shoulders and dragging our wheelie cases behind us.

'I'm relieved it looks OK so far,' Fay says in a stage whisper. 'You never know what to expect with these places. It's amazing what a wide-angled lens and a few fake reviews can do.'

'It looks perfect,' I say. 'Besides, don't pretend you booked it on a whim without forensic research – once a curator always a curator. I'm sure you tackled our wellness weekend with the same vim and vigour you approach a new exhibition at the library.'

She pulls a face. 'Still... I'm relieved. I'm fully expecting to leave this place feeling like a new woman. Or at the very least having been felt by a new man.'

'Uh, oh,' I say. 'She's on the prowl. Lock up your sons! And while you're at it, your divorcees, widowers and millionaire nonagenarians.'

We reach the window with the cat perched on the sill and Fay stops to stroke it along its back. It nudges its cheek into her hand.

'Or I could just become a mad cat lady. Cat or Cock? New game show idea.'

'Oof cat every time,' I say.

Fay gives me the side eye 'Yeah, you say that now, but the time will come when you'll want some fun. Can't wait to introduce you to the dating apps... they're addictive.'

'Feels so weird even thinking about kissing another man, never mind anything else. I've been with James for so long, I feel like I only know how to operate his body, I'd need an instruction manual for someone new.'

'I keep telling you – it'll all come flooding back.' The cat doubles back to Fay, its tail slipping through my fingers as it turns. 'As long as you don't put your life on pause because of some residue of loyalty to James. You know what men are like, they don't hang around. I reckon if we swiped later we'd stumble across your husband on one of the apps.'

'No! Really? Do you think so?'

She nods. 'Tenner on it.'

Inside, the entrance hall is deserted and instead of a reception desk there are plump armchairs dotted around a large gleaming table. The walls are wood panelled and the place has an air of faded grandeur about it. Two ladies glide past in fluffy robes and slippers, smiling beatifically.

'Sorry!' booms a voice. The owner of it is a surprisingly petite lady who seems to have appeared from nowhere. She's wearing loose khaki dungarees and has her hands on her hips. 'Mr Chaplin had some string coming from his bottom and I had to tackle it.' She holds out a hand. 'Don't worry, I've washed them. I'm Mary, welcome to Shearness.'

Mary has an impressive bosom and hair the colour of butter, which falls in waves to her shoulders. She looks a little older than us and has the bright eyes of a bird, carrying herself with the confidence of a seasoned head girl.

Before we can respond she points at Fay. 'I saw Mr Gable took a shine to you – he's very picky so you must be a special person.'

Fay, realising she meant the grey cat, grins. 'He's a great judge of character.'

'He actually is.' Mary nods earnestly. 'We once had a Tory MP here, real piece of work, was rude to any staff member who wasn't blonde, female and under thirty. Mr Gable did the biggest shit on his pillow.'

'Wow.'

'I know.' She shakes her head, growing misty eyed at the memory. 'It was the size of an eclair!'

The three of us fall quiet for a moment. I look at Fay and I'm pretty sure she's also pondering if she'll ever eat an eclair again.

'Cute name for a cat,' I offer.

'Thanks. All our rescues are named after stars of the golden age of Hollywood. Mr Chaplin is Mr Gable's brother but nowhere near as smart; what he lacks in intelligence he makes up for in gluttony – at least once a week I'm extracting string from his arse.' She pauses and looks at our confused faces. 'String from the kitchen bins.' She says it as if it is completely obvious. 'From the pork or beef joints. Right, check in? Quick bite then it's group meditation.'

After lunch in a room flooded with sunshine and dotted with more people in robes, dreamily browsing the buffet, we're back in our room, which is charming but cluttered with mismatched antique furniture closing in on our twin beds. On a shelf a stuffed rabbit is mounted in mid-dash, front legs at full stretch, rear haunches folded ready to propel it forward, though it evidently didn't propel itself fast enough. Its plastic amber-coloured eyes watch us. There are heavy drapes at the window and it smells faintly of rosemary.

We've unpacked and changed into the new yoga gear Fay has bought. Every inch is encased in stretchy Lycra. Both of us have slim figures but the fabric is so tight that my belly is trying to escape out of the waistband. We stand and appraise each other.

'We're very pastel.' I grimace, taking in the lilac and pink hues. 'Like we're sponsored by Petits Filous.'

'It's fine,' says Fay, 'in meditation everyone will have their eyes closed.'

We chuck on a hoodie each and head down to the ballroom, its high ceiling decorated with ornate mouldings. In the centre of the room stands Mary who has changed into a white vest and ankle-length skirt, both with a line of tiny silver bells stitched along the hems so that whenever she moves she tinkles. She's making an effort to talk in a soothing monotone.

'Welcome, welcome,' she murmurs. 'Come join us.'

Fay and I exchange a glance and I immediately want to giggle. I decide that I'd best not look at her for the next hour.

There are twelve mats laid in a circle, like a clockface, and most are taken. There are people of varying ages and varying awkwardness. Some people already have their eyes closed, some watch us dreamily, an older couple smile shyly at us. It reminds me of the nap room at Chloe's old nursery. We sit with crossed legs on the two mats closest to us.

Mary lowers the lights and we're enveloped in a blue-tinged gloom. She tinkles her way around the circle, her bare feet squeaking on the wooden floor, handing each of us a soft blanket.

She instructs us to lie on our backs and get comfy underneath our blankets. 'Place the palms of your hands one on top of the other where your heart is,' she tells us.

Mary returns to the centre and once we're all settled she begins her patter, talking us through a set of breathing exercises and visualisations that she says will help to clear our minds. She starts at ten and counts down through a series of feline-based scenarios. 'Next, count eight paw prints in the sand, one by one the tide washes them away', 'and there in the dark sky are two stars, shining brighter than a cat's eyes', 'one lone butterfly dances on a breeze past a basket of sleeping kittens'.

Next she encourages us to relax each part of the body, starting at the very tips of our toes all the way up to the tops of our heads. Her anatomical knowledge is impressive, not one area is left un-flexed then relaxed. I'm just grateful she doesn't move inside and start asking us to twitch our kidneys and spleen or we'll be there all day.

Despite our initial cynicism I feel very relaxed. Mary's sing-song voice is hypnotic and her words ring true so much that I feel a small lump form in my throat.

'You are a river, flowing through life. Like a river, there will be treacherous parts and calmer times. Seek out what you need, change course if need be. What is your destination, your personal ocean? Where are you headed? Visualise where you want your future to be.'

As I lie there I feel a single tear slide from the corner of my eye and tickle my ear.

Mary continues and ends with another meditation. 'Float away like an untethered balloon,' she says, so I do. I feel my eyes droop and my shoulders soften. Mum and her drama are a galaxy away, rather than just down the M6.

I steal a glance at Fay and she looks fully asleep, mouth gaping open slightly. She makes a tiny snorting noise and I smile to myself in the semi-darkness, pleased she's relaxing.

9

By early evening we're at dinner in a long bustling dining hall, a buffet laid out at one end, a handful of smiling staff milling around, pouring wine, offering water. Along the edges of the room are various-sized tables with white linen cloths softly lit by chandeliers. Pleasant chit-chat bubbles around the room, a large group of women in their thirties are laughing and raising a toast, clinking glasses. We find a table and I smile at the couple I recognise from the meditation session. One is voluptuous in an apple-green jumpsuit and matching wedges, and her companion is slender, with slightly rounded shoulders and wears a blue sailor dress with square white collar and matching navy Alice band clamped down over poker-straight blond hair.

'Sheila,' the first woman announces as she puts down her plate, piled high with slices of fruit and three large prawns, their heads lolling off the edge of the plate.

Her friend gently puts down a plate laden with olives and cheese.

'Join us,' I say, rather redundantly as Sheila has already sat down and is busy unfurling her napkin, while the other woman is awkwardly waving hers like a white flag of surrender before straightening it on her lap.

'I'm Josie, this is Fay.'

'Lovely to meet you,' says Sheila, lifting her plate up to her face and sniffing along a prawn's body like she's doing a line of coke from it. 'Got to be careful. Remember Corsica? I was nearly bumped off by a bad prawn. Three days I was out for the count, then when I came to my fever was so bad I was hallucinating. I was convinced Martin was Clare Balding and we were backstage at Crufts.'

Our blank faces prompt her to explain.

'Martin's my husband, lovely man, light of my life,' she sing-songs but she has mischief in her eyes and her friend shifts awkwardly in the seat next to her.

'Sorry, how rude, this is Ann-Marie.' She gestures to her left.

We've been so transfixed by the whirlwind that is Sheila that we've barely glanced at Ann-Marie but we do now.

She smiles shyly. 'Lovely to meet you.'

We take in the flawless make-up, classy French manicure and slight Adam's apple and know that underneath it all there is more to Ann-Marie than meets the eye. But it's not our business – everyone has a backstory and hers is one that clearly began as a male.

'I love your hair,' says Fay, eyes shining. 'Very beautiful.'

I know from the years spent helping Mum straighten and style her wigs that Ann-Marie's is a quality piece, a real investment.

'Thank you,' she says coyly, twisting a length of it through her slender fingers. 'I was brunette for a while but Sheila said I looked less Catherine Zeta-Jones and more Brian May.'

Sheila nods, snapping the head of a prawn clean off, a couple of drops of grey liquid landing on the table cloth. 'There was so much hairspray and backcombing going on her whole head was a fire risk. It's best to be honest about these things. We have learned over the last couple of years how to be honest with each other.' Her voice softens and I suddenly feel like Fay and I are intruding on a moment. 'All this glamour is... new to Ann-Marie. And to me too. However,' she sits up straighter and sniffs, 'it's lovely that we can enjoy a bit of pampering together, that's why we thought this weekend would be a good idea.' Shelia pulls away the rest of the prawn shell and using the tip of her scarlet thumbnail, burrows into its spine and gouges out its intestinal tract in one fluid movement. She wipes the sludge onto her napkin and takes a bite.

Fay is watching them rapt. 'Well, everyone needs to escape sometimes. Me and Josie certainly do, this weekend is her Christmas pressie.'

'What a lovely present,' Sheila says, 'and good for you too. I'm quickly discovering what it's like occasionally being in a same-sex relationship and I must say I've rather enjoyed doubling my jewellery and make-up collection overnight, though of course I can't get near Ann-Marie's bras – more chance of squeezing a Saint Bernard into a sherry glass!'

'Oh no! We're not actually together-together,' I say taking a sip of wine. 'Though even if we were, I doubt we'd wear each other's clothes. Fay endlessly ridicules me for my pashmina usage and I outgrew my Docs when I finished uni. In my opinion Docs are like slogan T-shirts and pigtails and should only be worn by the young.'

'Nonsense,' Fay says, poking one of her cherry-red boots out from under the table and looking down admiringly, turning it this way and that, like she's trying it on in a shoe shop. 'You'll have to wrestle these from my cold corpse when I'm a hundred and two.'

'Oh well, I'm sorry for the misunderstanding,' says Sheila, adding matter-of-factly, 'it was actually the Doc Martens that gave me the impression you were... a couple.'

Fay gives me a side-eye and I snort.

'I'm with you on the pashminas, Josie, I have a few myself – any day now they'll be back in fashion.'

It's Fay's turn to laugh now that I'm style-matched with the rather flamboyantly dressed Sheila.

'Fashion is cyclical,' she continues, waving another prawn. 'I keep telling Mar – I mean Ann-Marie – yesterday's rara skirt is next year's hot new thing. I've a collection of ice-wash denim in the loft that'd make Hasselhoff swoon!'

'It's true,' says Ann-Marie softly, voice breaking slightly, 'you should see the stuff Sheila keeps hold of, all labelled and dated, stacked joist to insulated rafter, it's up there. It's almost eerie. She'd make a good serial killer, so methodical she is.'

'Or archivist,' adds Fay. 'That's what I used to do.'

'How interesting,' says Sheila. 'We have a friend who worked at the Manchester Museum archiving – she's at an art gallery now, doing ever so well. One of the sisters who owns it had a stroke so she manages the place now; she's like family to them. Lovely girl, not remotely snooty seeing as she's fingering a Picasso one day and a Hockney the next. Right, who's for cava? Let's toast new friendship and fashion!'

10

The next morning I wake up early with an overwhelming urge to talk to James. I keep thinking about the photographs and I want James' point of view. I miss him. Not in a 'want to rekindle our love' kind of way – that ship sailed a long time ago. But I miss his advice. James is many things – occasionally daft, a teeny bit selfish but always kind and gives excellent guidance.

I'm only wearing my pants and a vest top and the room is chilly despite the sunlight pouring in through the gap in the curtains. Fay is snoozing off the cava and red wine we put away last night with our new friends Sheila and Ann-Marie aka Martin. After our second bottle Sheila cornered me by the traditional porcelain confessional: the sinks in the Ladies and it all came tumbling out. Ann-Marie is the alter ego of Sheila's husband Martin and since she discovered his penchant for cross-dressing some eighteen months ago, they've gradually reached a compromise they're both happy with: Ann-Marie can come to visit every Tuesday while Sheila's at her pottery class and every other weekend, including special weekends away like this one. Sheila's seemed thrilled to be able to share all this info, pausing only when another guest entered the Ladies. But once the hand dryer had fallen silent and the door swung shut again, she continued her tale.

'It's changed our relationship deeply,' she confided with a small hiccup. 'We're both more fulfilled – he feels he's truly himself with me now and as a consequence he's much happier. So to quote Lady Di, "There are three people in this marriage." Though Martin is both Charles and Camilla.'

'Well, Sheila,' I'd said, 'what an understanding and open-minded young woman you are,' and she looked pleased as punch with all three adjectives. 'Come on,' I said. 'Those two will be thinking we've fallen down the loo.'

Back at the table I could tell by Fay's face that Ann-Marie had been confiding in her too.

After a couple more drinks Sheila had dragged Fay up for a dance and I'd told Ann-Marie about being newly single.

'I'm not one for giving advice,' Ann-Marie had said. 'What I can say though, and this took me a long time to learn, is that it's not about what you do or where you go, but who you are. At your very core, who do you want to be?'

'That's a big question,' I'd said into my drink.

'I know. Maybe the answer lies in your past, in going back. Be brave, Josie. Life flies along too quickly to just be along for the ride. Take the wheel this time.'

I think of her words as I chuck on a robe. My forehead starts to throb and I rummage in my bag and locate some Nurofen, swigging two down with a glass of water in the bathroom. My face looks like a leather bag in a charity-shop window and I think ahead to the facial booked in for later. I don't know if it's the hangxiety, but the thought of having to lie absolutely still in a haze of ylang-ylang, listening to whale song fills me with fear. I feel jittery, like the time I had three espressos before a presentation in New York and couldn't string a sentence together.

I need some air. I grab my shades and push open the windows that lead to a tiny balcony, on which is squeezed a wicker armchair with faded cushions. I sit in it, resting my bare feet on the wrought-iron railing and breathe deeply. I start to feel better, though my heart races like I'm in flight-or-fight mode. Maybe I need to take flight, go and see the farm today? Ann-Marie's words are still rattling round my brain and I feel galvanised. I need to go there before this impulse melts away.

Our balcony overlooks a terrace where guests are eating breakfast under a cloudless but cool sky. They're sporting shades and puffa coats with the hotel's beige tartan blankets on their laps – think ski resort meets retirement village chic.

Beyond the terrace are stone steps leading down to lawns and a small lake edged with reeds. I spot a white footbridge at one end and a gentle waterfall at the other. Huge oak trees and weeping willows complete the picture. I breathe deeply and try to take it all in.

The urge to call James is still there. It's just gone eight a.m. and it's a Sunday but he's always up early, he's an insufferable seizer of the day, another hangover from boarding school where they were turfed out of their beds at first light for character building yomps over frozen moorland before tepid showers and hot porridge.

On the third ring I begin to doubt myself. What if he was out last night? I go to end the call just as he picks up. He sounds strange – husky voiced, panicked. 'Josie. Everything OK?' he asks. 'Yes, course,' I say, feeling foolish now for bothering him. 'Sorry, I just wanted a chat. Are you in bed, did I wake you?'

'No... no I was awake.' He clears his throat. 'Give me a second.' I think I hear a shower starting in the background. His bedsheets rustle against the phone like he's manoeuvring up from the bed and away from the noise of water. I can definitely hear it though. Fuck. He's got someone there! Barely a month since he was rogering me in the downstairs loo and he's back in the saddle.

'Are you there, Jose?' he says. It's quieter now and his tone has relaxed, he's clearly gone through to another room away from whoever is washing away their night of torrid sexual shenanigans.

'Yup, I'm here.' And in those three words I know that he knows that I know. And he knows that I know he knows I know. 'I just wanted your opinion on something but I can call you back later. I'm up North, in the middle of nowhere so the line's not great. You know what you always say... they've —'

'Barely got phone lines up there yet,' he chimes in awkwardly.

'Exactly. Look I'll call you later, or tomorrow maybe,' I say, then, 'Bye,' shouted cheerfully like I'm auditioning for CBeebies.

'Bye,' he replies.

'I did warn you,' Fay points out helpfully an hour later as we eat breakfast in the sunshine.

'I know.' I'm feeling a little sorry for myself, despite everything. James is a free man and I'm a free woman. I could have sex with anyone I fancy, right here, right now. I look up from my croissant to survey my options: a couple in their seventies each reading the *Telegraph* wearing matching plum fleeces, and a teenage girl enthusiastically vaping whilst feeding a very fat grey cat her leftover bacon. The cat is sitting on the other chair at their table for two.

'You were together a long time, Jose, it's bound to feel a bit weird.'

'I know.' My hangover isn't helping, my head feels like a burntout car and I'm worried about how last night ended. 'Are you sure everyone was dancing, not just us four?' I check again.

'Absolutely,' says Fay, who infuriatingly looks as fresh as a daisy. 'I told you – once they cleared away dinner the music began and everyone had a bit of a dance. Mary even led a conga, still tinkling in her outfit. Though at one point she was on her hands and knees looking for a bell that flew off during the locomotion. She was worried one of the cats would eat it.'

'Oh yeah, probably Mr Chaplin. Think that's him over there.' We look over to the cat. He's polished off all the girl's bacon and now seems to be chewing on a foil patty of butter while she studies her phone.

'No! None of that please,' booms Mary, appearing again from nowhere, carrying a cat we haven't seen before. This one is ginger with white splotches; it's very long and slung over her forearm like a fox fur.

She's heading over to the girl and I presume she means vaping is against the rules, but in fact she's talking to the cat. 'Mr Chaplin!' she shouts. The cat looks up at her like they're at a dinner party and he cannot quite place where he knows her from. 'Don't act all innocent. You know full well that butter gives you the squits, and I for one am not going to be clearing up your mess again. Here.' She swipes at the butter packet and grabs it from his mouth. He jumps down and with his tail slowly waving farewell, mooches away.

'Tsk,' says Mary with a shake of the head. 'Sorry. That cat has hollow legs,' she says to the girl.

Mary spots us and heads over, the cat over her arm swaying to and fro with her movements and wearing a resigned expression.

'Top party crew,' she says, giving a little fist pump with her free arm. 'What fun last night. Who knew my floor fillers' playlist would have such an effect on the dining room.'

'Yeah, well that and the copious amounts of booze everyone drank.'

'Yup, fair.' She nods, scratching her chin, looking off over the lawns.

'Aren't you going to introduce us?' I ask.

'Eh?'

I nod towards the bored-looking cat and I swear she almost jumps as though she'd completely forgotten it was there.

'Oh! Ha-ha, of course. Josie, Fay, meet Ms Monroe.'

The cat appraises us, twitches her white whiskers, then slowly closes her eyes and seems to fall asleep.

'Don't mind her. She's not herself – gets very blue some days and the only thing that keeps her on an even keel is her sister Joan Crawford, but I've not seen her all morning. We've come out to find her, haven't we, sweetheart?'

Ms Monroe opens her eyes but keeps them downcast to the ground.

'See?' whispers Mary. 'Not right at all. If you spot a ginger and white cat same as this one, except slightly plumper and more animated, that'll be Joan. Shoo her over to reception will you?'

'Course,' we both chime.

'Thanks, lovelies. See you for yoga in an hour?' She smiles but before we can answer she's gone, cat swinging by her side.

Fay looks at me. 'Uh oh.'

'What?'

'I know that face. It's the same one you pull when you're worried I'll be cross. It's the one you made at uni when you burnt my griddle pan to buggery.'

'Jesus, will you ever forgive me for that?'

'It was Le Creuset. So, no. Come on then, spit it out. Do you not want to do yoga, 'cos if that's it, I'm not arsed either?' She sips her coffee.

'I don't want to do yoga. Or the facial. Or any of it,' I say.

She looks up.

'I want to go.'

'Is this because of James?'

'No. It's because of Ann-Marie.'

We look across to where Ann-Marie and Sheila are sitting, they've joined the *Telegraph* couple and are playing cards.

'Something she said, about me going back. I think she's right.'

'Look, I'm trying not to be offended that you've been swayed by a stranger rather than your best friend, and I'm genuinely thrilled you want to go but we've got treatments booked – a whole night left.'

'I know. I'm sorry. I just feel like I need to go and see the farm. This morning. The photographs, the call with James, I just feel like everything is pushing me back there. I don't think I'll be much fun if we stay.'

Fay nods. 'Yeah, I can hardly hold you hostage in the hot tub.'

'Maybe we could come back here afterwards?' I say weakly.

'Look, I've been campaigning for you to visit the farm for years so I can't complain. Though you owe me a facial, my pores will have to remain blocked in solidarity with your mission.'

At that moment a fat ginger cat with creamy ears and tail comes sashaying across the lawn with Vegas residency energy. 'Joan Crawford!' we both cry and vape girl peers at us from her bubble of smoke.

'Maybe it's a sign,' whispers Fay.

'Really? Isn't it black cats that are lucky?'

'Yes. And ginger ones are for bravery, everyone knows that.'

We head off to find Mary, to explain our exit and to bid her farewell. We spot her by the bridge, crouched down stroking a leggy black cat, skinnier than the others. It darts into the undergrowth as we approach, 'Ms Garland,' says Mary. 'A troubled soul but we'll get there.'

We leave with her email address and a jar of honey from the hives she keeps on the meadow beyond the bridge.

As Fay starts the car I turn to her. 'You know the whole thing about how some people are radiators and they warm and enrich your life, and others are drains because they suck all your energy and positivity away? I think Mary is definitely the former.'

Fay grins. 'Radiator? Are you joking? More like a bloody furnace.'

11

We wind our way back along the country lanes, the Fiesta grumbling up the steep narrow climbs and all three of us seem to breathe a sigh of relief as the road broadens and flattens. We soon pick up signs for the M6 which would take us to the M1 southbound and home. Instead we head for another home of sorts, the farm where I grew up. If it's still there.

'I can't believe you were dragged from the only home you'd ever known just weeks after your dad died and you've never been back,' muses Fay. 'I think it'll be so healthy and healing to go there and say a proper goodbye to the area, to the farm, to your dad.'

'Or to reconnect to it...' I say.

I reach into the back seat and grab the photos, looking through them again. There's a familiarity there already, a comfort in knowing what to expect, like flicking through a novel you've read a dozen times.

'I've got butterflies for you,' Fay says as she slows down, approaching the turning for Lennington and Howlesden.

My head snaps up at the clicking of the indicator. It sounds like a ticking clock on a gameshow. 'Are you going to stick with the life you have, Josie?' whispers the smarmy host through his dazzling white teeth and orange tan, 'Or gamble and risk losing your happiness for the star prize – a peak into your past? The clock's ticking, Josie.' The audience shout, 'Gamble! Gamble!' Fay turns right into the road. 'She's gambling, folks!' cries the gameshow host. The audience goes wild.

The road towards Lennington is dotted with clumps of small terraced houses huddled together against the elements on the edge of the Pennines, which stretch out on either side of us now, a perpetual mottled green expanse as vast as a tumultuous ocean. We see an occasional farmhouse set back from the road, thin smoke curling up from the chimney, a tractor already buzzing around the yard, the busy life of a farmer.

'No one ever went into farming for the money and glamour,' Dad was fond of saying, usually through gritted teeth in the middle of the night when elbow deep in one of his heifers, kneeling in a wet sludge of cow shit and amniotic fluid, trying to tie a rope round the back legs of a large calf that was presenting breech. At times like this he'd joke to cover his panic, working fast to save the life of the unborn calf. I would stand watching, trying to hold a torch still despite shivering in my wellies as Dad's heavy breathing and the stricken cow's grunts filled the otherwise silent cattle pens. Occasionally the sound of straw shifting could be heard as one of the cows in the next-door pen strained their heads over the breeze-block wall to have a nosy at proceedings, her black eyes shining in the gloom.

After much heaving and a muttered swear word or three, the calf would slip out in a stream of glassy amniotic fluid and flop lifelessly onto the straw. Dad would work swiftly, clearing the gunk from its tiny pink nose with the palm of his hand, roughly wiping its head with fistfuls of dry straw, bullying it into life. After what seemed like a lifetime the calf would give a single raspy cough and gulp in its first breath of air, eyes blinking open at the new world around it.

Dad would smile at me in the darkness and push the calf close to its exhausted mum. Once the cow started to wash her new baby with long licks from her rough tongue, we'd leave them in peace to bond and head back to celebrate with Shredded Wheat and hot milk, sugar glistening on top in the half light of the kitchen, high from the night's drama.

The headlights from the vet's jeep would sweep across the yard just as we were finishing up. He'd stay for a brew once he'd checked over the calf. 'Grand job there, Fred.'

I always wanted to help during calving season so at the weekend and during the Easter holidays I made Dad promise he'd wake me in the night when he went to go check on the cows that were due to calve. I loved these moments, just me and Dad alone out in a sleeping world.

After Dad died, Mum would rue her time as a farmer's wife, a life never destined to bring riches as her husband had often pointed out. I would hear her late-night conversations at the kitchen table with her sister, my auntie Jo. 'How am I going to cope? He's left us penniless. I can't keep the farm going. We'll have to move.'

Within weeks of burying Dad we'd moved from the farm into a tiny two-up two-down in a rough part of Sheening, miles from where I grew up, away from my beloved primary school and down the hill from Loben Woods where Mum now lives.

Fay switches on the radio and Steve Wright's voice fills the little car. 'It's *Sunday Love Songs*, let's hear more of your messages.' He plays a compilation of voice notes from his listeners. 'Hi, Steve, it's Carol here from Lowestoft. Please play a song for my husband Gerry's sixtieth birthday, he's a wonderful husband, dad and grandad and he's my best friend and my rock.'

'Cute,' Fay and I say in unison and laugh as we sing along tunelessly to 'Secret Lovers'.

We drive along past a row of shops and a church then take a left and are plunged back into deepest countryside, as if the small high street is a Hollywood set masking the wilderness beyond.

The Fiesta rattles along, and at a crossroads with a wide tarmac road the satnav ushers us straight on, deeper down into a valley where the winding road darkens as the hedges either side of the narrow track rise up, penning us in.

I watch Fay's face as she drives, set in concentration. She's still very pretty and people are naturally drawn to her. She was always popular at uni – everyone seemed to know her and so by default they started to know me. A jealous housemate said I was 'Fay-mous with a y'.

Fay was studying history and did her thesis on anthropology of food, she was obsessed with cooking and could knock up incredible curries from whatever lay around the grimy student kitchen. She'd always have the munchies as she was never far from her biscuit tin stuffed with weed, loose Rizla papers, matches and other drug paraphernalia that reminded me of my mum's sewing box.

In autumn she'd take me magic-mushroom picking and we'd nibble while we harvested, so that by the end we'd be flat on our backs in the grass, watching the clouds and giggling, cheeks ruddy, high as kites. We even kissed once, just to see what it was like whilst tripping. Her lips were soft and hot and for a moment it was blissful, I was very high and felt a rush that seemed to travel from my mouth and spread down through my core. Our faces were so close that her skin appeared mottled with moving paisley patterns – the visuals were too much.

We broke apart from the kiss and rolled onto our backs, weirded out. She did an impression of my shocked face and I laughed so hard that I accidentally snotted.

She introduced me to James in the second year. He rented a room next door to her. 'He's sweet,' she said, 'but talks so posh he's definitely distant royalty.' The three of us became an unlikely crew and for the first time in my life I felt I belonged – they both looked out for me and I loved being looked after in a way I hadn't really been since I was twelve and my life had changed forever. Most people would say their uni years were formative but they were more than that to me – they were so very different from my childhood after leaving the farm, when life had been run through with loneliness like thick veins through the back of a hand.

Fay notices me watching her. 'What's that soppy smile for?'

'Nothing, just thinking.'

She slows suddenly. 'Bloody hell. This is getting a bit hairy.' She grimaces at the satnav. 'It's allegedly the right way though.'

Half a mile to go and we're in a tunnel of dark greenery. Fay puts the car's lights on. The trees above have joined forces to blot out the sky and it feels less like the magical green tunnel leading up to Shearness, and more like the area is trying to intimidate us. Steve is now playing the Piña Colada song but Fay turns down the radio and it fades away. 'Sorry, Wrighty, need to concentrate.'

Suddenly the Fiesta's front left wheel thumps into a deep rut at the edge of the road. Fay pulls the steering right to correct it just as a huge blue van careers around the corner coming straight at us and going way too fast, its front grille seemingly on top of us in a split second, inches away from colliding head on. We don't make a noise, no screams or shouts like in the movies. I brace for impact and in that fleeting moment I have enough time to acknowledge the irony of me dying in a car crash on the same roads that caused my father's death almost forty years before. I think of Mum as Fay wrenches the steering wheel sharply to the left and slams her foot on the brake, sending the little Fiesta careering to the side and bumping up onto the grassy bank where it lands with an almighty thump. The car rocks for a second. We look at each other in shock and then in unison turn in our seats to look behind us to watch the van as it disappears round the bend, a small dust cloud the only evidence it ever existed.

We are silent no longer. 'The bastard!' shouts Fay, her voice wobbling with shock. 'He nearly killed us.'

'I can't believe he didn't stop!'

'He was going too fast wasn't he?' she asks, seeking reassurance it wasn't her fault.

'Definitely. You did so well to get out of the way. Are you OK?'

'Yeah. Just. Fuming.' She looks down at her hands, fingers out-stretched. 'I'm shaking. You OK?'

I nod. I feel like I might cry.

'Do we call the police?' she says. 'For the insurance. That twat left the scene of an accident. That's illegal.'

'I don't know if that counts as an accident seeing as the vehicles didn't collide and the main impact was the front of your car with a bush.'

We open our doors slowly, wincing as they creak in agony. We climb out carefully as if avoiding causing the battered Fiesta any more pain. We meet at the front to assess the damage. The pas-senger side is worse as it took the brunt of the force and most of the front wheel is visible from under the wheel arch, sticking out at an unnatural angle like a footballer's ankle after a career-end-ing tackle. The front bumper seems to be hanging off but it's difficult to tell as that and the radiator grill are buried deep in a hawthorn bush.

I put my arm round Fay's shoulders. The wind is picking up and I get a gob full of hair as I speak, 'Sorry, Fay.'

'No,' she says. 'It's OK. Most important thing is we're in one piece.'

Her shoulders shiver and I'm not sure if it's the weather, which seems to be taking a turn for the worse, or the shock setting in after such an adrenaline dump; either way we need to make a move. Heavy clouds are knitting together in menacing clumps and we're in the middle of nowhere. We take out our phones but neither of us have any service. 'Balls,' we say in unison again, then laugh despite ourselves.

I look at the sky and try to read it like Dad always did. I'm sure a storm is brewing. I'm not great in thunder and lightning – unsurprising really. We hear a low rumble in the distance, which snaps us into action. 'Right,' I say, 'we need to get to somewhere where we have service or at least somewhere we can shelter and call for help.'

'OK...' Fay looks around. 'The last place we passed was a while back so maybe we push forward? Think we're less than a mile from Howlesden.' She goes and rummages in the glovebox, her bottom protruding from the open passenger door for what feels like an age. I think maybe she's getting snacks. 'Got a chocolate stash?' I ask hopefully when she eventually stands and stretches her back. 'I wish,' she says holding up a Sharpie. 'No, I've written a note, in case.' She places the folded bit of paper in the front window of the Fiesta.

'Clever,' I say. 'Not just a stunning face.' She replies with a wink.

We lock the car, which luckily isn't blocking the road on account of it being perched on the bank in a ruddy big bush, then step back onto the road.

'Hang on,' I say, 'there's no path, we can't walk on the actual road – any old nutter could come flying round the corner and pile into us.'

We clamber back up the bank and look at the barbed-wire fence; it is in a bit of a state with the odd fence post loose and leaning over, making the wire baggy enough for me to hold it down low so we can step over it and into the field.

'One advantage of having a farmer's daughter with us,' says Fay.

'My dad would never have let his fences get as bad as this,' I tut.

I recognise the ankle-length crop is hay and know right away there'll not be anything – specifically an aggressive bull – grazing and we'll be OK to follow the edge of the field until we reach civilisation.

We walk for a few minutes, scanning the horizon for buildings when we hear a louder rumble from the sky.

'Oh god,' I say, quickening my pace. 'Come up, let's go a bit faster.' I stride ahead and that's when I see it, a collection of buildings nestled at the lower edge of the field we're in. I feel a wave of nausea pass over me and my fingers tingle. Even though the buildings are tiny I know that beyond the modest farmhouse there is a paddock and some bullpens. There's a blue feed silo that looks like a NASA rocket towering over the gabled roof of a low-slung poultry shed. Etched into the peeling paint on the side of the silo will be the initials JSW for Josie Susan Wylde. Scratched into the paintwork by me in 1978.

I feel a fat drop of rain on my nose and before I can say anything to Fay there is a brutal crack of thunder directly above our heads and the heavens open. We shriek and run as fast as we can down the hill and towards the farm. I feel a lurch of excitement as we hurtle down along the edge of the field and towards my childhood home. We have no time to consider our game plan, focusing only on finding shelter and escaping the storm.

I start to grin as I run despite my fear of thunder. I'm bumping over the grass, excited and relieved that the place I fretted may have disappeared at the unscrupulous will of a developer is still here and (at least from what I can see) in one piece.

I'm ahead of Fay and slow a little to let her catch up. We're both sopping wet but at last the rain is easing. We reach the corner of the field and I know there is a stile where we can climb out of the field and turn left up the short farm track and into the yard. I hold out my hand to help Fay over the stile before clambering over myself. The moss-covered wood is slippery but the rain has stopped and we make it over, trotting the last few yards to the closed gate at the end of the farm lane. The stone gatepost and the sign attached to it is covered in ivy. I sweep the wet leaves to one side and Fay watches as I reveal the faded lettering 'Thistlefold Farm'.

12

'Oh. My. God.' Fay's reaction is priceless – disbelief, worry, joy all hurtle across her face in quick succession. Like I say, shit poker player.

'When did you realise?'

'I dunno… I mean the hawthorn bush you crashed into should've set the cogs turning but I didn't realise they were the actual ones on Dad's farm.'

'I was gonna say I wouldn't recognise a hawthorn bush if I crashed into one but I've literally just done that.'

'Yeah, I only know them 'cos I loved their beautiful white blossom. When I was little there used to be hundreds along the whole boundary fence.'

'Looks like they're still there.' Fay looks back along the route we've just run.

'Yeah. God, it was mad spotting the hen house and the feed silo… that's when I knew for sure.'

Standing here now at the end of the lane I feel ridiculous for not returning sooner. What was I so afraid of?

I glance at my phone and still only have a measly 3G. No use. We'll have to go up into the yard.

'Well?' asks Fay, following my eye line. 'Are you ready?'

'Nope.' I reply. 'After forty years' absence I'd imagined my return slightly differently. I thought I'd have time to collect my thoughts, to steel myself. Instead, here we are stumbling upon the place both looking like drowned rats.'

'I know.' She nods, looking down at her sopping jeans.

'And,' I continue, 'with no means of escape 'cos your car is currently residing in a bush.'

'Why do we need to escape?'

'In case the current farmer is pissed off that two randoms have rocked up in the middle of his yard.'

'Look, you made the decision to come here; something was pulling you back so keep the faith, you were worried the farm wouldn't even be here but it is. The hawthorns, the feed... lilo—'

'Silo.'

'It's all still here, it'd be crazy to not go have a look.'

'It's not that I don't want to take a look, it's more that I can't believe I've not come back until now.'

'Good. You're a badass, Josie, remember that.' She smiles, pulling me into a hug. 'And you're here now and so am I. We'll do it together.'

My phone suddenly buzzes into life, a text from James asking if I'm OK – guilty conscience probably.

Fay glances at his message. 'You know what that means?'

'That he's paranoid about our conversation earlier?'

'Oh yeah, I guess. But it also means we have phone signal.'

Ten minutes later we've called the breakdown service, hamming up the lone females in a deserted country lane element, and they've promised to get a local garage to us within the hour.

'Right,' says Fay. 'Plenty of time for a gander then we can head back to the car.'

We start to walk and as we do the sun appears. I look to the skies of course and there above the farm buildings is the biggest brightest rainbow I've ever seen. My eyes fill with tears. The appearance of one now is too perfect.

Fay hugs me tightly around the waist. 'See,' she says, 'it'll be OK, your dad's welcoming you home.'

The farmyard itself is reached through a metal five-bar gate. I'm pretty sure it's the same one from my days here, heavily rusted now. 'Hello?' we shout. No answer. The absence of activity, the peace and quiet – no tractor engines, no dogs barking, no machinery whirring – the absolute stillness tells me that the farm is deserted.

'What do you reckon?' Fay has her hands on her hips and looks at me, then at the gate, then back at me. Her cherry Docs are encased in mud and she looks freshly baptised by the downpour.

I nod and we climb over the gate. The adrenaline is now coursing through my body; I feel lightheaded and my mouth is dry. I'm being sucked through time with each step. To my right is the farmhouse and the cobbled square at the front where I came off my bike and needed stitches. I'm sure I feel the old scar on my knee throb now, like my body is synching with the surroundings. Every inch of the farmyard seems to hold a piece of my story. A faint smell reaches me, the familiar tang of well-rotted silage, the earthy tones of damp straw. Am I imagining them? If I concentrate could I evoke the sound of Dad calling the cows in from the field, the rattle of a few bits of feed in a bucket to tempt them to follow.

We stand in front of the house. I half expect a young me to trot out, mucky jeans tucked into wellies, off to play on the tyre swing Dad made for me, tethered to the yew tree. The house doesn't look much different – as far as I can see there's been no renovations to the outside at least. It's still white-washed but the paint is flaking and there are patches of grey where scabs of plaster have broken away from the brickwork.

The front of the house always looked to my young self like a face – the two upstairs windows the eyes, the sagging guttering creating a worried frown. The front door was the mouth, gobbling us up when we ran through it. I am eight years old and Dad is chasing me towards the house; I'm racing as fast as I can across the yard and through the front door to the safety of the living room, knowing full well Dad will be stopped by a force field – the 'no wellies beyond the lino of the kitchen' rule. Our farm dog Jet is joining in – confused but exhilarated with the kerfuffle and barking excitedly.

I kick off my sandals in the kitchen, crash through the lounge door onto the safety of the carpet and slide over the back of the low chesterfield sofa, like TV cops over a car bonnet. Dad is left stranded – panting and laughing in his mucky wellies at the kitchen boundary.

Dad wasn't particularly spontaneous but I was mid-water fight with friends and I'd sneaked up and sprayed him from my washing-up bottle that'd been repurposed as a weapon. I can hear the sounds of my delighted screams now echoing around the yard and the squeak of my wet thighs on the leather as I scoot over the sofa.

The heavy wooden front door is closed, fenced off by spiderwebs that sparkle with tiny raindrops, the biggest one stretched over the metal latch, smoothed by the pressure of a thousand thumbs.

The house seems small now but I know this is common – to return as an adult to find places have shrunk as you've grown bigger.

'How does it feel?' asks Fay.

'Weird. And kinda nice. But mainly weird. I'm glad you're here.' I feel tears well up.

'Always.' She touches my hand lightly.

Even though we're sure the place is empty it feels wrong to look through the windows. This was someone's home. But the pull is too strong. I take faltering steps and, shielding my eyes from the sun with a salute, peer through the murky glass. I'm braced for something, I don't know what, and as I squint into the darkness sure enough for a split second I see a tall figure standing there in the corner, but it's just a shadow cast by the gloom and my imagination. My eyes take a second to adjust and then I notice the seventies orange cupboards, Mum's pride and joy, are gone, replaced by pine, the eighties' equivalent. The worktops are cleared of all the usual detritus of a living kitchen – no toaster, kettle or breadboard. The small wooden shelf is still there but no longer cluttered with tractor keys, gloves in winter, Dad's tattered baseball cap in summer, piles of bills all year round.

'I wish I'd get letters,' I'd whinge to Dad.

'You can open mine,' he'd say, passing me a small selection of post, 'and you can keep the ones in the brown envelopes.'

'Really?'

'No, sweetheart,' he'd reply ruefully, 'you wouldn't want those ones.'

The shelf is empty apart from a grey layer of dust. My heart is thudding. I am conflicted, I am a stranger yet I'm home.

I step back from the window. I feel panicked, I think it's all too much. I'm overwhelmed. I take a deep breath and let it out slowly. Fay watches me.

'Can I have a tour?'

'Sure.' My shoulders start to relax as I concentrate on telling Fay about the yard. We stroll on past two low sheds. 'This was the coal shed and this was Jet's kennel,' I say. The old door is still on there and I squint through the rough square crudely cut out from the bottom of it and into the darkness. 'Dad made this little door down here so Jet could come and go.'

'His own little VIP entrance,' nods Fay.

'Exactly. Very Important Pooch. He slept on old hessian feed sacks in there.' I bob down but don't investigate further, afraid of something darting out – a mouse or worse, a rat. I'd told Fay all about Jet years ago, officially the best collie in the world and I can see his black and white face popping out now, investigating the sound of our footsteps. 'The skill when it was raining was to tiptoe from the house in your slippers to fill the coal scuttle quick enough to avoid getting wet and waking Jet, who would come wagging out for a cuddle and try to follow you into the house for the night.'

We walk across the yard past the hen house with its sliding doors on rusting tracks in the ground. The warm smell of compacted feathers, shit and heat is still in the air but maybe I'm imagining it. 'Hens,' I say, with a shudder. I can still hear the cacophony that came from in there when you shoved open the door. The deafening collective squawk of complaint that settled to a gossipy hubbub like dissatisfied customers waiting to speak to the manager.

'And there is the traditional farmyard space shuttle?' Fay points at the rusting rocket-shaped silo.

'Nearly. That's the silo, it held all the feed. Dad would wheel a massive wheelbarrow underneath, slide open a hatch and feed would pour out into the barrow.'

Like much of the yard the hatch is cobwebbed too, ancient specks of grain caught up like flecks of gold in a panner's sieve.

'Wonder how long it's been empty,' muses Fay.

'A while I reckon.' I head past the pig pens on the left and cross over the patchwork yard – concrete slabs stitched to gravel areas and cobbled sections, a mishmash of holes filled in and repaired with whatever was cheapest or even better, left over from another job. The farm always felt patched up, like a finger poked into a leaky hole until Dad ran out of fingers and the place became submerged in disrepair.

In the year before he died I remember the farm becoming more like a junkyard. Dad kept hold of all spare parts – bits of broken farm machinery, old timber and tyres – in case he could save a few quid repurposing them. As his budgets shrank the scrap heaps grew. I can see one now, lurking down the side of the pig pens; a modern art sculpture.

Once over the yard I stride down the side of the huge cow sheds, Fay breaking into a trot to catch up. I know what I need to see, my favourite view and I'm silently praying that it too, is unchanged. Over the years I've imagined a nightmarish landscape, scarred or destroyed by development. It was this fear, nestled amongst the other fears, that have kept me away.

We emerge around the back of the house with its small square of garden with its faded rockery and old apple tree. I beckon to Fay to climb up too as I step onto the bottom rung of the wooden fence. I hold my breath. This is it. I needn't have worried – if anything the view is more beautiful than the version I'd held in my mind's eye. Where other parts of the farm had shrunk and slumped this view is bigger than I remember and somehow brighter, in dazzling hues of spring.

From our perch the land opens up below us and I grin over at Fay, whose knuckles are white from gripping the fence.

'Wow,' she breathes.

We can see the whole of the back paddock and our fields beyond, a festival of greenery. The sun in beaming now and I feel a fresh breeze on my face, which makes my breath rush with joy. The doubt I felt minutes before melts away. I am back. I am hopeful Josie, happy Josie. I am no stranger to this land, I am bound to it by thick roots that plunge into the soil from my soul.

I notice first that the paddock is overgrown and looks all the more glorious for it, a flurry of orange-tip butterflies dance across the tops of the long grass peppered with meadow flowers and but-tercups. There is a scent that comes back to me, a fresh field smell of crisp country air that I gulp in giddily.

Beyond that the fields roll and undulate; the wind is picking up and the shadows cast by the hurrying clouds sweep over the land, causing the different shades of green to darken and brighten in turn. Tears stream from my eyes as I spot in the air above the fur-thest field a buzzard looking for lunch; it hovers as if tethered by a kite string to the earth. In the distance beyond our border a tractor trundles up the neighbouring field, huge funnel on the back distributing fertiliser onto the soil.

I close my eyes for a second to feel the breeze on my face; I open them again wishing my eyes could function like a wide-angle lens, I need to capture every inch of this view anew to store in my head and my heart, fold it away for safe keeping like a treasure map.

'This,' says Fay, 'is gorgeous.'

I can't speak for fear I might sob. I am home, home at last.

'It's like looking at a Constable whilst on mushrooms,' she breathes. 'The bucolic countryside but with such bright colours.'

I laugh and wipe the tears from my cheeks.

A loud honking comes from the yard. We climb down and scoot in the direction of the noise and there, rumbling away at the gate, is a ramshackle pickup truck which looks in need of being towed away itself. Hand-painted across the front in thick black lettering is 'Gordan & Sons Garage'.

'Damn. We were supposed to meet them at the car.'

We wave and the driver flashes his headlights in reply.

We climb back over the gate and I love the way I can still do it so naturally – left foot up on the second bar, swing right leg over and onto same bar on other side, swing left leg over, simultaneously jumping down as left leg almost meets the right. The dismount in one swift smooth motion is very satisfying. I hear a small yelp. Fay is slightly stranded on the third bar up with her legs crossed at the knees. I help her down giggling and we walk up to the driver's door.

The clouds of fumes being blown along the side of the truck from the exhaust engulf us.

'Thought you'd be here!' The man roars over the clatter of the truck. His face is buried under a thick thatch of black curly hair and beard, his eyes shining like two buttons. His protruding belly is wedged against the steering wheel and his hulk fills most of the cab, which is tipped towards us with his weight. The truck coughs another lungful of smoke.

'Saw your note.' He nods, grinning, and I recoil a little at his breath which is somewhere between hot tarmac and bacon crisps. 'This place is the only civilisation for a couple of miles so I thought you'd probably come looking for help. And I was right.' He beams then nods at the space next to him. 'Hop in then and we'll head back to the patient.'

We hoist ourselves up into the passenger seat of the cab, squeezing into the remaining space, slotting side by side on the padded bench, a double-width seat stripped back to a single by the encroaching outer boundary of his paunch. The black plastic is striped with gaffer tape and the grimy windscreen is decorated with the carcasses of a thousand miles' worth of bugs. I really don't want to be pressed up against the side of the man's girth so I put my left arm around Fay's waist and she presses her self tight against the truck's door, her right arm in my lap, heads pressed close.

'Hope you've not got nits,' she says.

'I can't promise anything.' I look at the man and shout over the din, 'Thanks so much. I'm Josie and this is Fay.'

'Gordon,' yells the man, crunching the truck into reverse and weaving back down the farm lane. I watch as the farm grows smaller and hear a whisper 'see you soon' – it's my voice.

'What?' shouts Fay over the engine.

'Nothing.'

The farm shrinks into the distance as we bump into potholes and the wing mirrors scrape through the hedgerow, becoming garlanded with strands of leaves.

Gordon swings backwards out onto the road and the truck settles as if catching its breath. 'Gordon Gordan,' he says with a wink, 'but you can call me GG.'

13

We roar back along the road to Fay's car, which GG quickly diagnoses as 'Absolutely fucked'. He makes a sign of the cross and drops his gaze.

'Are you sure there's nothing we can do?' pleads Fay, swatting away a small cloud of midges that have joined us to watch the drama.

'Sorry,' says GG, 'the front axle is more bent that a nine-bob note and to fix it would cost twenty times more than the car is actually worth. Would be madness to do that. She was in OK nick so you've obviously looked after her, but sadly it's the scrapyard for her.' He smooths his beard with his huge right paw then sniffs his palm, grimaces and wipes it on the bib of his overall.

Fay's shoulders sag with defeat.

'Where you off to? I can give you a lift,' he offers.

'London,' we say in unison.

'Ah. Well how's about I run you into the village and you can get a taxi to Lennington Station? There's plenty trains from there to Manchester, I think.'

'OK, thanks,' I say, turning to Fay. 'We can get a London train from Manchester.'

She nods and watches sadly as GG gets to work, attaching chains around the Fiesta and winching her awkwardly from the grass bank and up onto the bed of the truck, slowly reeling her in like a massive dead fish.

'What brought you round here then?' GG shouts as we set off towards Howlesden.

'She's a local,' Fay says and I nudge her in the ribs. 'Ouch!'

'Eh?' says GG glancing at us both.

'She said I'm very vocal, about what I want to do on my day trips 'cos I insisted on a ride to Howlesden – I know it's popular with walkers.'

'Aye.' He ponders this for a moment. 'Up in the hills there's a few decent "gastropubs", as they call them, popular with visitors, but not locals so much on account of them charging a fiver for a pint and double that for a Yorkshire pud. Madness.'

After ten minutes we rumble slowly into a small square and the truck shudders to a stop before falling silent. Gordan & Sons is a wooden structure with a forecourt upon which is piled a tower of wagon tyres on one side, and on the other a decrepit old-fashioned petrol pump with a faded 'Esso' logo on the front.

We climb down and GG stands over us, hands on his hips. 'Right. Bear with me while I sort out some paperwork. Shouldn't be too long.' He turns and disappears into a small shed next to the tyres that says 'Head Office' on the door.

'What's with all the secrecy?' asks Fay. 'Why can't he know you used to live round here?'

'I dunno.' I shrug. 'It just didn't feel right, blabbing on about it all. Plus it was so loud in there I didn't want to scream all my backstory over the noise of that engine.'

'OK,' says Fay, nodding.

'Sorry. You're not having a great day, eh? First we abandon the spa, your car is written off, you get rained on and then your best mate is a bit of an arse.'

'Don't be daft.'

We look around us. The little square looks very quaint in the spring sunshine, like the picture on a tin of shortbread biscuits. Across the street is a row of shops that swirl me straight back to my childhood. On the end is the chip shop where I spent most Friday teatimes queueing up with Dad for our chippy tea. I remember the owners, even back then, were older than god's dog so they can't still be about. I think it was called 'Village Fish and Chips' but is now rebranded 'For Cod's Sake' with an illuminated sign showing a cartoon fish with obscenely plump lipsticked lips, randomly wearing a top hat and giving a thumb-up with its fin. There's the smell of frying chips coming from the shop and my belly rumbles in response, a nudge to remind me we've not eaten since breakfast.

'Mixed messages with that sign,' says Fay. '"For Cod's Sake" is a nice pun but the name suggests some sort of exasperation and the over-sexualised fish seems to be dressed for a cabaret night.'

'Hmmm,' I reply. 'Ever wonder if you overthink things, Fay?'

'Every day.'

Next door is the newsagent's, then a greengrocer's, then a café that is next to a new estate agent's, in place of what I can't remember, but the shop on the end is unchanged. We cross the small road towards it and look up at the wooden sign above the window. 'Betty's Sweets' was a magical place to me as a child – floor-to-ceiling shelves holding countless jars of loose sweets.

'Ah, Betty's.' I do my best tour-guide impression. 'Run by the eponymous Betty.'

'Ooh, tell me more.'

'Always wore her pinny and slippers as if you'd walked into her front room, which I guess we had seeing as she lived out the back.' I peer past the window display of cut-price Easter eggs and into the shop beyond, which doesn't look any different. I am six years old again, eyes like saucers taking in all the jars, spending money burning a hole in my pocket. 'Wonder if they have popping candy? Remember when we thought it'd be funny to do some of that when we were tripping?'

'Ha, yes. Worst idea ever.'

'Betty knew the shelves like the back of her hand. Whatever sweet you called out she would locate it immediately, spinning on her flowery slippers in the direction of the jar containing your heart's desire. Sometimes I'd try to catch her out by asking for a quarter of a more obscure confection.'

'My favourites were cola cubes, rhubarb and custard.'

'Ah no,' I scoff, 'they would've been too easy to find. I needed to test Betty – cinder toffee, lemon bonbons – the trickier stuff.'

Fay nods slowly considering all this. 'You really didn't get out much did you?'

I laugh. 'That was our entertainment in the seventies. Poor Betty – probably clocked up thousands of steps on every shift.'

There was always a small queue as all the customers were children and spent too long gazing up at the sweets as if they'd arrived at the gates of heaven. Betty was patient though, resting her huge bosom on the glass counter while each child made their choice.

Dad would often run a few errands in the village and Betty would sort him out with a few Pontefract cakes, pressing the little paper bag into his hand with a wink. All the ladies liked Dad, even the old ones in their pinnies.

We push open the door and an old-fashioned bell rings. We're engulfed in a warm, sugary smell that again transports me. A woman our age comes through from the back, as slender as Betty was plump, sporting a huge orange jumper and a wide grin.

'Hello,' she says. 'What can I get you?' She has an accent that I can't quite place. 'Take your pick,' she says and it's on the 'your' that I detect a Cornish burr.

I glance around at the shelves. 'Quarter of Pontefract cakes please.' I smile. She turns and reaches up for the jar.

'I used to come in here when I was little,' I say to her back.

Fay looks at me with a 'Oh now you're ready to talk?' expression. I shrug.

'Oh really?' The lady turns with the jar and measures them out on the scales. 'How long ago?'

'Well, I left in 1982, when I was twelve but I remember the original lady – Betty?'

'Everyone remembers Betty!' The woman's face lights up. 'She was my grandma.'

'Wow – a grandma who lives in a sweet shop. Every child's dream.'

'I know right?' She hands over the bag of liquorice and I can't resist popping one in my mouth straight away. 'We lived a while away but I used to love visiting so much. She'd let me use the scales to measure out my own sweets.' She looked at the huge scales now with the polished metal dish on top. 'Grandma Betty kept working till about eight years ago and then I took over. She retired aged ninety-one. Can you imagine!'

'Wow,' I say. 'Amazing.'

'Yes, she was some woman. She passed at Christmas, just before her hundredth birthday. She used to say the secret to a long life was starting the day with a quarter of wine gums and ending it with a tot of whisky.'

'Well in that case,' Fay says, 'in honour of your gran I will have a quarter of wine gums, please.'

'Coming up,' says the lady, carefully reaching for the wine gum jar from a high shelf. 'You moving back then? Always happens. My parents moved to Cornwall before I was born but Mum was drawn back eventually and so was I.' She unscrews the lid and gently tips the wine gums onto the scales with a tinny clatter, the dial landing neatly on quarter of a pound. She screws the lid back on. 'Seems the most natural thing in the world to complete the circle. Return to where your tribe's from.'

I surprise myself by not really knowing the answer to her question, even though I know that of course I'm not returning; I'm just visiting.

The farm was amazing to see but I can't just pack up my life and return to a village full of strangers. She reaches over the counter, hands the paper bag of wine gums to Fay and, as if reading my mind, says, 'It's a lovely place to live. The people are very friendly – mostly. You'd quickly make friends – might as well start now, I'm Beth.'

Fay and I share a bag of chips on a bench in front of the church, St Mark's. Further along from the shops we spy a pub and a row of cottages before the road curls away into the countryside beyond.

'It is pretty,' says Fay, folding an extra long chip into her mouth.

'Yeah, it's lovely. These chips feel like a feast. I didn't realise how hungry I was.'

She takes a gulp from her can of Fanta. 'Me too. Writing off a car and stumbling upon a childhood home really works up an appetite.'

'The appetite of a fifteen-year-old – sweets, pop and chips.'

'I know – terrible. But bloody delicious.'

We're quiet for a moment while we finish the chips. There are few cars around and we can hear blackbird song coming from the trees that line the churchyard.

'Hey,' Fay says softly, nodding towards the church. 'Is your dad buried there?'

I sigh, which is all the answer she needs. I'd hoped she wouldn't cotton on.

'Do you want to go see him?'

'I really don't.'

'Why?'

'Well for starters it wouldn't be seeing "him", it'd be seeing a gravestone. Plus I can't bear to see it all overgrown and neglected. We have no relatives around here so there's no one to look after it.'

More than that I feel guilt. A hot shame spreads up my neck that I've abandoned the man I loved so much. That I've not been back to sit by his grave, bring flowers and chat to the headstone. As the years passed the guilt grew until it formed into a solid barrier, making me feel like I'd lost the right to visit.

We're quiet for a minute.

Despite the guilt I know she's right. Did I really think I could come all this way and see my childhood home, the village where I spent the first years of my life, and not visit the grave of the person I loved more than anyone else in the world? But the thought of his plot buried under ivy or weeds, thanks to my lack of care, feels so depressing. I have to do it, though. I don't have to stay long.

I stand up from the bench. 'Come on then,' I say.

Fay scrambles to her feet, folding the empty chip papers and cans into a package and tossing it into the bin by the bench.

St Mark's is a small parish church, with a noticeboard by the gate and multiple hanging baskets in full bloom by the door, where a few stragglers are saying their goodbyes after the Easter Sunday sermon.

The last time I was here was on a chilly October day almost four decades ago. Today the church feels less imposing and a much warmer place, with the spring sunshine illuminating the stained-glass windows. We slip past the parishioners and into the churchyard. I roughly know the route to Dad's grave and follow a small path that curves around to the left of the church, past a line of yew trees and towards a weeping willow, which thankfully is still there. I know Dad's grave is just beyond that.

I'm twelve and my mum, black veil fluttering in the breeze, leans against a tree for support. She looks frail, like she's in danger of blowing away herself up and over the cemetery. She felt faint I think, the other mourners gathered around her, all in black like a murder of crows. I look up at the weeping willow, a well-named tree for such a place. Though I don't think I shed a tear that day, I saved my crying for the following weeks, months and years, quietly hiding my sorrow so as not to upset Mum.

We keep walking slowly, Fay is reading out names from some of the headstones. She's always been a bit ghoulish, at uni she'd insist we'd walk through cemeteries so she could look at the angel monuments watching us from above, stone faces disapproving of our laughter and stoned chat.

The grass surrounding all the plots is like the baize of a snooker table and the newer stones we pass look polished and bright. Fresh flowers, candles and teddy bears cluster around them in silent vigil. As we walk further down the path the headstones are darkened by time and moss. The plots are largely bare and some are overgrown in a tangle of weeds and long grasses. Time has marched on and the mourners have moved away or become the mourned.

I know that Dad's is just beyond the willow on the right, not too close to the wall. I am braced, ready to have to delve through weeds and vines to free the stone and read the inscription.

Up ahead I see three stones and as I approach I take in the closest tombstone camouflaged green with grass. It looks pretty in a way, like it's been reclaimed by nature, and I decide there and then not to be upset by its abandoned state – his earthly resting place bears no reflection on where he rests in my heart.

Dad's plot is covered in grass speckled with daisies and butter-cups. I kneel by the stone and bow my head. My breath feels shallow and I need to take a moment. I breathe deeply and straighten my shoulders, braced to see his name etched in the stone. I push aside the tall weeds so I can see the lettering clearly. The name is spelled out in tall simple letters:

Abigail McCarthy, loving wife to Ernest. Born 21 March 1903 died 5 November 1981. Forever in our hearts.

Then below:

Ernest McCarthy. Born 30 December 1901 died 1 June 1985. Laid to rest with his adoring wife Abigail.

Fay has caught up and is reading the stone over my shoulder. 'Nice they're together again.' The breeze suddenly picks up and I wobble, reaching a hand out to the stone for support. 'Steady,' she says. 'Did you know them?'

'No... no, I'm a bit confused. I thought this was Dad's.'

We look at the next grave along, its neatness ruling it out.

'Hmm.' I stand up. 'Where is he then? I know he's not towards the back because I remember someone on the day saying "he'll be pleased he's not under the wall".'

'Random memories, eh?'

'I know. I can't remember who spoke or the songs we sang but I remember a quip about the bloody stone wall.'

I look further on but I'm sure it's near here. 'See it's not this one because – ' I stride to the next plot along – 'it's too neat...' But my words dry up in the wind as I look at the pristine grave, the clean pebbles on top, the vases of fresh flowers and read aloud from the stone as if to prove I'm not imagining it:

Frederick Wylde. 3 May 1944 – 10 October 1982. Rest in Peace.

Fay joins me and looks from the headstone to me and back again.

'Right,' she says. 'Someone is clearly looking after it.'

'I know that, but who?'

'Perhaps the gardener or vicar or something – aren't they supposed to keep the place nice?' We both glance at the neighbouring overgrown plot. 'OK, well maybe Abigail and Ernest offended the gardener at some point.'

'I literally can't think who would be doing it. Dad's parents are long gone obviously, and he was an only child.'

'Maybe it's a friend?'

I pull a face. 'Dunno. He just had his other farmer pals but yeah maybe.' I'm not convinced. I bob down and look at the flowers, a small bunch of cowslips. I recognise their golden centres and purple petals that fade to lilac on the edges. Mum used to have them on her rockery in the farm garden. She let me brighten up the rockery one year with leftover white paint. I must've been about nine and I remember being scared she'd be angry when the cowslips became speckled with white emulsion from my careless brushstrokes, but she just laughed saying they looked like a rare specimen. I love it when I remember a little snatch of happy time with Mum, it feels like when the sun comes out from behind a cloud and I'm warmed by the memory.

I look again. There is no note with the flowers, they're tied with string and sit inside a jam jar. I squint up at Fay. 'I don't know if I'm pleased or a bit jealous. He was my dad, why is someone else doing my job?'

'Well, sweetheart, you've not really been here to do it have you?'

I shrug. I know I'm being irrational. I take a deep breath and try to focus on the positive. I might not have been here to look after the plot but I'm here now. The knot of guilt that has lurked below the surface for years feels like it has loosened a bit at last. Fay turns and steps away. I touch the headstone, laying my palm flat on the marble, it is cool and smooth. The wording is simple – no mention of Mum or me, his only child. Just the dates. Thirty-eight years old. He'd barely had time to get his feet under the table of life. To enjoy the fruits of his labour, to see me grow up. I feel tears prickle at my eyes and my throat feels tight. I rock forward on my knees and gently place my forehead on the stone, the coldness is soothing and calms my breath. A single tear escapes the well of my eye and trickles down my cheek. I'm crying for Fred but I'm also crying for my mum and for twelve-year-old me, lost from each other in a tsunami of grief and complicated emotions swirling around us.

I don't know how long I rest like this, a few minutes maybe. I feel settled though, sad but settled. Eventually I sit back, get to my feet and breathe deeply. I look around and see Fay in the distance, reading a gravestone. She straightens and raises her hand in a wave.

Back at Gordan & Sons we duck inside the head office – a small wooden shed with just enough room for a desk and a couple of chairs. Gordon is snoozing with his feet up on the desk and his wide paddle hands resting on his acre of belly. With his dark beard and sizeable girth he looks like the evil twin of Father Christmas, the black sheep of the North Pole family. The beard is flecked with large flakes of pastry and the remains of a sausage roll lie abandoned on his desk, on a copy of the *Sun*.

'Can't believe he couldn't manage a whole one,' whispers Fay, eyeing the leftovers.

'You fancy it?'

I'm wondering what's the most polite thing to do in this situation – to gently nudge him awake, to clear my throat noisily or slam the door and re-enter?

Thankfully the decision is taken out of my hands when his phone rings. A tinny version of Meatloaf's 'Bat Out of Hell' rings out from somewhere on his person and he springs awake, swinging his boots down onto the ground and standing to touch his many pockets like a New York TV cop patting a felon down.

At last he locates the vibrating mobile and groggily answers, 'Gordan and sons. What can I do you for?' He nods gravely into his phone, which he switches to his left hand so he can luxuriate in a very thorough rearranging of his balls with his right. 'Aye. Yup. Yup. Okidokes. Will do.' He looks up at us now and nods, as if we should know exactly what has just been finalised on the call.

'Ta-ra,' he says and hangs up. 'Sorted.' He brushes a light snow-storm of crumbs from his beard.

'Sorry?' asks Fay.

'No need to be, was my pleasure.'

'No, I mean, sorry what is sorted? Was that about my car?'

'Nooooo. Sorted that out half hour ago. Where did you gals get off to? That phone call was Jim.'

'Jim?'

'Jim Taxi. He'll be here in a couple of mins.'

'OK. Good, thanks.'

'My pleasure.' He glances at the nub of sausage roll. 'I can never quite finish the third one,' he says mournfully. 'Can I tempt you?' He tilts the newspaper in our direction.

We both shake our heads.

'Fair enough. I saw you both stuffing yourselves with chips. I did shout to you but you were heading into the church. Weren't wasting your prayers on the Fiesta were you?' He chuckles at his own joke.

'No, actually my dad's buried there.'

His smile fades quicker than cheap fake tan.

'Oh right, I see.' He wipes his hands on his overalls. 'Sorry to hear that.'

'It's OK, he died a long time ago. Don't worry.' I look to Fay who's watching me quizzically. One minute I'm admonishing her for revealing my bloodline, the next I'm telling the sweet-shop owner and now GG. I don't know why I want to stake my claim in this village but I suddenly do. Maybe after the last couple of hours I feel a new connection that I can't deny.

'Do you mind me asking who your dad was?' says GG.

'Fred Wylde.'

'I knew it!' he shouts, slapping his thigh then, suddenly remembering the sombre tone of the conversation, looks serious again. 'My old dad and Fred were pals, he used to fix up your dad's tractors and all sorts. I used to help him sometimes, and I bloody KNEW I knew your face, you're Fred's daughter all right. It's uncanny, cor, I've got the shivers!' He shakes his head, rubbing the goosebumps from his outstretched arm. 'By 'eck, it's like he's standing in front of me now, apart from the obvious differences.' His eyeballs quiver with the strain of not flickering south to my chest. I appreciate the effort.

'People used to say I looked like him but I've not heard it for a while.'

'So you were visiting your old place then when I found you? I knew from the way you climbed that gate that you were farming stock.' He points at Fay. 'And that you definitely aren't.'

'Thanks,' she says. 'Who owns it now then? It seemed pretty deserted.'

'Oh aye. The third Earl of Lampston owns all the farmland round here, mainly renting to tenants, but your place – ' I like how he calls it my place – 'has been empty... must be going on for a year, eighteen months now. Old Pete Potter had it since the eighties when your family left but Pete didn't last long after his wife passed, they'd been married fifty-odd years. He died of a broken heart they say, though the half a tonne of silage bales that got dislodged and rolled onto him were definitely a factor too.'

'Right. How sad. It's a shame to see the place so run-down.'

'Well you could always take it on – dig out your old wellies.'

'Ha, that's not an option, sadly.'

'Well if you change your mind, it's up in the window of the estate agent's just over the road.' He turns and retrieves something from a shelf behind him. 'Now, you'll be wanting these I expect?' he says to Fay, passing her a small pile of stuff. 'From the glovebox.'

I see the car's log book, a packet of wet wipes, a couple of face masks and a four-finger KitKat. He hands them over like a nurse returning the deceased's personal possessions to their next of kin. Then he produces a biro and gestures towards some sheets of paper. 'I just need your autograph on a few things, please.'

I leave Fay and GG to sort through the paperwork and go and stand on the forecourt facing the village square: the church, the chippy, the bakery. Only about twenty metres stands between me and the estate agent's window, 'Martingale's'. A robin lands on the window ledge and cocks his head at me. Is it a sign? I'm getting more superstitious with age. I chide myself. It's easy to spot signs when you're desperate to see them. The rainbow over Thistlefold could've been a message from Dad, him beckoning me back to my birth-right. More likely it was the 'refraction of the sun's light caused by rain' – I still remember the deflated feeling in double physics when Dad's 'messages' were boiled down into scientific jargon.

The heel of my trainers teeters on the edge of the low cobbled kerb as my sensible head battles with my fantasy one. Maybe it wouldn't do any harm to follow a dream? Am I brave enough to start a new adventure at the age of fifty-one? So many things could go wrong. Yes, I argue silently with myself, but so much could go right. What happened to that brave young woman who headed off to New York all those years ago? She got old, I tell myself. 'Bollocks,' I say out loud and step off the kerb.

I spot it right away, thanks to the feed silo prominent in the foreground of the photograph. 'Available to Rent. Small holding with 62 acres and 4-bedroom house'. I take a photo of all the rental details, feeling a rush of excitement.

We arrive back at London Euston early evening after a mammoth trek of minicab, cross-country train then eventually the 16.05 from Manchester Piccadilly.

It's Easter Sunday and the station is busy with day trippers carrying voluminous rucksacks, tired kids holding balloons that bob into the faces of fellow travellers, the concrete beer garden of a nearby bar packed with a rowdy crowd. The capital's hubbub that I used to love, now feels claustrophobic. The gurning faces of the drinkers, the squeal from a grizzling baby, the hustle and bustle of the city close in on me after the space and distant horizons of the countryside. Here, pushing through the pulsating crowds, I barely have room to breathe.

14

The weeks that follow our trip pass by in a new but still familiar rhythm; I find comfort in the roster of my regular appointments and activities. From the moment I wake till the moment I drift off at night, I mull over the pros and cons of upping sticks and moving away. I dream about the near miss on the same lane that claimed my father's life. My internal monologue is stuck on a loop of what ifs. This is a big decision and one only I can make.

I try not to fret that some usurper may, at that very moment be signing a ten-year tenancy agreement on my place of birth. The ink drying on the dotted line while I rattle around my big house hundreds of miles away. I scold myself for romanticising the situation and try to discount the rainbow-hued welcome mat laid out in the sky by my deceased father.

Instead I concentrate on yoga on a Monday, coffee with a friend on Tuesday, blow-dry on a Wednesday and volunteering at a homeless helpline every Thursday. By Friday I'm knackered – seems treading water requires as much energy as swimming.

It's a Saturday when the doorbell goes and I find Chloe standing on my doorstep, grinning. I love her visits home and I'm excited to have some mum and daughter time after so long.

'I have my key!' she protests before I can even open my mouth. 'It's just buried in here somewhere.' She nods towards the humongous backpack currently weighing her down. She is stooped under its weight, like she's giving a pal a piggyback.

'Come in, come in,' I say, hoisting the bag from her back by the thick straps as she steps into the hall. 'Jesus, feels like you've got an extra person smuggled in here.'

I spin her back round to me and fold her into a hug. Her soft skin is damp with the exertions of carrying the rucksack. Her hair smells of fig shampoo and tobacco – I try not to judge. I pull her out of my embrace and study her face, she is the exact same height as me these days, a thing I will never get used to. Her round face is sprinkled with sweet freckles and her hair falls in syrup-coloured coils to her shoulders.

'I missed you,' I say.

'I missed you too, Mama.' She calls me this whenever she wants to get around me; I feel my hackles flex gently. She has news?

She does indeed.

'Well I don't have anyone in my rucksack but I *do* have someone with me.'

She smiles sheepishly, the stud in her nose twinkling in the sun.

'Right.' I look over her shoulder and from the side of the door steps her companion.

'This is Aspen,' she says.

Aspen is tall and willowy like a sunflower and beams down at me from behind a curtain of peroxide hair. He's in camouflage shorts and conversely a luminous lime-green top. Does he want to be seen or not seen?

'Hiya,' he says, holding out a bony hand decorated with a simple line drawing tattoo of a triangle at the base of his thumb. 'Great to meet you. Wow! You really look like Chloe. Same eyes. Yours are just a bit more...'

We all wait as he searches for the right words in this conversational cul-de-sac he's just zoomed up. I help him out. 'Old?'

'No! More... lived in.'

'Right.'

'Sorry about the slight ambush, Mama,' Chloe says as Aspen nods. 'It's just we're only stopping for a couple of days then we're seeing Dad.' She crinkles her nose in excitement like she's always done. 'We're off to Cornwall for the month – Aspen's mum has a house there.'

'Well come in,' I say, ushering them through to the kitchen.

'I need to err...' says Aspen to Chloe, eyes pleading.

'Oh right, yeah the loo. Just down there on the left.' She points him in the direction of the downstairs toilet.

'Thanks. Too much kombucha on the train.' He winces.

'You won't notice he's here,' Chloe whispers conspiratorially as we walk to the kitchen. 'He doesn't eat much or smell, he's like a really easy pet.'

I start to make coffee. Chloe sits on the unit, the flesh of her thighs pressing on the worktop where her denim shorts end, her tassled ankle boots tapping against the cupboard door. I busy myself with the coffee, pouring Rwandan medium grind into my beloved machine. There's more to come from her I can tell. She's my daughter and I love her and would lie down and die for her, but also her arrival on my doorstep is often like having a handful of tiny grenades thrown into your day. Things are never simple. I dump extra coffee into the filter paper.

'I spoke to Gran earlier,' she says breezily and hops off the counter. She opens the fridge.

'Please can I make a snack?'

'Course you can.'

She gets a knife and a chopping board and starts slicing a chunk of cheddar and an apple into thin slivers.

'She was not happy,' she says, still slicing.

'What now?' I switch the machine on and it starts to gurgle reassuringly.

Chloe pauses and looks at me. Her lips have flatlined and her eyes are wide.

'Oh shit,' I say.

'Yes. Oh shit. Honestly, Mum, why didn't you tell her?'

'I was getting round to it, I had to find the right time. You didn't need to tell her.'

'I thought she knew!'

'I know. I wanted to tell her when I visited but I just couldn't find the right moment.'

Aspen walks into the kitchen. I see he's taken off his shoes and is sliding along on stripy blue socks. I like him a bit more.

'Such a cool house,' he says. 'You two talk so similar too, I can really hear where Chlo gets her northernisms. I quite like them, they're quaint.' I wonder when he'll stop pointing out our similarities. 'She talks a lot too, always yakking on aren't you, Chlo?' He chuckles.

'Charming,' she says.

'I don't mean it badly, you could just edit yourself a bit more, that's all.'

Chloe looks a little annoyed.

I look at Aspen. 'I've never thought Chloe needed to edit herself. Surely the whole point of being comfortable with someone is never having to edit yourself?'

He shrugs and holds his palms up as if he's the one under attack. 'Uh oh! Mama Bear is protecting her young!' He steals a slice of apple from the chopping board. Chloe rolls her eyes.

'So, come on, what happened with Gran?' I ask.

'Well,' says Chloe, layering a piece of cheese between two slices of apple and nibbling delicately at it. 'She rang to say "congratulations on uni ending" and then was asking where I was staying and I said "Mum's" and that I'd be "going round to Dad's at some point".'

'Right.' My heart is thumping with adrenaline at this development. I pour some coffee into a mug and see my hand is trembling.

I also suspect I might even be a tiny bit relieved; the worst is over – the cat is out of the bag. All I have to do is call the cat and calm it down.

Except I know Mum will be furious. When we married she loved to say she'd acquired the son she'd never had in James. Despite these supposed maternal feelings she'd always flirted with James in a distinctly unmotherly way. Her eyes would twinkle at him as she coquettishly giggled at his every quip like a hen fluttering its wings at a new cockerel in the coop. James had everything she admired in a man – good breeding, private education, wealth, and the confidence that comes with such an upbringing. She was especially wowed by his wealth, cooing over his latest car, gushing over how hard he worked.

She used to joke that we could never split up, trilling 'because then I'd have to choose!'

She will very much see our divorce as my failure to hold on to such a glittering prize.

'When did you speak to her?' I ask.

Chloe looks at her phone. 'About half an hour ago.'

'Right.' I take a glug of coffee. 'I'd better call her.'

Chloe exchanges a glance with Aspen, who looks very much like, if there was a spare one-way ticket to Mars leaving immediately he'd jump at it.

'What?'

'Nothing... she was just upset, that's all.'

The phone rings twice before she answers. She dispenses with the need for a hello, saying instead, 'At last.'

There is already a quiver in her voice, a ripple on the surface that hints there will soon be a flood. I've stationed myself by the window looking out over the garden, hoping the view of the greenery will keep me calm.

I wished Chloe had arrived with this news later in the day so I could self-medicate with a glass of wine but it's eleven a.m. and so coffee will have to be my crutch.

'Mum —' I start but she cuts me off.

'I'm sorry but what hurts the most is that you couldn't tell me yourself.'

'I know, sorry.'

'I mean, were you ever going to tell me? You've had plenty of chances. We speak every week, you were even here, sitting at this very table eating my cottage pie. I'm surprised you didn't choke on it knowing what secrets you were keeping from me.'

'I wanted to tell you, I nearly did but then you brought out the photos.'

I hear a sharp intake of breath. 'So it's my fault?'

'Of course not. It's just, getting the photos was such a big deal for me I forgot everything else.'

'I feel a fool. I imagine everyone in your life knows apart from me, and I'm sorry but as the saying goes, you've treated me like a mushroom – kept me in the dark and fed me you-know-what.'

'I'm sorry.'

'This isn't easy for me you know,' she says. Here we go, I knew she'd be the victim in all this. 'I love James, you know that.'

'So do I, Mum, we still love each other, we're just not IN love. We really weren't happy. Don't you want your daughter to be happy?'

'You have to work at it, Josie. James is the best thing to happen to this family in a long time.'

'Mum, don't you think we tried? If I'm OK with it, and James is, and even Chloe understands, then surely you can be?'

'Well clearly you've all had time to get used to the idea. I'm still in shock. You've let something very special slip through your fingers and that hurts me deeply. I'm going to need time to get over this.'

I sigh. 'I'm sure you will eventually.'

I love how I'm comforting Mum over my failed marriage.

Her tone is still accusatory but softens slightly. 'Well all this is digging up some long-buried memories for me. And I gather he's moved on already! Though I'm not surprised – he was always very good-looking. A man like him won't stay on the market long.' She tuts to herself.

My stomach drops. 'What do you mean? Moved on?'

'Chloe said, she said she's going round to "James and Ella's". I suppose you were going to keep that from me too?'

I feel the floor below me shift. I know the saying is to pull the rug out from underneath someone but I didn't know that that sensation could actually be real. My legs buckle slightly, the same weakening as when boys at school would nudge me on the soft flesh behind my load-bearing knee. I lean against the window frame for support.

Mum pauses. She sounds out of breath like she's just crossed a finish line. She speaks in a small voice now. 'You didn't know did you?'

I can hear the triumph in her tone, a smug victory lap wearing the shoe that's now on the other foot.

I find my voice but the slight croak gives me away. 'I didn't but it's OK. I'm sure James has his reasons for not telling me. For starters he's been in New York for the past two months and is only just back so I've not seen him.' There follows an uncharacteristic silence from Mum, which is unnerving. She's enjoying me scrambling to justify James' lack of communication. After twenty-three years of marriage he could've at least given me the heads-up. Must be the woman I heard when I called from Shearness. Or perhaps the latest in a long line. I plough on. 'Besides, we're no longer together, haven't been for ages.' I say this to wind her up. 'He isn't obliged to tell me every cough and spit of his life. I don't need to tell him if I'm seeing someone.'

She speaks at last. 'Well are you?'

'No,' I say, 'I'm not but that's not the point. The point is, if and when I am I won't need to run blabbing all about it to James.'

What's hurting me more than anything is that our daughter has obviously met Ella. That's clearly what she was going to tell me earlier before she thought better of it. I know it's not Chloe's job to tell me about this Ella, and it's certainly not my mum's, it is James'. That's what stings, but I'm not about to let Mum know that.

'Well sorry to be the bearer of bad news.' She's clearly not.

'It's not bad news, Mum, it's fine.' The name Ella – she's obviously young, no one born before 1990 has that name.

'Bottom cupboard on the left,' Mum whispers.

'What?'

'I'm talking to Simon. He's my student lodger, over from Malaysia. Remember I told you? He's trying to find the colander. He's a wonderful cook, he's about to knock up a laksa.'

'Right.' I'm startled by the brutal change of gear Mum is capable of – from my personal life to a noodle soup without pausing for breath.

'Most of his friends have gone home from university for the holidays and the campus is empty. He can't go to Malaysia –' she drops her voice conspiratorially – 'his parents are in politics,' before adding at regular volume, 'they're off travelling. So instead he's here with me for a couple of months and I'm sorry but he's an absolute pleasure. Mouse is obsessed with him.'

We end on a reasonably chatty note. Mum is clearly already fixing up Simon as a surrogate son to replace James, especially now he has her whippet's approval. I finish the call and flop onto the sofa. Is it still too early for a wine? It is.

15

Chloe peeps around the door from where she's clearly been ear-wagging.

'Safe to come in?'

'Wish you'd told me.'

'I'm sorry. I let it slip to Gran and was hoping she wouldn't mention it. I think Dad could've told you.'

'I know.' She perches on the other end of the sofa and allows her top half to fall like a felled tree so she's lying down with her head on my lap. I twist a lock of her hair gently in my fingers. 'I missed you,' I say.

'I missed you too. It's mad to think I'm done now, no more studying.'

'The world is your oyster, sweetheart.'

I twirl her hair, picturing the squidgy cute five-year-old whose curls I'd plait for school.

'What's the deal with Aspen?' I ask eventually.

'We were friends for a bit then got together at a party, he did textiles too. He's sweet and he makes me laugh.'

'Good, that's important. Your dad has always been able to make me laugh.'

'I know, I remember when I was little you and Dad laughed a lot. I was lucky – you were so clearly in love when I was growing up, it was nice to be surrounded by that.'

'Really? Is that what you remember? That makes me happy.'

'Yeah, your and Dad's relationship is something to aspire to.'

'Hmmm... not so much any more though, now we've split up, hardly "couple goals" as you say.'

'No one says that any more, Mum,' she corrects me gently, 'but just because you've split up doesn't mean your marriage isn't something to be proud of.' She thinks for a minute. 'If a jumper unravels or a vase breaks after twenty years, it doesn't wipe out the comfort or the beauty that thing provided for all the time it was in one piece.'

My nose tingles like I might sneeze or cry. I roughly rub away the feeling with the back of my hand. 'Ah you're lovely.' I squeeze her.

She turns and lies on her back. 'Talking of jumpers,' she says to the ceiling, 'Aspen and I really got into the constructed textiles bit of the syllabus this year.'

'Right... what's constructed — ?'

'Basically knitting and weaving. We're thinking of exploring sustainable knitwear using wool from British sheep. We've got a meeting set up with a farmer down in Cornwall when we go see his mum.'

'Amazing.' I smile. At her age I was an analyst at Silverman Stein, one of the oldest established banks in the City, trying to break into wealth management. In my head I was a sharp suited badass but really I was trying to prove to myself that I was good enough. I planned on earning enough that I could stack it into a staircase up and away from my troubled teenage years. Now here's my daughter hoping to make jumpers from the wool of native sheep. Maybe my dad's countryside genes skipped a generation.

'Your grandad would be so proud,' I say, kissing the top of her head.

'Do you think so?' I can hear the little smile in her voice.

'Course. Supporting farmers, using British produce, working within the rural community – he'd love it all.'

'Did Grandad have sheep then?'

'No, he didn't. His pal did though, so occasionally we'd be given a newborn lamb to hand-rear when its mother had died or it was one of twins and the mother couldn't feed both.'

'Cute!'

'Yeah, you would've loved it.'

We're quiet again for a moment.

'Mum, do you think if Grandad hadn't died you would've stayed up north? Maybe I would've been raised on the farm?'

'Maybe. Though if your grandad hadn't died maybe I wouldn't have been so determined to take myself off to uni and that's where I met your dad. Thank God I did or you wouldn't be here, and that just doesn't bear thinking about.'

'What did he have? I know he had some cows.'

'Pedigree Polled Herefords. In fact, stay there.' I extricate myself from underneath her, sliding off the couch and go to grab the photos that Mum gave me. I'd been wondering when would be the right time to show her. I've carefully put them into an old-fashioned album, only the first seven pages are taken up, a photo at the centre of each, the rest lie empty. Seven photos to sum up so much.

'Your gran gave me these last time I was up.' I say it casually, nervous to add any more weight to the moment for fear it may raise unanswerable questions – like why she'd never seen family photos of her grandad before, apart from a grainy shot in newspaper archives. I'd told her mostly the truth, processing camera film was expensive and more of a faff than in today's digital age, plus Grandma didn't like to talk about the past. I edited out the bit about my mum destroying photos, ripping up my memories. Clearly Chloe was curious though and had confessed that like me at that age, she had looked up her grandad's accident online.

Chloe sits up now and I sit next to her and place the album on her lap.

Aspen comes in and I inwardly sigh. I really wanted this moment to be just the two of us. Chloe senses the shift in the atmosphere and says, 'Babe, can you give us a minute?' Aspen sweetly complies, spinning a 180 in his stockinged feet and slipping back out through the door.

Chloe races hungrily through the snaps, lingering longest on the one of me as a toddler with Dad on the tractor. 'Ohmygod! I looked just like you when I was little.' She gets to the seventh picture and carries on, checking the following few empty pages in case I'd accidentally left a gap.

'That's it?' She is disappointed.

'Yep. That's it.'

A thought occurs and I'm saying it before it's fully formed. 'Maybe you'll see the farm one day, in real life? We could go there.' I give her a potted version of the trip up north, the crash, the farm visit. I even tell her about my dad's grave being looked after by a 'mystery mourner', as she puts it. It feels great to share all this, to let these hemmed-in thoughts loose. Her eyes are wide as she takes it all in. I reassure her I won't be making any rash decisions about the farm.

'Mum, why not? Be rash! You've got to follow your heart on this one. I'm doing my own thing, Dad definitely is.' She grins ruefully. 'Take the plunge. You've looked after us long enough and it's your turn for adventure. I KNEW something had happened,' she squeals. 'I've just had a feeling something is different about you, there's a new energy around you.'

I laugh and heave myself off the sofa. 'New energy?' I say. 'Ooh lovely, I could do with some of that.' I chuckle to hide the lump that has inexplicably formed in my throat. Is this the catalyst I need? My daughter giving me permission, untying the apron strings one final time?

The next few days fly by and we make little mention of the farm. Chloe knows I need space to let the decision percolate. She throws herself into sorting out her teenage bedroom and I can hear her and Aspen laughing as she goes through her One Direction memorabilia – T-shirts, a clock, countless posters.

Aspen has made himself quite at home and mainly drinks kombucha whilst concocting all manner of meals from the deepest recesses of my kitchen cupboards. 'I like to earn my keep, least I can do is cook,' he says, whilst dishing up a vegan paella that tastes like someone has soaked the contents of my hoover bag in a Cup a Soup. Still, he's a nice boy. Beyond the home-bleached fringe lies the face of a bonny baby contest winner, all bright blue eyes and peachy skin. He is no trouble, sliding around in his socks, sweetly asking about my day and offering to make mint tea.

Chloe and Aspen finally head off to James' before going down to Cornwall and I arrange to meet up with Fay in town for some lunch.

'My treat,' she says. 'I have news.'

She wouldn't tell me any more details so I find myself sitting in a booth at our new favourite restaurant, nursing an elderflower spritzer and nibbling some edamame. Tow Bar and Grill is housed in a former bank, the cool marble pillars and high ceilings now vibrate with the noise of diners sitting at dozens of wooden tables and in cosy booths.

Huge Jurassic plants in pots the size of tumble dryers provide ample leafy coverage for those not wanting to be on display, though those are in the minority here. The clientele have no problem being watched, slinking around with their bare midriffs and chunky boots, laughing the sort of laugh that dares you to stare.

We hated this place the first time we came a few months ago. Fay had seen a five-star review from a brilliantly witty but notoriously hard-to-please restaurant critic and so we booked for dinner. We were met by a bustling restaurant like a crowd in a Renoir – everywhere we looked people were hanging over the back of chairs, engrossed in lively debate, some swung a partner through the air in impromptu dance. Instead of nineteenth-century Paris with the bonnets and boaters it was modern-day central London with undercuts and polka-dot micro-dresses. We braved it and once the sweet waitress with a pierced lip welcomed us like long-lost friends, bringing us our cocktails within minutes, sensing we needed to soften the edges of the room, we were charmed and vowed to return for lunch. Lunchtimes are calmer and I'm quite at home sipping my drink and people watching. I half-wish Chloe and Aspen were with me though, I could've basked in the glow of their youth and cool.

'Gotcha.' Even though I'm facing the entrance, Fay manages to creep up from behind having come in through the side. 'Bloody hell, Fay!'

'Sorry, babe. Over-excited.' She hugs me harder and for longer than strictly necessary. Oh god. A cloud of foreboding suddenly hovers overhead. She's buzzing with a fizzing energy. What is her news?

The waitress from our first visit comes over beaming. She looks stunning. She has a gypsy scarf tied around her hair and looks as if she may produce a crystal ball. 'My favourite ladies!' She beams. 'What can I get you?'

'Champagne please,' says Fay and I look at her then at my watch.

'Coming up,' says the waitress.

'Don't you have to be back at the library?'

'Nope. On account of the fact that I'm leaving and it was finally signed off today.' She watches me, enjoying this bombshell rock me in my seat. She carries on before I can speak.

'Well I'm not leaving-leaving, of course. They can't get rid of me that easily. I'm off on a placement, like a job-swap really. For a year.'

'Oh wow.' I find my voice. 'That's amazing, Fay! Where, what, why... I need all the deets.'

'OK, I'll start with "why" then build up.' She grins excitedly. 'Why? Well why not? I love the British Library but I've been there for eighteen years so I need a new challenge.'

'Right.'

'When? In about a month.'

'Wow, so soon?'

'Yup, but it's been in the pipeline for ages. I just didn't want to jinx it by talking about it. Hope you understand?'

'Course,' I say a little too loudly. She looks relieved.

'What? Well, I will be taking over the role of Head of New Exhibitions in Food and Social History, concentrating on sustainability, local lobster and their famous beans.'

The waitress arrives with champagne and two flutes in one hand and an ice bucket in the other.

'Beans? Is that a clue? Coffee beans?' My mouth goes dry at the thought of Fay leaving me for a whole year to go to Brazil... or Rwanda? Are there famous libraries in Rwanda?

She ignores me. 'Which brings me to where.'

Only now does Fay look a little nervous. 'I'm off to Beantown.'

'What?'

'Boston.'

Pop! The champagne cork is loud and makes us both jump. Froth spills out of the rim of the bottle and flows down the neck. 'Oops, sorry,' the waitress grimaces but the distraction gives me a few seconds to reset my face from devastated to ecstatic. How will I cope without my bezzie? And how can I be so selfish to instantly think about myself in this moment?

'Oh my god, that's incredible,' I nearly shout, pulling her in for a hug.

'You've got to come and visit,' she says into my hair. 'Promise you will?'

I release her from the embrace; her face is shiny with excitement. 'Well, we'll see.'

'"We'll see" means "no".' She pouts.

'Look, never mind me, you must be so thrilled. You must have so much to do?'

'Mountains of stuff. I just feel so alive though, Jose.'

'I bet.' My face is aching from propping up a big fat smile. What will I do without her? There's been so much change in my life recently, I'm falling behind. 'A toast,' I say, touching the rim of my champagne flute on hers and holding it there fleetingly like a tender kiss. 'To new adventures.'

Our food arrives and Fay tells me all about the history of Boston – the famous beans originally cooked by Native Americans with maple syrup, venison and corn.

'It's going to be brilliant, I've got so many ideas. There'll be a whole month looking at the slave trade's role in bringing molasses to Boston, which was then added to the beans. We'll have historians and authors doing Q&A sessions, there'll be theatre pieces, plus we'll be exploring the art depicting those times.' She takes a gulp of champagne. 'Sorry, it's boring. I'm just so happy.'

'It's not boring, it's brilliant.' It's great to see her so energised.

'We're even talking to some of the Boston Braves baseball team. They'll be doing signings and meet and greets at local schools – they used to be known as the Boston Beaneaters.'

I smile. 'Wow. It's honestly so magnificent seeing you this excited. I'm thrilled for you.'

'Thanks, darling,' she says, leaning in for another hug. 'I love you. You're the best friend a woman could wish for. I'm going to miss you. We can zoom though? And you must try to visit, none of this "we'll see" business. It's got some excellent bars, I've researched that already obviously.' She grins.

'Obviously.'

'Work related, I'll have you know. We're doing a Christmas street food festival celebrating the local Boston Lobster.'

'Christmas?' I say, the champagne has loosened my reflexes and I can't mask my disappointment. 'Aren't you coming home for Christmas?'

Fay is accustomed to my childlike obsession with the festive period. I know it's pathetic but she's always indulged me. Until now. Her face falls. 'No way sadly. Flights are so much at that time of year, plus the festival. Hey – ' her eyes widen as an idea dawns – 'why don't you come? For the festival? Babe that'd be so cool. Imagine, Christmas in Boston scoffing lobster with your bezzie! You could even get your claws into the local men.'

I groan at the pun. 'I might be busy,' I say. The champagne has loosened my tongue too.

'Where? At your mum's wrestling over the roasties?'

'You know a few weeks back when we'd found the farm and you were chatting to GG about the car, sorting out the paperwork?'

It takes her a second. 'Yes?'

'Well I popped over to the estate agent's. Thistlefold *is* for rent after all.'

'Oh. My. God. You never said! Are you going back? I knew you seemed quiet in the taxi! Why didn't you tell me?'

'I dunno. I needed to think it through.'

'And have you?' She takes a glug of champagne, leaning in eagerly.

'Yes. I mean, I think so. It's a massive decision. Anyway – ' I wave a hand – 'today is about you, about your news.'

'Fuck that,' she says. 'Come on, what are you going to do, Jose? What have you got to lose?'

'My sanity?' I laugh. 'Isn't it a completely mad thing to do?'

'Yes.' She smiles. 'But that's what makes it so exciting.'

16

The next evening I'm on the two Chrises' front step. I take a deep breath and ring the bell. I hate the first five minutes of any social gathering, scanning the faces to find a close ally, the disruption your arrival brings, people pausing chat or moving away, like you're the jack in a game of bowls, manoeuvring into conversations, rolling others out of position.

It's in these moment that I miss James. I would usually slink in behind him at social occasions, lurk in the shadow of his public-school confidence as he dazzled everyone with his easy charm. I savour the emotion for a moment, these heady seconds of feeling bereft. Single. I allow myself a little wallow. All of these thoughts cluster and crackle in my brain in the time it takes between me ringing the bell and the door swinging open.

'Welcome,' smiles a middle-aged woman in dark trousers and white blouse. They have the caterers in, wouldn't expect anything less. She has an accent, Polish perhaps.

'May I take your... blanket?' she asks, looking at my pashmina. Relieved Fay isn't hearing this, she'd love it.

I smile at the woman. 'No, I'll keep it thank you.' She nods. 'Is it filling up out there?' I ask, looking along the sage corridor, through the navy kitchen towards the hubbub coming from the back garden. Someone shrieks with laughter. 'Yes, quite busy.' She smiles. 'Right,' I reply but don't move. She seems a little confused by this.

'I'm Josie,' I say apologetically. This is my way of trying to ingrati-ate myself with the staff at parties like these. I want them to know I'm one of them, I'm working class, I'm here through a twist of fate but it could so easily be me standing there holding a platter of tuna tataki. I want them to know I'm different from the other guests who take a canapé without a glance their way, never mind a thank-you. I'm absolutely like them despite the fact I've just hopped over the low wall from my equally huge house next door.

'I'm Alina,' she says at last.

'Lovely to meet you.' I rub my hands together. 'Right then,' I say, rolling my eyes in mock horror, 'I suppose I'd better go through, can't avoid it any longer!' I squint, trying to see if Ruth is out there. I turn back to Alina but she's slipped away and is now busying herself at the kitchen sink. I cringe. She probably wants to get on with her job then get the hell out of here. She's not here to help a random partygoer untangle her complicated feelings about entitle-ment, class and belonging, not for the wage they pay her. After my visit to Thistlefold I feel even more like a chewed-up jigsaw piece, not quite fitting in anywhere any more.

The garden is busier than I was expecting. A DJ is stationed at the back of the garden on the raised seating area playing chilled Balearic beats, and two chefs with matching combats and ironic mullets are busily turning skewers over a coal barbecue by the clematis-clad trellis.

I feel too hot. It's the anxiety or the menopause or both – they go hand in hand these days. I feel self-conscious in my grey T-shirt dress and pink pashmina – am I smart enough? With relief I spot a couple of neighbours who I know to say hi to. They're with Chris Crab, who is holding court under a golden shade sail stretched taut and glistening between two trees and their garden office. He has Muffin tucked under one arm like a clutch bag. Gold bunting is strung between the house and the trees and huge golden '5' balloon dances on its weighted string next to its '0' partner. It reads to me like a question: 'SO?'

Crab has his back to me, Muffin's bottom poking out from under the candy-pink striped sleeve of his shirt. I head over and am grateful to be intercepted by a waiter with a tray of drinks. 'Champagne, Pimm's, elderflower or a Chris-tini?' he asks.

'Oh lovely,' I say, grabbing a glass of Pimm's and one of champagne. I neck the latter hoping no one is watching and put the empty glass back on the tray. 'Thanks.' I turn with my glass of Pimm's just in time to hear Crab say, 'And off he roared into the sunset, a mid-life crisis on two wheels.'

I know he's talking about James because of the mid-life crisis comment, but mainly because the couple he was talking to had in unison widened their eyes on spotting me approaching and glared at Crab.

'Oooh, are we having a good gossip?' I say, drawing level with Crab who doesn't miss a beat.

'Mrs Perry! My favourite neighbour! I was just telling these two about James' departure. It was quite dramatic.'

'Well, yes.' I smile at them and they grin with relief that I'm not cross and they're not busted. 'To the untrained eye it may have seemed dramatic him zooming off but it's less Hollywood block-buster when you know he kept having to pull over to allow the removals van to catch up because the driver had a dodgy sat nav.'

The couple are Sukey and Paul from Number Five, the other side of the two Chrises. They are in their early forties and annoyingly young to be so successful. They created then sold a very successful carbon neutral smoothie brand called Sup – an amalgamation of their names – and flogged in overpriced health-food shops around the UK.

Tall and slim, Sukey wears her mousey hair in a simple centre parting and Paul is balding with round, wire-rimmed glasses. James says they look like the pair from the 'American Gothic' painting.

Though they're holding glasses of champagne, not a pitchfork, and Sukey is nibbling a spring roll, Muffin's nose twitching at the smell. 'I imagine you won't miss his motorbike, Josie, the noise that thing made!' She slots the last of the spring roll into her mouth. What she actually means is *she* won't miss the disturbance.

'Oh I'm looking into getting one for myself,' I reply. 'With a side-car for Crab.'

'Oh absolutely, count me in,' he nods. 'I can rock a headscarf and shades – I'll be the Louise to your Thelma. What fun we'll have.'

Then Crab's face falls. 'Oh who are we kidding? You won't want me cramping your style as you go gallivanting Josie. Spending the settlement, taking a tomboy in every town! '

'Don't worry, Crab I'll keep you posted,' I say

'Well, if you ever up sticks we'll be devastated… the only comfort would be you naturally giving me and Chris first dibs on Number Three… you know I've been fantasising about knocking through to your lower ground for decades. Not a euphemism,' he adds with a wink.

I laugh. 'Yes, Crab, don't worry you'll be the first to know.'

There's a silence and we all study our drinks for a moment.

Sukey clears her throat. 'It is nice to see you, Josie,' she says, her head angled to the side, the edges of her voice trimmed with a subtle sympathy. 'You're very brave, always so full of banter – ' she says 'banter' as if saying 'gonorrhoea' – 'but are you actually doing OK?' She grips my forearm now and attempts a deep look into my eyes. 'Anything we can do – anything – you must ask.'

'Well yes, there is one thing,' I say, and she nods sincerely. 'You can let go of my arm so I can drink my Pimm's.'

She laughs at my little joke though I can tell she's irritated. Fuck it. They've never been good friends of mine and I don't want their sympathy now. I drink my Pimm's and feel the booze starting to take effect, I stand a little taller.

'Self medication – it's the only way, babe,' says Crab, touching his champagne flute to mine before taking a swig. 'You must try a Chris-tini – gin with a drop of lychee syrup. Just like the birthday boy it's strong, sweet and will have you on your back in no time.'

We all laugh. 'I could do with a bit of that, now I'm single and ready to mingle. Lock up your husbands, especially you, Crab!' We laugh again though Sukey gives Paul a look for laughing a little too loudly.

'Hands off, bitch,' says Chris. 'He's all mine.'

We all turn to survey the man of the moment. His slender frame is elegantly clad in dark jeans and lemon sweater. The kind of outfit that looks casual but probably cost more than an overnight stay at the Ritz. He suddenly opens his arms wide, smiling into the distance and we all watch as Ruth bowls through the garden and into his embrace. She's wearing what seems to be something found in a skip round the back of the *Strictly* studios. An ankle-length dress in royal blue satin with a frilly trim.

'Happy birthday, you bloody legend!' she hollers. She only comes up to Chris' armpits and squeezes him around his waist in a rugby tackle. On hearing her voice Muffin starts to wiggle ecstatically and Crab puts her down so she can scamper over to Ruth, yapping excitedly.

'Charming,' says Crab forlornly. 'Guess I know where I rank in Muffin's most loved chart.'

'Don't take it personally – Ruth is a legend to all the dogs round here. Plus she always smells a bit of chicken.'

'True,' says Crab.

Ruth spots me and envelopes me in a hug. 'Drink?' she asks and, smiling beatifically, whisks me away towards a low bench, grabbing two more glasses en route. 'Oof. I'm getting too old for this.' She scowls, settling down and looking at the crowd. Her bare arms are a mottled strawberries and cream from the exertion and the sun, the skin on her shoulders a crinkled pink.

'For what?' I ask.

'This bullshit.' She nods at the party.

'What happened to Raver Ruth? This isn't like you?'

'Sorry, don't mean to be a party pooper.' She takes a breath. 'I'm a bit fed up, Josie. The arthritis in my ankle is playing up and today I've had two dogs conspire against me to find three – THREE! – different types of poo to roll in. Fox, badger and a mystery third turd that I'm praying isn't human.'

I wrinkle my nose.

'So my car smells like Satan's bumhole. Plus the heat, it's too much.' She sweeps her fingers across the perspiration that has settled like dew on her light moustache. 'See? I'm sweating like a pig in a butcher's back room. Then to top it all I slipped on a pizzle.'

'A pizzle?'

'Yes.' She looks at me as if I'm a moron. 'A dried bull's penis.'

'Of course.'

Ruth drains her glass and waves at a waiter who heads over with a tray. 'Thank you,' she says and takes a glass and sips while placing the empty flute on the tray. 'The booze is helping. I just feel... grouchy. Especially at something like this, surrounded by buffoons.' On cue, Sukey's shrill laugh rings out above the music. Sukey seems to be getting uncharacteristically merry.

'Well you've never been a people person, Ruth, you've always preferred dogs.'

'Yeah, well I've even gone slightly off them after this morning's shenanigans.' Her shoulders lower as she starts to relax. 'I'm OK. I just think, to be honest, that even though I'm surrounded by people and pooches, I'm lonely.' She sniffs. 'You know it's coming up to Maud's birthday?'

I squeeze her hand. Shit, I should've realised. I've been so caught up in my own head I forgot. This time of year is always tricky for Ruth.

'I just miss her so much still, Jose. I miss the smell of her, the feel of her in bed next to me. I've still got most of her stuff you know? When someone passes so suddenly it's like there's still their energy left behind in the most mundane of things – the coffee cup she'd drunk from that morning, her pillow... they all fizzed with her. I still sleep with her favourite jumper, I spritz it with her perfume.'

We watch the dance floor for a moment.

'She wouldn't want you to be sad, Ruth.'

'Oh I know,' she chuckles, her voice suddenly thick with tears. 'I can hear her now – "Come on, Ruthie, chin up my duck".'

She reaches into her bag for a tissue and blows her nose with a loud honk. 'Ignore me, I'm just feeling soppy.' She dabs at her eyes.

'Stick with me,' I say. 'I'll look after you. Might even get you on that dance floor soon. And Fay's coming tonight, she'll sort you out.'

'Is she? Oh marvellous. I DO love Fay. You're lucky to have her.'

'Funny you should say that,' I reply and fill her in on Fay's news, which seems to naturally lead on to my nearly news about the farm. I also tell her I couldn't live without her friendship, that whatever happened, we'd always be there for each other. I feel bereft that my decision means I'd be leaving Ruth behind.

She shushes me. 'Don't you worry about me. That's the beautiful thing about you, Josie, you think about others too much. You need to think about Number One for a change.'

'It's all so scary though, Ruth.'

'You know, Josie, sometimes it's healthy to be frightened. Look, it took me many years to accept who I am, that I was worthy of love. Then when I met Maud it felt so good it frightened me. But you must be invigorated by that fear, by change.' She grabs both of my hands in hers and says earnestly, shouting slightly above the music,

'Because there's nothing to fear in life more than fear itself – never let it hold you back, Josie. Promise me that much. Life is short, my love, you must throw yourself into it feet first while you can.'

By ten p.m. Chemical Brothers' 'Block Rockin' Beats' is playing and the small dance floor on the decking is packed. The two Chrises are at the centre, performing some sort of drunken jive and Ruth has definitely rallied. She is next to me and bouncing her bottom up and down as if knocking in a fencing post with her coccyx.

I'll miss them when I go, I think, the emotion and the Pimm's getting to me. Hang on, where did that come from? It seems subconsciously I'm already mentally packing up and preparing to leave. I feel a tickle of excitement that it's happening.

'Jose!' I hear a shout over the music and I spin and there, like a vision, is Fay. She promised that if she could slip away early from her latest exhibition at the library she would make it to the party. Her peroxide hair is as ever cropped close, her petite frame clad in a tight black jumper dress with red patent pixie boots to match her lipstick. Huge gold hoops gently knock against her neck.

'There you are,' I shout and fold her into a hug. She feels like a little paper doll that I'm in danger of crumpling. Her hair tickles my chin and I take a moment to breathe in her familiar aroma. She still smells of honey, a buttery sweetness. She disentangles herself and grins up at me. 'I think I need to play catch up, I'm annoyingly sober and desperate for a drink. Shot?'

'Yup,' I say and link my arm through hers, steering her towards the kitchen.

I spot the lady from earlier. 'Alina!' I shout like she's an old mate. 'This is Fay and she needs a shot of vodka, please.'

Alina disappears and comes back with a bottle of Absolut and some small glasses on a tray, which we take and make our way back out to some wicker sofas framed by twinkling fairy lights.

'Go on then,' Fay says. She's had two vodka shots in quick succession and then produced a travel sweet tin from her bag containing a neatly rolled joint. Its glowing end dances like a firefly in the night as she gesticulates. Fay has always been a big gesticulator. She puts it down to her 'Sicilian heritage', though her mum once told me both her and Fay's dad were pure Blackpool stock and as far as she knew there was no Italian in there, unless her grandma had been romanced by a tourist over for the donkey rides.

She offers me the joint and I take a puff, feeling Sukey's eyes on me from the other sofa. I hold down the urge to splutter as the smoke hits the back of my throat.

'So?'

'What?' I ask.

'The farm? Have you thought more about it?'

I laugh. 'Fay, I only saw you yesterday, so no. How's "Churchill's Cheese War"?' I say, changing the subject to her latest exhibition.

'"Churchill and Cheese – How Rationing Won the War",' she gently corrects, 'is going brilliantly thank you, the big bosses are very happy.'

'They'll miss you when you go.' I feel gloomy now. 'And so will I.'

'I'll miss you too. Hey, guess what I got for old times' sake?' She glances around then rummages in her bag. 'Have a piece of this.' She produces a small bar of chocolate from her bag and breaks off a piece. 'Mushroom chocolate.' She smiles. 'Super mellow, honestly, it will just make you a little wavy.'

'Oh god,' I say. 'Go on then.' I pop the square of chocolate in my mouth. It's more powdery than normal chocolate but actually tastes quite nice.

'Leftover from my recent little dalliance with a surfer dude from Abersoch,' she adds wistfully. 'Any nice men here?'

'Hardly,' I say.

'It's a pretty OMG crowd.'

'As in "OMG there's so many hotties"?'

'No – as in they're all either old, married or gay.'

I chuckle. 'Hey, when you leave the dating pool here to plunge into the one in Boston I can take your place – entertain all the bereft men you leave behind with my feminine charms.'

'Absolutely.'

Fay has never found 'the one', though, as she puts it, she's 'had a LOT of fun searching'. A broken heart in her early thirties meant she missed the boat to have her own kids but has always been her usual pragmatic self about it. 'I like being cool Auntie Fay who can still bugger off to a food festival in Seoul at a gnat's knacker's notice without worrying about anyone else.'

'I may need tips from you on how to date New York style.'

She takes the joint back. 'Easy – you can sleep with as many people as you like. Not all at once. Unless it's a very successful night.'

'Oh I dunno,' I say. 'After so many years married to the same person I've no idea what I'd do with another man's penis.'

She laughs, accidentally inhaling smoke and coughs. 'Think it'd come back to you.'

'Besides... I think the biggest hurdle I've yet to overcome is the ski-panted one they call Sandra.'

'Ah, yes,' says Fay, 'she must have an eighties' dealer sorting her for Anais Anais perfume and ski pants. Is she worried her feet will drop off if there's no elastic holding them on? She's found a fashion she likes and is fully committed to it, you're not that dissimilar to be fair.' She smiles sweetly and eyes my pashmina.

'Piss off.'

'So what *is* going on with mummy dearest? Have you mentioned the farm?'

'No. I'm too scared, I know she'll freak out. Don't suppose you want to tell her for me do you?'

'No thanks. So it's happening then?'

'I don't know. Maybe.'

'I think you should go for it.'

'Really? OK, that's that settled then.'

We laugh.

'Well, whatever you decide to do, I think you're awesome.'

'Ah. Thanks, babe.' I hug her. 'I love you.'

'I love you too.'

'What a beautiful scene.' I look up and it's Ruth, face bright pink from exertion. She plonks herself in-between us and plucks the remaining spliff from my fingers.

'What are you two plotting? Sitting here thick as school custard?'

'Josie's next move,' Fay says.

'Ah that!' she says, wincing as a thin spiral of smoke reaches her eye. 'Presume you're telling her to do it?' she says, tossing the spliff butt over her shoulder and into the shrubbery. I see Sukey twitch her head in disapproval. 'Dance?' Ruth shouts, and pulls us both up and towards the decking.

Half an hour later I'm feeling pleasantly fuzzy around the edges when the music dips and Crab takes to the mic. 'Just want to say a big thank you to you all for coming tonight. Chris as usual would prefer it if I didn't make a fuss and speak – ' we all look to the birthday boy who looks pink cheeked and chuffed despite the sudden attention – 'but I just have to say a few words. Like me, I'll keep it short and emotional. Chris is a very special man, he works hard, he certainly plays hard –' a few cheers from the crowd – 'and we've been together for twenty-six years now. You might think he deserves a medal for that rather than a cake but I just want to say we love you all, we love our friends here on the street, you're more than neighbours, some of you are like family.'

'Just "some of us"?' says Sukey. 'Frigging charming.' A few people laugh but there's an edge to her voice. I glance at her, she's leaning drunkenly on Paul and he looks embarrassed. Crab smiles and carries on but I can tell he's off his stride. 'OK, I love you all,' he says sarcastically, widening his eyes at Sukey, 'but mostly I love my Chris, the kindest, most handsome —'

'Too fucking late,' she slurs loudly. This time no one laughs and there's an awkward pause. Paul shushes his wife. 'Don't you fucking shush me,' she says. Sukey clearly can't handle her booze. I've never seen her like this. 'Paul,' I say gently, 'maybe take Sukey for a glass of water so we can get to the cake?'

Paul tries to steer Sukey away from the crowd as she snaps wildly at me, 'Don't you tell my husband what to do. This is none of your business.'

'It is my business when you're spoiling my friend's party,' I shoot back.

'Oh so sorry, little Miss Divorcee.' There's an audible gasp from Crab who looks torn between jumping to my defence and enjoying the drama. 'Sorry you're not the centre of attention as usual.'

Ironic really, seeing as at this very moment along with her I'm very much the centre of attention. The crowd is rapt, I feel frozen to the spot.

'I see through your act, your forelock tugging, salt-of-the-earth northerner routine, charming everyone on the street with your ironic asides and eye rolls at all our middle-class lives when really you envy us all our success.'

'What —' I start, but she cuts me off.

'Don't like it now, eh? You can give it but you can't take it, clearly.'

Other Chris steps forward. 'OK, Sukey, come on.'

'No!' she shouts without taking her eyes from me. 'I see you sneering at me, getting high with your little coven – ' she sweeps a pointed finger at Ruth and Fay – 'when really you've got nothing, no career, no husband now and no life.'

All the air seems to have been sucked from the garden. Paul looks horrified and tries again to pull her away and she almost overbalances. 'You'll be stuck here thinking you're better than us for the rest of time, a bitter lonely old woman,' she spits.

'Now that's enough,' roars Ruth. Fay too opens her mouth to speak but I hold up my hand. 'Sukey, I don't know where all this has come from but you've actually done me a favour.' I feel a calm wash over me, only the slight wobble in my voice betrays me. 'Your nasty little show has helped make up my mind. I'm leaving. I'm moving back up North, away from this bullshit. I'll miss the friends I love but I won't miss dickheads like you.'

Just then two waiters emerge from the house carrying out a huge cake covered in glowing candles with the rest of the staff in pursuit singing, 'Happy Birthday'. Crab tentatively joins in and everyone follows suit and sings to Chris who blows out the candles and gives a bewildered smile. I look back to Sukey but she and Paul are gone.

17

The showdown and my unexpected announcement seemed to reinvigorate the party. Guests who were ready to call it a night were suddenly recharging their glasses and staying for the gossipy debrief. Chris Crab had swiftly sidled up to ask if I was selling the house. After a while Paul returned briefly without Sukey, who he'd put to bed. He apologised on her behalf, blaming mixing booze with the strong painkillers she'd taken after dental work. I told him not to worry and waved him off before inviting Ruth and Fay to join me in another round of slippery nipples. The cute waiter making the sickly sweet shots of Baileys and Sambuca watched with amused fascination as we necked them.

'What are you smiling at?' I'd slurred before seductively purring, 'Wanna join the party?'

'No,' he'd said. 'It's just you remind me of my mum and her mates at Christmas.'

I'd groan at the memory but I know it'd hurt my head too much. I'm now cowering in a foetal position in a shady corner of the garden on a sunlounger, regretting my life choices. My brain feels like it's being repeatedly trapped in the doors of a lift, a rhythmic thud on either side of my temples.

When I think about taking over the farm I feel I may vomit – is that the hangover bringing on a sense of doom about the whole thing? There's also a small feeling of nervous excitement right in the pit of my stomach. Dread and exhilaration. Two mismatched feelings sitting side by side, like a goose and a sparrow sharing a nest.

I manage to smother the pain under a blanket of painkillers, tea and a snooze. I fall into a deep sleep but a sixth sense drags me from the depths of my slumber as I gradually become aware of someone standing over me. I manage to creak my eyes open.

Silhouetted against the blue sky is the familiar shape of James. Broad shoulders blocking out the glare of the sun and blond hair glowing like a halo.

'I'm really rocking the "Prince Charming" vibes here, standing above a gently snoring sleeping beauty.'

I stretch and yawn, feeling my jaw creak.

'I would've tried to awaken you with love's true kiss but then I spotted the dribble.'

'Never used to stop you,' I say, wiping my mouth with the back of my hand and attempting to shuffle into a seated position. 'Anyway, I hear I'm not deserving of your love's true kiss any more?'

'Ah yes.' He at least has the grace to look a little bashful. 'Sorry. I never really knew when to mention the... situation.'

'Well she's not a "situation" is she? She's a woman.'

'Yes.' His smile is stuck in place like a big plaster.

I'm rather enjoying his awkwardness. 'So?' I say, budging up and patting a little space on the lounger. 'Come on, why don't you park your lil' tush here and tell me everything I need to know? Height, weight, date of birth – all the stats.'

He plonks himself down on the edge of the lounger, almost tipping us both over, and I give a little scream. 'In fact, I'll go here.' He sits on the lawn, legs crossed like a six-year-old in assembly.

'Well, I've known her a while, through work –' he holds up both hands – 'but obviously nothing ever happened, until now. Anyway, she lives half the year in New York where she's from and we spent a lot of the last month together and... she's cool.'

'Right,' I say, absorbing this information. James and I are well over. Kaput. So why is my heart thudding? Maybe because my husband of twenty-three years seems to have replaced me as quickly as one would replace a broken kettle. Ella is from the States? Some sexy, successful New Yorker; so irritating. And intimidating. I picture a Carrie Bradshaw clone strutting up Fifth Avenue in head-to-toe Chanel. I suddenly feel self-conscious in my crinkled tee and mumsy denim shorts.

'And Chloe saying to my mum she was going to "yours and Ella's"? Is she living with you?'

'No.' He shakes his head quickly. 'In fact the opposite. I've moved in with her, but only for a few weeks. The quarterly lease is up on the temporary place and there's a few niggles to sort out with my new apartment, so it was either the Hilton Canary Wharf or hers and she kindly offered me hers. We spent most of it in New York anyway. But I think that's where Chloe got confused.'

'OK.' I wait a beat. 'Go on then.'

'What?'

'James don't.'

'What? Even after all these years I can't read your mind, Josie.'

I don't know why it matters so much to me. 'How old is she? Is the figure more than my waist size?'

'What? You're a size ten! Yes she's older than ten.'

'Don't be an idiot, I mean in jeans – I'm a twenty-eight.' (On a good day.)

He laughs but doesn't answer straight away. Oh god, how old is she? Twenty-five? I hate myself for caring. I hold my nonchalant expression firmly in place though a wave of nausea betrays me.

'If you must know she's forty-six.'

'Oh.' I say. The sickness subsides. Forty-six I can work with. Beyond forty-five, not crossed over into fifties yet, but hurtling towards it.

'Why are you surprised? Thought I'd "do a Mike"?'

To 'do a Mike' was our shorthand for any kind of mid-life crisis behaviour ever since James' colleague left his wife and kids for a twenty-two-year-old dental nurse. He also had a hair transplant and so many fillers that he looks like he had an allergic reaction to a facial bee sting.

'Well I hoped you hadn't. It's just the name Ella belongs to twenty-something pop stars and influencers.'

'It's short for Isabella.'

'Right.'

Despite my initial bravado and forced matey bants, I feel a bit sad. I busy myself picking off a bit of fluff that has settled on my bare thigh. I rub at my eyes, my lashes crispy with slept-in mascara.

'Hey, it's OK.' James gently takes hold of my wrist to stop me rubbing.

I realise he thinks I'm close to tears. 'James, don't flatter yourself, I'm not weeping, my eyes are knackered from sleeping off a big night.'

He lets go of my wrist and looks chastised, then clears his throat. 'So how was the party?'

'Good, though I got up to too much mischief,' I say.

'Who with?' he asks.

'Wouldn't you like to know,' I say saucily.

'Yes, I would rather.'

'Fay,' I reply, and he looks relieved. What's good for the gander clearly isn't good for the goose.

'How is she?'

'She's grand, she's off to Boston for a year, a job swap.'

'Wow,' he whistles, picking at a blade of grass. 'She's always been impressive, eh? How do you feel?'

'Excited for her, bit gutted for myself.'

'I bet. A year is a long time stuck here without your best friend. Though you could fly over and see her?'

'I can't actually, I'll be too busy.' I take a breath. 'I'm moving to Thistlefold, my dad's farm.'

James takes a second then half laughs as though I'm winding him up. Of all the reactions why did he have to laugh? Is the idea of me undertaking a new challenge, changing my lifestyle, so unbelievable?

When I don't laugh along with him, nudge his ribs in a 'nearly got you' kind of way, his features slip from amused to worried.

'Hang on, are you serious? Where's this come from?'

Because I'm following my gut for a change rather than worrying about what everyone else is doing. I'm ready to go back, in fact I need to go back. I don't say that of course.

'Look, it's not all signed and sealed yet – ' and the award for understatement of the year goes t... drumroll, please – 'but I'm seriously looking into it.' I plan to ring the estate agent first thing tomorrow. 'I'm hoping that by autumn I'll be able to move in.' I'm literally pulling answers out of my derrière at this point.

'And this house?' Not an unreasonable question.

'Well, there are lots of options. We could rent it out, Fay's doing that with her place and she said she would introduce me to the guy who sorted hers.'

'OK.' He nods slowly, digesting it all. 'Well, I guess it's up to you.'

'You guess right.'

'I don't mean it like that. Look, I care for you, Jose. I know in the past there've been a few times where you've wanted to try a new career, make a change—'

'This is different.'

'It's just I know you get really excited about a project but sticking at it can be... a challenge.' I can tell he's choosing his words carefully, rolling each sentence round in his head to check its suitability before bowling it at me. 'Maybe in the past if I'd had more support or encouragement I would've stuck at things.' I shoot back petulantly.

He winces.

'Sorry. It's just it's a bit depressing that you clearly think I'm not up to it.'

'It's not that. It's just in the past, well you've had me and you've had Fay. We've always been there for you and – '

'Well I don't need you any more,' I snap.

He looks hurt.

'James, I'm a grown woman. I know you two have always rallied round, protected me, ever since uni, but you know, before you guys and even after, I survived. I was all alone in New York, remember.'

He studies my face. I need him to understand because if he does then he will let go of me.

'I can be strong. Just 'cos I've just not needed to be strong when you and Fay have been there to catch me, doesn't mean I can't be when you're not around.'

He shakes his head. 'It's going to be tough though, Jose.'

'I can be tough,' I say now. 'I had it tough growing up. I need to find that inner strength again. The old Josie. I have to do this.'

'I just want you to know what you're getting yourself into. Running a farm will be a lot harder than your past projects like... Cupboard... Queens – '

'Wardrobe Warriors.'

'Sorry – Wardrobe Warriors.'

'James, this is so different. This feels like fate. I was with Fay and we stumbled across the old farm and it's empty. It felt like it was waiting for my return. There was a storm and a rainbow and we crashed the car and – '

'What?' He looks alarmed.

'It's a long story but I feel it in my gut. This is the right thing to do, in fact the only thing I can do.'

Just like that, I'm telling the truth. I'm not trying to convince James or Fay or even myself any more. I feel this truth in my bones. In my core. Now I just have to make it happen.

The phone rings twice before a gruff voice answers. 'Hello, Martingale's Estate Agent's, Jonathan speaking.' In the background there is laughter and chat. 'Hello?' he says again, impatient, like he's irritated by the youth and exuberance of his colleagues.

'Hello. I wanted to enquire about a farm I saw advertised in your window, please?'

'Oh aye?' says the man. 'Which one would that be, please?'

'Thistlefold. Thistlefold Farm.'

'That's funny,' says the man.

'Is it?'

'Funny peculiar not funny ha-ha,' he clarifies.

'Right.' He's not forthcoming so I ask again, 'Why?'

'Well, that place has been empty for over a year with not a sniff, not a whiff of interest then boom!'

I hear the office quieten down, listening in.

'Boom?'

'Yes. Boom. This is the fourth enquiry about Thistlefold in as many months.'

'That doesn't seem a lot.'

'Well, I imagine you don't know the market round Howlesden and Lennington quite like I do and I can tell you, so many enquiries out of the blue is unusual. There's been a flurry of interest.'

'Right.' The noise in the background swells again.

'Sorry about the clatter,' he says breathily. I can tell he's cupping the phone so his words can't be overheard by his co-workers. He speaks in a hoarse whisper. 'Only Amber from the office has just announced she's finally engaged to Simon and, bless her, with her funny-shaped face we never thought she'd find "the one". In the twelve years she's been here she's had her heart broken no less than seven times, and I think we're all just so happy that the tears today are ones of joy – and, from our side, relief.'

'Well that's lovely. So, what's the —'

He cuts me off. 'Thing is, for such a meek lass she's a bad drunk and until Simon swept her off her tootsies, she's ruined a fair few works' drinks and Christmas parties getting maudlin and weepy, occasionally violent...' He trails off.

'Right. Yes well,' I steer the conversation back on track, 'Thistlefold. Is the leasehold still available?'

I hear my own blood rushing past my ears.

'Oh yes,' he says, 'very much so.'

Part Two

18

It is mid October. I am a farmer. I have the paperwork to prove it. For the next twelve months, at least, I am official custodian of a farmhouse, fifteen outbuildings and the surrounding sixty-two acres of farmland divided across five fields, which include two ponds and three protected oaks.

On the M1 I lose sight of the truck containing almost all of my life at the junction with Finchley Road. I am free. I am happy. I am terrified. I can't quite believe it is only seven months since I clapped eyes on the farm again and now I'm returning.

The motorway is mercifully quiet for a Monday lunchtime. Jeremy Vine is on the radio and his familiar voice is a welcome distraction as he talks to Josh from St Helens about a disgraced MP.

'Thing is, Jeremy,' insists Josh, 'I don't really care what politicians get up to in their personal life – chem-sex parties, dogging – as long as my bins are collected on time.'

'Well thank you, Josh. I'm sure your local MP will be relieved to hear that!' Jeremy laughs, then his voice dips into a deeper, more serious tone. 'Coming up next, as Halloween approaches, are trick or treaters a dangerous nuisance or a bit of harmless fun? We speak to one woman who doesn't like them and has an unusual way of discouraging them and it involves, wait for it – ' He takes a breath then exclaims, 'GEESE! That's after "Dreams" from the fantastic Fleetwood Mac.'

I sing along, murmuring the lyrics, self-soothing like a baby cooing to itself. I wonder if my heart will hammer in my chest for the whole 184 miles. The last few hours have been a blur. Ruth popped round for a farewell coffee, noisily blowing her nose making her latest charge Sylvie the Saluki jump. Finally, I closed the front door and double-locked it, laying my hand on the smooth wood one last time. It was through that door that James carried me when we first bought the house, it was the door I bumped backwards through with Chloe in her buggy, the handles laden with shopping bags like a pack mule. For over two decades that door had been the portal to peace, security, comfort. Also years of mind-numbing routine when one week would melt into the next.

The two Chrises waited on their path ready to wave me off, their words still ringing in my ears. 'It's going to be fabulous, good luck, you know where we are when you decide to sell up!'

My phone rings. It connects through the car's Bluetooth. It's James. 'Hiya.'

'Hello.' He sounds very formal. 'I wonder if you can help me, I'm looking for Farmer Josie, thought to be heading northbound following the whiff of pig poo and inbreeding.'

'Ha-ha, very funny.'

'Happy moving day, Jose!' I can hear he means it.

'Thanks. Can't quite believe it's happening.'

'Neither can I.'

'You never thought I'd see it through did you?' I can't stop a smugness creeping into my tone.

'You know what, from that first conversation we had I knew you would. Though I could tell you were still trying to convince yourself as well. But you're actually doing it, Jose.'

'Thanks. Have you spoken to Chloe?'

'Yeah, last night. She seems very relaxed about her childhood room being packed up in her absence. I remember a time when she wouldn't let me over the threshold without first solemnly swearing not to touch any of her Barbies or cuddlies. Must be the combo of Cornish life and Aspen's hippy vibe rubbing off on her.'

'I just think she's happy. You know she's got farmers across six areas interested in the wool scheme, it's really taking off.'

A large tanker overtakes and swings into the slow lane in front of me.

'So the house is all sorted?' he asks.

'Yup – tenants move in at the weekend. Fay's guy was very efficient. It's rented out part-furnished. I'll only be needing the one bed for now.'

'Where will Ruth sleep?'

'What?'

'Come on,' he chuckles. 'You think you'll be able to keep her away?'

'I'll bed her down with the hens.'

'She'd probably love that.'

There's a pause. I can feel a build of pressure, like a swollen crisp packet on a plane, ready to burst open.

'Jose?'

'Yes?' The tanker in front brakes, the red lights like a warning.

'Your mum rang.'

I slow down, the tanker now has its hazards on, there's obviously some kind of problem up ahead. Great, now the M1 insists on being a metaphor for my relationship with my mum. I'm reduced to a crawl. It's probably for the best. I remember a study once showed that listening to loud music makes people drive faster, for me the equivalent is stressful conversations about my mother.

'Jose?'

'Sorry, traffic. And there's me thinking you'd called to wish me well.' I know this is unfair. 'Course she called you, James, makes perfect sense.' I hear him breathing, allowing me my little rant. 'She's also been calling Chloe for updates, freaked out poor Fay by waking her in the middle of the night in Boston with an "urgent" call and even got hold of Ruth through her Hound Stretcher website – they've only met a handful of times.'

'I know,' he groans.

I roll to a standstill. I reach for my coffee, sip at the lukewarm dregs.

'She told Ruth that what I was doing would be "the end of her". That Ruth had a moral obligation to stop me doing something so damaging.'

'Yup, she said that to me too. What did Ruth say?'

'Apparently she said, "Sandra my love, you're as crackers as a collie with two cocks."'

He laughs and despite the stress it's contagious and I can't help smiling.

'Well at least we can always rely on Ruth for a random dog/dick analogy.'

'Always. Mum is being impossible. I know you can't be expected to put her straight, it's just so over the top. I mean, I'm not plotting to steal the moon or poison Father Christmas – I'm moving back to my childhood home.'

'I know. Look, I know all this, Jose, and I tried my best, I promise. I told her she was being unreasonable.'

'Bet she loved that. The worst thing is – ' I put my coffee cup back in the holder and rummage in the centre console for my lip balm – 'she won't take my calls, won't even talk to me. Instead she's floating around connecting with everyone else in my orbit like a big dramatic... satellite.' I find the chapstick and smudge some on my lips.

'She'll get over it, Jose. She'll have to. She can't stay on her perch of indignation forever. Everyone is on your side and everyone is gently telling her – with the possible exception of Ruth when it comes to the gentle bit – that she's being unfair on you.'

We speak for a few minutes longer. I can tell James is trying to steer the conversation into less hostile territory – he wants to know what animals I'll be buying first, if I've ever driven a tractor. I say I don't know, and yes Dad let me have a few goes when I was ten. But the mood has passed and I'm keen to get off the phone, this light-hearted chat feels strained after the discussion about Mum. As we say our goodbyes I can't help feeling a little deflated.

My last call with Mum echoes around my mind. 'Why do you have to make everything about you? I'm the one who's moving to the farm, not you.'

'Don't you see?' she spat. 'It *is* about me. The farm, that house, the whole area was *my life* until it was taken from me.' I pictured the darkness that shadows her eyes when she shouts; I saw it often as a child. She took a breath, lowered her voice, perhaps aware her lodger was nearby. 'For you to go and hijack the place because you've watched one too many episodes of *Countryfile* is selfish and unfair,' she hissed. 'I'm sorry but I want to keep that place buried in my past, while you seem intent on digging it all up for your own entertainment.'

'Entertainment? It's my heritage. It was my home too, my life too! My dad!' I protested but by then, she'd hung up.

The traffic continues to crawl and I pull alongside a mum and daughter in a pale blue Range Rover, their matching blond pony-tails swinging as they chat. The girl looks to be about twelve, the age I was when everything changed.

I'm back in the tiny kitchen of our rented terraced house and Mum is trying to light the ring on the hob of the gas cooker. The numbers on the dial have been rubbed off by years of use. The ignition switch is broken and each time she holds a match close it is blown out by a puff of gas that refuses to catch. I try to help, hovering next to her, suggesting she turn the dial less.

'Josie, you're not helping by getting under my feet.' She's swaying a little as if moving in time to a soul record but the only sound is the occasional hiss of gas and Mum's mutterings. 'Bloody smart arse,' she grumbles. 'I've had enough of being stuck here with you in this shitty little house.' I wince. Mum never used to swear in front of me and I'm yet to get used to it.

She is drunk. She would take a while to get steaming on account of the Schweppes lemonade she mixed with the white wine. She nurses this spritzer all day from lunchtime, topping it up as and when. Always in the same glass – a tall commemorative pint pot celebrating the engagement of Prince Charles and Lady Diana, engraved in white etching with both their faces. It is not official merchandise and Diana looks more like Barry Manilow – her nose too long, her hair too short.

Mum strikes the last match from the box but she's holding it pointed downwards and the flame licks up burning her finger so she drops it onto the linoleum floor. I instinctively stamp on it with my school shoe before it can melt the plastic. She shouts, 'No!' but it's too late. A sticky scorch mark is left and she seems relieved to be able to focus her fury on me now instead of an inanimate object. Her foul mood needs justifying.

'Look what you've done,' she snarls. 'No wonder I'm stressed. Trying to look after you and cope with all this.' She points an accusatory finger around the room as if at a jeering crowd. 'It was about to light and now we've no way of heating our tea and, thanks to your stupidity, we'll be charged for that damage.'

I look at the glass, trace the curve of Prince Charles' jaw, his unsure smile. For the last couple of months I'd become expert at shrinking away as Mum's moods became unpredictable. Somehow, I could vacate my own head. I let Mum rant and rave – answering back or defending myself only fuels her fire, best to let it burn out. Mid-gesticulation she manages to knock the small pan onto the floor with a clatter and chilli con carne splashes out, the majority coming to rest in a sludgy puddle half in the pan, half on the lino. She looks down at the mess and makes a sort of strangled laugh noise. I brace, expecting more fury. Instead she turns on her heel to the fridge and refills her glass with a shaking hand, gives a sigh that seems to deflate her whole being, then stumbles out of the kitchen.

The house falls quiet and I scoop most of the food off the floor and back into the pan and put it into the fridge. I make myself a jam butty. The bread is old but I pick off the green bits and it's better than nothing because I'm starving. I wolf the butty looking out of the back window into the tiny brick backyard. I think about the view from the farm kitchen window that looked out over the paddock and how Dad would spot me daydreaming and wave from the tractor. I miss him and my old life so much it gives me a stomach ache.

By the time I go into the lounge she's fallen asleep on the sofa and is gently snoring in front of *Tomorrow's World*. Her head is at a weird angle, her chin pushed forward onto her chest. I want to move the cushion behind her head so she doesn't wake in an even worse mood because of a cricked neck and also because, despite everything, I want to look after her. Gently I take hold of the cushion and start sliding it out from underneath her very slowly. It all happens in a split second. I realise too late that I've trapped a lock of her hair to the cushion under my thumb and I'm about to pull her hair, waking her up. Instead I'm confused because as I brace for the hair to tug at her scalp I realise it's still trapped under my thumb and isn't attached to her head, the greasy coil of hair is still lying across the cushion as I straighten up. It has come away in my hands.

*

The tanker in front starts to pick up speed. I accelerate to keep up with the flow of traffic, whatever slowed down the traffic has disappeared as suddenly as it arrived.

Five hours, three coffees, two toilet stops and a sizeable pasty later I find myself bumping up the lane of Thistlefold Farm. It takes me a moment to realise all of it belongs to me – the rusty gate, the lane, the blackberry bushes still bearing September's fruit. Well, for the next twelve months anyway. Then after that, who knows? I gulp involuntarily. An actual gulp, like people do in the movies. Then I giggle out loud. Unbelievable. This is ludicrous. I must be actually insane. What the hell am I doing?

I make a mental note to fix the gate. I imagine it will be the first of many such notes and a second later as my car dips with a loud thump into a deep pothole. I add 'Sort lane' to the list.

It's coming up to six p.m. The last time I was here I was welcomed by a huge rainbow on a spring day but now autumn has arrived and dusk is fast approaching, a strip of dark concrete sky lies across the horizon.

The golden beam of my headlights sweeps across a car parked in the yard. I had arranged with Jonathan from Martingale's to meet me with the keys. A chunky man unfolds himself from a canary yellow Mazda and salutes, then I realise he's shading his eyes from the glare of my lights.

'Blimey,' he says as I climb out of my car, 'I thought you were about to interrogate me, dazzling me like that.'

'Sorry,' I say, mildly miffed that my big moment – the first time I step onto the yard that is my new home – has been slightly ruined by a quip from a man in a cagoule and shiny suit. I hope it's not a bad omen. I stand for a moment and look around me. The farmhouse, the buildings and the barn look as if they've just appeared before me like the pages of a pop-up book; the story of my childhood. The grey wooden sheds look foreboding and spooky in this light. The house cold and unwelcoming. It's familiar and alien at the same time. Over the last few months I hadn't visited in person but I had pored over the dozens of photographs emailed to me by Jonathan. 'It's best to know what you're letting yourself in for,' he said on the phone.

Every building had been photographed and every fault highlighted – no loose guttering, cracked wall or damp patch had remained undocumented. I guess he was trying to be helpful, managing my expectations. He had filmed around the farmhouse and buildings too, Blair Witch-style footage dropping into my WhatsApp. Shaky camera work and booming voiceover. 'See this.' A podgy finger hovering into shot like an uncooked sausage in space, pointing at a patch on a bedroom wall: 'Penetrating damp. It'll dry out in the summer months but just so you know.' The faults were so many and so well documented it was as if he was trying to put me off the place, like the caretaker who's got something to hide at the start of a murder mystery.

'Don't apologise,' says Jonathan now. 'I have very sensitive eyes, my mum is the same, wears sunglasses all year round, she looks like Roy bloody Orbison.' He laughs. 'Anyway. Welcome. Nice to meet you again.' He smiles mischievously.

'Again?'

'Yup.' He grins but doesn't reveal any more details, waiting for a penny to drop, though no penny is forthcoming. It's been a long day and I'm not in a riddle mood. I could really do with getting into the house and putting the kettle on before the removal lorry turns up.

He spins the house keys on his fingers, clearly enjoying his little game.

'Sorry, Jonathan, it's been quite a drive and I'm keen to get indoors.'

He speaks in a voice usually reserved for asking toddlers what the magic word is. 'What's short for Jonathan?'

'John?'

'Nearly.'

I bite my bottom lip. 'Jonny?' I say through gritted teeth.

'Correct!' he booms. 'Jonny Beadle. The last time I saw you was at school. Though we weren't friends. I was in the year below. I remember you cried at the school disco 'cos I spilled my drink on you, though it was actually not my fault, Cathy Pinkton shoved me.'

It's Jonny the imbecile. From the photographs. Course it is, now I look closer at the round brown eyes set too close together, the long chin that could've been shaped by a heavy-handed potter. All I can manage is a weak, 'Oh wow.'

He's still grinning.

I glance at the keys again. 'Well, I suppose I'll keep bumping into old school friends now I'm back, eh?'

'I was going to tell you over the phone but I wanted to see your face.'

'Right.' I'm pretty certain my current expression wasn't worth the wait.

We fall into an awkward silence.

'Oh god, the keys. Here you go. Sorry, was back in the school hall then drinking my lemonade.' He holds out the bunch of keys on his index finger.

'Cherryade,' I correct, taking the keys.

'Pardon?'

'It was cherryade.'

'So you do remember!'

'Yes. The pink wouldn't wash out of my blouse.' I say the last bit through a smile but I'm aware I still sound like I'm peeved about a ruined Lady Diana blouse forty years ago.

'I forgave her though,' he says to my back as I walk towards the front door.

'Who?'

'Cathy Pinkton! For shoving me into you. I forgave her enough to walk up the aisle with her and she's been Cathy Beadle for going on twenty-five years now.'

'Lovely!' I shout over my shoulder. From the big reveal to the punchline to the reprise, I've disappointed him I'm sure. A five-hour drive, a brimming bladder and an estranged mother can do that to a woman. I daren't look back at him. Instead I shout, 'Fancy a brew?' as I waggle the key into the lock.

'No thank you. I'll leave you to it – let you explore your new home, if that's OK?'

Wow. Jonathan in a 'reading the room' shocker. I try to keep the relief from my voice. 'OK, if you're sure?'

'Yup. Looks like rain. I'm going to go pick up Cathy and the kids from her mother's, get me some husband points.'

'Good for you, she's a lucky lady!' I'm overcompensating.

'That's what I tell her. Her mum's just had her hip replaced so it's been quite full-on recently.' I didn't strictly need to know this last nugget. I nod, still holding the key in the lock, my head twisted around awkwardly over my shoulder. 'Anyway,' he opens his car door and squeezes himself into the sporty car, a half-deflated lilo being stuffed into a suitcase. 'Bye for now. Sorry again about the blouse!' And, at last, he's gone.

The key turns on the third try and I push open the door and almost fall into the farmhouse kitchen. I feel like I've stumbled out from a time machine. The place I've dreamt and daydreamed about for the past four decades.

The videos from Jonny, the visit with Fay and peering through the grimy windows may have given me a sneak preview but nothing could prepare me for this physical feeling, like a hand gripping my stomach and squeezing. There is a smell that still lingers from my childhood, though surely that's impossible? It could be the wooden beams, the brickwork, maybe the paddock beyond. It is an earthy not unpleasant scent.

I stand still and survey the room. I feel a swell of sadness. Being back in this room brings Dad's death sharply into focus and my heart aches with the unfairness of it. A visceral feeling like he's been torn from this house too soon. I take a breath. All the times I've imagined coming back here and now I've made it, so I try to focus on the positive and savour the sweetness of my return. I long to hear my dad's laughter or Mum singing along to the radio as she makes a tower of sandwiches for the lads helping out with haymaking. I know this is impossible. It is up to me to make new memories now.

I look downwards and see the limestone floor is the same one I played on and slid across in my socks. It's the floor I would lie down on by the AGA, stroking Jet's silky black ears, a dusting of her dander clinging to the front of my school pinafore.

The units, the wallpaper and curtains left behind are alien to me but I notice the old door still has the curled iron coat hooks. They are empty, expectantly tipped up like a dog's nose at the dinner table, waiting to be hung with wax jackets. The table itself is different but the same square wooden sort we had, and I see Bill the vet chatting away while Dad leans against the AGA putting the world to rights over a brew.

I shiver and realise the darkness has brought with it a chill. I need to crack on. Jonathan had reassured me numerous times that the electricity and gas would be reinstated but still I hold my breath as I flick the main switch in the kitchen. I breathe a sigh of relief as a warm glow is cast around the room, which reignites the butterflies in my tummy. Shit. It's really happening. My phone buzzes with a text – the removal lorry is twenty minutes away.

I check my pocket for a tissue and nip to the downstairs loo, then go out to the car to grab my overnight bag and the one box

I need for now packed with essentials. I carefully unwrap the jug of my coffee machine and plug in the unit on the kitchen counter with a little squeal of excitement as it lights up. Now I'm home. Coffee or wine? I decide I need both.

With the machine gurgling away, I'm distracted by the glow of lights from the neighbouring farm across the fields and make a mental note to go say hello to my new neighbours at some point. I open the wine and unwrap the newspaper from around the Merlot glass I'd packed a few hours and a hundred lifetimes ago. I feel giddy. 'Toto, I've a feeling we're not in Kansas any more,' I say out loud in my best Dorothy voice. Hampstead could be a different planet compared to where I am now. The wind whistles a faint tune against the windowpanes and I remember the sound from my childhood, Mum making hot malt drinks on wintry nights. I used to be irritated by her fussing around me with extra layers, not knowing then that this caring version of mum wouldn't be around forever.

I light the AGA without blowing myself up thanks to the YouTube tutorials I'd studied all week, then stand with my hands on my hips in the centre of the kitchen. It needs a proper clean before I unpack – each drawer rattles open making the tiny mouse droppings inside dance and the cupboards are strung with spiderweb bunting.

For tonight I just need to get cosy, direct the right boxes and furniture to the right rooms and flop into bed.

19

I wake the next morning and for a few seconds I have no clue where I am. Then it comes to me. I'm in Mum and Dad's room. I settled in the master bedroom last night, only deciding when the removals men had wrestled my huge bed to the top of the stairs. My super king-size bed fitted perfectly in the Hampstead house but in this modest low-ceilinged room it gobbles up all of the space. I don't care. I love my bed, my acres of space to stretch out, especially as I'm now the only one to occupy it.

A soft light is warming up the window and I reach for my specs and go look outside. My breath catches in my throat, the paddock and the fields beyond are washed in an orange glow from the rising sun and the deep green of the grass is made more vibrant by the generous soaking of dew.

I can hear birds singing and... well, that's it. In London when you listened closely there was always low static, a barely audible rumble of traffic, of planes overhead, punctuated regularly with a whirr of a leaf blower, a dog's bark or a distant siren. Even the birdsong seemed more businesslike in the city, as if the blue tits were running through the day's itinerary.

Here though, this was the definition of the purest peace and quiet. I breathe deeper than I have in a long time. Close my eyes in a moment of meditation. Then, a scrape. My eyes spring back open and look upwards. A noise overhead, like someone tapping acrylic nails along the attic floor, scratching at the joists with the teeth of a plastic comb. The sound is skittish, lively and therefore alive sounding.

My heart sinks. I am not alone.

I pad downstairs in my slippers, past piles of boxes abandoned in doorways. I try not to let my mood be dampened by the thought of the ceiling above my bed collapsing with the weight of ten thousand rats tumbling down on top of me and burying me in a writhing, squeaking mass. I need to deal with it at some point but I have a big day ahead.

By mid-morning I've cleaned and scrubbed the kitchen so at least I can start unpacking some boxes. Occasionally a memory bubbles to the surface as I open a certain cupboard – the place where Mum used to stash the choccie biscuits away from Dad or the stone ledge above the AGA where she would keep matches; the small black nail in the surrounding brickwork upon which Mum would hang an oven glove.

I forgot the joy of an AGA, the comfort of its gentle warmth, a steadying influence sitting there, an ancient tor to be revered and gathered around. When we left the farm I remember Mum missed it so much. We moved on a rainy cold November day, Mum tracing a hand along the shiny silver rail on top of the AGA, almost patting it goodbye.

She'd been positive at first, verging on the manic. 'We'll make it cosy, Josie! Oh that rhymes – I'm a poet and I didn't know it!' she said as we stood in the damp chill of the small terraced house, our few belongings from the farm looking uncomfortable in their new surroundings, like unexpected visitors who've arrived during an argument.

She soon became tired of the place. Within days she was crying a lot again, about Dad, the unfairness of the cruel cards dealt her in the past weeks. The friends who'd gathered her up in their arms in the aftermath of Dad's death slowly faded into the background, busy with their own lives, their own kids. The phone stopped ringing and visitors became a rarity, especially as Mum's grieving morphed from sorrow to anger, fuelled by drink and exhaustion. So we were left to it, to pick up the pieces. Being around Mum became uncomfortable. Her moods were unpredictable and she even pushed away her own sister eventually, accusing her of not caring.

The new place only exacerbated our estrangement from all that was familiar. It felt like we were trapped there, just me and Mum, with our grief and loneliness, our moods clacking together like two little marbles forgotten in a pocket. She would wear the same grey leggings and faded T-shirt that hung off her thinning frame. On nights out with Dad she always applied her eyeliner elegantly, a thin liquid line of black flicking up at the edges of her eyes, but now she barely showered and she was just as likely to use make-up as she was a flame thrower.

I had started at a new school and tried my best to slip into the playground and my new life unnoticed, as if I'd always been there. I refused Mum's offers to walk me to school and could see the relief in her eyes when I said there was no need. She would smile, her lips quivering with teary pride that I wanted to be independent. In fact I was embarrassed by her – the greasy hair, the ghoulish dark rings around her eyes, and I felt guilty that I was ashamed of my own mum.

The day after Mum's hair had first come out on the pillow I heard her crying in the bathroom. Fistfuls of her hair filled the sink and lay strewn on the mildewed lino. Her doctor just sent her away with pamphlets about alopecia and a prescription for Valium. When she left the house, which was rare, she wore my old blue bobble hat. Her lashes thinned, her eyebrows too.

One friend did call round still, Trish, who with her squished raspberry pout and wide eyes heavily rimmed with blue pencil looked like a Picasso portrait. Trish was kind though, appearing in a flurry of cardigan, enveloping us in a cloud of perfume, never empty-handed. After she'd hugged me tightly enough to make my bones creak, she'd head to the kitchen, putting the lasagne or cottage pie she'd made into the fridge.

I sat on the stairs in my too-small nightie, the worn carpet itchy on my thighs, and listened through the thin wall as Mum cried in Trish's arms. 'Look at me,' Mum would wail, 'it's the last straw.'

'Hey, come on,' Trish would coo.

Mum was slurring, almost incoherent. 'Everything has been taken from me – my husband, my home, now my hair.'

Trish would hold her and try her best to give her a pep talk. 'It's probably from the stress. Didn't the doctor say as much?'

'It feels like it's punishment.'

'Come on, that's nonsense.' There was a muffled response from Mum, speaking into her friend's woollen expanse, then from Trish, firmer now, 'It's stress, San, you need to start looking after yourself for Josie.'

A silence, then just Mum hiccuping, trying to regain her composure, drained from the crying.

'No more drinking, San, you need to get a hold of it before it gets hold of you.'

Little did Trish know that the drinking already had Mum in its grip. I sneaked back up the stairs then and into my bed. I was confused and scared. I wanted to sob, scream and kick out at an unfair world. I missed my dad too, but I knew I had to be strong for Mum, so instead I'd bite down on my thin duvet, unleashing a silent roar that made my temples throb.

Once the kitchen is unpacked I pour a coffee and sit at the table. 'Well, Dad, I'm back,' I say out loud.

The farmhouse seems strange without at least one dog roaming around, sniffing for scraps of food or affection. I'll get round to filling this place with animals but there's no rush. Besides, top of my to-do list is getting rid of some animals, the ones in the attic, presumably rats or preferably mice, even better just one random squirrel. Please, God not bats that come with some kind of preservation order – I do not want to be the mad bat woman of Thistledown.

I can't bear the thought of another chat with Jonathan just yet so I think about my options and I'm struck with a feeling of isolation. In Hampstead James was always at work whenever there was an emergency but I had the neighbours – whether it was a leaky roof, a problem with the electrics or a worry that there was a dodgy-looking pair sitting in a car outside. A message on the street WhatsApp group would result in either a flurry of phone numbers for recommended tradesmen or one or two neighbours scanning the street from their doorstep, with chests puffed out, to check out the suspicious vehicle. Here though, I'm entirely alone.

It is at the same time, undeniably thrilling.

I could call GG for a rat catcher number, though I reckon before any pest controller had a chance to smell a rat, half of Howlesden would know about my infestation. That's not really the conversation opener I want for my first forays to the village.

Then I remember Beth from the sweet shop. I'll ask her. Who knows, I may get a recommendation and a quarter of bonbons into the bargain.

Before I do any of that I need to properly reacquaint myself with the farm. Moving in at dusk and this morning's jobs in the kitchen mean I've barely set foot outside. My wellies are by the kitchen door that leads straight out onto the yard. The boots look too shiny and clean. Red designer numbers are all very well on Hampstead Heath or at Glastonbury, but round here they'll mark me out as a novice. I've come from five generations of farmers but those red wellies scream townie and I make a mental note to buy some basic green ones ASAP. Nevertheless I pull them on now and head out to the yard, Notes app open on my phone ready to... to do what exactly? I had an inventory of the buildings already. I tap in 'Gate. Lane. Wellies' then I put my phone in my pocket and resolve to walk round the fields, to just 'be' on the farm.

I realise the worth of Jonathan's emails when I come across a rusted door or faulty gate and I'm not surprised or disappointed. All in all the buildings themselves are in pretty good nick, they just feel very empty. I'd only ever really known the yard to be a hive of activity so seeing it now so desolate feels strange. Just the birdsong and the wind whistling through the trees. A slick of panic washes over me – what was I thinking? I've left behind my life to come here, an empty farm full of ghosts and memories. I rub my face as if to wipe away those thoughts. *Embrace the quiet*, I tell myself, *it's not for ever, new life will be breathed into the farm soon enough.*

I zip up my jacket and walk past the paddock and towards the field, climbing the five-bar gate with ease. The panic subsides. This is more like it, I think. Here I am, just a farmer checking her fencing.

I make my way around the edge of the first two fields. I even remember their names – the imaginatively titled Front Field and Figure of Eight, named after the shape of the pond in the top corner. On to Three Oak Field where I follow the fencing in a clockwise direction as that will lead me eventually to Goose Pond Field, so called because of the Canada geese that settle there every winter. Then on to the last field, Blacksmiths, named after the lane that borders its right-hand boundary.

The barbed wire and posts in Three Oak Field seem to be holding up. I make a note in my phone of any slacker sections that'll need fixing before it's fit for keeping livestock in. The first three fields are full of lush green grass, thick tufts fold beneath my footsteps then spring back into position as if I'd never passed by. The summer's leftover meadow flowers speckle the green with occasional red, blue and lemon. No herds have trampled, munched or shat on these fields for a good year or so. Thistledown has accidentally embraced the current trend for rewilding I'd read about in the Sunday supplements.

When I was a girl the first three fields were mown for hay and Goose Pond and Blacksmiths were barley straw. Haymaking was a busy time at the farm. Dad's pals and some lads from the village were roped in to help on the promise of being fed and later on at the pub, watered. There was a real sense of community and all the farms helped each other out – mowing the grass, turning it to help it dry, baling it into prefect bristly oblongs, then once completely dry, bringing it in from the fields and stacking it in the barn. All this was a race against time so machinery and manpower were shared, with everyone trying to get it all done before the weather broke and rain came. I remember thinking Dad was so important, always at the wheel of the tractor pulling the baler, making perfect parallel rows of cut hay across the fields as neat and uniform as the lined paper in my school books. If I idolised Dad I coveted the young lads helping out, my twelve-year-old self spying on them as they stacked the bales. I wasn't quite strong enough to help so instead was charged with taking mugs of tea to them, blushing at their sinewy arms and fruity language.

Walking now I can see from Three Oak that Goose Pond Field looks different to the others. In fact it looks like it used to after the haymaking seasons of my childhood. There is no grass, instead there is stubble, a short bristly yellow covering of crop left behind after a barley harvest, an uneven regrowth on a chin. From a distance the field looks golden but close up it's scrappy and strewn with large stones; the stubble is difficult to walk on. I carry on along the fence and can see the next field along, Blacksmiths, is stubble too.

I'm torn. Someone has been using these fields without permission as far as I know but on the other hand, why not? At best it's a practical use of land to grow food and bedding for livestock, at worst it's... well, a bit cheeky? Still, I'd like to know who did it. Things are different now, these fields aren't unclaimed any longer, they are mine. For the next twelve months anyway.

I head back to the house along the perimeter of Blacksmiths, pleased most of the fencing seems in good enough nick. There are a couple of spots that need sorting including the area where Fay and I gingerly climbed through after the car crash all those months ago. I smile at the memory now of us legging it through the rain.

I can see where the wire's been stretched by a cow using one of the posts as an arse scratcher, rubbing back and forth until the post is waggled so violently it widens the hole it was originally thumped into. Once the fence post is loose, the wire is stretched and twanged until it becomes distended and hangs sloppily like a washing line whose ends are strung too close together.

As I turn and walk from the top of Blacksmiths back towards the yard I feel the first drops of rain. I look up and see I've been ambushed by a fat cloud blacker than a cassock despite the morning being fair and bright up until then. I remember Dad lamenting that 'Up here we get four seasons in one day' whenever he banged through the door into the kitchen soggy and dripping onto the stone floor, having started feeding the cattle in bright sunshine.

The rain starts to fall in thick sheets now just like it did with Fay and I wonder if I'll ever get to walk in these fields without starting off dry and ending up wet. The stubble is hard to run on so I settle on a brisk walk – a sprained ankle is the last thing I need.

With my head down against the worst of the rain, I notice with satisfaction that the dampened ground is muddying my townie wellies. The rain soon starts to ease off then stops as promptly as it started. The black cloud above has gone, like a cartoon bad mood. I'm alongside the Blacksmiths Lane side of the field when something bright catches my eye in a tree. I think it's a bird of exotic hue but as I peer closer through the hawthorn hedge to the other side of the road, I see it is brightly coloured ribbon used to tether a small posy of flowers to the trunk of a tree. The purple flowers look a little battered by the elements. I recognise the flowers as purple cowslips like the ones on Dad's grave. Then I'm suddenly struck by a realisation that winds me. Today is 12 October, two days after the anniversary of the car crash that killed Dad on Blacksmiths Lane. The tree I was now squinting at through my damp fringe must be the tree the car hit on that stormy night. Someone around here obviously still cares about him.

I stumble my way back towards the house. I'd forgotten about Dad's anniversary in the busyness of packing up and moving. It was a date Mum never commemorated and whenever I did ask about it, she'd snap that it was a date to forget, not to remember.

20

Back at the house I realise I don't want to be alone, spotting the memorial to Dad has shaken me. I also haven't eaten and so I drag a brush through my damp hair and jump into the car to head into the village. I need something to distract me from picturing that tree, the flooded road, the car skidding out of control.

Besides, I want to pick up a few things and I can't hide up on the farm, I need to start familiarising myself with the village and its inhabitants. As I spin the Volvo round in the yard and bump down the lane, I feel ridiculously nervous. I read an article once about how nervousness is the same chemical reaction as excitement so I try, as the article suggested, reframing these feelings from mild terror into something resembling elation.

'I *am* excited,' I say out loud to Jeremy Vine on the radio as I pull out from the lane and on to the road, thumping through a deep puddle. 'I've moved two hundred miles to the middle of nowhere on a whim, I'm entirely alone apart from a vermin infestation, someone is using my land for their own profit and a Scooby-Doo style mystery is forming about who is still marking my father's death after four decades. So yes! I'm definitely excited, Jeremy!' In response, he plays Coldplay's 'Fix You' and my manic shouting at the radio turns to tears as I drive through the winding country lanes, singing at the top of my lungs. I open my window to blow away the cobwebs and any small doubts.

The ambush of so many emotions all rushing at once is like being on the losing side of a snowball fight. I am pelted with feelings – I'm sorry for myself, sad for my dad, thrilled that I'm here, nervous about the next twelve months. And very, very hungry.

I pull up in the village square and realise the radio is still blaring. Bobbi the traffic reporter is talking about trapped traffic on the M4 and a passing elderly couple give me a disapproving glance.

My empty stomach growls and I buy a warm pasty from the baker's, a pale girl at the till only glancing up briefly from her phone to take payment.

I eat it in the style of a seabird with a fish, and I'm still brushing the spots of pastry from my chin as I push open the door to the sweet shop. The bell clangs and Beth appears like a genie summoned. 'Ah-ha!' she says and looks not a little smug. 'Welcome home, Josie.'

She remembers me!

'I had a feeling when we met that you'd be back. You had a glow about you after seeing the farm and you struck me as someone who follows their gut.'

I liked this; I've never been described like that before – it made me sound brave.

'You were right,' I say. 'Though I'd keep your fortune-telling skills under wraps or there'll be a queue round the block wanting next week's lottery numbers.'

'Ah well, I have to confess I had a tip-off – everyone in the village knows you're here. GG from the garage popped in this morning, he'd bumped into Jonathan who'd sneaked in for a pint at The Three Keys last night 'cos he was in Cathy's good books and apparently he was telling the whole pub you were officially back at Thistlefold. By all accounts he was lapping up the attention. Your return is the biggest news since the Davies' barn burnt down. Don't get me wrong, he's nice Jonathan, just don't tell him any of your secrets, he's like the unofficial town crier.'

'Luckily I've no secrets.'

Beth snorts softly at this. 'Everyone has secrets.' She reaches for the Pontefract cakes. 'Your usual?'

'God you're good,' I say, 'but I fancy some strawberry bonbons, please.'

She nods in approval. 'I remembered you liked liquorice 'cos they're not a big seller – in fact there's only one other person in the village who ever buys them.'

'Wow, I have a confection twin, how exciting.'

Beth laughs. 'Yup. That's not the only thing you have in common, he's your neighbour too – Will over on Creekside Farm.'

I wonder if Will is the one harvesting my fields. Maybe I need to pop round with a box of Allsorts to break the news that we'll need to come to some arrangement. If he's got all the machinery to plant, spray and cultivate the barley and bale the leftovers into straw, it'd be cutting off my own nose a bit to demand he stops outright. After all, he's got a combine harvester, I've got a Volvo.

Out loud I say, 'Interesting, thanks for the intel.'

'You're welcome.' She does a small bow then pours the bonbons from the scales into a paper bag and hands them over. 'How was your first night?' she asks.

'It was fine. Though I have company.'

'Urgh god, let me guess – mice? Rats? Bats?'

'I dunno. The first would be manageable, the third would be annoying but if it's the middle one I'm moving in here.'

'Ha, that won't be necessary.' She gets another paper bag and scribbles the name 'Alex' on it. 'When you call mention my name.' She winks.

'Oh aye.' I smile. 'Is Alex one of *your* many secrets?'

'Maybe,' she says with a waggle of an eyebrow.

SARA COX | 180

We both laugh. She scribbles something else on the paper. 'My number,' she says. 'When you feel brave enough to come and meet the locals I'll take you to the pub quiz night on a Thursday, people are so wrapped up in it that at least you won't be the centre of attention... just a side show.'

'I can live with that,' I say and thank her, popping a bonbon in my mouth as I leave, the bell clanging above the sweet shop door.

Maybe because of a bit of human interaction or maybe it's the sugar entering my bloodstream, but I feel gung-ho and put 'Creekside Farm' into my satnav and within minutes I'm swinging the car into the bottom of a narrow lane leading to my new neighbour's farm.

The yard and house are much more compact than Thistlefold, a simple cottage on a courtyard of smaller redbrick outbuildings. The place is neater though, no piles of junk or sagging roofs. 'Hello?' I shout lamely into the ether. Somewhere a dog barks. I start to lose my nerve, is it rude to just rock up like this? I'll just introduce myself and maybe invite them round for a coffee and some cake at a later date. That's when I'll mention the hay field, not today. I head to the door of the house, trying to stride confidently. It feels like someone is watching me.

Before I can knock, the dark wooden door opens a few inches and a voice growls, 'He's not in.'

The room behind is dark and the owner of the voice is a small man, maybe mid-seventies though it's hard to tell in the gloom. Silver whiskers on his chin under a thin wet mouth clamped shut. There is a stale smell coming from him, an unwashed sourness. Half his face is obscured by the door.

I'm caught off guard. Is this my liquorice-loving neighbour? 'Will?' I almost whisper to the crack in the doorway, which seems to be slowly closing.

'I said, not in!' the man snaps.

'Right. Sorry to pop up out the blue, I just wanted to say hello, I've moved in next door and—'

'I heard,' the man says. 'All the way from London, eh? Flashing your cash, rubbing our faces in it.'

I open my mouth to speak but nothing comes out.

'You've got a bloody nerve, swanning up here like this. I don't want you on my land or anywhere near it. I thought I'd seen the last of your lot. You are not welcome up here or in this village.'

My hackles rise. 'Now hang on—'

'No *you* hang on.' The door opens a little wider and I see his bulging blue eyes for the first time, their yellowing edges quivering with fury. '*You* have come up here and I'm telling *you* now to *leave*. Or I will be forced to take action to get you off my land.' He glances to his right and I'm sure in the shadows I see the silhouette of a rifle leaning up against the wall. Or maybe it's my imagination. I don't want to find out either way. I turn on my heel as he slams shut the farmhouse door, and on wobbly legs make it back to the car. I swing the Volvo round with jelly arms and once I'm back in my own yard and safely stopped, the tears come. My hands are shaking. What the hell was that?

21

That night I lie awake, the old man's words rattling around my brain. In turns I'm furious – how dare he? Then bewildered – maybe it's a case of mistaken identity? Then a little sad – is he unwell? I replay the scene again and again but instead of my standing there with my mouth opening and closing like a goldfish on a rug, I return zinger after zinger that leave the old man silent and thoroughly reprimanded.

The next morning I resolve to evict the grouchy old git from his residency in my brain by turning to the best therapy I know: cleaning. It works.

The house isn't filthy, just dusty, so as I wipe down skirting boards and door frames, run a damp cloth across shelves caked in grey fuzz, I do some thinking. Mind-numbing tasks are perfect for this. I still haven't heard from Mum. I tried to call her after my disastrous encounter at Creekside Farm but it went straight to voicemail. Maybe she just needs time. The monotonous work combined with the silence soothes me; the confrontation with my neighbour is placed up out of reach on a high shelf to be dealt with later.

I start to feel cocooned from trouble up at my lovely farm, in my childhood home. Back in London problems seemed bigger. Life here feels simpler, steadier. I notice that a certain tightness, from secrets hidden, from walking on eggshells with my mother, that had

WAY BACK | 183

hardened like a nut within my breastbone for – what? – months, years, is finally loosening.

Chloe calls on FaceTime as I clean. She's ruddy-cheeked and windswept, showing me a flock of sheep in the distance on a Devon farm she's visiting to talk wool. I take her on a tour of the upstairs, angling the phone to show her my old bedroom, the wooden beams above and the views from the small window. She can't wait to visit.

The walls had been painted and the carpets replaced but the views from the windows haven't changed at all in forty years, so while wiping the ledges I pause the longest here. Looking through the window is like watching a snatch of film from the past. I half expect Dad on his tractor to rumble into shot or Mum to stride into the garden in wellies and apron to peg out a basket of washing, glancing skywards for rainclouds.

On the Thursday morning I hear an engine outside and see a red van with 'Simply the Pest' emblazoned on its side. Out hops a willowy woman, blond hair in a French plait and dressed in a red boiler suit.

'Hiya.' She grins as I come out of the house. 'I'm Alex.' I'm slightly surprised she's a woman – and didn't Beth hint they'd been involved? Then I silently chide myself. 'That's so heteronormative, Mum,' Chloe would say. 'Lesbians aren't like tube stations, they don't just exist in London.'

Barely half an hour later we're having coffee and Alex has set mousetraps and poison up in the attic. 'They've come inside now the weather's getting cooler,' she explains, taking a sip. 'I'll pop back in a week to check the traps.'

'Thanks,' I say. 'I feel a bit bad – they're not doing much harm up there.'

'Yet,' she adds, 'they breed like wildfire and you don't want hundreds up there, chewing through wires. We're just nipping it in the bud.'

I look out through the kitchen window, the cobbles in the yard are glinting in the sun. The farm is weirdly quiet. I've no idea where to start with filling it with animals. I was kind of hoping that I'd know through osmosis, that just being near Dad amongst the animals all those years ago might've rubbed off on me? But so far it doesn't seem like being here has activated any long-dormant farming instinct.

As if reading my mind Alex asks, 'So apart from mice, are you planning on any other livestock?'

I laugh nervously. 'Course!'

She looks at me expectantly.

'Well... it's a big decision,' I stutter.

'You could start small?'

'Oh yeah?' I was keen for any guidance.

'A cat.'

I laugh but she looks completely serious. 'It'll keep on top of any pests – best deterrent to keep mice and rats at bay, which'll come in handy when you move on to bigger animals.'

'OK, yeah, thank you. Good advice.'

'You're welcome.' She pauses, draining her cup and standing to stretch her arms back into her overalls. 'So, how do you know Beth?'

'I don't,' I say and she looks a little relieved. 'Well I know her from the shop. She's been very kind to me, recommending you and of course keeping me stocked up on sweets.'

'Cool. Typical Beth.' She smiles.

'Have you known her long?' I know I'm being nosy.

'A couple of years. Right, I'd better be off – pests won't exterminate themselves.'

'Good job or you'd be out of business.'

'Exactly.'

*

By my one-week anniversary of being at the farm, I've got it in good shape. Things that looked odd at first – my bookshelf and my sofa – no longer looked like they were trespassing. The familiar things from my current life eventually finding their place in this space from my past, within these thick walls so dense with memories.

I lurch between being very still (drinking copious amounts of tea, daydreaming and googling local livestock sales) and being focused, and almost manic. I speak to GG and he gives me the number of a chap who can come and fill in the worst potholes on the lane with aggregate. Mick arrives with his teenage son and a small tipper truck and fixes up the lane in no time for cash in hand.

Mick tells me about a decent farm store nearby and I go shopping. I buy a basic tool kit, overalls and a pair of proper wellies. I fill the Volvo with a shovel, fork, squeegee – to muck out any future animals – and arrange for them to deliver the wheelbarrow, feed tubs, stepladder and new hose. I purchase some WD40 to spray on rusting hinges and spend a very enjoyable couple of hours liberally spritzing anything that's metal and dares to squeak. YouTube is my best friend. I return to the shop for some plaster and patch up the front of the house. I will whitewash it in the summer. It feels good to take charge, to make right those things that have been neglected. I feel my confidence grow by the day.

During one of my walks I head for Goose Pond Field and before I even get close to the water I hear a honking chorus that sends me tumbling back through time. The Canada geese are back, they've returned as they did every year when I was little. We never knew where they came from, Dad used to tell me they arrived the year I was born. 'We nearly called you Lucy Goosey after them,' he'd say. Mum would cluck and roll her eyes at these tall tales.

The geese would stay over Christmas, roaming through the three top fields looking for grass to eat, using the pond as their base, then they'd be off to the next stop on their constant tour. Dad didn't mind them, only getting annoyed when Jet occasionally rolled in their lurid green poo. 'Bloody hell, Jet,' he'd say as he hosed down the dog in the yard, 'this stuff's like summat from outer space.' I was always sad when the geese left.

I'm delighted now as I watch perhaps two dozen of the birds sitting in a group by the pond, their chests made even broader as their feathers puff out against the chill wind. The whole farm feels as if it's now leaning into late autumn and the geese's arrival seems to kickstart the process, or maybe kickstarts me noticing. The three oaks are multicoloured, green with a golden and orange wave of colour moving through the branches like fire. The blackberry bushes that hug one edge of the field intertwined with the hawthorn are speckled with the dark crumbs of fruit that has withered on the vine, blackened as if burnt.

From the distance comes a throaty rumble and I turn to follow the sound. On the far side of the neighbouring field is a quad bike with huge chunky tyres. There's something cartoonish about it – like a kid's Tonka toy that's been magically magnified to real life size. It's bouncing over the ruts and I can make out a man driving it. Balancing behind his seat on a little platform is a dog, legs planted. I'm presuming this is Will from the next-door farm. I wave from my spot in Three Oak Field but it's pointless, he's too far away and seems to be on a mission, going at a fair clip. I know I could hop in the car and drive round to their house to introduce myself but I can't quite summon the courage after the confrontation with the mad old man.

As I'm walking back my phone goes and it's Fay. It's 11 a.m. here so I know it's early in Boston.

'Everything OK?' I answer.

'Hello,' she mumbles sleepily. 'Yes course. I just woke up, I had to call you, I dreamt about you. You were riding a big bull around a village so I thought it might've been a sign of something...'

'Ha! I'm not riding anything sadly.'

As expected, Fay is loving Boston. The library staff adore her, her first exhibition has had great reviews and she's been seeing a car mechanic in his forties who, as she put it, 'fixed my fender and I couldn't fender him off! Honestly, Josie, he looks like the guy from the old Athena poster you used to have in your room, the oiled-up mechanic holding a couple of tyres.'

'Wow, really?'

'Well, yes – if you squint a bit.'

Wherever Fay goes she still manages to find romance and adventure. She retained the same allure she had at uni all those years ago when people of all persuasions were drawn to her like horny moths to her sexy flame. We chat about Christmas and I tell her it won't be the same without her rocking up in a naff festive jumper

'I'll miss you too Jose, I'm so proud of you though.' She's muffled now, holding the phone under her chin. 'It's insane to think it was only a few months ago over a boozy lunch that you told me about the farm and now there you are – you've done it. What's it like? Are the villagers friendly?'

'Mostly.'

'Go on...'

'I had a bit of a run-in with a neighbour but it's fine, nothing I can't handle.'

I hear rustling as Fay sits up in bed, her voice sharper. 'Who? Why didn't you ring me?'

I realise the old Josie would've been straight on the phone blubbing to Fay. 'Ah it's not a big deal, just a grumpy old codger, I'll sort it.'

I'd also not told her about the flowers tied to the tree. I'd handled both things on my own, not needing any hand-holding from Fay – or James for that matter.

'Furry muff,' she says, relaxing. 'As long as you're OK. Suppose there's not much I could do from over here anyway. I'm hoping to come back for a fortnight in February though, can't wait to come and cuddle all your animals, Farmer Jose.'

I don't correct her – by February I should at least have a cat.

The good news is the scratching above my bed has slowed to a deathly silence as one by one, the mice succumb to Alex's poison. As promised the woman herself rocks up a week after her first visit to 'do a body count, clear up and reset the traps'. She tells me over coffee how, after a few failed jobs she hated in retail, she found herself chatting to a friend's dad who was not far from retiring from his one-man pest business. She ended up being trained by him and eventually took on his customers when he hung up his pressure sprayer.

She is so easy to talk to that I confess my failed business ventures over the years, and she politely acts impressed by my former career as a New York banker.

'It was so long ago,' I say, 'I feel all the mistakes I've made since then have wiped out any kudos of my early career.'

She laughs but not unkindly. 'I don't think that's a thing, Josie. Some folk round here have only ventured as far as Blackpool or if they're very daring "costa del fry up". You should feel good about your time working in a high-stakes industry in one of the world's coolest cities. Then you raised a child! Neither thing is to be sniffed at. Besides,' she continues, 'you have a whole new career now. What's next here on Thistlefold? Award-winning honey?'

My face must be a picture as she laughs again. 'OK, maybe not bees. How about a farm shop selling organic eggs from your hens and world-class sausages from rare-breed porkers?'

I feel squeamish at the thought of slaughtering pigs I've reared and chatted to every day – some farmer I'm going to be. 'I don't know yet. I've got to start somewhere but I'm not in any rush – it's got to be right. Anyway,' I want to steer the topic away from me, 'what do you like about your career? How did you know you'd found the right thing?'

'I just like helping people, as "Miss World contestant" as that sounds. Every day is different, every pest poses a new challenge.'

'Are people ever surprised that you're a female, not some hairy-arsed geezer?'

She shrugs. 'Were you?'

I blush slightly, caught out. 'A little.'

She smiles. She really is very pretty – no wonder her and Beth had something going on. 'Yeah, well, you're not alone.'

'You must be the best-looking exterminator people have ever seen, no wonder they're a bit surprised.' Jesus, did I say that out loud?

Her pale grey eyes sparkle at this and she looks amused, like a cat playing with a mouse.

My cheeks grow hotter.

'Thanks,' she says, 'I'll definitely be coming back here, great coffee and excellent compliments, you're my new favourite client.'

'I'm thrilled though, you kinda have to come back anyway to check those traps.'

'True,' she says putting her empty cup on the sink. 'Hey, what are you doing tonight?'

My heart thumps – oh god, is she asking me on a date? I start to stutter that I have no plans really and she cuts me off.

'It's quiz night at The Three Keys, I'd insist you join my team but I know Beth has already mentioned it and she could do with some fresh brains on her side.'

'Oh.' I'm sure I've gone bright red, what's wrong with me, acting like an awkward teenager with a crush? I busy myself rinsing the mugs so I can avoid looking up at Alex. 'OK, cool, yeah maybe. Can't promise my brain is particularly fresh but I'll bring it anyway.'

22

By seven p.m. I've changed my top six times and I'm in a sweaty state. My hair is unhappy at so many T-shirts and jumpers being pulled on and is standing on end in a wavy wall of frizz. I don't want to look too townie or wannabe bumpkin.

Eventually I wear the plain white tee I first put on and chuck a chunky cardi over the top.

I wrestle my hair into submission and set off. As I drive down the track, pleased my fillings no longer rattle now the potholes are gone, I start to swing towards the right and my headlights sweep across a van parked up across the road from the end of my lane. It takes off swiftly as I approach, travelling away from the village. It's dark but a cloud of exhaust fumes is left hanging in the night air like mist from a mouth and I also see the van is blue. Something jolts me and I pause before pulling out onto the dark road. Then I remember – the van that caused the crash with Fay was a big blue van. Is it just coincidence? I wind my way through the lanes to The Three Keys, my thoughts at last distracted by the noise coming from inside the pub as I pull up outside. The chaotic sound of thrashing guitars jars within the stone walls and hanging baskets of the quaint pub – it is Blur's 'Song 2' blaring at an ear-splitting level.

'Woohooo!' I hear the people in the pub whooping along to Damon's lyrics. I nearly get back in the car and drive home. I've got a nice Malbec I could crack open.

No, Josie. I force myself out of the car and towards the pub. I'm worried the music will fade as I arrive and all eyes will swivel in my direction, like in the spaghetti westerns Dad used to love watching on a Saturday afternoon – 'You new in town?'

The song ends just as I push open the door but I'm largely ignored – people are still bobbing about, chatting and shouting hellos. I pick my way through the sea of faces, most of them pink with exertion and the heat from the roaring fire and head for the brightly lit bar. The place is packed and noisy so it's a minor miracle when I hear 'Josie!' and see Beth waving at me from the corner. Relieved I mime 'Drink?' and she shakes her head so I buy myself a G&T and head over. She's sitting with a small group, though there's no sign of Alex. I'm introduced to the team members that make up 'Agatha Quiztie' and as I take a sip of drink I almost spit it out as a familiar voice booms over the mic, 'GOOOOOOOOOOOOD EVENING THREE KEYS QUIZZERS!' A cheer goes up. 'Here we go, I'm GG – car mechanic by day and by night, well Thursday night, your quiz host extraordinaire. Now that we've kicked things off with the traditional Blur singalong, get ready for the GREATEST PUB QUIZ IN THE LAAAAAAND!' Another roar from the regulars. I take a glug, wishing I'd ordered a triple.

'Phones off, pencils up, brains on, LET'S GET QUIZZICAL.'

The crowd settles into near silence and remains that way for the first half of the quiz, just a low murmuring as the team members corroborate their answers. I'm useless and remain quiet, nodding thoughtfully as the answers are scribbled down. Luckily I know that Yazoo's debut single 'Only You' was released in 1982 and am pleased my Alison Moyet obsession has finally come in handy.

GG announces half time and I offer to buy a round of drinks; that's when I spot Alex, she's sitting with a different team around the other side of the bar. Out of her work gear and with her hair unplaited, falling instead in pale waves around her face, she looks gorgeous. She sees me looking and mouths 'hello'. A few moments later as I'm ordering the drinks, I see the barman grin over my shoulder at someone as I hear a gruff voice.

'Do you come here often?' I know it's Alex messing about and enjoy the feel of her breath on my neck. I turn and notice she smells sweet, like she's been sucking on a fruit lolly.

'First time actually. Was invited by some weird woman who wears overalls and smells of mouse poo.'

'Hmm... I should be careful with that one,' she warns.

'Oh really?' I say back over my shoulder. 'Why? Could she be a bad influence?' It feels good to flirt a little, emboldened as I am by the gin and tonic – though it's probably for the best I've ordered a lemonade this round. The barman places the drinks on the bar in front of me and I tap on my card.

'If you get lucky.' She's a little merry herself and leans close to me from behind to order a pint of water from the guy. I can feel the softness of her small breasts push into my back and a warmth flood my crotch. *Good grief, Josie. Get a grip.*

I gather the five drinks and clutch them awkwardly in both hands and turn to her. She looks innocently at me. 'Good luck.'

'What with?' I ask dumbly.

'Round Two.'

The rest of the quiz passes by in a blur of South American flags, scientific breakthroughs and Oscar-winning films and I'm relieved when GG instructs us to swap papers so we can mark the answers. There are occasional whoops and the odd heckle as we go through the answers and we come a respectable fifth. I start to say my good-byes to Beth and the others when the winners are announced, 'The insurmountable Blood, Sweat and Beers', and the team stand to take a bow to some applause but mainly good-natured jeering. Amongst them is a chap who looks very familiar, he turns from his rowdy pals and the room seems to melt away as he nods at me, a faint smile playing over his lips. I can't place him but my heart thumps with an unexpected rush of adrenaline. He has dark wavy hair, is tall and broad-chested. I am ambushed with a strong need to head towards him, so I do. Emboldened by alcohol I intend to introduce myself.

The barman rings the brass bell and the whole pub surges towards the bar for last orders. I push through the wave of chatting locals, repeating a mantra of 'oops... sorry... 'scuse me' and emerge from the other side as if spat out from a rolling sea on to a beach, but the mystery man has disappeared. I notice the pub door close so push my way towards it and go outside into the crisp October air just in time to see the same blue van from earlier roar off up the street. Whoever that mystery man is I now know he nearly hurt Fay and me that day and was hanging around the farm earlier. I suddenly feel very tired and climb wearily into my car. I see the door to the pub open and Beth and Alex leave, arm in arm, weaving up the road towards the sweet shop.

23

I gradually tick more things off my to-do list, the old gate is back on its hinges, I've enquired about how to spruce up the sign, and I join Beth's Agatha Quiztie team again, even making sure I arrive on time for the Blur song to warm up.

I sense a frostiness from Beth when I mention Alex. I decide there and then that whatever's going on there is complicated and I shouldn't add any more fuel to that particular fire with my own slight crush on the hot pest controller. I don't know what I was thinking, a trippy snog with Fay and a couple of drunken dalliances on nights out with the girls in New York does not make me bisexual.

No, Alex is cute and sexy but I need to nip that particular frisson in the bud.

I don't see the blue van man and don't ask after him – the whole blue van mystery would no doubt just sound daft and I don't want the guy getting a heads-up on my enquiries. On the way to the loos I spot a poster advertising the village bonfire night for the following Friday and promise myself I'll go.

When I was growing up on the farm bonfire night was a huge affair. Dad always had some spare wood to burn, saving up offcuts and split pallets all year round so that by November he could build a massive bonfire. The kids from the neighbouring farms used to come and we'd clutch sparklers, writing our names in the pitch black while the dads lit rockets, running back and forth through the dark. The mums perched on bales of straw near the warmth of the fire eating black peas and parkin.

When we left the farm Mum never wanted to do anything for Guy Fawkes night and I daren't ask. The one time I did was when we'd just moved after Dad died and I'd wondered out loud about our having a mini bonfire in our new tiny backyard. I can still remember how she glared at me as if I was completely insane. 'Josie, don't be ridiculous, there's not a cat in hell's chance we can have a bonfire, not here. And we definitely can't afford fireworks, so don't even bother asking.'

Instead I watched other peoples' light up the night sky from the window of my little bedroom.

The days since I arrived have blended seamlessly and it's a pleasurable sensation. I have been busy fixing up the farm to the best of my ability and have a blackened toenail to prove it after dropping a gate on it. Steel toecap boots go on the shopping list. I've also found balance: outside jobs in the morning while I have the energy, then in the late afternoon a spot of yoga on my mat in front of the AGA or reading.

Thanks to James, I'm comfortable and have enough money to keep me going for a while, so there's no rush to try to make any kind of income from the farm. Shame is starting to creep in though. What was the point of moving hundreds of miles if I'm not going to attempt to honour my dad's legacy and do some actual farming? I have to at least make a start with procuring one small animal, as recommended by Alex.

I call Shearness Manor and ask for Mary.

'Mary speaking! *No, Dirk*! Sorry, hello, who's this? I've got a territorial ginger spraying my reception area – no one seems to have told Mr Bogarde he was castrated last month! Hello?'

'Mary, it's Josie, we came to your wellness weekend back in – '

'Josie!' she shouts, sounding thrilled. 'How could I forget you and your friend... Kay wasn't it?'

'Fay.'

'Exactly. Bogarde, no! Pssssss get out of it.' I hear a clatter. 'Sorry, Josie, ammonia from stale cat piss is not the scent I want welcoming my guests at check-in or they'll be a-moaning – at *me*!' She chuckles then lowers her voice into a stage whisper, 'I confess I just lobbed a roll of sticky tape at Mr Bogarde, but don't you worry, he dodged it. Like Usain Bolt that cat, though he's built like Hitchcock. Right, how are things with you?'

I tell her all about my move. 'We're near enough neighbours!' she booms.

'Well, not quite, but yes, only an hour or so away. I hoped you might be able to help. I'm after a cat, to help with the mice and also for company, of course, and as you're the expert on all things feline, I thought I'd ask if you knew of any shelters where I might find a cat or two.'

Mary gasps theatrically and I think for a second Dirk has returned. 'Well, this is meant to be! It was only last night I looked up to the stars and wished for a solution. It's like I've cosmically ordered this phone call. Wasn't it Noel Edmonds who believes in all that? I used to like him on that *House Party* show, Crinkly Bottom wasn't it? Very funny – though I couldn't stand that Mr Blobby.'

'Right. So, hang on – you were saying you need a solution? To what?'

'To Doris Day.'

'OK,' I say. 'Doris, cute name.' I feel my heart flutter with excitement.

'Cute name, very cuddly with humans but she's a cold-hearted killer. Oh she's a *beast*! Only been with me a month, was found in a box by the gates, so whoever had her before knew we took in cats here.'

'Poor thing.'

'Oh don't you worry about Doris, as long as there's small fluffy things to massacre she's quite happy. Not a day goes by without the feathered, furry or slimy meeting a grisly end by her claws. We had Billie Piper here last month, filming scenes for a Netflix thing nearby she was. Great woman. Incredible teeth. Anyway, Doris Day caught a toad the size of a cauliflower and left it by Billie's feet as she had a nightcap with a girlfriend. Billie was lovely about it of course but I felt terrible.'

'I bet.'

'I can't bear her bringing in another tit or robin. It's lucky there's no endangered animals round here, she'd bring down a panda given half a chance. Now –' she takes a breath – 'apart from the relentless killing sprees, Doris also abhors other cats, literally wrinkles her nose at them like Princess Anne looking at the paparazzi.'

'Well she'd be the only cat here. In fact the only animal.'

'Don't worry about that, once Doris arrives things will snowball, you just need to break the seal. Right, when do you want her? Tomorrow is my day off, I was going to go bra shopping but I'd be very happy to have a good excuse to get out of that, nothing strikes fear into my heart like a woman in plum lipstick and court shoes wielding a tape measure.'

We agree she'll bring Doris around lunchtime the next day and I get off the phone with Mary's instructions ringing in my ears to not buy a single thing for the cat – she'll bring everything with her. 'Because you're doing me a favour to be honest.' It's only when I put the kettle on to make a celebratory cup of tea do I realise I didn't even ask what colour Doris is.

My excitement at her arrival is tempered slightly by the fact that today is an unhappy anniversary – it's two months since Mum slammed the phone down on me, accusing me of ruining her life.

These deafening silences have pockmarked our relationship since Dad died. Most years there would be a period of weeks where she'd freeze me out before eventually thawing if I apologised enough. Whether I'd done anything wrong or not, I always felt guilty.

During my university years she fell out with me for three whole months over a silly squabble; my banishment stretched over the festive period so I spent it instead with Fay and her family in Blackpool. It was one of my best Christmases ever: mulled wine after windswept walks on the beach, charades and board games in their cosy front room. It all beat watching Mum getting maudlin in front of the telly, drinking herself to a stupor.

Another memorable estrangement was when I lived in New York. I rang her and she was asleep – it was only lunchtime at home and she knew that I knew she'd been drinking. Her effort to sound sober gave it away – the over-straightened voice clipped and telling. Humiliated, she picked a fight then stopped answering my calls for weeks.

So it continued, eventually easing during the golden Clive years when he gently maintained her like a gardener dedicated to a rare shrub. He kept her on a sober, even keel. My marriage to James and then Chloe's arrival was also extra incentive for her to stay in touch. Back then when we three were a team and Mum could only reach them through me.

But now she has her own relationships with them I am no longer needed as a conduit. She swore to Fay and to Chloe that there was no coming back for us from this 'betrayal' and a part of me wishes that were true.

24

The next morning I wake early to distant shouts, a man's voice repeatedly calling over the growl of an engine. Sounds travel well here if the wind decides to ferry them in your direction so I couldn't be certain how far away the man was.

I look out through the window. The man on the quad bike is back and he's now hurtling over my field towards the back of the house. The cheek of it.

Wearing joggers and a vest top I nip downstairs, cramming my bare feet into my cold wellies. I slam out the front door. I know I look like a wild woman but I don't care. I climb the gate and drop over the other side and wait, hands on hips, for the quad bike to rumble to a stop. The man on it looks flustered, his face set in a stressed grimace. It is the guy from the pub on quiz night, the one who roared away in the blue van – the same van that I'm sure caused us to crash that day, the man who's been lurking around at the end of the lane and is now here, killing the engine whilst barely looking in my direction. Instead he's scanning the horizon to his left and looking beyond me across the yard.

'Can I help you?' I ask, aiming an equal measure of indignant and authoritative.

'Only if you've seen my dog.'

This catches me out a bit. 'I've not seen a dog but I did see you roaring over what is now my field and therefore private land.'

He looks back over his shoulder as if spotting the route he'd come for the first time.

'Aye, right.' He smirks. 'Sorry?' He says it like a question, as if English isn't his first language. His dark blue eyes glint a little. My authority and indignation are not having the desired effect. It doesn't help that he's so good-looking. I straighten my back and my resolve, fixing my mouth to 'not amused'.

'She's a collie, nearly all black bar her white socks and nose. She's in season and she got out, which could be a disaster for me if any mongrel gets a whiff of her.'

I feel the wind leave my sails a little. He's about my age and even when worried he looks handsome, the stress causing a crinkle above his dark brows. Plus he clearly cares for his dog. A dashing pet lover – it's impossible to remain too affronted. I glance at his wedding-ring finger, then hate myself for it. Still, it is bare.

'Well… good luck.' I fold my arms across my chest, aware of the cold now the adrenaline is subsiding. My upper body seems to be turning the colour of corned beef.

He looks me up and down for a split second too long – is he enjoying my discomfort? 'Thanks. I'd better crack on,' he says. 'I'll let you know.'

The quad bike grumbles back to life and he nods just beyond me with half a hopeful grin, eyebrows raised in a question; it takes me a moment to realise he wants me to open the gate for him.

'I'm Will by the way,' he shouts back over his shoulder, 'from next door.'

'Josie,' I shout and point at my chest like a simpleton. He waves and roars off down the lane.

I head back inside for a hot shower and a couple of hours later a cauliflower curry (made during one of my many 'thinking days' when I chopped vegetables as my thoughts swung from intense joy at my new adventure to absolute despair at my rash decision) is now bubbling away on the AGA, awaiting the arrival of Mary and Doris Day the cat.

The kitchen is filled with the smell of cumin and coriander and the steam from the boiling rice has made the windows mist over. I'm listening to an author on *Woman's Hour* talk about her recent trip through Nepal. The kitchen feels cosy and like a home for the first time since my return.

A horn honks announcing Mary's arrival. From the window I spy her battered Land Rover and by the time I have my wellies on and get outside she's on all fours on the back sear, her sizeable bottom blocking my view.

'She's like ruddy Houdini,' she shouts. She seems to be wrestling with something. Has she brought me a cat or a tiger? She emerges a moment later, shuffling backwards on her knees and clambering down from the vehicle. She has a pet carrier in one hand and throws her free arm around my neck in an embrace that borders on a throttling.

'Welcome to Thistlefold,' I say, enjoying the feel of the phrase. Maybe this is what I've been needing, real-life company. More humans. I've been rattling around the place like the last biscuit in the tin.

Once inside Mary plonks the cat carrier down on the kitchen table with a smile. 'Something smells good? I presume it's not your perfume?' She seems very pleased with her quip.

'It is actually, I always wear a dab of eau de cauliflower on special occasions.'

She roars with laughter at my lame joke and I remember why I was so drawn to Mary when we met her at Shearness. She's like a one-woman band – quite loud but fun. You can't take your eyes off all the moving parts, the cymbals and whistles. She's also very kind. 'Well. What a magnificent place. And you are surely the bravest, most awesome woman I know! What an exciting time for you.'

I almost believe her.

A tiny scream comes from the pet carrier.

'Right, to business. Now, as you can hear, despite being just about a full-grown cat, Doris has not learned how to meow. She has her own version – a little shriek – it's very cute. As is she.'

On Mary's instruction I check all exits are blocked and she swings open the pet-carrier door. Despite managing to escape into the back of the Land Rover Doris is now very keen on staying put in her crate. I peep into the darkness and two bright amber eyes stare back at me. 'Hello, Doris,' I whisper and there's movement. She emerges slowly from the crate and on to my kitchen table. She is beautiful. Her body is mottled in cream and brown like a seventies' carpet but her face, ears, paws and the tip of her tail all look like they've been dipped in milk chocolate.

'She's sort of seal point, but not full,' says Mary. 'I reckon her mum's a well-bred Siamese and some tortoiseshell moggie had his wicked way with her.' The cat stretches luxuriously, sticking her bottom in the air. I gently scratch at the base of her tail and it instantly curls at the top into a question mark. 'She likes you,' coos Mary. 'I like her,' I say, continuing my gentle scratching. Doris looks at me as if to say 'Left a bit'.

After lunch I take Mary on a tour of the farm, leaving Doris to explore her new home in peace. An unfamiliar sense of pride swells up as I show Mary my attempts at DIY and watch her admire the view. I tell her of my encounter with Will, the van drama, and the strange old man at the farm.

'You need to talk to this Will properly, invite him round for a drink, get to the bottom of it.'

'That feels a bit intense – he's probably too busy anyway, he's got a farm to run.'

'Or,' says Mary, her eyes lighting up, 'throw a little house-warming to meet your new neighbours? And may I be the first to accept your invite, thank you very much, I'd be thrilled to attend. I'd love to meet the mysterious Will.'

'Well,' I say, looking across the yard and down the lane at the now familiar blue van bumping up the lane, 'here's your chance.'

Will swings the van to a stop and hops down. On the passenger seat is a collie.

'You found her then?' I say.

'Aye.' He smiles ruefully. 'Though I don't know if I was too late. She was over on the Yates' land gambolling around with their spaniel. She looks worryingly pleased with herself, don't you, Fliss?' The dog cocks her head, giving nothing away.

'Oh dear,' says Mary. 'Nice to meet you, it's Will isn't it? I'm Mary, Josie's friend and cat dealer.'

He looks from me to Mary as if for the first time he's noticed her. 'Yes, hello! Sorry, I promised my new neighbour that I'd pop back with an update on my dog.'

He looks back to me and is studying my face. 'We've definitely met before,' he says slowly. God he's good-looking. Tall too. Such a shame he nearly killed us with his van. Though maybe I can forgive him. There's definitely something familiar about him.

'I was thinking the same thing,' I say. 'Look, I know you're probably rushed off your feet but if not, fancy a coffee? Would be good to get to know you apart from brief encounters in windy fields.'

He looks at his watch and my heart sinks. Mary, who's been a rapt audience of one, looks on with eyes like saucers in anticipation. Will grimaces. 'Go on then. I've got a feed delivery coming but they'll manage without me. As far as they know I'm still searching hill and dale for the dog.'

'Great.' I grin.

Mary says her goodbyes and clambers back into her Land Rover. 'Still think a house-warming could be a good idea,' she says as she fires up the engine. 'I love a party.'

*

Will is warm and funny and it's hard to hold on to my misgivings. He meets Doris and she approves too, hopping on his lap for a bottom scratch. I make a pot of my favourite coffee, even getting out my milk frother and my new neighbour is suitably impressed. He seems genuinely fascinated in my whole story and how I've ended up returning to the farm. As he talks I try to find the right moment to bring up the reception I got at his farm the other day but I'm loathe to ruin the genial atmosphere. He saves me the job.

'So, Dad tells me you popped up t'other day?'

'Yes.' I grimace awkwardly – how truthful was his dad about the encounter?

'Let me guess – Dad was a moody old bastard and ran you off? Excuse the language.'

I nod. 'Yeah, he was. He seemed so angry at me. He proper kicked off.'

'I'm sorry. He's... irrational at the moment, getting angry at the smallest thing. His bark's worse than his bite, but still – it's not nice. I'm sorry.'

'I know this sounds dramatic but I thought he had a gun?'

'Noooo. No, he doesn't, not one that works. I've got a rifle for the farm but by law it's locked away in a cabinet. There's an antique musket that's usually up on the wall but it doesn't fire. Please tell me he wasn't waving it around?'

'No, I just thought I saw it.'

'Bloody hell,' he mutters to himself. He takes a breath. 'I think it comes from fear, a fear of change. Maybe he's worried you arriving will change things.'

My heart skips a beat. How? By stealing away his son when we fall in love? I blush at the thought.

'You know, with the fields and that, the hay,' he says.

'Oh yes.' I nod, blushing more, concentrating on pouring more coffee. 'I was going to ask you about that.'

'Aye, course.' He looks at me seriously from under his dark brows. Those eyes. Christ on a bike. 'I'll have a word. With Dad,' he says solemnly.

I backtrack. 'I don't want to make things worse, don't want him thinking I've been telling tales.' *Especially as one day he'll be my new father-in-law*, I silently yell in my head.

'No, he needs telling, he can't be behaving like that.'

I try to lift the mood. 'Still, must be nice, just you and your dad running the farm together? A real family business?' I'm fishing.

'Aye, it can be nice, though it's a lot of work. Luckily there's three pairs of hands to muck in, or muck out.'

'Oh?' My heart sinks.

'Aye, we have a young lad from the village helping out a few days a week.'

Is that a twinkle in his eye? He knows my game. I don't care, this new Josie is bold and I'm enjoying her.

No mention of a wife or girlfriend. Seems too good to be true, surely he's got some comely wench who lives in the village? Or maybe a hot young stud.

We get down to business. It turns out Will has harvested both top fields – Three Oak and Goosepond – for the last few years. He started helping the then farmer Pete Potter as he was getting on a bit and the deal suited them both. Will did the donkey work and they got equal share of the barley crop and straw from Pete's two fields. 'So I owe you some barley feed and straw. Although...' He pauses. 'Do you have any cows to eat it or lie down on it yet?'

'Ah – good question.'

'Well if you need some help when you're ready to get animals bigger than a cat let me know, I'll take you to the sales. Least I can do after driving over your private land.' His eyes shine again, teasing me. 'You'll need someone with you otherwise you'll come back wi' all sorts – they'll spot a townie a mile off and send you home with a three-legged sheep and a cockerel wi' no cock-a-doodle-doo.'

'Oh aye,' I say. Crikey, where did that 'aye' come from? 'We'll see. I might know more than you think.' This is a bluff, but I can google can't I? I resolve to do some proper swotting up before the sale trip. 'But yes please, that'd be great. I'd love to be chauffeured there and back, especially if you have a trailer. I imagine I won't fit many cows into the back seat of my Volvo.'

'OK. Deal.'

We chat for a while and decide we definitely must have met each other before. 'Our paths would've crossed when we were little – especially if you were next door when I first lived here.' A long buried name pops into my head. 'Is your surname Jones? I'm pretty sure that's the name of our old neighbours but I don't remember them having kids.'

He nods. 'You're right, Barry and Elsie Jones. They moved off our farm twenty years ago and we took it over. Before that we lived in the village, though my dad used to work on your farm.'

'Right,' I say, my brain ticking overtime.

'What year were you born?' he asks.

'1970.'

'Oh really?' He's polite enough to look shocked. 'I'm 'seventy-three so a little younger.'

'Ouch.'

'You'd never know it though.'

'Thanks for lying so convincingly.'

He laughs. 'I wasn't – you look in great nick. If you were one of my cows you wouldn't be anywhere near ready for the knackers yard.'

I clutch at an imaginary string of pearls around my neck. 'That's the most beautiful thing anyone's ever said to me.'

Then I have an idea – the photographs! Why didn't I think of it sooner? 'Stay there,' I tell him.

'I've no choice,' he says, looking down at Doris who's now sound asleep on this lap.

I go up to the bedroom and grab the photo album from my bedside drawer, quickly flipping through to my birthday party picture, slide it from its cellophane holder and head downstairs. He studies it for a second and laughs. 'There I am! I'd recognise those dungarees anywhere, I loved them.' He points to the little lad wandering through frame.

'Yes!' I say, a little too loudly. 'The mystery is solved, though I'm surprised we don't remember each other better if we were pals back then.'

'Well looking at this pic I don't think we were particularly close.'

'You're right. You don't look that excited that I'm about to blow out my candles.'

'Maybe,' he says, holding my gaze and looking suddenly serious, 'it was the age difference that kept us apart.'

I laugh. 'Maybe. Or perhaps I just couldn't emotionally connect with a boy who dressed like a tiny painter and decorator.'

We fall quiet for a moment and it doesn't feel awkward. But all that is about to change, I can't not mention the blue van incidents.

'So,' I say breezily, 'I do have two other teeny bones to pick with you.'

'Right...' He looks uneasy.

'On Easter Sunday I came to look at the farm and we ended up writing off my best friend's car.'

He looks confused but doesn't speak so I continue.

'It happened on Blacksmiths Lane.'

He looks blank. 'OK?'

I decide to just spit it out. 'And I'm pretty sure it was your fault. You, in your very blue very big van.'

His eyes widen in surprise. 'Oh no, that wouldn't have been me.'

'Well, it was a van just like yours.'

'It might've been the van, but I was in Amsterdam on a stag do last Easter weekend. I've got the pictures to prove it, though I don't know if you'd want to see them.'

'Right,' I say, deflated yet relieved this handsome man's not a psychopath.

'What happened?' He looks worried.

'What I'm pretty sure was your van came hurtling round the corner and forced us off the road.'

'Were you hurt?'

'No, but only because my best mate Fay managed to steer us out of the way and up a bank.'

'Jesus.' His face darkens. 'I think I know who it could be – there's only two other people who drive that van, my dad and Noah. He's young and I've told him often enough not to go like a bat out of hell. He's a dickhead.' He looks genuinely furious then adds as an after-thought, 'Excuse the language. I'm really sorry, I'll talk to him.'

'OK.' I silently debate whether I mention the van parking on the lane that time.

'What's the other bone?' Will asks, giving me no choice. 'You said there were two.'

'It's probably nothing, it just spooked me at the time seeing as I recognised the van. It was parked up on the end of my lane the other night and sped off when I drove towards it. It just seemed weird...'

His face softens as he rolls his eyes.

'Again, Noah. He'll have been romancing some lucky lass who doesn't mind the stink of diesel and silage. He probably doesn't know you're here, Thistlefold's been empty for a while. Bet he shat his pants.' He looks embarrassed. 'Again, excuse the language.'

'I've heard swearing before.'

'Yeah, well I don't know – maybe your time in London has made you all posh?'

'Hardly.' Something still doesn't feel right but I can't put my finger on what. 'After the quiz,' I say, 'you roared off in the van. That's what made me realise it was you. I connected the dots because bright turquoise is a striking colour for a van.'

'It's a beauty, eh? Bought cheap from Yorkshire Water when they upgraded their fleet. In a certain light you can see the logo and phone number we spray-painted over.' He drains his coffee. 'Well if you're not going to charge me I believe I'm free to go?'

'Ha-ha,' I say. 'Just don't leave the county.'

'Chance'd be a fine thing. Nice to meet you, neighbour.' He smiles, gently lifting Doris Day and placing her, still curled up, on the kitchen chair next to him. She opens an eye and glares at him indignantly. 'Better get back to Fliss,' he says, half to the cat. He straightens. 'Anyway I never drive on quiz night 'cos I need a few pints to oil up my old grey cells, so it wasn't me behind the wheel that time either – Dad picked me up. I can't remember him speeding off, but if he did he was probably annoyed with me. He hates leaving the house after dark these days... mardy old bugger. As you know, right?' he says, pulling on his coat. 'You've got my number, I meant it – call me if you need owt and let me know when you wanna go shopping.'

25

I arrange to meet Beth and Alex at the pub's bonfire night on the Friday in the hope of cementing our friendship and putting any residual flirtations thoroughly to rest. I spot them both sitting on a picnic bench watching the huge bonfire, whose bright flames illuminate the pub car park. I take a sip of my drink and make my way to them through kids twirling sparklers. Cheers ring out from the small crowd as a rocket zips up into the sky. Both women wear matching bobble hats and their cheeks glow from the heat of the fire and the mulled wine they clutch.

'Here she is!' they chorus tipsily.

I spot Will over by the fire and they notice as he grins in my direction.

'Oooh, I see!' says Beth. 'So my shop is no longer the sweetest thing in the village?'

'What?' I squeeze in next to them on the bench.

'Oh come on,' chimes in Alex. 'We heard from Pat Yates that Will stopped by yours when he was looking for his dog. Pat said he pulled Will's leg when he mentioned he was gonna call back to Thistledown to update you and he blushed bright pink according to Pat.'

Beth leans in. 'Most out of character for Will, you must've had quite an effect on him.'

I swallow my pleasure at the tale. 'Bloody hell. Do the jungle drums ever stop beating round here?'

'Nope.'

Alex stands up unsteadily. 'Right. Loo, then same again?' We nod and she heads off.

I look at Beth. 'Anyway, we're neighbours, we had farm business to discuss.'

She smiles knowingly. I'm glad she can't see my cheeks burn.

'Oh aye?'

'Yeah, he's taking me shopping.'

'Very *Pretty Woman*.'

'Hardly. I'm the one paying and we're not hitting up Rodeo Drive but the cattle sales.'

'Exciting! He's a nice guy Will. The village's last remaining eligible bachelor, if you don't count GG.'

Result. 'I was lucky enough to meet his charming dad the other day,' I add.

'Old Jack? Give you shit did he? Don't worry, his bark's worse than his bite, he's had a tough time of it with one thing or another.'

Alex comes back and hands me a glass of mulled wine.

'Thanks!' I stand up. 'Right, wait there.' I wink to wind them up. 'I'm off to seduce bachelor boy.'

They laugh bawdily as I do my best sashay towards the fire.

I look through the crowd for Will. I'm keen to speak to him because I'm feeling rather pleased with myself having done a bit of livestock research. The previous evening I'd spent a lovely couple of hours by a roaring fire with a nice Malbec and my laptop, merrily googling away and making notes. I was in my element – it was like swotting for my exams again. I began with 'Best way to start a cattle herd', which suggested starting with three or four females. I know I want

Herefords, as that's what we always had, and happily they come up when I google 'friendliest cows' and 'easiest cows to raise'. Heifers (a cow that's not bred or has only had one calf) range from £900 up to £2,000, depending on pedigree. By my third glass of wine I put my laptop away before I find myself buying something there and then from the breed's official website. Still, I feel less green and more excited about the cattle sale.

I spot Will looking ridiculously handsome, jacket collar pulled up against the chill. We chat over steaming-hot potato pie and he agrees to take me shopping as promised. It'll be good to take the plunge before the real winter weather kicks in. The farm is already feeling more remote and by three p.m. the vast skies above close in darkly. I head for home before last orders, hugging Beth and Alex on the way out. 'Well?' they chorus expectantly. 'It's a date,' I say and they beam at me as if I've just announced our engagement.

The following day Will drops round a trailer of straw that fills a big corner of the barn, he also brings hay and some sacks of cattle ration – the stuff I'll feed them. 'It's like muesli for cows, I remember now.'

He nods. 'Promise me you won't say that within earshot of anyone at the sales.'

We perch on a bale of straw. I try not to look at his thigh, which is inches from mine. Even clad in maroon overalls it's hot. Instead, I stare straight ahead, businesslike.

'I just need to familiarise myself with everything again. I trailed round after Dad like a pup at his heels, I must've picked up some knowledge along the way.'

'Yeah, I bet.'

'It's just been buried under decades of other stuff – uni, work, child-rearing, school runs...'

He nods. 'You'll unearth it.' He looks me up and down. 'You're already looking like a local.'

I glance down at my slightly mucky wax jacket, manky nails and the hole in the knee of my jeans. 'I'm taking that as a compliment.'

'You should. Right then, Tuesday's livestock sale over in Clitheroe is our best bet and you're thinking of starting just with cattle for now?'

'For now?' I laugh nervously. 'Yes. Cattle. If I can get a trio of heifers I reckon that'll be a good starting point.'

He looks surprised by my sudden confidence. 'Good. What did your dad have again?'

'Herefords. Or "brown and white ones" as my friends used to say.'

'OK. They're beef as you know. We're dairy over at ours but I don't imagine you want a couple hundred Friesians to milk every morning as well.'

'Absolutely not.' I smile sweetly. 'I'll leave that to you.' Quite a substantial part of me can't believe I'm having this actual conversation. About buying actual cows. 'I'm hoping we can pick up three or at a push, four decent heifers for around fourteen hundred a head. I don't want to go much above that.'

He nods. 'Sounds about reet.'

'And,' I add, 'I don't know if I'll still be here in a year so we need to get ones that'll hold their price if I want to sell on.' There's a silence. 'Will?'

'Yup, sorry,' he says. 'I will say, you might need to go up a bit higher on the day – up to two grand apiece if they're decent? Depends what's there and who's bidding.'

'God, I won't feel *too grand* if I have to pay that much, eh?' I nudge him and he groans at the corny pun.

'Well let's see, I'm not after cow royalty, but if I'm starting a herd I might as well begin with something proper. I'd be happy going up to eighteen hundred apiece,' I say firmly. I surprise myself at how self-assured I sound, though my mouth has gone drier than a pot-pourri sandwich. What the hell am I doing?

'Right. Well, I'll pick you up Tuesday morning eight-ish? Do you want to bid on the day or shall I?'

'I will.'

'Quite right.' He looks somewhere between amused and impressed. 'You'll be grand. Tuesday it is, I'll sort you out.'

If only, I think. 'Can't wait,' I say. I'm terrified. 'Do I owe you anything? Diesel for the van?'

'Nah. You could bring some of that fancy coffee of yours in a flask as payment for my services if you fancy?'

'Done.'

Later, Fay FaceTimes me and I give her the lowdown on Will and tell her all about Beth and Alex. She makes me promise they won't replace her as my best friends. Fay is making friends too and loving Boston. She is seeing a scientist who works in food preservation and seems smitten. We laugh at the madness of Mary popping round with a spare cat and I angle the camera round to formally introduce Fay to Doris Day. I tell Fay about the six mice Doris has caught since her arrival like a proud mother talking about her daughter's piano recital. My actual daughter rings right after Fay and Chloe and we chat for over an hour. She went back to London for a long weekend for a birthday party and bumped into Ruth on the heath with her pack of hounds. Chloe says she's fine but missing me.

I put the phone down and feel topped up with love. The overriding feeling is that everything is going to be OK – the world is still spinning, people are getting on with their lives. And finally, it feels like I am too. I've been given the fresh start I didn't know I needed so badly.

Then comes the wave of guilt. Mum. How can feel happy and settled when I'm estranged from my own mother? Then a new thought occurs: maybe that's exactly why I feel so good, because we're estranged.

Tuesday morning dawns bright and crisp, I can see my breath as I stroll across the yard to Will's van. I try to give off the air of a woman who's both businesslike and worldly, rather than a woman who tripped over her cat before stepping barefoot on a mangled mouse. I was washing rodent guts from twixt my toes at six a.m. At least Doris is doing her job of chief exterminator.

Instead of a traditional greeting, Will says, 'Did you bed down?'

For a second I think he's flirting then realise he's talking about the cattle pens.

'No,' I say firmly, 'I was feeling superstitious.'

He laughs and shakes his head, slowly turning the van round and bumping us down the lane, his empty trailer rattling along behind us.

He may well laugh but I didn't prepare Chloe's room before she was born and I'm sticking to those principles today. If we end up coming home with no livestock, leaving a deep bed of shaken-out yellow straw untouched would be too depressing.

I can see Dad now, letting me help bed down the sheds, which would occasionally turn into a kind of pillow fight as we chucked armfuls of straw at each other, the golden strands floating feather-like, landing in our hair and down our welly tops. One time Mum caught us and joined in. We both battled Dad till he tackled Mum and gently wrestled her down onto the straw before planting a smacker on her lips. 'Urrghh, that's disgusting!' I'd howl but I secretly loved how in love they were. In the happy times.

The van is cosy with the heaters on full blast and I steal a glance at Will, his wavy dark hair and strong jaw. He has big hands too – what is it with farmers and big hands? Dad's were the same.

It's a beautiful morning and as the traffic slows I pour Will a cup of milky coffee from my flask. My phone buzzes in my pocket. It's Mum. It's been two months since we last spoke – can the frost have melted already? A tangle of emotions knots up my stomach as I stare at the phone. Relief that perhaps this means repairs can start on our relationship but also anxiety. I sag under the weight of emotional baggage that seems to weigh us down when we come together.

Will seems to sense me bristle and glances over. I smile weakly at him. 'Hello, Mum,' I say.

A crackle down the line. 'Mum?'

'It's very noisy, Josie, I can barely hear you. Where on earth are you?'

'I'm in a van.'

'Well, I'm sorry but it's too loud. What are you doing in a van?'

I brace myself. 'I'm off to market.' I sound like I'm doing the 'this little piggy' rhyme Chloe used to love: 'And this one cried wee wee weeeee all the way home'.

Another silence. A tactic of Mum's as familiar and well worn as all her others. In a game of Mum bingo I predict she'll also mention a medical complaint and will definitely guilt-trip me before the end of this call.

'Off to market? Whatever for?'

'I don't know yet. A couple of bits of furniture maybe, just a browse with a friend.'

I see Will look puzzled at my white lie.

'Well, the noise is unbearable, I'm getting one of my headaches.' Bingo! 'Call me back later if you can make time for me in between all your gallivanting!' Full house!

And that's it. Weeks of her not taking my calls, no support, no housewarming card as I move halfway up the country, we are back to our version of normal: her picking at me, me placating. We will not discuss this latest void in our relationship though. We will edge around it and pretend it's not there, an ominous stain on a hotel room carpet.

If I ask for an explanation or, god forbid an apology, she'll snatch back the gift of communication she's deigned to bestow. So we'll continue to sweep stuff under the rug and the lump beneath will grow even more mountainous.

After a minute Will speaks. 'Your mum not approve of your new farming life?'

'Slight understatement there.'

'I thought she'd be chuffed, you following in your dad's foot-steps.'

'No. The very opposite. She sees it as a personal affront that I've moved back. She's never really got over his death and I think me returning rakes up all sorts of pain for her.'

'What about you?'

'What about me?'

'I mean – ' the traffic slows to a standstill and we see blue flash-ing lights ahead. He sips his coffee – 'I'm sure it was hard for her but she was an adult. I imagine it's not been easy for you? How old were you when he died?'

'Twelve.'

'There you go.'

It still amazes me how naturally, instinctively, friends, colleagues, boyfriends have always seemed to immediately understand my grief. Mum could never acknowledge it – it was all hers. She was very much the star of her own sorrow show. I was there in a supporting role. It's only through other people's eyes that I started to see that was wrong. Especially once I had Chloe, who I'd do anything to protect.

We crawl past a crumpled car that's spun into the central res-ervation, the walking wounded standing by an ambulance on the hard shoulder.

'Bad do with your dad,' Will says quietly.

I study the trees and the fields beyond. I will not cry. I think Mum's call shook me up.

'Yeah, it was pretty tough. I was so sad to leave the farm too.'

'I must've been about nine but I remember it. The whole village was in shock. Things took a while to get back to some sort of normal.'

'Well, Mum never really got back to normal after that.'

I seem to have been slipped some sort of truth serum as we drive the last few miles. I tell Will about Mum's depression and obsessive cleanliness, alopecia, drinking and my eventual escape to university and then New York. A potted history of the life and times of Sandra and Josie. Will is a good listener. 'Sorry, I've been wanging on at you. Bet you're regretting bringing me now.'

'No.' He looks shocked. 'Not at all.'

We fall silent for a minute. 'It's worth it for the coffee.'

I watch him as he manoeuvres the van and trailer through the traffic. 'What about your folks?' I ask.

'Pfft.' He makes an exasperated noise. 'Let's just say you're not the only one with an... interesting family. Mum left Dad about... must be about twenty years ago, not long after we took over the farm. It was a relief when she left. Jesus they could argue. Screaming matches, throwing things and then a silence would settle over the house, which was almost worse than the rowing.'

'What did they row about?'

'Money. Always money. We were always scraping by. I remember one year I'd outgrown my school shoes over the summer but daren't ask for new ones 'cos I knew we were proper skint. It was only when the games teacher saw my bleeding toes that Mum found out I'd kept it secret. She hit the roof, she was mortified.'

'Oh, Will, that's awful.'

'My toes are all reet now like,' he smiles, 'but Mum, bless her, couldn't stand the stress of watching every penny. Farming's a tough life and I don't think Mum was cut out for it. She liked the finer things in life. She never really fitted in, she was quite a character.'

'Was?'

'Eh?'

'You said she "was" a character?'

'Oh aye. She died, about fifteen year ago now, cancer. She'd remarried, to a nice enough bloke over in Bolton, and was happy and seemed settled at last then bam... it took her.'

'God, I'm so sorry, it's so cruel.'

'Aye.' Will coughs and clears his throat.

'And your dad?'

'He never really got over her leaving. Then blamed himself when I couldn't go to uni – there's no way we could've afforded it. I needed to help him keep the farm going. I told him it didn't matter.'

'Did it not matter?' I ask gently.

The traffic slows suddenly and he puts on his hazards for a few beats. 'Well,' he blows out a long breath, 'course it would've been grand to go, get my degree in agriculture or animal management.'

'So that was the dream?'

'Yeah but it had to stay a dream, sadly. Would've been nice to have a different career alongside running the farm that would've brought in more cash, used this a bit more – ' he taps a finger to his temple – 'but I couldn't let the farm just sink.'

'You're a good son.'

The traffic has stopped and he looks at me. 'You reckon? I do me best. When Mum died Dad was a mess. I tried to help him through that too.'

'Sounds familiar,' I say.

'Yeah.' He smiles at me then turns back to the road. 'These days he just stays in, always brooding. I'm worried he's not well,' he says grimly, 'he flies off the handle. He's fuming I'm helping you out, which is plain irrational for starters. I had to sneak out after feeding up this morning. It's pathetic, I'm a forty-eight-year-old man skulking about behind his dad's back like a teenager.' He laughs sadly and sniffs. 'Sorry. It's like we're on bloody Oprah or summat.'

'Can't be easy living with him?'

'Nah, it's not. But I love the farm. I just throw myself into that.' Will flashes his lights, letting a horse box pull out slowly in front of us.

'Your dad worked at Thistlefold didn't he, before you got the farm?'

He looks over. 'Aye, when I was really little. Our dads were quite pally at one time, I think. I never went up with him though – too dangerous Mum said, all that machinery. Shame or we might've been good mates.'

'Well at least you made the guest list for my birthday party that time.'

We see a sign, 'Clitheroe Sales and Auction House', and pull into a large car park already busy with trailers and lorries. I'm wide-eyed taking it all in.

'Look at you all perked up.' Will laughs. 'You look like Fliss when she sees the sheep in the distance.'

'I'll take that.' I smile. 'She's a very cool dog.'

As we walk our way around the livestock on sale, all contained in a seemingly endless grid of small metal fenced pens, I'm eight years old again, following my dad's wellies through the crowds. I was always on best behaviour, fancying myself as his co-worker rather than a kid getting under everyone's feet. Dad would know a few of the other farmers and there'd be banter over bacon barms and polystyrene cups of tea from the snack van.

I'd listen, enjoying seeing this other side of Dad while I sipped my instant hot chocolate; this was a different Dad – joshing with his mates, occasionally bursting out laughing then lowering his voice to impart a sly bit of gossip.

Today I'm following Will. He's quite a bit taller than me and keeps glancing back as we make our way past all the livestock. I notice more than one passing female check him out. When a gate suddenly swings open he puts a protective arm out to catch it before it gets to me. I swoon a little. Despite my feminist beliefs I'm enjoying this sensation of being protected. If I was with James he'd be bowling off ahead like a kid and would lose me in minutes. Throughout our marriage he'd bounded off and left me, over-excited at a gig or rushing ahead at a foreign airport. What would James think if he saw me now, I'm only up the M1 from our smart Hampstead house but this feels a million miles away. Chloe told me on the phone last night that her dad is still with Ella, apparently very happy. Good for him I think, as I follow Will's broad shoulders along the concrete walkway.

Will stops suddenly and leans on a gate, looking closely at three cows in a pen. They're bonnie and watch us curiously with bright eyes. Most importantly they're Herefords, their cinnamon brown fur interspersed with creamy white on the face, chest and underbelly, with matching creamy socks and tail tip. I feel my heart flutter. Could this trio mark the start of my farming life proper? Will reads the cows' information in the catalogue, screwing up his nose and looking disappointed. He turns on his heel and strides away.

I catch him up at the pig section. 'What was wrong with them?' I ask, unable to hide my disappointment.

'Nothing, they were perfect. Just didn't want the seller to see we think that. Lot No. 254 – ' he pulls a tatty biro from his pocket and circles the number on the page of the catalogue – 'fingers crossed we'll be taking them home with us, if you approve.'

'Definitely.' My disappointment has turned into excitement. 'They looked spot on. Your BAFTA-winning performance back there fooled me.'

'Ah well, I'm a man of many talents.' He winks.

I look around the pig section, at the younger stock huddled together for warmth. Most are snoozing, blissfully unaware of their fate – a new pen somewhere or the plate. All is calm; the quiet is only occasionally punctured by the clanging of metal as the animals are herded in or out of the pens.

That's when I spot her. She's calmly watching me and she's alone – a huge pig, pale pink with black splodges all over her, like she's been paint-balling. She sniffs the air and tips her snout up in greeting. She looks as if she's smiling at me. She trots up to the gate.

'Uh, oh,' says Will.

I can't take my eyes from her, 'What?' I say.

'I'm just watching your face. This is like something from *When Harry Met Sally* or summat. May I remind you we didn't come here for a pig?'

'Look at her though,' I breathe. As he starts to warn me 'careful!' I've already slipped my hand through the rails and she snuffles her soft pink snout on to the palm of my hand. 'Watch your fingers, sows can bite,' he murmurs but she's gentle and sweet.

Will leafs through the catalogue. 'She's not in here so probably an add-on. She's a Gloucester Old Spot, reckon about two years old.'

The sow looks at me then, really looks at me, white blond eyelashes fluttering and I know she's mine.

'What's she doing here?'

'Probably barren so no use. Here for –' He stops.

'What?'

'Oh god, if I say the next word you'll definitely want her.'

'Go on.'

'Meat.'

A sudden burst of rain catches the farmers as they make their way from the sheds to the various auction rings and by the time they're sitting on the tiered plastic seating that surrounds the cattle ring in concentric circles, steam is rising from their backs like they themselves are the livestock.

We sit about halfway up, looking down on the action. There's a Roman amphitheatre energy in the room, all eyes on the stage in the centre. Some buyers cluster closer to the action, leaning on the metal bars that rise high above head height to keep them safe from any beasts that may fancy their chances of leaping into the crowd. The ring has two metal gates spaced at 10 o'clock and 2 o'clock – one is in, the other is out, the same as saloon doors on a restaurant kitchen.

Animals are herded from their pens along a corridor of metal fencing and straight into the ring. Once final bids are accepted they leave through the other gate, back along to another holding pen while payment is made, then up on to a wagon and away to their new lives – or their demise.

The auctioneer, a distinguished-looking chap in a tweed suit with bristly grey sideburns steps up on to a raised platform, gavel in hand. He has the best view in the room and he'll need it. As the auction starts those bidding barely move – a twitch of the catalogue or a barely noticeable nod of the head is enough.

The tension in the room rises with each lot. The auctioneer's patter races along at breakneck speed. 'Who'll give me 875 – 875 – 875 – 880 – 885 – 890 – 890 – once, twice, 890 SOLD!' Then, as the gavel thwacks, the out gates are slid open and as they're shut, the in gates clang open and in trot the next animals. Some of the cattle look panicked, eyes rolling, breathing deeply, clouds of steam billowing from their noses. Their herd instinct making them move as one jostling mass, trapped in the ring.

'It's a new place – all the smells and noise, that's all,' says Will.

I don't know how I feel about it. Have my years in London made me soft? I feel for the animals. I came to market enough when I was little but maybe I was more focused on my hot chocolate.

Before long Will taps my thigh with the rolled-up programme. 'We're up next. You said eighteen hundred apiece so that's—'

'Five, four hundred.'

'Yup, bob on. Don't be in a rush, keep an eye on the room. I know this sounds daft but keep track – don't get carried away and bid against yourself, I've seen it done before. I'll touch your leg if you lose track.'

I don't think that'll help with my concentration. 'Right,' I say.

'Good luck. Remember to breathe. You'll be grand. Enjoy it.'

The out gate slides open and a cow with her calf at foot exit as the auctioneer says, 'Lot 254, three maiden Hereford heifers, eighteen months old, breeder T. Richardson of Burnley.' Will sits up slightly straighter. The three cows look skittish, overwhelmed by the whole experience and careering round the small ring before settling, chests heaving, withers twitching. They watch the crowd.

'Bidding starts at fifteen hundred pound for this trio, who'll start me off for these three lovely heifers?'

A chap in a flat cap and navy overalls leaning on the ring twitches a finger and the bidding begins. Even though we're on the third row of seats the auctioneer spots my first nod at eighteen hundred. I suppress a squeal. A third bloke, a big fella in a wax jacket seems to be bidding just with a raised eyebrow. He drops out and before long the auctioneer is rattling along between me and overalls man, barely pausing for breath and the price is going higher and higher. He looks back to me. 'Five? Do I have five thousand?' I nod, my eyes on the auctioneer, but I can see my opponent in my peripheral vision. The adrenaline is making my focus sharp and I feel invincible, though my heart is threatening to burst through my chest. The auctioneer and the crowd glance back and forth between me and overalls man like they're watching a tennis match. They lean in en masse, this is game on, both of us want this win.

'Five-one hundred. Do I have five thousand one hundred? Five thousand one hundred for these three well-bred heifers here.' Overalls man twitches his finger. Damn that finger. I want to chop the bloody thing off.

I have 5,400 ringing through my brain but I feel like I could keep going up to a million if I had to, just to win. Will's words come back to me. 'Remember to breathe.' I refocus. Perhaps it wasn't meant to be.

'Back to you, madam, five thousand two hundred? Do I have five thousand two hundred pounds?' It feels like the whole shed is holding its breath. I nod and everyone's heads whip round to watch overalls.

'Five-three? Do I have a bid for five thousand three hundred pounds, sir?'

I hold my breath. Overalls will never stop. I watch his finger. So does the auctioneer. So does the crowd. It stays still.

The auctioneer asks again, trying to tempt him. 'We are on five thousand two hundred pounds for these three Hereford heifers – do I have five thousand three?'

The crowd leans in. I can't breathe. 'On five thousand two, going once...' Overalls gives the tiniest shake of his head. '... going twice...' THWACK! The gavel comes down 'SOLD! Five thousand two hundred pounds to the lady in the green jacket!'

I want to scream, plant a smacker on Will and possibly do a victory lap hi-fiving the crowd, but instead I stay cool and allow myself a small smile, as Will throws an arm around my shoulders in jubilation.

The gate clangs open and the three heifers bundle out.

A young bull trots into the ring and the crowd refocuses and sit up a bit straighter. My moment of glory is over, forgotten by everyone but me. I'll treasure this feeling forever.

A young woman in a branded jacket squeezes through the crowd with a clipboard and card machine and takes all my details as I pay.

'Well done.' Will grins. 'You're a natural. A shade over seventeen-thirty, you got a decent deal.'

I'm absolutely buzzing. 'I want to do it again.'

'I bet. Nowt much else that'd suit though in the Herefords...' He tails off, unsure if I'm joking.

'I know. How's about I try for that pig if we can squeeze her in the trailer?'

We head back over to the pigs, lots of the pens are empty now and my heart sinks. She's gone. I *knew* I should've come over for her earlier. We turn and start to walk slowly back towards the cattle area. Will is quiet – he seems to sense my disappointment and doesn't try to offer any words of comfort.

'G'wan! Git on,' a man shouts behind us, making a pssst noise and there, trotting along the narrow metal corridor from the auction ring back towards the pen is my pig. As the gate swings shut behind her ample arse she begins busily snuffling the corners of the pen as if there to do an important job. I approach the man, who is himself rather porcine. Around dark eyes pushed into flushed full cheeks like fat raisins in dough.

'Excuse me,' I say and instantly hate how posh I sound away from the streets of north London. I try again, in a proper northern accent. 'That pig yours, love?'

The man lifts his flat cap to scratch the sweaty curls underneath. 'Aye, she is.'

He looks confused and quite rightly – in the general order of a conversation it's traditionally my turn to speak. What do I say? The poor man has just bought a pig and here I am, enquiring politely after it like Jessica Fletcher in a rural episode of *Murder She Wrote*.

'She's love-ely.'

'Aye, she is that,' he agrees.

'I would love to buy her from you. I know you've just bought her yourself but I saw her earlier so—'

He shakes his head. 'Well the thing is—'

But I don't let him continue. I have to have this pig. I feel a connection with her. I know it's ridiculous and emotions shouldn't get in the way when it comes to farming, but I have to have this pig – I know she'd fit in brilliantly on the farm. 'I'd love to have her, it'd be such a waste for her to go into pies and sausages when she could live out the rest of her days at my little place.'

I see Will glance at me and I realise 'the rest of her days' is a bold statement seeing as I keep reminding whoever will listen that I might only be at the farm for a year.

'What I'm saying is—' he tries to interject but I know I have to be assertive.

'Double,' I say firmly.

'Eh?' he replies, taking a crumpled ball of tissue from his pocket and wiping his nose.

'I'll pay double what you just paid for her.' Will wilts slightly next to me.

'Not possible,' he sniffs.

'It is,' I say, jutting out my chin like a cowboy in a western. 'Try me.'

'It's not possible, lass, as I was trying to say, I've not just bought her, I didn't sell her, she's mine but I couldn't bear to part with her for pennies.'

I laugh like a mad woman, mainly from relief. 'Ohhh... right. OK, well what's your price?'

He rubs his chin. 'Well. She's more like a pet to be honest so it's difficult to put a price on her... if I want to sell at all.'

At this the pig looks up at him as if even she realises he's pushing his luck.

'OK, well if you're not selling, come on, there'll be others,' Will says, starting to turn and giving me a stern look.

'Hang on,' the man calls as I follow Will. 'She won't get in pig, she hasn't taken from last three servings and I can't afford to feed her if I get no return... so if you promise me she'll have a good home?'

I nod eagerly.

'Then three hundred quid and she's yours.'

By nightfall all three heifers and the pig are bedded down in deep clean straw and Will heads off home. I fall into bed exhausted but feeling more content than I've felt in a long while.

26

Life at last feels like it has a new rhythm and direction. The cows and I have got into a routine and I'm back on speaking terms with Mum, a polite truce, and we speak on the phone every couple of days. The conversation falters whenever I mention anything to do with the farm, so I try to avoid the topic, which isn't easy seeing as it's the number one thing in my world right now. No matter – when did anything ever going on in my world impact on Mum's? Instead we stick to safe subjects – her, her lodger, Chloe and her sweater business and occasionally she asks after James. There's not much to update her on. We're in no rush to officially divorce and her voice goes weirdly sing-song when I say that, like there's still a flickering hope we'll rekindle our love and I'll give up this ridiculous farm fad.

That's not going to happen any time soon. I'm loving this new sense of purpose, the feeling for the first time in a long while that I'm truly needed. I wake every morning to the heifers calling me for their breakfast – feeding up is my favourite thing – all three cows at their gate watching me as I head across the yard and into the shed to fetch them their feed. The pig (named Penny after my formidable banking boss in New York) is getting fatter by the day and follows me around the yard while I go about my jobs, occasionally nibbling the tops of my wellies as I pause to lean into the heifers' pen with their hay. I call Will who agrees to loan me his smaller tractor to help with mucking out, an upgrade from the wheelbarrow I've been struggling with. He accepts my offer of some dinner that night in return for the favour.

Will arrives later on a small cream tractor with a front loader, and a large bucket on arms at the front that'll be brilliant at scooping up muck and wet straw from the cattle pens. I hear him before I see him, the engine making a throaty rumble as it crosses the field, the pale headlights struggling to illuminate his way, the bucket at the front raised high as if in greeting. He pulls up and lowers the bucket to reveal a small bunch of flowers and a bottle of red wine, cushioned by empty hessian feed sacks. I laugh with delight. Too cute. The tractor coughs and splutters then falls silent.

'All yours,' he says, hopping down and handing me the gifts and the keys. 'It's no Lambo but it'll do you.' He looks chuffed at my reaction and grins broadly. He's wearing dark jeans and a checked shirt – classic rural smart casual. He looks freshly showered, his dark hair still damp.

'It's awesome. Thanks so much,' I say, tearing my eyes away from his handsomeness and looking at the tractor. I'm grateful Dad taught me to drive his the year before he died. This vehicle looks much like his one back then and I'm sure I'll work it out.

We head inside. 'I can drive you home later,' I say as he prises off his wellies. He eyes the champagne chilling in a pan of iced water and smiles. 'I can always stagger back over the fields.'

We chat about how Penny is getting on. 'Perfect name considering how much you paid for her,' and his dark eyes twinkle as he laughs yet again about the extortionate price I paid for the pig. 'You got a bargain – if her trotters turn out to be solid gold under all that pig shit.'

I bat away his ribbing because I'm very happy with my new livestock and open the champagne I've been saving for a special celebration. Starting the farm off and the arrival of my loaned tractor to save my aching back definitely falls into that category. This does all feel like a real turning point.

Will wrinkles his nose as he takes a sip. 'Those bubbles get everywhere,' he says. With his face bathed in the glow from the fire I've lit in the lounge he looks even more handsome. The smell of paraffin on my fingers from the firelighters takes me back to Dad. He taught me how to light a fire the night before my ninth birthday. 'Right, Jose, build a noughts and crosses grid with your tinder then slot bits of firelighter between them then balance the coal on top... careful.'

Dad, always frugal, would use half a piece of white firelighter, chunks crumbled off like a stock cube and spaced strategically. I use two or three whole ones these days and every time I do, I imagine how horrified Dad would be at the extravagance.

Doris darted across the yard when Will arrived and she's clearly thrilled he is here and a fire is lit. As we drink, she curls up on Will's lap.

We polish off the bottle and I put some chicken and veg soup on the AGA – not exactly wooing him with oysters but it'll have to do; besides it is home-made and delicious. As I butter some crusty bread, Will stands at the AGA. 'Good arse warmer these things.' He nods. Doris is becoming obsessed with Will and is now, after much mithering, perched precariously on his shoulder like a parrot, her long tail occasionally gliding across his face, a moving moustache.

I feel giddy with the booze and the company. There's a silence as I stir the soup. I can feel him watching me. My heart starts to thump a little. Surely he can't move in for a kiss with a cat on his shoulder? We have a connection, I can feel it.

As if reading my mind he says, 'It's like I've known you much longer than a few weeks y'know.'

'Same.' I look up from my stirring and smile. Doris is now nuzzling his ears. 'Looks like you've got a fan there.'

'Yup.' He glances sideways at the cat. 'Always got on well with animals, people less so.'

'What? You seem very popular in the village.'

'Oh aye, yeah, when summit needs fixing, catching, moving, I'm always called upon. No, I mean, you know – in a romantic way.' He clears his throat. 'Relationships and that.'

'Oh I see.' I keep stirring, playing back the words. 'And when you say you've always "got on well with animals"?'

He laughs and Doris has to mind her balance on her now shuddering precarious perch. 'Purely platonic. Unlike some in the village.'

'Shut up, who?'

'Well, it's an urban myth, but some kids started saying that Gordon or "GG" is only called that 'cos he's very keen on horses and was caught fondling one in a field.'

'Ha-ha. Oh my god, that's disgusting.'

'I know – absolute bollocks. Luckily poor GG has no idea.'

'I thought with your dashing good looks you might've woo'd every gal in the village?' My flirting is clumsy but what the hell.

Will doesn't seem to notice. 'There's been a couple. I was engaged as a teenager but luckily for all involved that fell through. There's been a few relationships since but nothing serious.' He pauses. 'Until now.' I look up sharply and he points to Doris. I laugh too loudly and busy myself getting bowls out of the cupboard, relieved I don't have the main light on and can hide my blushes.

We eat and drink and laugh a lot. He loves the sound of Ruth and the dogs from Hound Stretchers, saying he'd like to meet them one day and I mention Mary's idea of a house-warming party.

Will tells me about past relationships, about the ill-fated proposal to a local girl when he was nineteen which involved a £15 Ratners ring and a bottle of Blue Nun. He tells me all about his mum Ruby, who was widely regarded as the most beautiful woman in the village when she was young. 'Everyone reckoned she was the spit of Liz Taylor, with her dark hair and blue eyes.'

'Wow,' I say.

'Yeah.' He nods. 'Apparently it was a shock to all when she started going out with Dad.'

He tells me his dad Jack's family, the Hockleys, were known to be trouble in their nearby village of Totton. Will's dad was the youngest of four brothers always in and out of prison. 'Dad was whatever the opposite of "black sheep of the family" is,' says Will.

'The "white sheep"?' I ask.

'Aye, I suppose so,' he says. 'Anyway they made a go of it, Dad became estranged from his family over the years and instead threw everything he had into working for us, trying to keep my mum happy... which wasn't easy really.'

'Oh?' I ask.

'Mum was always a bit of a romantic. She thought life was for living and wanted to be swept off her feet – not just some tea out or a trip to the seaside. She had expensive tastes and would spend money quicker than Dad could make it. On daft stuff too – trinkets and dresses and perfume.' Will shakes his head. 'They argued a lot about it. Dad tried his best, but he wasn't very affectionate and just thought that if he worked hard and kept making money then that'd be enough. But I guess he never really felt enough for her and was scared of losing her.' He pauses and for the first time looks uncomfortable. 'Mum was... a flirt. She'd wind Dad up by saying she was wasting her life with him and that any number of men would give anything to whisk her away.'

'Crikey. A live wire was Ruby then?'

'Yeah and then some. That's probably why she didn't have many female friends, none of the women trusted her. She was only really close to Betty from the sweet shop, saw her as a bit of a mother figure, I think. Though everyone loved Betty.'

'Yeah, she was quite the village legend.' I nod.

'Her and Mum would chat for ages, shooing me out the shop, and I'd be sat in the drizzle on Betty's step with a bag of liquorice.'

'Beth said we have that in common, a love of liquorice... plus of course, as we're now discovering, rather "complicated" mums.'

'Yours was quite pally with mine for a bit but they fell out, I think.'

'God they must've each met their match. Why did they fall out?'

'Dunno. My mum fell out with everyone in the village at some point. She had quite a mouth on her and wasn't afraid to use it. I loved her but she could be cruel.'

I nod. 'I know how that feels.'

Will drains his glass. 'She had a reputation, there were rumours about her that Dad would hear and confront her; she'd always deny everything, of course.'

I stand to clear the table and start to open Will's bottle of wine. 'What were the rumours?' But before he can answer I stop to look out the window and I'm surprised to see headlights sweep into the yard and across the window, temporarily dazzling me. I shield my eyes with my arm but before I can reach the door to go see who it is, it swings open, slamming against the wall and almost hitting me.

A man charges in. He's small but sturdy looking and is clearly absolutely furious. I recognise him as Will's dad Jack, looking even angrier than the day I met him at his farm. Spittle has settled on his grey stubble as he glares frantically around the room. 'I knew it!' he roars on spotting Will. 'I bloody knew it!' He lurches towards Will. Doris scrambles out of the way as he leaps up. Jack grabs hold of Will's arm and attempts to clumsily wrestle him away from the table. He may have been strong once but he's no match for his son who shakes him off with ease. In all the chaos a glass is upended on the table and rolls onto the floor, smashing.

'STOP!' Will shouts, shoving Jack away. 'Get off me, you bloody lunatic.'

The old man stumbles and steadies himself, boots crunching on the broken shards of glass. They are both out of breath. 'You lied,' the man gasps croakily. 'You're just like your mother, always lying.'

'Dad, what the hell?'

The man spins now and glares at me. 'You look just like your dad,' he hisses. 'It's like he's come back from the dead after all these years. To bloody haunt us.'

I physically flinch at his words.

'Dad!' shouts Will. 'That's enough.'

'No it's not.' He doesn't take his eyes from my face. 'It'll never be "enough" – not till she goes. You –' he jabs a finger towards me – 'you come back here to gloat have you? Here to look at the havoc your father left behind? You stay away from my family, do you hear me? Your lot have done enough damage. Your dad was a liar and a cheat and I reckon you're no better.' His voice grows louder with each word. 'You leave my son alone, do you hear?' he roars.

I'm shaking and look to Will who, red-faced and furious, has started to bustle his dad towards the door. 'I'm sorry, Josie, I'll call you when I can. I'm so sorry about this.' He wrestles Jack out of the door and into the blue van. They roar off moments later, Will at the wheel, his profile set in fury.

I clear up the glass and the dishes as if in a daze. What the hell just happened? I feel sick. Why would Jack hate me so much? Why was my dad a liar?

I open the red wine Will brought and see my hands are shaking. I put a log on the fire, which hisses, and sink onto the sofa. On spotting the flowers sitting so pretty in their vase, the tears come. How could a lovely night suddenly turn so dark? I look around the room, at the dancing shadows cast by the flames and feel so alone.

I miss my dad. Miss his hugs, him ruffling my hair. How could Jack say such cruel things about him? Doris comes back from wherever she'd scarpered to and kneads my tummy with her paws before settling on my lap. Her claws poke through my sweater but the pain is a distraction from feeling so numb.

I call Fay but it's late afternoon in Boston and I know she'll be busy at work – it goes to voicemail.

Chloe answers but is in a noisy pub. I keep checking my phone in case Will is calling. Eventually, three glasses of wine and two sobbing sessions later, my phone buzzes. It's not Will, it's Mum. Straight away I regret picking up. 'You sound funny. Have you got a cold?'

My voice is thick with tears and too much alcohol and she seems worried. It all comes tumbling out – after all, isn't that what mums are for? I tell her about the tractor, the lovely evening then, of course, Jack arriving like a grenade lobbed into the kitchen.

She surprises me by sounding genuinely concerned. No 'I told you so's' about my decision to move back to the farm, instead she listens in silence, before telling me everything will turn out OK and to get some sleep. As we say our goodbyes she falls quiet and I can hear her thinking.

'I know what you need – your mum. I'm going to come stay,' she says.

I feel silly, I'm being dramatic crying over such a ridiculous confrontation and start to gently dissuade her but then think better of it. Why push her away if she wants to help? Plus, it's time she finally returned to the farm.

27

I wake to the sounds of the heifers mawping, calling for breakfast. It feels like someone has removed my tongue and replaced it with some overcooked liver dipped in sawdust. Once I unstick it from the roof of my mouth I drink copious amounts of water from a mug in the bathroom, looking in the old mirror above the sink and feeling very sorry for myself. I can't handle my booze any more. My eyes are swollen from last night's crying and look like two overripe split grapes. I have the fear. Hangxiety they call it, I read about it in the Sunday supplements. The middle-aged not coping well with the crushing anxiety that accompanies every hangover beyond the age of forty-five.

When exactly did Mum say she was coming? It's all a bit hazy.

I feed up, slightly cheered by Penny and her waddling gait as she potters along behind me. My hangxiety returns as I watch her though – she's looking fat and bloated, her tummy is hard and I worry she may have something wrong with her. Twice she's broken into the feed shed but not for a couple of weeks, so how is she getting so fat? I may need to get the vet up. Correction. I may need to call Will later to find out which vet he recommends. Ten a.m. and he still hasn't called. Even a text saying he'll call later would be appreciated. I'm starting to feel like the whole thing was a bad dream without a proper debrief with the other victim.

A strong coffee later and I'm ready to call Mum who reminds me immediately of the date of her arrival and I'm relieved I don't have to ask. I'm also relieved that she can't make it for a couple of weeks due to 'commitments' – Thursday 9 December it is. She says she'll not be bringing Mouse, 'that Pennines wind will rattle his ribs', and as a cat owner I'm relieved. I didn't fancy refereeing that battle.

I mention to Mum the idea of a house-warming party to coincide with her visit. I think a bit of me hopes she'll dismiss the idea so I can use her as an excuse, but surprisingly she seems keen. We agree the Saturday would be perfect, giving us a couple of days to, as she says, 'be together, just me and you before everyone else piles round'.

I get off the phone feeling perkier and get a tickle of cabin fever so grab the flowers Will brought round and head off to the village in the direction of the church graveyard. In a bag I have a brush and dustpan, a cloth and a bottle of warm soapy water. I spruce up Dad's grave, sweeping the fallen leaves and dust from around the stone, then giving the smooth marble a wipe. It isn't that dirty at all and I get the eerie feeling someone is still tending it. Still, it feels good to make it look all nice. I sit on the grass, cross-legged like a little girl. I can feel the damp from the ground soak through my jeans to my bottom.

'Sorry I've been a bit crap, Dad, not visiting. I've been busy.' I feel silly talking to the headstone and glance around self-consciously but there's no one nearby. 'I've got three heifers, hoping to get them in calf in the new year.' I look up to the sky, the breeze blowing small clouds across the blue. 'I've even joined the Hereford Society so I could get their pedigree papers through. Spoke to a lovely lady on the phone. When I gave the farm address she remembered you – she sounded very fond of you, Dad. Mind you, you could always charm the ladies.'

The wind picks up and a fistful of curled leaves float around me like confetti. I stand up and gather my cleaning bits, hoping my wax jacket is covering my damp rear. 'Love you, Dad, so much.'

I stroll through the graveyard for a catch up with Beth at the sweet shop. After all the drama with Jack, I think I deserve some liquorice.

'Have you heard?' she asks as she comes through from the back. 'Will's dad was rushed to hospital last night.'

I don't get through to Will till dusk. His phone has been off all day and I start to fear the worst.

'I'm so sorry,' he starts.

'Never mind that,' I say, 'how's your dad?'

He doesn't answer straight away. 'He's... OK. Gave me a scare though. He had a bit of a funny turn when we got home. I was so angry with him when we got back and we rowed, then he clutched at his chest and I thought, "bloody hell he's gonna have a heart attack and it's my doin'." I called an ambulance and they said it'd take an hour and to get him there myself. Worst thirty minutes of my life that journey. Turns out it was a severe panic attack. They want to run dementia tests – he wasn't making much sense and was very angry still. Anyway, I've just got him home. They said he'd probably rest better in his own bed.'

I don't see Will for the next few days, though we speak a couple of times on the phone. Jack's doctor popped in to see him and did a few of the basic dementia tests, asking him various questions. He concluded that Jack seemed to be 'not showing the traditional red flags of cognitive struggle or decline but definitely showing signs of being extremely... cross'. The doctor, despite knowing Jack for all thirty-five years of his career, tells Will he couldn't extract from his patient the reasons behind this anger. 'He remained tight-lipped, Will, but maybe he'd open up to you?' Will tells me he hasn't dared try. He does however confirm he's very up for the house-warming party.

I barely have time to stress about Mum's visit. The weather has turned very wet and the tractor is an absolute lifesaver. The muck heap takes some maintenance and I can't imagine how I would've coped with just a fork and wheelbarrow to keep all the crap piled up and pushed back. The rain soaks the midden, running through the piles so a huge brown lake appears on the concrete around the edge of a moat of shit consommé. My long-handled squeegee – a relic from my childhood farm memories – was fun to use for the first two minutes but now gathers dust. Instead I spend a happy half hour a day pushing back the pile with the bucket on the front of the tractor, the base of it scraping noisily along the ground as I accelerate towards the heap.

A few months ago I considered reorganising my spice shelf a job well done, now I'm thrilled to be shovelling shit.

A sense of belonging washes over me that I never had in Hampstead. I loved my house and thought I enjoyed my life in leafy north London but here, now, in this moment I feel at home. I'm in waterproof trousers with my wet hair plastered flat by the rain next to a massive pile of stinking crap and I've never felt happier.

On the Monday before Mum's visit I'm up early, texting all the locals an invite to my house-warming party. Will, of course, plus sweet shop Beth, Alex the exterminator, Mary from Shearness and even GG. I text Ruth but I imagine it may be a bit late notice for her, depending on what dogs are currently staying with her, though she's usually off weekends when people deign to walk their own dogs, so maybe she'll come.

Invites texted I finish my breakfast feeling very pleased with myself and walk through the ever-present drizzle to feed Penny.

I find her pacing in the corner of her pen. Something isn't right. She's kicked all her bedding into a big pile and seems distressed. Her jaw is slack, she's mouth-breathing and gasping. She doesn't seem to notice me. It's like she's been poisoned, delirious as the toxins rush through her body. 'OK, sweetheart, OK.' I reach out to stroke her pink, bristly back and she flinches, she's clearly in pain. I fumble for my phone, cursing myself for not sorting this sooner. She'd seemed so content in the last week I just didn't get round to calling a vet and now it's too late. I'm an idiot – not fit to look after live animals. The heifers start calling for their breakfast and I press a finger over one ear as I clamp the phone to the other. Over the din I can just make out the ringtone as I cross everything, hoping that Will answers. He does. He forwards on his vet's number and says, 'I'm on my way,' as I ring off.

The young lad I speak to at the vet's is brilliant as I gabble on in a panic. He promises me the vet out on call will ring me back in minutes and he does. 'Thistlefold? OK, I'm not far away, I'll be with you in the next twenty or so.'

I put the phone down and gently stroke Penny. I feel completely useless. Penny drops onto her front knees, I'm sure she's breathing her last. She's gasping harder now and her eyes seem unfocused. She falls down into the straw lying on her side, lifting her rear leg in pain.

I hear an engine in the yard and seconds later Will appears. He climbs over the gate and into her pen with one leap. He's stony faced as he lowers to the floor by Penny's head and takes one look at her before pushing through the straw on his knees towards her back legs. He glances under her tail and then smiles up at me, brushing the damp hair back from his eyes.

'What?' I say, confused.

'She's not ill – she's farrowing!'

'What?'

'She's in labour and I reckon the first piglet is only minutes away.'

I laugh in shock. 'What?' I shout the word this time, making Penny jump slightly. 'Shhhh,' I say, stroking her shoulder and lowering my voice. 'But how?' I ask Will.

He pauses and cocks an eyebrow.

'Well, I know *how*... I mean...' I stutter.

Will laughs gently. 'A pig's total gestation is easy to remember – three months, three weeks, three days – and sometimes you can't tell they're in pig for the first eighty or even ninety days... seems she was sold in good faith as not in pig, then a month later here we are. Very much in pig and about to pop.'

Pop she does. A minute later I can see Penny's contraction, a wave of tension rippling down her long stomach and she lifts her tail and out flies the first piglet. I can't believe the speed of it. The piglet's tiny snout first pokes through then in a smooth motion is followed instantly by the rest of its wet little body. There's no crowning, no easing the head out. Pigs are built to breed, they have it down. I look up at Will in shock as the first piglet, which landed about a foot away from Penny, starts to snuffle about in the straw sniffing out its mother and her milk.

'What about the vet?'

Will says, 'I'll call and cancel.'

'Really?'

'Yup.' He shrugs. 'She should be OK, looks like she's just cracking on.'

Each pig that slithers out is covered in a slimy coating of mucus and blood and is accompanied with a gush of fluid, a white cord trailing from its stomach like a piece of overcooked spaghetti. I think back to Dad's pigs in the seventies. I can't remember being shocked by the brutal yet beautiful way the piglets entered the world. Maybe I was too caught up in hoping for a runt to nurse and fuss over by the fire. *Charlotte's Web* was a massively popular book and all the local farm kids knew they were lucky if they had piglets to play with.

'Maybe grab an old towel though,' says Will.

Every ten minutes or so, Penny lifts her tail and with one push a piglet is expelled, each one coming out head first. After an hour and a half she has nine perfect piglets, each one pale pink with a scattering of random black spots. Penny's breathing seems to slow, she relaxes and makes low grunting noises. Will and I watch as the squirming piglets feed. Occasionally she squeals and kicks.

'They have teeth sharp as needles,' Will explains. 'If she was in a crate and couldn't escape them maybe you'd clip their teeth to stop them hurting her teets, but she can move and escape them when they get too much.'

I'm relieved, I'm not great at the dentist myself and feel squeamish at the thought of clipping off the piglets' teeth.

'We'll keep an eye on her though. It's not a big litter so there's plenty of space and teets to go round so less jostling and fighting for milk.'

I nod. It's a lot to take in. When I woke up I had five animals including Doris and now I have fourteen. 'Not a big litter?' I say, incredulous. 'There's *nine* piglets there.'

'I know, they can have twenty.'

'Jesus,' I mutter.

'Shame there's not an even number, makes it easier for them to divvy up the teets.'

Penny gasps then as if on cue. Her back leg twitches. She grunts softly and lifts her tail. A tiny piglet slips out, like an afterthought. This one is half the size of the others, about the length of my hand.

It lands in the straw and is still. Will and I spring up from where we've been sitting in the corner on a bale and Will tells me to pick up the piglet. I quickly kneel and lift the tiny limp creature. It is warm and wet but I can feel it cooling in my hand.

'Wipe its face,' Will tells me, handing me the towel. I look up at him. 'Quickly,' he says.

I snap to it, and wipe the gunk from the piglet's eyes and snout. 'Use your fingers to clear its mouth,' he says. He sounds calm. I think in that moment how life and death are all an everyday part of farming.

I thrust my forefinger into its tiny mouth, instinctively using a sweeping motion across the tongue, like I was taught in the infant first-aid classes I went to when pregnant with Chloe. Surely a choking baby can't be much different from a choking piglet? There is mucus on the roof of its mouth that is stretched like a thick bubble across its airways. I pop it with a thumb and quickly pull the gunk out. Its mouth and snout now look clear.

'We need to get it warm,' says Will. 'Give it a good rub with the towel, be quite rough, we need to get the blood circulating.'

I hold the tiny piglet with one hand under its tummy and with the other, rub the towel up and down its back like I'm trying to work up a shine. As I rub, Will occasional says 'stop' and reaches over to slap the pig firmly along its spine with his open palm. 'Go on,' he says.

I keep rubbing and massaging the piglet, willing it to live when suddenly its little pink legs twitch and its eyes spring open. I turn it so we are face to face. It looks at me curiously, and wrinkles its snout. It has a black patch over one eye like it's been in a bar brawl. Quite fitting really I think, it's certainly a little fighter. I laugh as its little legs start to gallop in mid-air, trying to run.

'You did well there.' Will grins, glancing at her rear end. 'Put her in the middle of her brothers and sisters, there, where its warmest.'

I squeeze her in amongst the hot squirming bodies of her bigger siblings and she starts snuffling towards a teet. A little girl.

She was hovering in the space between life and death and I pulled her towards life and made her live. She's alive thanks to me. It is the best feeling in the world. I also don't think I can ever eat bacon again.

After twenty minutes Will is pretty sure Penny is done. She seems settled. Will builds up a low wall of straw around the pigs to stop any draught while I make some tea and cheese butties. We eat them sitting on bales and they taste like a feast after all the excitement.

'She'll not be the only new mum round here in a couple of weeks,' Will says, draining his tea. 'Seems that bloody spaniel over at Yates' did get to Fliss that day. Vet reckons she'll pup in a week or so.'

'Oh crikey,' I say.

He shrugs. 'No use getting stressed about it. Noticed she was a bit slower moving the sheep and knew right away. We might have to train up Doris.'

'Oh aye.' I laugh. 'She'd be good I reckon.'

Will nips home and returns with a heat lamp and we hang it above the corner of the pen where Penny and the piglets are gathered. Most of them are still feeding but some are full and snoozing, piled on top of each other like socks ready for the wash. He plugs in the lamp and it casts a buttery glow all around the new family, cocooning them in a cosy snow globe safe from the chill of the farm.

28

To say Mum will expect a clean house is like saying a Korean dictator expects his crowds to clap.

I spend days on my hands and knees scrubbing the stone floor, wiping all the surfaces, hoovering the stair carpet. The house now looks fit for my visiting dignitary. It's exhausting, plus I've not been getting much sleep thanks to the piglet with the black eye – Nicola (named after Nicola Adams the boxer).

Nicola the Piggola as I sing to her, half delirious in the dead of night, is feeding well from her mum but as instructed by Will I'm topping her up every few hours with a baby bottle of multimilk, a formula designed for whatever runt or farmyard orphan happens to be in need of some extra TLC. Once I've dragged my weary arse out of bed, chucking my jacket and bobble hat on over my pyjamas and wellies, stumbling across the yard, it's actually very cute wrapping Nicola in a towel and giving her a feed. Takes me back to Chloe as a small baby, though thankfully Nicola doesn't need burping. Each time I flop back into bed Doris wakes momentarily from her slumber to glance at me with one eye as if to say, 'You must be crackers,' and I think she has a point.

The house looks beautiful though, and by Thursday morning I'm sitting at the kitchen table, Doris on my lap, enjoying the calm before my whirlwind of a mother blows through. I sweep a critical eye around the room, trying to guess what fault Mum will immediately point out to burst my bubble. Or maybe she won't – maybe she'll arrive in high spirits and full of encouragement. Half of the anxiety with her is never being sure which mum to expect; what scale of stressed she'll be on and how much I'll have to manage her. The not knowing is harder than dealing with whatever drama or illness she comes carrying, weighing her down like a heavy bag.

I had this feeling all through my teenage years – as I walked slowly up the street to our little terraced house I'd count the paving stones; there were one hundred and twelve. Each day I counted, walking slowly, studying the ground to avoid the cracks, trying to delay the moment I turned my key in the front door and felt either the chill of her indifference or a hot blast of her anger as she grabbed me and scrubbed my hands in the scalding water over the kitchen sink.

I watch the clock. All my outside jobs are done, the house is perfect and I have a couple of hours before Mum arrives. I might even put on a bit of make-up, make myself presentable, otherwise Mum will say her favourite go-to insult wrapped in faux concern, 'tired'. Maybe I'm over sensitive with Mum's comments, my judgement is blurred after so many years of put-downs, constantly alert to potential threat like an impala grazing on an open plain, ears twitching to detect predators.

I locate my make-up bag on the floor underneath my thermal socks, chucked there after one of Nicola the Piggola's night feeds. Funny how I'd make a bit of an effort in London but putting on mascara on the farm seems as appropriate as wearing a feather boa. Pulling a brush through my hair I suddenly hear an almighty kerfuffle come from behind the chimney breast in my room – a loud squawking, a scraping of feet or wings or both. Whatever is in there (a bird, a massive bat, a dragon?) has settled lower down inside the chimney and is either stuck there or is currently cavorting around

SARA COX | 248

in my front room with its soot-blackened wings, a Rio carnival dancer gone goth.

I almost throw myself down the stairs, using the bannisters to take them two at a time and thump through the door into the room. Well, it was a room five minutes ago, now it's like I've walked on to a battlefield seconds after a dozen cannons have been fired. There is a haze over the room, a grey cloud hovering cartoonishly around the fireplace and quickly settling on my newly polished surfaces.

There is no sign of the creature but every few seconds comes a smacking sound, followed by the sound of falling soot. I try to peer up the chimney but it's pointless, decades of soot have settled and thickened solid in there like fat in an artery. That was another thing on my to-do list – arrange to get the chimney swept before I started using it properly for winter. What is my problem? I scold myself.

I call Beth who sends me the number of Arthur Larkitt of 'Super Larkitt Sweep' and he agrees to come around as soon as he's finished the job he's on. 'Round midday, I reckon,' he shouts over the noise of machinery. At least the chimney beast has fallen still. Please don't let it be dead, what if its carcass becomes lodged up there, filling the house with its festering stink?

In the meantime I follow his hollered instructions and grab a bedsheet and gaffer tape it over the fireplace to catch any more dust. I wipe the coffee table and windowsills but this just seems to move the dust around the room rather than get rid of it. I catch my reflection in the mirror. The tiny particles of soot have stuck to my tinted moisturiser and I look like Pathé footage of a miner. Mum and the chimney sweep are both due around midday. I'd hoped to be standing on parade ready to welcome Mum in a relaxed manner. Instead she was about to arrive in the middle of a minor drama.

I call her and it connects through her car's bluetooth.

She doesn't say hi, sensing I'm after an ETA – she knows I'll be on pins waiting for her. 'I'm on Willows Lane,' she barks, 'about ten minutes away, though the traffic can get sticky as we get to the village.'

'Oh. OK great. Was just checking you'd not got lost.'

She tuts. 'I'm sorry but I'm not completely senile yet, you know.'

'I know.' I pause. 'It's just I know you don't trust satnavs and you've not been here for decades.'

She falls silent. This is so unusual I presume we've been cut off. 'Hello?'

'Yes, yes I'm here.'

'I was worried some of the roads may have changed, but if you're fine – '

'Yup, I'm fine,' she snaps. 'It's all exactly the same. I did live round here for donkey's years you know. Why are you fussing anyway? What's wrong?' Ol' bloodhound Sandra on the scent of drama.

'Nothing. We've got a creature stuck up the chimney but the sweep's on the way, so nothing to worry about,' I babble. 'See you soon, byeee.' I hang up.

Predictably I see a van bumping up the lane just ahead of Mum's trusty blue Polo. They both pull into the yard and I'm not sure who to go to first, but the decision is taken out of my hands when Arthur hops out, slamming the van door behind him. Mum very much stays put in her car, a thousand-yard stare boring through the windscreen. Probably waiting for the red carpet, I think, then feel snide. It's been a long time since she pulled up into this yard. I imagine memories are flooding back. She was a young widow when she left, a lot of water has flowed under the bridge since then. She's wearing a dark-blond wig with big curls that tumble on to her shoulders; she looks like a country singer.

'Howdy,' shouts Arthur. He is ruddy cheeked and very tall with thinning black hair sticking out at all angles like he's just gripped an electric fence. He looks like one of his brushes and walks with a slight limp as if he has a stone in his boot. He watches me expectantly.

'Hi, sorry, yes... the err...' I glance back at Mum's car. She is still staring straight ahead. I feel the anxiety build in my chest. I wish she would just get out of the car at least. She is stock-still and her hesitation seems performative now, for my benefit.

'The fireplace is this way, inside.'

He nods and begins to follow me. 'Yup they usually are.'

'What?'

'Inside. Fireplaces.'

'Oh god, yes, sorry. I'm a bit distracted. That's my mum in the car there, I need to go get her.'

'Don't worry.' His eyes crinkle, he has a kind face. 'Show me the way, then go sort your mum.'

I do just that then I head outside and open Mum's car door. 'Hiya.' I force fake cheer into my voice, sounding like a jolly girl guide. 'You OK? Chimney sweep has come to remove an intruder.'

She doesn't respond. 'Come on then.' I nod towards the house, smile stretched thin across my face.

She gets out slowly and looks more frail than I remember. It's been a few months since Fay and I visited and she's aged. I can see down her cowl neck sweater, her collarbone stretching the surrounding pale skin taut like the knuckle end of a chicken drumstick. I fold her into a hug and she allows herself to be held for a moment then inevitably grows rigid, the awkwardness of affection overwhelming her.

We don't speak, instead I grab her bags and lead her inside and settle her at the table by the warmth of the AGA. She is looking around the room dazed as if she's been picked up by a tornado and spat out in my kitchen. I remember feeling like I'd fallen through time when I walked back in this room again.

I leave her to acclimatise and go through to the lounge.

'Reckon it's a crow,' Arthur says, 'though most birds look like crows when they've been in a chimney for a bit'. He has spread white sheets all around the fireplace and over the sofa like the train of a bride's dress. Arthur is in mask and dark overalls. Every time he glances over he dazzles me with the beam of his head torch. 'Oops, sorry, I'm always doing that.' He grins ruefully, switching it off. 'It's quite high up though. I can't reach it to grab from the bottom so ideally it needs to exit out the top. I'm going to use a brush to hopefully give the bird some purchase, something to perch on. I should then be able to raise it up and persuade it out.' I obviously look worried. 'Whatever happens, your chimney will be bird free within the hour. I ought to sweep it too, looks like it's not been swept for a while.'

'Definitely,' I say. 'Thank you. I was getting round to it.'

'Aye,' he says, 'well old Pete who lived here never had me round, so no wonder it's in a state. I wouldn't say he was tight but I heard he liked to sit round the fire every night and if it was really cold he'd even light it.'

I laugh.

'Right,' he says, looking serious, 'I need one other crucial bit of kit.'

'Cup of tea?'

'Exactly. Milky, three sugars.'

In the kitchen I find Mum is standing by the window looking out at the paddock. She turns and watches me silently as I put the kettle on the AGA.

'I'm sorry but I still can't quite believe it,' she says eventually in a low voice. 'Can't quite believe I'm standing in this kitchen again after all these years. I never thought I'd see it again.'

I grab some mugs as the kettle starts to softly whistle. 'How do you feel?'

The mum before me is softer, more gentle than the usual sharp-edged, brittle version I'm used to. I feel a little on the back foot, surely there is still the old familiar wolf lurking there under the fleece?

'How do I feel?' Her eyes glint a little. 'Now you ask me how I feel?'

There she is.

'You hardly cared about my feelings all those months ago when I begged you not to come back here.'

I feel twelve again. Standing in this kitchen in the days after Dad's death, cowering while Mum's temper builds like the hiss of a pressure cooker. The kettle sings in its highest pitch and I move it from the hotplate.

'Mum —' I start but she cuts me off.

'As it happens it's not as bad as I thought it would be, considering.' She almost sounds disappointed, she loves to suffer. 'I've been through so much within these four walls, Josie. A lifetime's worth of pain, heartbreak, betrayal.'

'Betrayal?'

'Yes.' She tilts her chin up now and holds my gaze steadily. She takes a breath as though to say something but the door swings open from the front room as Arthur comes in.

'Right, we're all set,' he says. 'Be helpful if you fancy watching from outside so you can spot the bird as it hopefully flies out – ' he crosses his fingers – 'or drops out. It's still alive but being trapped can put a lot of stress on their little hearts...'

He stops and looks at Mum, mouth agape.

'By 'eck,' he says. 'I'd know those eyes anywhere.'

'I wondered when you'd cotton on,' replies Mum coquettishly, swishing her cowgirl curls, miraculously recovered from her trauma.

'Do you two know each other?' I ask.

'Your mum here was the prettiest girl in the village when I was growing up. I was just a daft teen working with me dad when your mum moved to the farm. She was, well still is, a real bombshell.'

'Oh Arthur, get out of it.' Mum beams.

'I knew I recognised you,' he says to me, 'you're the spitting image of your dad but 'cos you're a Perry not a Wylde I didn't put two and two together.' I notice Mum's smile has frozen a bit like a TV on pause. 'You though, Sandra, you've not changed a bit in all these years.'

I pass him a cup of tea and Arthur takes a slurp. 'Right. No rest for the wicked, and I'm very wicked.' He winks at Mum and she giggles. 'I bet you are, Arthur.'

Urgh. Are they flirting? Mum hooking up with a toy boy chimney sweep was not a twist I was expecting.

'Right,' I say a little too loudly, 'let's go outside shall we?'

Mum and I wait out in the yard. We have to walk quite far back, dodging the puddles, to get a good view of the chimney stack. After a few minutes we spot movement at the top and we're astonished to see Arthur's brush slowly rise from inside the chimney and sitting atop it is a crow. It looks around for a second or two, perhaps adjusting its eyes to the daylight after the darkness of its temporary prison, then crouches low before springing upwards and taking flight, circling the house once then swooping down into the tops of the trees along the edge of the paddock. We cheer and Arthur's brush jiggles up and down in a celebration dance before disappearing back inside the chimney.

He nips out to the van then fetches a vacuum cleaner, which is tall, yellow and cylindrical with a thick hose attached, and heads back into the lounge.

'He was just being friendly,' says Mum once we've returned to the kitchen. 'Sorry but are you jealous?'

'Yes. You got me – I've always wanted to be seduced by a chimney sweep with a limp.'

'Well there's no need for sarcasm.'

At least we're back to normal.

Mum glances at her watch. 'What's he doing in there? We saw the bird go.' She seems suddenly anxious.

'He's still got to sweep the chimney. I imagine it's a big job seeing as it's not been done for so long. No rush is there, though? Or are you waiting for the grand tour?'

She doesn't seem to hear and keeps watching the door.

'Right,' says Arthur. 'All done.' He's loaded his stuff in the van and is standing by the sink, scrubbing his hands under the tap. 'Lovely to see you, Sandra, I must say.' He keeps his eyes on the job in hand as he says, 'Not much has changed since you left but if you fancy a refresher course I'd be happy to take you on a tour now that you're back.'

'Oh she's not back,' I blurt out at exactly the same time Mum says, 'I'm only visiting.' We laugh awkwardly.

'I mean,' Mum says, 'I'm just here for Josie's house-warming party.'

'Oh aye?' says Arthur, eyes lighting up. 'Oh I love a good party.'

I'm left with no alternative as both of them look at me expectantly. 'Please come, Arthur. Saturday night from sevenish. You're very welcome, though it's only a few friends from the village, nothing wild.'

'Not till I arrive anyway.' He wiggles his hips and motions as if he's just joined an invisible conga line. Mum grins. 'And, of course, don't forget, us chimney sweeps bring good luck.'

He turns for the door. 'Whoops nearly forgot with all the party talk.' He spins and fishes something from his pocket. 'Found these in the chimney, on the collar they were. Very strange but seeing as the chimney's not been swept for years who knows how long they've been there. Probably no use but thought I'd better give them to you.' He places on the unit a small collection of keys.

'We find all sorts up chimneys. Folks used to hide their heirlooms up there away from burglars. Can you believe my dad once found a sawn-off shotgun wrapped in a towel! I've found a Roman coin and a Christmas card from 1945 that must've slipped down behind the mantle... Anyway...'

He looks to us but I've stopped listening, instead I'm transfixed by Mum who has gone deathly pale.

'Wow. Thanks.' I pick up the grimy keys. There is a metal key that stands alone and three smaller ones connected by a metal hoop. I put them in my pocket and show Arthur out.

Mum is silent and sitting studying the palms of her hands as I close the door behind me.

'What's the matter?' I ask. 'You look like you've seen a ghost.'

'What a horrible thing to say seeing as I've come back for the first time since your dad's death,' she snaps. 'There are ghosts hiding round every corner of this damned place. Sorry... I just...' She softens. 'Ignore me.' She holds up a hand. 'It's been a long day. I think I'm just hungry that's all.' She purses her lips as if afraid of what might slip out from them.

The keys feel like they're going to burn a hole in my pocket but I know from Mum's reaction it's best to let her settle and not to push her. I have her for three whole days. We have plenty of time to chat and I resolve to look at the keys more closely when I'm eventually alone.

We have sandwiches after which she brightens, but an afternoon stroll up to see the geese on the pond makes her sullen and silent. I deliberately cut back through the front field so we avoid Blacksmiths and the site near Dad's crash. Mum seems exhausted and allows me to send her to bed to rest. It's bizarre seeing her settled in my old room, which I've bought a nice new bed for. She seems childlike as she curls up on top of the duvet and when I return with a cup of tea a few minutes later she's already fast asleep.

Under the light of Penny's heat lamp I retrieve the keys from my pocket to study them. Two of the smaller ones seem to be to unlock some sort of equipment rather than a door or a vehicle, the third is a slightly bigger Yale-style house key. The biggest key is definitely a car key, though it ends abruptly and the top area, the bit you'd hold it with, is missing.

My heart thumps as I allow a thought to resurface from the depths of where I've pushed it down all afternoon. On the night he died, Dad was driving Mum's little car. I'd always wondered why. I presumed because the Land Rover was out of action. Maybe he was rushing and couldn't find the keys for his own 4x4, which would've been much more suitable for the rain-soaked lanes. I open Safari on my phone and search 'Land Rover key 1970s UK' in google images and cross-check the photos with the soot smudged bit of metal in the palm of my hand. A match. The length of the key and its jagged tooth design look exactly the same, the bit missing at the top according to the photographs, was hard black plastic, obviously melted away.

Why would Dad's keys be in the fire? Who'd wanted to stop him going out and why would they do such an extreme thing?

I check myself. Dad had a Land Rover and now I'm adding two plus two and coming up with thirty-six. Dad died four decades ago, who knows what's been going on in the house since then? Maybe Pete Potter found the keys and chucked them in the fire or they're nothing to do with Dad, just some random keys that ended up there due to a freak accident? Perhaps a magpie stole them and dropped them down the chimney from above. Didn't Arthur say that mag-pies loved to build their nests on the chimney pots?

I spend an hour mucking out the heifers, there's something sooth-ing in the thrum of the tractor engine and the to-ing and fro-ing with the loads of wet mucky bedding from the pens to the midden. I'm a dab hand with the tractor now, reversing out left-hand down, swinging right in a neat semicircle to the pile, clambering down intermittently to unhook a bit of stray twine or to switch the cows into different pens. The task is just about mindless enough for me to be able to think. Though my thoughts just circle around the keys like a buzzard circling carrion, unable to land.

I'm bottle-feeding Nicola the Piggola by the time Mum finds me. She is silhouetted against the blackening sky and I swear with her standing over me in her woolly hat and wellies we are back in 1980.

'Tip the end of the bottle up, she's getting bubbles,' Mum says gently and I correct the angle of the bottle, which had drooped as I watched her approach. Surely she can feel this too? This full circle feeling? Like we're back where we're supposed to be? I can't find the words, weakly saying, 'This is nice,' but she doesn't hear. She pulls back the spring bolt on the gate with ease despite her years. Her strength seems returned, brought out by her being stood on this land.

'She's a nice sow.' She smiles, watching Penny with her litter, half of them sleepy drunk on milk, the others busily feeding.'She's a good mum then?'

'Tries her best,' I say.

'We all try our best,' Mum says.

I don't want to burst this bubble, I want to cast it in copper so it can't melt away. I can't remember the last time Mum looked so at peace. Her edges have softened in the glow of Penny's heat lamp as she kneels down on the thick clean bedding to fuss over a curious piglet that's trotted through the straw to say hello. She scratches its back gently then chuckles as it nudges her hand when she stops. 'You like that eh?'

In fact I do remember when she looked like this, it was when I was a little girl here on this farm, Mum kneeling in straw, helping a sow with her piglets, instructing me what to fetch and carry. A patience and a kindness in her that was all shattered the day Dad died. What happened to her? People die all the time, and those left behind survive and somehow carry on.

Ruth always said about Maud passing, 'One doesn't "get over it", the grief is like a huge black hole you get used to living alongside, you make room for it but it's always there.' What was it about Dad dying that made a huge part of Mum die too? The good part of her.

I need answers. I feel a rush of adrenaline as it dawns on me that I can't pull down the shutters on this any more. I need to find out why Mum changed, why my life was uprooted and my childhood innocence allowed to curl and rot like roots in frost.

She was a victim too. Her drinking, her alopecia, her OCD all engulfed her, each hot on the heels of the last before joining forces to almost break her. No wonder I fled to university, then New York and London. I've never really stopped running from her. Until now. Wasn't that a huge part of the motivation for moving back here? To stop running from her, from the secrets of the past?

I suddenly feel powerful. Mum is back on what was her old turf but this is now my land and she's not leaving till I've squeezed everything I need to know from her.

I place Nicola back in with her siblings and straighten up. 'Mum,' I say, and my voice sounds loud over the gentle snuffling of the piglets.

She looks up at me warily, as if knowing what is coming.

'What happened with Dad? Why were you so angry when he died?'

She stands too now, the blond curls of her wig held in place with the woolly hat.

My throat dries, this is the first time in years I've dared to ask.

She lifts the piglet, reaches over and places it in the deep straw near Penny; it is hungry again after its adventure and latches back on to drink.

'Your dad,' she says quietly, 'made some bad decisions.'

I don't speak, willing her to fill the silence she's left.

'He... I guess you could say invested unwisely. Kept it a secret from me. I found out.'

'When?' I ask, vaguely remembering arguments around money, hushed exchanges dripping in fury.

'Money had always been short, no one ever became a farmer to make their fortune. We were always scraping by, but then I found out there was even less money, he'd been lying to me.' She's speaking quickly now, breathlessly as if it's a relief to spit the words out. 'We were in danger of losing the farm and he was trying to stop us sinking by reinvesting, but it always went wrong. We had debts, some I never knew of...'

There is the sound of an engine in the yard and I'm irritated that any second now someone is going to appear and she will close up again, snap shut like a mussel shell.

'What did he invest in? When did you find out?'

She winces at the memory. 'The day before he died,' she says.

'Helloooo!' booms Will, making us both jump.

'Jesus, Will!'

The pig pen tips on its axis. If Mum found out about Dad's debts the day before he died she probably wasn't on speaking terms with him on the day he died. I can't imagine how much that would eat away at a person. Or maybe I can; after all I've witnessed Mum's bitterness and sorrow all these years.

I felt like we had made progress, the nut hadn't cracked but it had creaked. Maddeningly I can't process this new information right now thanks to Will's interruption.

'Sorry – didn't know you had company.' He reddens slightly and despite my irritation I can't help but smile. He looks cute when he's bashful.

Mum stands up and turns. She stares at Will and I see her face harden. We are flung forward through time and we're back now in the present. The softer mum has gone for now, but I will get her back.

'You must be Will.' Her voice sounds strong but she looks weak, as if our conversation has taken its toll. 'I'm sorry,' she says and suddenly reaches out towards me, looking panicked. Her knees buckle and Will leaps over the gate and we help her to a bale of straw to sit on.

I feel awful. What was I thinking? She's not a young woman, why did I need to confront her out here? Couldn't I have waited till we were inside in the warmth and at least sitting down. I feel guilty for ambushing her with my questions.

'I'm OK. I got up too quickly, that's all. It's my blood pressure medication.' Mum smiles weakly, looking at me. She is ignoring Will, refusing to look at him, but he doesn't seem to notice.

'You must be Sandra? I've not seen you since I was tiny but wow, Josie looks just like you.'

We both look at him then in surprise. Mum drops her head again and says to her lap. 'No, she looks like her dad, not me.'

'Well,' he says, sounding awkward now, 'I'll go and make you some sweet tea, shall I? Maybe that'll help.'

Half an hour later I've lit the fire and settled Mum in front of it with her tea. She continues to ignore Will and I know I'm responsible – after all I'd been the one crying on the phone to her, telling her all about his dad bursting in on us, and upsetting me. She probably thinks he's a wrong 'un and is looking out for me. 'Kick one and we all limp,' she's always said.

Unless she knows something about Will's dad she's not letting on? Maybe there's history there? Oh god please let's not have some failed romance between the two of them. Arthur did say Mum was the prettiest woman in the village back then, though by all accounts Will's mum Ruby gave her a run for her money.

Either way none of this is Will's fault and I'm embarrassed by her behaviour. Mum heads up to her room and I apologise to Will for her like I used to back in the day to neighbours, my teachers, her friends. 'She's not well, I'm so sorry. She doesn't mean it.' My words follow a familiar route, like water spilled on a table always finding the same grooves in the wood.

'It's alreet, I'm a big boy.' He sips his coffee. 'Besides, I don't have a leg to stand on when it comes to unruly elderly parents being rude.'

'True.' I smile. 'How is your dad?'

'He's back on form, well enough to give me a bollocking about the sheep's water trough this morning...'

'Excellent,' I say. 'I told Mum about that night. I think she's still cross about it. Do you know if she and your dad were pals? He doesn't seem keen on our family. I just wondered if maybe something went on between them.'

'God knows. All I know is it's easier if I fib about where I am, prevents a barney. I'm currently picking up a tractor part, not sitting here drinking fancy coffee with my fancy lady friend.'

'Lady friend?' I ask and we both laugh, embarrassed.

He reddens slightly again, making my heart beat faster. 'Well, you are my friend,' he says gruffly and our eyes meet. I feel my cheeks grow hot. I didn't factor in falling for someone so soon after James but I feel like I am tumbling gently in love with my blue-eyed farmer from next door.

He really is gorgeous but it goes deeper than that, I feel comfortable with him, like we're cut from the same kind of cloth.

'So,' he says, spotting Doris making a beeline for him across the stone floor and scooping her up, clearly relieved to have a distraction from the intensity of the moment. 'This party then. What's the dress code?'

29

Friday dawns grey and damp and once I've fed the animals it's almost lunchtime, so Mum and I go into the village. I've left all the Christmas decorations in the loft back in London so we plan to buy a few twinkly lights and maybe even a tree to make the house a bit Christmassy for the party. Mum is wearing festive red velvet ski pants with a bright green fleece and some gold moon boots and looks like a retired elf.

On the way she calls her neighbour Sally to ask after the dog. 'Thanks again for having him, Sal. He would've hated the farm – no place for a whippet like Mouse.' Sally fills in Mum on all the local news and I drive as Mum replies with a rally of responses. 'No! Really? Well, no surprise there, she always did have a face like a slapped you-know-what... He didn't?!'

I'm astonished there's so much gossip to catch up on, she's only been away for twenty-four hours.

Mum rolls her eyes at me and glove-puppets her hand into a yapping mouth. At last she falls silent then says, 'She's fine thank you, very happy, doing a great job on the farm, pedigree cattle, a rare-breed sow.' Mum pulls down the sun visor and pulls at her fringe in the little mirror on it. 'And she rescued the most darling cat. The house is beautiful, very cosy.' A pause. 'Yes I am,' she replies, 'very proud.'

I know Mum is just showing off to her neighbour but I'm touched and swallow a small lump down in my throat. She may not be able to say it to my face but maybe she is proud of me? She hangs up with 'Thanks again, Sally, don't know what I'd do without you, you're a good friend' just as we drive into the village square. 'Sally sends her love,' she says to me. 'She was very impressed with the farm, though you never know what she's really thinking, she's got more faces than the town hall clock that one.'

I park up, acutely aware that in front of us is the church and the graveyard where Dad is buried. I pretend to look for something in my bag and try to steal a glance at Mum. How must this feel? To return here after all these years? The last time Mum was here she was burying her husband, made a widow at thirty-seven. Like me, she must have tortured herself with the same if onlys – if only there hadn't been a storm, if only the cattle hadn't escaped, if only he hadn't used that stupid car. On top of these shared if onlys, I now knew about her own personal one: if only me and Fred hadn't argued before he left.

Mum is looking up at the church spire. 'Would you like to go take a look?' I ask gently.

'What at?' She looks genuinely confused.

'Dad's grave?'

'Oh, no thank you. Best not.'

She quickly gets out of the car and heads away from the church at a determined pace. I'm stunned. I don't know what reply I was expecting but certainly not one so callous. It's like I'd asked if she wanted to visit a Christmas market, something that wasn't quite up her street rather than the grave of her husband, my dad. If she feels nothing but resentment towards him in death (for leaving her? for his money troubles?) surely she could at least pretend for the sake of those still alive? She's heading for Gordan & Sons where on the forecourt are a dozen or so Christmas trees for sale.

'Ho, ho, ho,' booms GG, appearing from his shed office with a synthetic white beard on elastic over his actual beard and a Santa hat skew-whiff atop his head. He still has his oily overalls on.

'Didn't know your sister was in town, Josie.' He smiles.

'This is my mum Sandra.'

GG bows low, keeping his small button-like eyes on Mum's face. Mum flutters her stick-on eyelashes. Then he gasps, pointing, 'I *knew* it!' He slaps his thigh. 'I *knew* you looked familiar when we bumped into each other last month! It drove me bloody crackers for days trying to place you and now I know, Fred's missus, god rest his soul.'

'No,' we both reply at once, then she laughs. We are in sync sometimes at least.

'Mum's just visiting.'

'No, no,' insists GG. 'I never forget a face, I remember because you dropped some flowers you were carrying and as you walked off I remember thinking your face rang a bell.'

'No.' Mum calmly but curtly corrects GG. 'It wasn't me, I must have a doppelgänger.'

GG, whose skin is clearly thicker than a rhino's flank shrugs. 'Yup, you must have.' Though I notice him keep studying Mum's face.

We select a nice tree and GG lobs it through his netting machine and carries it to the car for us.

There's a festive feeling in the village and it looks as pretty as a Christmas biscuit tin. Lights are strung between the lamp posts and doors are decked out with holly wreaths. I take Mum into the Keys and we share a bap stuffed with local roast beef. Everyone welcomes Mum warmly and I can see she loves being the latest attraction in this sleepy village. Old Frank, who props up the bar most days, remembers Mum and his rheumy eyes grow wet when he recognises her.

In a bid to smooth the way for tomorrow's party I continue taking Mum on her meet-and-greet. We find Alex propping up the counter in the sweet shop chatting to Beth and they are both charm personified – the latter woos Mum with some complimentary wine gums. Then we stop by at the farm store for a few sets of twinkly lights.

I'm struck by how quickly Mum can turn – the mask doesn't slip, she just swaps them in the blink of an eye. I should know better than to be hurt by her disinterest in Dad's grave or pleased with her fleeting pride in me – I can't tell now in retrospect if she meant either of them.

I'm losing my determination to get to the bottom of what happened all those years ago – juggling her many moods all day is exhausting. I make us dinner and I give myself a pep talk. I need to know what Dad did wrong – how did he lose money? And, perhaps more importantly, why has Mum remained so hateful and bitter? What happened on that stormy night in 1982?

Over dinner I try again. I clear my throat. Before I can speak, she does.

'You've made some nice friends,' she says.

'Yeah, Beth is lovely. I'm lucky. Ruth is coming tomorrow too, all the way from Hampstead. She's getting a lift with the two Chrises. It's turning into a bit of a bash. Also a friend called Mary is coming, you'll love her, she's quite a character.'

'And Will?'

'Yes. Will is coming. I'm worried I gave you a bad impression of him and his family when I was upset last week.'

She looks at me now. 'I know the Hockleys well enough thank you very much. Nothing that you said altered my opinion of them.'

'Meaning?'

'Meaning, you should stay away from Jack Hockley. Admittedly he's the best of a bad bunch compared to his criminal brothers but he's always been a sad, bitter little man and I imagine the apple hasn't fallen far from the tree with his son.'

'You're wrong,' I say. 'Will is a good person. I like him.'

'You like him?' She sing-songs in a mocking tone. 'What are you? A teenager mooning around over a pop star? You're not even divorced from James yet. You did *so* well to bag a man like James, you should be concentrating on winning him back, not gallivanting around with a crush on some bumpkin.' She looks furious.

So this is why she doesn't approve of Will, she still hopes James and I can get back together.

'For god's sake, Mum, can't you accept James and I are over? He's moved on, so have I and it's about time you did.'

We silently eat our food but I've lost my appetite, mashed potato carpets my tongue, making me almost gag. I pick up my glass of water with trembling hands.

Cortisol is flooding my veins. I can't resist picking at the scab. 'I don't know why you pretend to care so much about what I do. It's always been all about you.'

'What on earth are you talking about?' She lowers her cutlery and sits back in her chair.

'Growing up you made all the bad stuff that happened about you. I was never given a chance to grieve for Dad. You stole all the limelight, all the grieving time...' My voice wobbles.

'Not now, Josie, I don't want to talk about it,' she says calmly.

'Well I do, Mum,' I say, 'though today it seemed like you couldn't give a shit about Dad. You didn't even have the decency to visit his grave. Poor Dad – lying there unloved because for nearly forty years you've been too busy playing the poor widow.'

'Josie,' she warns.

'No,' I say firmly. 'No, I won't stop. Do you know someone else looks after his grave? Puts ribbons and flowers on the tree where he died alone and in the rain and darkness.' My voice cracks, years of pain pouring out.

She looks up at me now, shocked.

'See?' It's satisfying to see her hurt. 'Someone cares, out there someone at least loved him!' I know I've gone too far but I can't help myself. Her eyes fill with tears.

'I loved him,' she whispers.

'Well, you have a funny way of showing it!' I shout. I stand up and my chair scrapes back noisily startling Doris who scampers from the room. I want to escape before my own tears come, I don't want her to see. I'm not quick enough.

'I do show it!' she shouts, which stops me in my tracks.

'How?' I scream back.

'It's me.'

'What is?'

'The flowers, the grave, the ribbons on the tree, it's all me.'

I turn. 'I don't believe you,' I whisper.

'It's true.' She takes her napkin and dabs at her eyes. 'That's why that stupid man recognised me today.'

'GG?'

'I tried my best to look incognito, hood up, but I dropped the flowers and he helped me. Would've been more suspicious if I'd hurried away.'

I let this sink in. 'So, you're telling me that you've been coming back to the village, the place where you drummed it into me you'd never return? All the years I wanted to visit Dad's grave... it would've helped me.'

'It's only been a recent thing, the past few years,' she says now, in a smaller voice, 'since I've got older. Since Clive died.'

'He died years ago, Mum, why couldn't you have told me?'

'You were down in London. I just came every few weeks...'

The room tips. I can't believe this. 'You're the most selfish person I know.'

'Well you know nothing!' she retorts.

'I know nothing because you won't tell me.'

'All these years you've hero-worshipped your dad, but he broke this family.'

'How?' I croak. 'Tell me.'

'I can't,' she says. 'Don't you see?'

'No, I don't, Mum. I need answers. Were those Dad's car keys in the fire? I looked them up. Seems a bit of a coincidence. Land Rover keys don't just end up in a fire, so how the hell did they get there?' I might be grasping at straws but I just want to keep hammering at her with whatever tools I can grab until the dam bursts and she talks.

She straightens, her voice is icy. 'I knew this was a bad idea. I should go.'

'No,' I say.

'Yes.' She stands, placing her napkin on the table. 'I'm an old lady now, Josie, and I want to make things better, but I don't know how.'

'Let me help.' I'm crying now.

'You can't,' she says quietly, 'and this is making me ill. I will leave first thing, let you enjoy your party.' And she walks unsteadily from the room.

I barely sleep, the night's events playing over and over in my mind, fury at my mum mixed with guilt for confronting her. I must have dozed off because I wake to a watery grey light coming through a gap in the curtains.

It is late, eight a.m., and already I can hear the heifers starting to call for breakfast. The coffee is strong and hot, soothing me and making the room click into focus. I spot Mum's car keys on the side near the sink and slip them into my pocket. I don't want her running away from me, from the past again.

30

When I get back from feeding up I'm feeling better. Penny and the piglets cheer me and Nicola the Piggola, who has now caught up with her siblings, always wants fuss and nuzzles up against my wellies until I give in and drop into the straw for cuddles. Back inside, the Christmas tree is still bare, standing in the corner of the lounge, so I busy myself winding lights around it and drape more along the windowsills. Simple but effective, the farmhouse immediately feels festive and cosy.

Mum comes down the stairs just as I'm sweeping out the grate to make a fire. I notice she's dressed and looks ready to leave. Today is party day and I do not want her to go or the small progress we've made will be lost.

'Morning,' I say brightly from my kneeling position by the fire. 'I've made coffee and there's croissants too.'

She pads silently through to the kitchen. I feel the car keys in my pocket.

When I go into the kitchen I decide to come straight out with it. By 'it' I mean, if not the truth then an embroidered version of it, made pretty to appeal to her ego. I know exactly what she likes to hear because it's a script I've been reciting a version of for most of my adult life.

'I'm sorry. Let's forget last night.'

She looks up as though she doesn't remember what was said.

'Please don't go. Let's have a nice time. It's my party today and I'm nervous – I need you, Mum.' She goes to speak but I rattle on. 'I really want everyone to meet you, I want to show you off.' She snorts. 'Come on,' I cajole. 'You're so good at these things.'

'It would be a shame to miss the party.' Bingo!

'It won't be the same without you,' I add.

'Really?' she says. 'You really think that?'

'A hundred per cent.' I do my best smile.

The day flies by. I take delivery of a huge tray of fresh pasties that just need baking off and Beth drops round surprising me with a pile of home-made choc-chip scones she's rustled up. I see a small van bump up the lane and a young lad wrestles a huge bouquet of flowers out from the back and hands them over with a bottle of Dom Pérignon in a gift bag. I know only one person who is this thoughtful and this flash, and I'm right. The card attached says: *Good luck with your new home, have a great party, sorry we can't be there, James xxx*. I presume Chloe told him, the sorry we can't be there clearly a jokey reference to his lack of invitation. I just about squeeze the bunch into two vases and a water jug, though they look slightly out of place in their farmhouse surroundings.

Chloe confirms by text she can't make it and Fay sends an email with a dozen pics of us from past parties through the ages with the words: *You'd better not have this much fun without me. Love you.*

Mum and I concentrate on not talking about anything of importance and instead on party preparations, spending the day tidying the house and pushing the sofa and chairs to the walls to create more space. At teatime the food shop arrives, which is mainly wine and posh crisps.

Our house parties and Christmas get-togethers in London were usually catered. 'Why stress yourself?' James would say. Even the tree we had was always eight-feet tall, otherwise it'd look ridiculous, dwarfed by the high ceilings. I look over to our squat little number from GG's strewn with fairy lights. Its bottom is full and the top wonky, the flames from the fire reflected a dozen times over in the silver baubles. It feels twinkly and cosy, like the Christmases of my childhood.

Even the outdoors feels more festive up here, the fields glistening with frost at dawn and dusk, the robin perched on the bare hawthorn – a real life Christmas card. London never felt properly festive at Christmas, just busier. And noisier. The streets, the pubs, the shops full of people clamouring over each other. Like Christmas was just another task to tick off on the capital's to-do list. I sigh contentedly and adjust the mistletoe dangling down from the kitchen doorway, hoping to lure Will underneath it at some point.

I leave Mum mopping the kitchen floor and go to feed up. I hear the throaty rumble of Will's quad bike pull up.

'By 'eck, I love a woman in a waterproof trouser,' he says and I lift my jumper to show the attached braces, giving one a twang. 'Saucy.' He grins.

I'm thoroughly loving this flirty development in our relationship. 'I need to get a lock for that front field gate,' I tease, 'all sorts of ruffians keep cutting through.'

I see he has one hand behind his back and feel a blush spread to my neck as he reveals he's holding a little posy of fresh flowers – primrose and holly.

'For me?' I ask coquettishly.

'No, for the pig,' he deadpans.

I prop them up in the water trough and he helps me bed down Penny.

'All ready for the big bash?'

'Yes, I suppose, a bit nervous but it'll be fine.'

'You'll be grand,' he says. 'Why nervous?'

'Well, you know, worlds colliding and all that.'

'Speaking of that, I was thinking of maybe bringing my dad... just for the first hour or so, thought it'd be good for him?' His voice has grown gruff like he's embarrassed. 'He's... calmer and unless I force him out he's going to get more... weird... stuck inside like a bloody hermit.'

'Course.' I grin. *Shit, what if he causes a scene?* Then I catch myself – I've done nothing wrong, I can't control the way everyone feels, I can't be responsible for his behaviour or my mum's for that matter. If there's old wounds there, maybe it's not such a bad thing they're opened instead of festering. 'You should definitely bring him,' I say.

We finish up and he makes to head off, first stopping to give me a hug. 'Good luck, see you later,' he says into the top of my hair. It is unexpected but welcomed. His jumper is warm and smells of hay and diesel. His chest feels firm underneath, like I could happily nestle there for say, a thousand years. Instead, the hug is fleeting. He opens his arms and releases me though I stand motionless. 'Better get these in water,' I say awkwardly, gesturing to the flowers he brought. 'Aye.' He smiles, then strides away to his quad bike.

In the house Mum is busying herself straightening the kitchen chairs. I can tell right away she was nosying through the window and witnessed the hug. I don't say anything, I don't want to rock the boat. I put the flowers into a little tin milk jug and they look perfect.

Mum side-eyes them. 'How... quaint,' she sing-songs.

I don't care and instead enjoy the butterflies that are still dancing deliciously around my tummy.

I shower and even shave my legs, armpits and bikini line, just in case. Having embraced my inner bumpkin I'm out of practice with this beautifying malarky and nick my shin, scarlet blood gushing down my leg. I dab at the cut and pull on black tights, black heels and a little black cashmere dress that feels obscenely slinky against my skin after so many weeks of overalls and wellies.

There is a tooting of a car horn and I rush to the door. Ruth's arrival is like the rush of heat when you step out of an airplane on holiday. 'Whit-woo! Look at you! Stunning!' she shouts as she engulfs me in a huge hug and her familiar scent of spearmint gum and lavender fills my lungs. The two Chrises unfold themselves from their car and pick their way around the puddles in the yard. It is barely six p.m. and pitch dark, though a floodlight illuminates the yard enough for Chris Crab to spot the pale faces of the heifers watching curiously. 'Oh my god, cows!'

'Yes,' I laugh, 'well spotted.'

'Now you've got to be the sexiest farmer I've ever seen,' they say in the light of the kitchen, making me give them a twirl.

All three gush and wow and gasp as I show them round the house. 'So rustic, which is *huge* at the moment,' offers Other Chris with a smile as he opens a bottle of champagne.

'We can hardly take it all in,' says Crab. 'Our Josie, so far away from civilisation and many many miles from a Waitrose but here you are – not just surviving but thriving.' His voice is filled with emotion. 'So, a toast to you, Josie and to thriving.' We clink glasses.

'Delicious,' I say as the vintage champers hits the back of my throat.

'Well count yourself lucky we're not toasting your new life with a glug of SUP.'

Other Chris shoots Crab a look. 'What?' he says theatrically. 'We can't not tell her, Chris! Anyway, Jose, you'll laugh.'

'OK, go on.'

'So as we were packing up the Tesla, Paul walks past and we get chatting.'

'Neighbour Paul?'

'No, Paul Hollywood.'

'I wish!' swoons Other Chris.

'He's obsessed!' tuts Crab. 'Anyway, yes, neighbour Paul. And I mentioned we were off to see you.'

'They ham it up obviously,' interjects Ruth. 'Made it sound like you were having a get-together at your country estate that'd put a Balmoral shindig to shame.'

'And Paul says "Hang on a mo" and trots off as fast as his Clarks can carry him. By the time we've locked up the house he's brought Sukey out with him and they're lugging a massive box of their SUP smoothie drinks between them.'

Other Chris leans in and says in a simpering voice I instantly recognise as Sukey's, 'For Josie's house-warming. Please send her my best. I know we didn't always see eye to eye but hopefully she'll enjoy these.'

'Wow,' I snort, 'so her calling me a "bitter old woman" in front of a hundred party guests translates as us not "seeing eye to eye"?'

'Yup. I know right? We were running late and still had to drop Muffin off at the dog sitters so I just bunged them in the car.'

'I tasted one on the way up and honestly, grim,' shudders Ruth. 'I wouldn't tip that stuff on my weeds. Spirulina and matcha tastes like licking a goat's undercarriage.'

'Urgh,' I say, 'so where are they now?'

'Well, imagine my horror when en route I accidentally left them on a picnic bench outside Watford Gap services – though judging from the people there, shuffling around chomping on burgers, they could do with the vitamins so every cloud...'

I laugh. 'You're a very wicked person, Crab.'

'I know! That's why you love me.'

We sit around the table and finish our champagne before the madness of the party commences. It feels like we're back in Hampstead, the four of us drinking and laughing and putting the world to rights. Then I feel the stone floor beneath my shoes and hear the occasional moo from outside and breathe a sigh of relief that I'm properly home where I belong, not stuck in London.

They fill me in on the journey and the hotel they're staying at in the next village. 'Makes Fawlty Towers look like the Four Seasons,' says Chris Crab.

'Nonsense,' chides Ruth, 'you're just spoiled. Not all hotels offer kimchi martinis and hot and cold running celebrity clientele.'

'Hot and cold water would be a bonus though.'

I'm loving their light-hearted squabbling, it's like the good old days.

Mum comes down from her bath, glammed up to the nines in a bright red trouser suit and, of course, the two Chrises make a huge fuss of her. 'Always so glamorous,' coos Other Chris. 'Didn't know you were cabin crew for Virgin Atlantic, Sandra,' teases Crab, but Mum just giggles and says, 'Cheeky!'

Ruth is polite and warm to Mum. She knows the stress Mum has put me through over the years so I can appreciate she's making the effort for me.

Mum of course asks all about James, which the trio deftly sweep under the carpet while pouring her a glass of Shloer bought especially for her.

Mary arrives from Shearness sporting wide-legged trousers and an impressively big blow-dry. She holds aloft two jars of heather honey 'to bring you years of sweetness in your new home'. I remove one of the lids, the smell of honey always reminds me of Fay and ridiculously I feel tears spring to my eyes. Luckily nobody seems to notice. Ruth brings Mary a glass and fills it with champagne.

'Thank you...?'

'Ruth.'

'Ruth.' Mary smacks her lips as if tasting the word then takes a sip and they clink glasses. I study the label on one of the jars and above a simple sketch of a cross-eyed cat looking at the fat bee landed on its nose is the word 'Shearness' in curly script. 'Yes,' Mary says proudly, 'from my own hives – we have six now. The hotel must keep evolving, Josie, and tempting new people with our delicious produce, because without guests I'm just a mad cat lady in a tumbledown wreck.' Ruth laughs a little too loudly at the quip and I see her touch her hair self-consciously.

'I'm still relatively new to the beekeeping game, about a year into it. I collected every drop in these jars and have the stings to prove it.'

'Well if you need anyone to suck out the poison I could help,' Ruth offers.

Mary pauses for a second and I hold my breath. Then she roars with laughter and Ruth looks thrilled and relieved in equal measure. I do believe they're flirting.

Guests start to arrive and before long my kitchen is heaving. GG, Beth and Alex are holding court in one corner, Mary and Ruth are swaying to the Christmas music chatting away like old pals and Mum is laughing at Arthur the chimney sweep's jokes. The two Chrises are deep in conversation with Jonathan Beadle, the estate agent, and his small but very vocal wife Cathy making me briefly wonder if they're grilling him on a potential holiday home up here. Looking at the crowd – the pub landlord, the girl from the bakery and her pal – it clicks that about half are here because they heard about the party on the village grapevine, then collared me on my errands and invited themselves. This is what community feels like, right here in my kitchen, getting sloshed and listening to Wham!

The only person very much not here is Will. I keep scanning the yard for his van; unless he's going to quad it over the fields? Not with his dad on the back surely? I envisage the big bike on its side in my freezing field, the two of them trapped underneath it in the darkness. Or maybe his dad has had one of his episodes again and is refusing to come. I check my phone again. Nothing.

'You OK?' It's Ruth. Her breath smells of champagne. She's glowing.

'I'm fine. OK, I'm not. Will is very late, I'm just a bit worried.'

'He's a farmer,' she says, 'you know yourself that he could've been delayed by any number of animal-based issues.'

'Yeah,' I say weakly.

'Come on away from the window, a watched pot never boils. Let's get you a drink. I'm starving by the way.'

'Oh shit.' I remember suddenly. 'The pasties need going in.'

Ruth helps me to load trays of pasties into the AGA then pours me a drink, links my arm and pulls me into the lounge where she steers me towards the sofa. The girls from the bakery are in there, chatting in a corner.

'You and Mary seem to be getting on well,' I say.

'Yes. I must say it's rather lovely to flirt. It's been a while. You know I shut up shop down there years ago but still... it felt lovely.'

'She's great you know. Shearness is beautiful.'

'Yes she told me all about it. Been in the family for generations but the upkeep is astonishing. I think she's a marvel.'

'Absolutely. You should go one day.'

'She's already invited me! I may even extend my trip and stay a night before heading back to London. I've no dog duties till Tuesday.'

'Great,' I say, then add in mock warning, 'did she mention the cats though?'

'I love cats,' Ruth says. 'I'd be quite happy to be surrounded by so many pretty pussies.'

We laugh.

'You must miss Fay?' she asks. 'How's she doing?'

'She's great, very happy in Boston. She knows me better than anyone and knows Mum too. I could do with her support now, it's been quite the time with Mum.'

'I'm no Fay,' says Ruth, 'but you could try me.'

I give her a potted version of the story so far – Mum saying Dad had money troubles, the keys in the fireplace, Mum secretly visiting the village.

'Keep going with her,' she urges. 'I feel like the whole truth is just around the corner.'

I'm distracted by headlights sweeping across the yard. Will. I leap up and Ruth smiles at me knowingly.

I tug at my dress a little and head into the kitchen to welcome him. Ruth follows. The door swings open with a rush of cold air and standing there is not Will but Chloe. My jaw drops – I'm ecstatic and astounded all at once. I look round in surprise and catch Ruth's eye. She knew all along.

'Surprise!' says Chloe and the room gives a cheer. I hug her tightly to me. She smells of the cold and I bury my face in her hair. 'But... how?'

'Well, I didn't want to miss the party of the year and see the place that's my heritage.'

I glance behind her at the retreating minicab. 'And Aspen?' I ask, expecting him to be hiding like the first time I met him. Her face clouds over and she gives a little shake of the head.

'Right, come on,' I say pulling her through the crowds as she struggles out of her coat. 'Grandma is over here, and the two Chrises and I can't wait to introduce you to my new friends.'

'Hang on, Mum.' She pulls me back. 'Can we go somewhere quieter?'

I stop. 'Oh my god, what's wrong?'

She breaks into a broad grin. 'Nothing is wrong, I just want to give you your present.'

We slip upstairs and into my room. I sit on my bed, close my eyes and hold out my hands like a child, which makes Chloe laugh. 'OK, hold on.' I can hear her rummaging in her bag then a package is placed on my palms and I open my eyes. It is the shape of a hardback book. I gently rip the purple tissue paper and inside is a thin box. I can feel Chloe's eyes on me. 'Go on,' she says gently and sits down next to me on the bed. I open the box at one end and slide out a silver frame. Inside it is the photograph of me and my dad, the one where we're on the tractor together, my favourite one.

I gasp. 'Oh god, Chloe, you're gonna wreck my mascara.' I pull her into a hug.

'You still have the original but I nicked it and got it copied when I was down staying with you, I just needed to find the perfect occasion to give it to you.'

'This is the perfect moment,' I say, dabbing at my eyes with my little finger.

'I wanted you to feel like grandad was here with you.'

'I do. I love it and I love you, my darling.'

We go downstairs and I place the picture on the windowsill in the kitchen, the place where I often stand at the sink looking out on to the yard, daydreaming about seeing Dad rumble past on his tractor.

The party really is in full swing and by ten p.m. I'm feeling quite drunk. The pasties were a hit and soaked up some of the booze but I keep glancing up hoping to see Will, just arrived, rosy-cheeked with the cold and full of apologies.

On Chloe's advice I ring him but it goes straight to voicemail. 'Sorry,' she says. 'Don't know why I'm giving relationship advice, I'm clearly useless.' Turns out Aspen, despite the floppy fringe and organic socks, is a bit of a control freak and put down Chloe one too many times. They're on 'an extended break. For the next decade or so', she smiles ruefully.

'Seems to me,' I say, 'you're very good at relationships – half the skill is knowing when they're not working.'

I go to tickle up the kitchen and find Crab in there amongst the crowd, topping up his glass. 'Hey,' he says putting an arm around me, shouting a little over the hubbub. 'I know I told you earlier but I just want to say, me and Chris are extremely proud of you. We were so worried when you left.'

'I know, I could tell by the way you kept saying, "There's no shame in coming back if it's not for you".'

'Yes... and we may have had a teeny bet on how long you'd last.'

'You didn't?' I laugh, outraged.

'I said two weeks and Chris said a month, so neither of us won.'

'Unbelievable.'

'We're so pleased you've proved us wrong, Jose.' He hiccups. 'We bloody love you and we miss you terribly but we're beyond thrilled to see you look so at home. It suits you here. This place is impressive. *You're* impressive.'

'Thanks, Crab,' I say, 'I love you too,' and I mean it. I extricate myself from his hug as he heads off to find Chris and I take out some of the empties. It's so noisy in there, the music is cranked up and the lights are dimmed – everyone going wild to Rihanna and Calvin Harris' 'We Found Love'. The bass is really thumping and I think not for the first time it's a good job our nearest neighbour is over a mile away. Talking of my nearest neighbour, where the hell is he?

I slip my heels off and put my wellies on and stagger outside with an armful of empty bottles, heading for the recycle bins by the coal shed. The cold hits me like a slap as I crunch over the ground, my warm breath visible in the chill black. As I put the last of the bottles in the bin I feel a hand on my shoulder. I drop the bottle the last few inches and it lands with a deafening clang as I yelp. Who is out here lurking in the pitch darkness? I spin to find Will standing there.

'What the hell?' I shout.

'I'm sorry, I'm sorry.' He's half-laughing, holding his hands up like I'm pointing a gun at him. 'I thought it'd be funny, I'm so sorry.'

'Fuck's sake you gave me such a fright!' I feel dizzy with the adrenaline dump. I lean on the bin for support. 'You don't look that sorry... Oh my god,' I say, heart thumping.

For now I've forgotten the cold despite wearing a thin dress. The yard security light springs on, illuminating his dark blue eyes, his mop of hair, his shy smile. God, he's gorgeous. Even in the same navy jumper he always wears. My stomach twists.

'Honestly.' I playfully thwack him on the arm.

'I know, I messed up.' He's laughing properly now. 'Your face though. And that noise, you sounded like a goose laying a rugby ball. Look at that dress though.' He gives a low whistle.

'You're an idiot,' I state matter-of-factly.

'And you're cold,' he says, putting an arm around me, opening up his jacket like a bird's wing and folding me in under it. He's much taller than me and twice as broad, making me feel small and secure nestled under his arm.

'Where have you been?' I ask, sounding grumpier than I mean to.

'I'm a grandpa,' he announces.

I stop and turn to him. 'What? How?' I ask coolly.

'Fliss,' he says, 'started pupping the minute I was in my finery ready to leave for here. Ruined my one good shirt an' all.'

My heart restarts. 'Oh wow, congratulations. She OK?'

'Yeah, she's grand. Got five pups, Sprollies I believe they're called thanks to her visit to the Yates' springer spaniel.'

'Are they cute?'

He nods begrudgingly. 'Yeah, yeah I suppose so. Some are chocolate spotty, others black with patches. You'll have to come round and pick one, I'll do you a deal.' He grins. 'Dad's stayed home to look after them, think he was chuffed to have a legitimate reason to not come.'

We stop walking. The yard light blinks off but I can still see his face in the golden glow of the kitchen window. He looks serious now, his eyes searching my face. 'Sorry I was so late,' he says. He gently tips my chin up with his finger so our eyes meet. His lips part slightly as he leans down. We are going to kiss. At last. I feel suddenly woozy with the champagne and the excitement. I rise slightly on my tiptoes to meet him halfway. I feel his sweet warm breath on my upper lip as our mouths come together.

'JOSIE, NOOOOOOOO!' screams a voice.

We spring apart like startled teenagers, a fraction before our mouths meet. It is Mum, she's on the doorstep and looks distraught. She hurries towards us and grabs me. 'No!' she shouts again, pulling at my arm as though saving me from an attacker.

'Mum, get off.' I wrestle my arm from her grasp but she claws at the sleeve of my dress. 'What are you doing? Mum calm down.'

'I will *not* calm down,' she shrieks again, looking at Will fearfully.

He takes a step towards her and she backs away, dragging me with her. The commotion has attracted a small audience – the two Chrises, Chloe and Beth are all spilling out from the kitchen and into the yard. Mum is making a huge scene.

'Mum what's going on?'

She only has eyes for Will. 'You stay away,' she hisses at Will. 'You stay away from my daughter.'

'But—' he begins.

'NO!' she shrieks again. Has she been drinking?

'Come on, Sandra.' It is Ruth, by Mum's side, trying to gently lead her back towards the house but she still has a hold of me. I'm thirteen again – Mum wild-eyed and drunk, causing a scene, hurting me. The other guests have heard the shouting and someone's stopped the music. People tipsily wander outside.

I loosen the grip of her fingers from my dress and step away from her towards Will. Chloe is now at Mum's other elbow, trying to pull her away too.

'OK, OK, if this is what you want,' Mum screams at us. 'I didn't want to tell you this now but you leave me no choice.'

'Mum, are you drunk? Get inside, you're crazy.'

'I'm not crazy,' she shrieks. I've hit a raw nerve. 'And I've not touched a drop. I'm trying to save you from him.' She jabs a finger towards Will who flinches. He glances at me confused.

'What? But why? Why can't you be happy for me?' I realise I'm crying.

'Whatever is going on, let's get inside and sort it out,' says Will, putting an arm around my shoulders and gently steering me towards the house.

'He's right, come on, Sandra,' urges Ruth.

'I will never let you be with him,' she screams.

'Why?' I scream back. She shakes her head. 'Why?' I repeat, even louder this time.

She looks at me, her face stricken. 'Because he's your brother,' she whispers.

I laugh. An ugly, tear-sodden laugh that catches in my throat with a wet gurgle. I don't understand. What the fuck? The ground tips towards me and I sway, I feel like I've been shoved. I think I'm going to be sick. I look to Will but his eyes are fixed on Mum, his face twisted, frozen in shock like a mask.

Mum is panting like a dog that's been dragged from a fight. She looks pale too, and is leaning on Ruth.

Chloe snakes an arm around her other shoulder. 'Come on, let's get you inside,' she says softly.

The party is over.

31

Chris and Crab come to find me, hugging me tightly. 'We're only round the corner, yes? We'll be there all tomorrow morning, promise you'll call if you need us.' I nod dumbly. The rest of the guests slide away into the night, some squeezing me sympathetically on the shoulder or awkwardly murmuring, 'Thanks for a great evening.' No doubt they're all off to reconvene at the pub; this undignified scene will keep the local gossips going for the next three Christmases.

Will is sitting in silence at the table with Mum surrounded by leftover party detritus, bowls of crisp crumbs, a corkscrew, crumpled napkins. I want a drink, so walk past them and glug red wine into a glass. Ruth is at the AGA, boiling the kettle while Chloe picks her way around the room, putting empty paper cups, plates and beer bottles into a black bin bag.

The kettle begins to whistle, tearing a strip through the silence.

I sit heavily in a chair.

Mum tries to lift her mug of tea but her hands are shaking and it spills, the liquid looking blood-like as it seeps through the scarlet tablecloth. Ruth dabs at it then gives up and quietly pads from the room, Chloe following.

'I'm sorry, Will.' Mum shakes her head. 'I really didn't want it to all come out like this.'

'I don't understand,' Will says almost to himself. I feel wretched for him. And for me too.

Mum sighs heavily, the world on her shoulders as ever. Please don't let her twist this into her own personal tragedy. She's not the only victim here.

'This is madness. Why would you say that?' Will says, clearing his throat and looking straight at Mum, his dark blue eyes shiny with tears. 'Hello?' he almost shouts now, waving a hand close to Mum's face. She flinches. 'How can you sit there so calmly, you need to explain.'

'After Fred died there was a mountain of paperwork to go through – mainly unpaid bills. We'd been dragged through the mill finan-cially and we were on our knees.' She sniffs. 'Fred was never very organised with his accounts and I was naively hoping to find some-thing in the paperwork that would save us and the farm. In fact I found the opposite.'

'Go on,' I say. Mum has a rapt audience of two. Does she relish this drama?

'I found Fred's life insurance. I had no idea he'd taken any out. It had only been taken out a few months before so it wasn't worth much and I didn't want to cash it in because – ' she looks up at Will guiltily – 'alongside me and Josie it named you, Will.'

Will's brow crumples in confusion. 'Me? Why?'

Mum smirks then softens, as if speaking to a small child. 'Why do you think, Will?'

'I don't understand?'

'You are Fred's biological son, Will. He and your mother always flirted. Mind you,' she can't resist, 'she flirted with most of the men in the village.'

Will winces at the sting of her words. He sits straighter now. I curse myself for noticing his broad chest, his long straight fingers splayed out on the table – this man who an hour ago I hoped could be my lover, who now could be my brother. My head swims.

'Hang on, you're saying they had an affair? Did Dad tell you this?'

'No.' Mum juts out her chin and looks up to me. 'There were rumours about her though, and me and your dad had been through a rough time. I did the maths and you would've been about two when she fell pregnant. I was still in a bad way...'

'What do you mean?'

'Well, now I suppose they'd call it post-natal depression but back then it was baby blues. I was in a very dark place, Josie, and I'm afraid I took it out on your dad, something I'll always regret. You know we were very much in love for a long time, me and Fred. I think I will always love him despite what he did.' She sniffs, becomes more businesslike. 'Anyway I know it was tough for him. I presume he turned to Ruby for comfort and got that and then some.'

Post-natal depression? She's never told me this before. I'm back in the little scruffy terrace, her screaming at me one minute, weeping the next.

Will, who'd been fiddling and folding a paper party hat slides it away from him now, as if it's the incriminating paperwork we're discussing. 'This is all a load of bollocks. Jack is my dad. A document doesn't prove anything.' Will shakes his head in disbelief. 'Let me see it. Where is it now?'

For the first time she looks guilty. She starts to tear at the edge of the balled-up tissue in her hand. 'I don't have it. I panicked. I was in the attic, surrounded by dusty boxes and clutter. It was claustrophobic. I didn't really understand – the words, the numbers all blurred together, I got in a real state, imagining all sorts. I had a lot to cope with.' She glances imploringly at both of us. 'First the shock of Fred's death, then finding out about you, it was all too much. I convinced myself the policy meant that you'd be entitled to a third of everything – that even in some way we might owe you.'

'What did you do?' he whispers.

She looks upwards now, studying the ceiling.

'Mum?' I almost shout. I hate the way she's slowly dragging Will over the coals like this.

'I was trying to protect you,' she says, glaring at me, her voice growing louder with each word so the 'you' rings out like a warning.

'Where is it?' I hiss.

'Gone,' she says. She softens as she looks to Will and she tips her words out like she's emptying them from a sack, relieved to be free of their weight. 'I was not in my right mind, I was grieving. I thought nobody would ever need to know. I burnt it in the sink. I wanted to forget what I'd seen and let sleeping dogs lie. Those papers proved your mum's infidelity, Will, and might've meant we owed you inheritance. They were dangerous. I wanted rid.'

'Oh my god, Mum.'

'Don't "Oh my god" me. It was different times – we couldn't google back then, I didn't understand what all the implications were, I was entirely alone. I just know that Will was named on there, clear as day alongside you. I knew we were moving away and your two paths would never meet. But then they did.'

So that's why she was so upset I was returning. So keen to play the concerned mother dashing to my side when I mentioned Will.

She looks to Will. 'I presumed your mum either didn't realise or wanted it to be kept a secret. I just tried to forget what I knew. You've always been the apple of Jack's eye; with Fred gone what would've been the point of ripping your family apart? They'd been through enough, I actually felt sorry for your mum—'

Will cuts her off by standing up unsteadily, his chair screeching on the stone floor. As he does, a beam of light sweeps across the yard and a door slams. A figure strides towards the house. The door swings open and there stands Jack. He looks taller than the last time I saw him, clean shaven and younger as if invigorated by the fight before him.

'Dad!' Will says. 'You OK?'

'Aye, lad I am.' He looks at each of us with a grim nod. 'Well I was. I was enjoying a nice quiet pint down The Three Keys to wet the puppies' heads when all hell breaks loose, half the village tumbling through the door squawking like hens with a fox in the chicken run.' Mum looks mortified. 'But they all fell quiet when they saw me, looked like they wanted the ground to swallow them up. T'was only Beth brave enough to take me away from the gawping crowds and fill me in on the twaddle that madam here – ' he nods at Mum – 'had been spouting about me and my son.'

Will goes to Jack now and hugs him. Jack looks surprised but not displeased with this sudden show of affection.

'Hey, come on, come on,' and I realise that Will's shoulders are shaking as Jack holds him. 'Come on, lad, let's sort this out, eh?'

Both men sit down opposite me and Mum and I almost laugh with relief. I know Mum sees it too. Until now I'd never seen Will sitting calmly side by side with his dad. Everything, from the shape of their eyebrows, the matching frowns, the squareness of the jaw to the Cupid's arrow of their top lip are identical. It is almost spooky. Will's face like a neat pencil tracing of Jack's, just on less wrinkled paper. I want to crack open some bubbly, spraying it like I've won the grand prix. Will is one hundred per cent not my brother.

The two times I'd come across Jack his lips had been curled into a furious sneer, his face obscured by a darkened doorway the first time and by rage the second. Now, next to Will, I could see the handsome young man Jack once was, both in his own features and the carbon copy to his left.

Mum studies their faces. 'Well,' she says in a small voice, 'I know what I saw, I saw your name on Jack's life insurance document, Will, and I presumed it meant he was your father. But... looking at you both now... I mean, don't forget you were a little boy when all this happened and you favoured your mum but now...'

Jack clears his throat and speaks slowly, holding Mum's gaze. 'You mean to say that half the village – in fact probably most of it by now seeing as gossip spreads like wildfire round here – believe that Will is not my son because of a piece of paper you saw forty years ago?'

Mum goes to speak but Jack cuts her off. 'You know what, Sandra, we go way back. I've not seen you for decades. And you've not changed one bit – ' I see Mum's eyes brighten but I know this comment has a sting in the tail – 'you're still a nasty meddling bitch.'

Mum's mouth forms a perfect 'O' and I go to speak, but Will beats me to it. 'Now, Dad.'

'Don't, Will,' Jack says, his eyes still firmly planted on Mum. 'Don't defend her. You owe her nothing. Her and her family ruined us.'

Mum draws her head back like a snake about to strike. 'Oh here we go, Jack. You still clinging on to that belief are you, like a man clinging to the wreck of a sinking ship? A ship that *you* helped sink by the way!' Jack's face hardens, his lips thinning. 'You were a grown man when you and Fred made all those decisions – you have to take some responsibility for your actions instead of just blaming Fred. He didn't force you to sign on the dotted line, you gambled on an investment and you lost. You and Fred were as bad as each other, throwing away your families' futures on a hare-brained scheme behind our backs! Me and Ruby should've banged your bloody heads together.'

Mum's accent, refined over the years by dinners at the golf club with Clive, has grown broader during this sparring match, her vowels flattening into the local vernacular. Will and I regress too, watching wide-eyed as the grown-up argue.

'Oh aye,' Jack snarls, 'Fred had nowt to do with me almost losing the farm, being up to my eyeballs in debt... losing–' He stops and gulps in air. He glances at Will. His voice lowers, 'We lost everything. It broke us. And Fred bloody knew it. Why else would he try to look after Will financially through the bloody life insurance? Because he *knew*. He *knew* it was his fault. I've hated the man these last forty years but at least *he* had the decency to know he'd messed up. Fred named Will on those documents because he was guilty and was trying to make it up to us, not because he was secretly Will's father. And if *you* can't at least see even now that it was all his fault then you're more stupid than I thought, which is saying something.' He slumps back in his chair, spent.

The room falls silent. The coloured fairy lights I've strewn along the windowsill look garish in this new sombre world. They pulse on and off behind Mum, in turn illuminating then plunging into darkness the photograph of Dad and me on the tractor. One second he's there, the next he's gone.

'So this is why you didn't want me coming home?' I say to Mum. I surprise myself that I call it home. 'Because of a feud over money? Over a get-rich scheme? Because of a stupid assumption about Will? And you,' I say shaking my head at Jack, 'that's why you hate me? Because of what my dad did? Was it you ringing the estate agent's, nearly running me off the road, spying on me from the bottom of the lane?'

Jack meets my eye. 'How do you think it felt the day I heard you'd been snooping around up here?' he growls. 'Coming up from London, splashing the cash, when thanks to your father my son was denied the privileges you had growing up?'

The kitchen falls quiet.

'Dad.' Will speaks now. 'You're wrong. She didn't have it easy growing up, she probably had it harder than me.' He glances at Mum as he speaks.

'Well she – ' Jack jabs a finger at me but keeps his eyes locked on Will – 'at least went to bloody university didn't she? You didn't!'

'She worked for it, paid her own way,' Will shouts now. 'You know nothing, Dad, none of this is Josie's fault.'

I'm touched at Will's attempt to defend me. Then a thought occurs.

'Hang on, Mum, is that why you argued on the day Dad died? About Jack and the money?'

Mum doesn't respond. Instead she looks up at Jack. He gives an almost imperceptible shake of the head.

A voice comes back to me. The shouting. The doors slamming. A second male voice, raised above Dad's. More doors slamming. An engine starting outside.

'You were there,' I say to Jack. A statement, not a question.

Both he and Mum sag.

'The night Dad died. The voices I heard, the arguments, why were you there, Jack?'

Will is watching him now. 'Dad?' he says gently.

32

Jack and Mum look at each other. A thousand memories seem to pass between them in that moment.

'Go on, Jack,' whispers Mum.

I can barely breathe, desperate to hear what secret they're hiding but terrified of what is to be revealed. I'm back in my childhood bed, fingers pressed against my ears, sheltering under my duvet as the storm rages outside and downstairs a different storm blows.

'I was there,' Jack says, 'the night your dad died. I was there.'

'Why?' This time it's Will, his voice sounds hoarse.

'I'd gone round to confront Fred. The day before me and Ruby had spent the whole day working out how much we were down. I'd invested all our money – emptied what was in our joint account, everything – even a nest egg from her folks.' He glances at Will, ashamed. 'That was meant to help you go to university, to follow your dreams.' Jack studies the palms of his hands, as if cradling something there. 'Your mum was against the idea, Will – said it seemed too good to be true. Over a few too many pints one night Fred persuaded me. We felt brave, daring. I fantasised about doubling, even tripling the money, playing over and over in my head the moment I'd tell your mum we were rich. She'd be cross I'd lied but only for a second – once she realised how well I'd done, what a hero I was.'

Will sighs and rubs at his eyes.

'Of course it didn't go to plan. I had to tell her I'd deceived her and lost the money. We were going to be scraping by for the rest of our lives. No holidays, no meals out, no treats. We'd be forever nose to the grindstone just to survive.'

'You already knew it'd gone wrong though, Jack,' says Mum. 'Why come round and confront him like that? We were going under too. I was struggling to cope – we had enough on our plate.'

'Yeah you had enough in your glass too I seem to remember, Sandra?'

Her face hardens. 'I'll have you know I have not touched a drop of alcohol for thirty years. Lord knows I could do with a drink now though. Don't try to shame me for my drink issues, Jack. Yes I'd been drinking that day, I was stressed about our future. You coming round shouting your mouth off was what triggered everything that came after.'

'Triggered what?' I say, almost to myself.

'I had to come and see your dad,' Jack says in a whisper. 'I wanted to look him in the eye when I told him. That thanks to his advice, his persuading, my family's life was ruined. My son would probably never go to university and escape this life of graft. And...'

He pauses. His eyes go glassy with tears.

'Go on,' Will says gently. I feel like the whole room is holding its breath.

Jack studies the floor. 'We lost our daughter because of it. The baby we were told time and time again we'd never have. Then your mum became pregnant and the same doctors said, "Well, nature sometimes finds a way."'

'A sister?' Will breathes.

'Aye, lad,' says Jack. 'Your mum could still hide her little bump from you and everyone else under baggy clothes 'cos we didn't dare get our hopes up too much. We thought by six months along we'd be OK. The stress of losing everything was too much though, your mum collapsed that morning and your little sister arrived too soon to save.'

The kitchen is deathly quiet. Jack seems to have aged years in the last few minutes. He takes a jagged breath. 'We had time with her, the nurses wrapped her in a yellow blanket. She was perfect, like a little doll.' He rubs his eyes roughly. 'I was in a state. I drove round to Thistlefold straight from the hospital. I was so angry at the world. And at your dad. I wanted to strangle the life from him. Pulverise him. Destroy his life like he'd destroyed mine.' White spittle has collected at the corner of Jack's mouth and his eyes narrow as he looks to Mum.

'What did you do?' I say. I look to each of them in turn.

Will stands and walks to the window, holding on to the edge of the sink for support. His little sister didn't make it because of some stupid decisions made by two stupid men.

Jack looks up into my eyes. 'I pulled into the yard and she was out there.' He nods to Mum. 'Clearly drunk. She was just walking through the rain in her slippers. I shouted her name but she ignored me.'

Mum looks away embarrassed, the night's events no doubt coming back to her.

'Your dad was surprised to see me. I told him he was a murderer. We argued – we were shouting, going round in circles, him refusing to accept responsibility. The cheek of it. But I wouldn't have signed on the line without Fred's persuasion and reassurance. I wouldn't.' He looks imploringly at Will.

It's there in my memory. The angry male voices. The shouting stops. The phone is trilling in the kitchen. It rings and rings. It's so loud. Do I dare go down? No. I stay where I am. The ringing stops. Doors slam. Thunder rumbles above as the rain hammers on my little bedroom window.

'The phone rang?' I say now and Mum snaps her head up, like a shop mannequin suddenly brought to life.

'Aye,' says Jack, 'it was a neighbour. The cows were out. Your dad said he'd have to go. I wouldn't let him.'

'Why?'

'What, dash off to his precious cows? How dare he – when I was talking about my dead child?' He's almost shouting now. Will, still standing by the sink, dips his chin low onto his chest, blows out a breath as if he's been submerged. 'He grabbed his car keys and I tried to stop him. I threw myself at him, caught him across the eye and tackled him to the ground. I just wanted him to stay and have enough respect to listen to me. I lobbed the keys into the fire as we fell. It was a fluke. They went straight in. He grabbed a poker and I thought for a second he was going to come at me with it but he didn't. He raked the coals like a madman, hot cinders flying everywhere, but the keys were gone. He was holding his eye, he was in a state, he grabbed your mum's car keys and ran out.'

I see the whole scene play out. The keys landing on the chimney collar, Dad holding his face, staggering to the car. 'How could he drive properly, he might've been concussed.' I look to my mum. 'Why didn't you tell me all this? Why have I been left to wonder all these years? Someone played a part in my dad's death and you've never thought to tell me?'

Mum meets my gaze. She looks resigned. She shakes her head.

'Why didn't you stop him, Mum? Where were you when all this was happening? Drunk, in your slippers out in the storm – where were you?'

She takes a breath, her throat making a shallow death rattle. Jack watches her, his eyes wide.

She mumbles a response.

'What?' I say.

Louder now, she replies clear as a bell, 'Up at the cattle pens.'

It takes me a second.

The final pieces slide together with a sickening thud. She let out Dad's cattle. She's the reason he was out there in the rain, driving through the storm in a panic, squinting through an injured eye in a crappy little runaround.

'Why?' I breathe.

Her face is grey, her wrinkles deep in the low light of the kitchen. 'I was angry, Jose. Angry at the mess he'd got us into. I just wanted to hurt him and the only way was through his beloved cattle. Before I knew what I was doing I'd swung open the gates and shoo'ed them out on to the lane. I just wanted him to have a miserable night out in the rain rounding up cattle. I didn't know things would... go so wrong.'

I can't stay in the kitchen a second longer, I feel like I'm underwater. I try to speak but my head is rushing, the room tips as I stand. I have to get away from this pair.

'No wait, Jose, please,' Mum shouts.

I stagger outside. It's raining. Of course it is. The sort of rain that soaks you within seconds. I stumble through the sheets of grey water towards the warm glow of the pens and grab on to the gate for support. The sobs come then, ripping through my body. The heifers eye me curiously from where they lie on their straw beds, blinking slowly. I weep for the dad I lost and for the life that I left behind. I weep for the wasted years of guilt and bitterness and the repercussions for both families. I weep for Will, his mum and the lost little girl.

I rest my head on the cool metal of the gate and let the sobs subside. As the rain starts to ease so does my breathing. I rest a while listening to my own breaths and the sound of Penny's snuffling in the next-door pen. I feel an arm around my shoulder then. It gently pulls me close and holds me steady. I feel instantly warm, suddenly safe. It is Will.

33

I'm gifted a split second of blissful ignorance before my world crashes around me again as I recall the secrets revealed three days ago.

I'm in bed but can't really remember getting here.

I glance at the empty wine glass on the bedside table and feel shame that another night of drinking ended with someone – Chloe? Ruth? – putting me to bed.

I need to pull myself together. This grief, this anger, I have to let it go or it will tighten its grip on me. I don't want my daughter seeing me drunk and crying for a fourth night. I know better than anyone how horrible that is. I have a hot shower but my skin feels papery and sensitive to the touch.

My teeth are chattering as I pull on a hoodie. When Will held me in the rain that night then hugged me goodbye, it felt kind of final. As if the chasm that had opened up now separated us.

Mum had left on the Sunday morning and I've not spoken to her since. Ruth slipped into my room and asked if I'd seen Mum's car key and I'd pointed at my fleece. She slid the keys from the pocket silently like she was robbing a corpse. Mum murmured through the door, 'I'm here when you're ready to talk. I'm going to head back home.' There was no protest from me. I wanted nothing more than for her to leave.

Since then Ruth and Chloe haven't left my side. I've gone to call Will a few times but couldn't bring myself to.

I feel wretched for Will and his family. The guilt is unbearable – me returning to Thistlefold has unleashed a whole world of pain on him.

My anger towards Jack has withered over the three nights going round in circles with Ruth as I worked through bottle after bottle of wine. It's hard to remain furious about a tussle that resulted in some keys being lost in a freak event forty years before. Besides, I think Jack had every right to thump my dad that night.

My feelings about Dad now? I don't know where to start. He's always been my hero, but he caused such heartache with his get-rich schemes.

As for Mum? She claims she only meant for Dad to spend a rotten night getting drenched trying to fetch his cattle. She envisaged the worst that would happen would be a stinking cold. Instead, it led to Dad lying cold on a slab hours later. I think ironically I will eventually forgive her for that before I can make peace with the consequences of that night: a childhood wrecked by her self-hatred and guilt.

In the kitchen Doris is getting cuddles from Chloe, who is curled up with a coffee in the squishy armchair under the window.

I pour myself a mug and peer at my daughter from under my pulled-up hood.

'How are you feeling?' she asks gently. Not a trace of judgement in her voice. What did I ever do to deserve such a lovely daughter?

'I'm OK. I'm sorry.' My voice quivers and I sigh. 'I'm done. No more drinking.'

She gives me a little smile and sips her coffee. Doris watches me.

'Where's Ruth?' I ask.

'She's popped to the village, we were running low on supplies.'

Oh god. I bet the streets are still trembling with the aftershocks of all the revelations.

I eat some toast and feel a tiny bit better. For the first time in days the rain has finally eased and the sun is peeping out from behind the clouds.

The next few days trundle by. Once I'd reassured Chloe I would be OK and promised to call her the second I wasn't, she left with Ruth, both of them piling into Beth's little car and bumping off down the lane to catch their trains.

The good thing about a farm is that it needs you, you're the cog that makes everything turn. I'd allowed myself a few days to lick my wounds and Chloe and Ruth had muddled through helping feed the heifers and looking after Penny and the piglets, but now there is work to catch up on.

The vet visits to vaccinate and help ear tag all the piglets and I overcome my squeamishness as I don't want to seem soppy. The first dull click as I squeeze the metal instrument, pierce the soft pink flesh with the yellow plastic tag, makes my stomach roll but I keep going and by the end, as the vet roars off down the lane I feel like I've passed a farming milestone. I want to call Will to show off, my first instinct is still to call him for approval.

I go to call him or message him a few times a day, then something always stops me. I think about his twinkly eyes, his smile. Then I think about the harm my family did to his a generation ago; will things ever be the same between us? Instead I make do with sending him a photo of Nicola the Piggola with her new ear tag glaring displeased into the camera. He sends a laughing emoji and a thumbs-up emoji. Then my phone buzzes again. 'Fancy a brew?'

As twilight starts to fall I switch on the main lights in the barn. I've been reorganising the bales and despite the light frost on the fields making everything look Christmassy, I'm boiling hot. I strip off my fleece and then my padded gilet, whose pockets are filled with fencing nails, my penknife and some twine. Proper

farmer's pockets these days. I sweep the barn floor till the concrete is bare and dust free, though I know it will be carpeted in
loose straw and hay within hours. Still, it feels good. I'm down to
only a bobble hat and vest top. I'm fitter these days without trying, my arms toned not from yoga or body pump classes but from
manual labour. I feel strong and capable. It's a good feeling, as if
I've pushed through the pain and staggered out the other side.
This place, this farm, despite the heartbreak it witnessed decades
ago and days ago feels more like my home than ever. Whatever
happens with Mum, with Will, I know I will remain here. My
future is right here on this land. I can't imagine being anywhere
else. I resolve to speak to Jonathan at Martingale's estate agent's
in the New Year and start the ball rolling. I make this decision
standing in the middle of a dusty barn and weirdly it doesn't feel
that momentous. It feels obvious. I think deep down I've always
known I'd spend the rest of my days here, from that first moment
Fay and I stumbled upon this land.

No champagne corks popping in celebration, instead I roll my
overalls down into trousers and brace my core as I attempt to sweep
away the cobwebs slung high up across the rafters, swinging the
unwieldy brush as high as I can like a metronome.

'Missed a bit.' I'm concentrating so much that the voice makes
me drop the brush and I yelp, jumping out of the way as it clatters
to the floor. I turn to see Will.

'Oops,' he says cringing, 'sorry.'

'It's you,' I say.

'Yes. At least I think it is.' He looks down at himself as if to check.
I smile at the old joke. He's wearing jeans and a wax jacket.

'You look knackered,' I say. God is that the best I can do? His face
falls a fraction. 'Not that I can talk,' I babble on. 'I look knackered
and probably insane.' I point to my bobble hat to illustrate my point.
My hair is swept up inside it away from the clouds of dust and dirt.

He looks at me for a moment and his face softens into a smile. 'I've missed you,' he says, then quickly adds, 'I've missed our chats, missed hanging out, missed your... unique fashion sense.' I raise my hand to gently primp invisible curls. He laughs. My stomach flips.

'Yeah, I've missed you too.' Standing still I start to feel cold and grab my fleece off the bales. 'Brew?'

'Aye go on then.'

In the kitchen Doris wakes from her snooze in the basket by the AGA and relocates to Will's lap.

'Seems I'm not the only one who missed you.' I start to make coffee.

'What a mess, eh?' he says eventually.

'Yup.' I nod.

My phone buzzes and I see it's Fay trying to FaceTime me. I last spoke to her drunk and sad on Tuesday night and although we've been texting since, I know she'll worry if I don't pick up.

'Sorry – do you mind?' Will shakes his head and I grab my iPad and open it to see a tousle-haired Fay holding a mug of coffee and smiling expectantly.

'Ah look at you!' she says, beaming. 'You're all ruddy cheeked, like a proper farmer now.'

'Actually,' I say, 'there's an actual, proper farmer here. Will's just popped by. This is Fay, my bestest friend in the world and this –' I spin the iPad so he's in view – 'is Will.'

'Well hello, Will,' says Fay, her voice all mischievous. 'I've heard a lot about you.'

'Yeah, I bet you have.' He smiles at the screen. 'Sorry about that. Nice to meet you. Josie has told me all about you two.'

The three of us chat for a bit and it quickly becomes clear Fay is just checking up on me. It's also pretty clear she approves of Will, her voice has taken on an uncharacteristically twinkly pitch. It's mid-morning over there and she's off to meet pals for brunch.

'Before I leave you two lovebirds,' I feel my cheeks burn, 'have you thought about plans yet?' she asks.

'Pans?' I say.

'Plans. For Christmas.'

'Err... no,' I say, then a thought occurs and I gasp. 'Why, are you coming over?'

'I wish,' Fay says. 'Can't afford it sadly; you two are welcome here for a traditional Boston Christmas, ice-skating, their famous hot chocolate...'

I feel suddenly coy, Fay talking about us as if we're a couple when the repairs haven't even started on our faltered budding romance. I've kept my eyes glued to the screen the whole conversation so Will can't see my pink cheeks.

'Sounds dreamy but I think three Herefords, some pigs, a cat and an entire dairy herd would have something to say about that,' I say, 'not to mention the sheep.'

After we say our goodbyes to Fay I pour us both some coffee and we go through to the lounge. The fire is lit, which always feels the height of decadence during the day but it is nearly Christmas after all. The room is toasty and we sit on either end of the sofa. I can't help staring at Will's feet – he's taken off his mucky wellies at the door and seeing his navy ribbed socks feels weirdly intimate. God knows what I'd do if I ever saw him naked – probably combust. I blush at the thought and look away from his feet and into the flames. The same fire where the drama between our families reached its dramatic climax all those years ago.

'I'm sorry about your sister,' I say.

He gives a small shrug. 'It was a long time ago. Hard to feel sad about someone I never even knew about. Weird though. She would've been forty now. I do feel bad for what Mum and Dad went through though.'

'I'm sorry, it's awful. And the uni thing—'

He cuts me off. 'Josie, stop apologising. You were a little girl when all this happened. It has nothing to do with you, with us.' He really holds my gaze as he says 'us' and I fear my thumbs might drop off with longing. Those eyes. Jesus wept. He clears his throat. 'So,' he says, 'be honest with me if you think this is a terrible idea, I won't be offended.'

'Go on.' My heart is thumping.

'Christmas. At mine. With my dad and your mum. And Chloe. Maybe Ruth? Why not?'

'Why not?' I say, incredulous. I can only think of a dozen reasons why not but I stay quiet.

'The whole gang. Back together,' he says in a mock American accent.

I let out a small laugh that is more of a squeak. 'Really?'

'Really.' He nods.

'You make it sound like a rock band reuniting or a scout jamboree but... you *do* remember what just happened with our families or have you banged your head on your silo?'

He pushes his hair back off his forehead and nods earnestly. God, stop looking so damn handsome. 'I know it sounds mad, Josie, but I think the only way to fix all this bad feeling is to chuck everyone together in the same room with loads of food and booze. What can go wrong?'

I look at the little crinkle under his eyes and want to lick it. Must concentrate.

'I'm just not sure what Chloe's up to. Or Ruth.'

'It's next week you know?'

'Shit,' I say, 'it is. It's sneaked up, eh? Thing is, I kinda wanted my first Christmas at Thistledown to be... well, here.' I look around the room. He sighs and looks defeated. God he's even cute when he's downcast dammit. What the hell? What's the worst that can happen, apart from we ruin Christmas *and* wreck both our families? 'I mean, you're welcome up here, you and your dad of course,' I offer.

I must be bloody mad. 'I don't actually have a turkey yet but you're welcome to join us for whatever we can rustle up.'

'OK, I'll do you a deal.' He tickles Doris under her chin as he speaks. 'Reckon I can get my hands on a decent-sized turkey, I will roast it and bring it up and you take care of the trimmings?'

I falter. 'Do we really want to put ourselves through this? Can't we have pot noodles and a nice Merlot, just me and you?' I feel bold, the 'me and you' tripping off my tongue.

He moves closer on the sofa, leans forward towards me. 'Because Christmas is about family and friendship and – ' I feel giddy at his sudden proximity. The coffee on his breath smells rich and sweet – 'coming together.'

I struggle to stifle a giggle as his face moves closer. He's about to kiss me. This time it's actually happening. We both lean in together and then I feel it, a warmth spreading through my crotch. A heat that feels... a little too hot and, hang on, wet. We realise at the same time as does Doris that Will's coffee cup has tipped pouring its contents in both our laps and all over her. Doris leaps up, her cream and brown fur sodden on one side. As she makes her escape her head connects with the underside of the mug, knocking the remaining dregs on to Will's top.

'Oh my god.' I stand up gingerly, the crotch of my jeans is sopping wet and so is Will's. A pool of coffee remains on the sofa cushion, slowly sinking in.

'I'll get a cloth,' Will says and dashes into the kitchen.

Doris, most unimpressed, resettles in front of the fire and starts to lick herself dry, all the while glaring at me. The moment has passed though it takes all my willpower not to follow him into the kitchen and finish what we nearly started. Will I ever get to kiss Will Hockley? One day, I smile to myself. Maybe I should write to Santa or make a bloody Christmas list. It's all I want. My phone buzzes. It is Ruth, checking up on me.

*

Christmas Eve morning rolls around and I can hear Chloe gently snoring next door; I poured her into bed past midnight after we'd been to GG's special Christmas quiz at The Three Keys. I took a lot of persuading but eventually Will and Chloe cajoled me into it. I was expecting a few whispers as we walked in but no one paid much notice. Alex even defected from her team to join Beth's and they flanked me on either side just in case any busybodies approached. None did. Seems we were old news already. Will joined us too but Chloe binned us off in favour of some younger people, students home from uni for Christmas. She took quite a shine to a lad whose parents have a large pig farm over Robbworth; I get the feeling she might be coming to stay at mine more and more.

In the car on the way home she drunkenly informed us that she'd been teaching the barman how to make cocktails and she'd had 'Three screaming orgasms' to which Ruth replied, 'I should be so lucky.'

Ruth is staying with us and happily Mary is joining us for Christmas Day. Then we're all off to a buffet and party at Shearness on Boxing Day. Mum is arriving later on today. I'm braced but I feel surprisingly calm. We've spoken on the phone a couple of times and she seems different; like her shoulders have lowered. Lugging the burden of those secrets around must've been exhausting. No more secrets, no more dwelling on the past; as we head towards a new year I want to think only of the future, my future on the farm.

Mum says she's looking forward to seeing her granddaughter for Christmas before Chloe heads off to Brighton for New Year's Eve. Chloe's already seen her dad to exchange presents – they did it early as James and Ella are spending Christmas in Oman. Course they are, while I freeze my nips off here; still, I wouldn't swap it for the world.

I feed up in the cold and crisp early morning. There's a sharp breeze blowing that could slice through a stale loaf and I pull my woolly hat low. I hear a rumble in the distance and know it is my potato delivery man. I smile to myself. Will's quad bike comes to a stop outside the cattle pens and I lean on Penny's gate. The pig looks up from her munching to have a nosy. She, like all the animals on the farm (me included) is sweet on Will.

'I come bearing spuds,' he says, holding up a large carrier bag. 'Late crop beauties freshly harvested especially for you.'

'Lovely! Thank you.' I smile 'Did you grapple them from the ground with your bare hands?'

'Summat like that. Jim over on Blackstones still owed me a few bags after I helped him fix his baler.'

'Right.' I nod, smiling. The tip of his nose and his lips are pink from the cold. He clears his throat and looks serious.

'I wanted to come and see you before the Christmas madness starts.'

Oh God. Is he about to launch into a 'It's not you it's me' speech? Has he got cold feet? Maybe he's right, maybe it'd never work with our families' history.

'I wanted to get you by yourself.'

'Right.' I'm genuinely worried my heart is going to explode out of my chest and land in Penny's feed trough. Get it over with Will.

'Look, that night at the party, you know I was going to kiss you?'

'Yes, I think I remember.'

He smiles bashfully. 'Ha. And the other day, on the sofa?'

'How could I forget? Doubt Doris will either.' I'm waffling now.

'Well I wonder if we could try again?'

Oh. Hello. I can't look into his eyes. Or at his mouth; it's too much. I focus instead on his nose.

'A kiss?' I ask his nose. My voice cracks a little.

'Yes.'

'Here? Now?' This slow build-up, just talking about it in such a practical manner like we're organising a straw delivery is making my internal organs clench in an alarming manner. He nods and takes a small step closer.

'Yes. Please. I'd like that,' I whisper.

I move closer to him, I'm gripping the top bar of Penny's gate, otherwise I might faint. I wish I wasn't wearing a manky bobble hat. I tilt my face up to his. He's so tall. I look into his eyes now, the dark blue of a dozen clichés – a swirly ocean, a winter's dusk, a peacock's undercarriage. God I wish I could mute my internal dialogue, just for a second.

He leans closer, his breath smells minty, did he brush his teeth before setting off to woo me with spuds?

It's happening at last. We lean in closer, I see the darkness of the long lashes as his eyes close. Our lips meet. His mouth is soft and warm, his kiss starts sweet and gentle but becomes more urgent. I return the pressure, I feel lightheaded like I'm on a swing, floating through the air, my stomach flipping.

I feel something firm nudge urgently against my thigh. Will reaches down and gently pushes Penny's pink bristly snout away.

We smile as we continue to kiss. Nothing's going to stop us this time.

I reach a hand up to touch his hair, his cheek, to make sure this is real, that this is actually happening at last, that I got my Christmas wish after all.

We are sitting under an umbrella on the bench overlooking Dad's grave. It is October, the fortieth anniversary of Dad's death, ten months since the truth was revealed about the day my dad died and the events leading up to it.

We have placed sunflowers by the headstone.

Mum takes my hand gently in hers. We do not need to speak.

All the talking has been done. The recriminations, the tears. The late-night phone calls, raking over the past. Mum, to her credit, has never refused to answer my questions come day or night. The dam finally burst and she has succumbed to the relief of opening up. We have talked ourselves dry but through the pain has come a new beginning for us and I am starting to make peace with the horror of my teenage years at the mercy of Mum.

I hear footsteps and turn, it is Will. He is carrying a plastic bag. His hair is damp from the light rain that's just subsided. I put down the brolly. By his side is his loyal collie Fliss and one of her pups who bounds along on a lead by his side. On spotting them, my own pup leaps up from between my knees, straining at the leash desperate to go and play with her sibling. Soon they are a wriggling mass of choc-chip fluff.

I stand and walk to meet Will on the path and we hug. 'It's nice that you came,' I say.

'Course,' he replies, pulling me close and kissing me full on the mouth. I feel my body become light as air and a giddiness momentarily overcomes me. Surely it's blasphemous to feel aroused in a churchyard?

Mum slips from her daydream and turns to look at us, smiling. She is pleased Will and I have grown so close, she says she can see how happy I am.

'How are you feeling?' he asks now.

'Excited.'

'Scared?'

'Nah, not a bit,' I say.

'Good.' He kisses me again. 'I'm gonna roast a chicken for tea later to celebrate. Dad's even attempted to make a cake. He bloody loves you now, eh?'

'Don't be jealous.'

'I'm not. Though I hope I've no reason to be?'

I nudge him in the ribs. 'Don't even joke about it, we've had enough drama in our families, we don't need another plot twist.'

Turns out living on next-door farms is pretty handy for a relationship; some days I can't believe that the hot neighbour who roared over my field a year ago is all mine. Will feels the same, insists he's 'punching above his weight' and says all his friends say the same, too often for his liking.

Most days he pops over on his quad bike or I go to his on mine, a birthday present to me from James, at Chloe's suggestion. Good old James, again thoughtful and a teeny bit flash.

Divorce proceedings have started, it'll take a couple of years but we're in no rush. James has been brilliant about the London house, we didn't even need to put it on the market; as promised we gave the two Chrises first refusal and they snatched our hands off. I get updates from Crab – photos of him in a yellow hard hat as the works pick up pace knocking the two houses together. I'm glad they got their dream, just like I got mine.

Chloe is living with me now, sourcing wool for her fledgling eco knitwear business from local farmers, including from Will. Even I am in the family firm, helping with the accounts, fundraising from investors – my old banking skills coming in handy at last for 'Wylde Wool'. I, of course, am thrilled she's using her grandad's name.

Fay returned in August as promised after her year placement in Boston; she was only visiting though, wanted me to meet her scientist fiancé Todd, whose dazzling smile and gym bunny bod belie his impressive brain. The pair of them seem perfect together, Todd can barely take his eyes off Fay and she is genuinely happier than I've ever seen her. They're planning their wedding in the States; we'll all be going over for it.

Ruth now lives only an hour away, her business has evolved from Hound Stretchers to 'In the Dog House' holiday kennels within the grounds of Shearness. She and Mary are making a go of things despite the latter being a cat person. They both come over at least once a month for a Sunday roast with us all. Will, I've discovered, is not only drop-dead gorgeous but a fine maker of Yorkshire puddings. Just when I think I couldn't love him any more...

Yesterday I met with Jonathan and the lawyers representing the Earl of Lampston who owns most of Howlesden. I finally signed on the dotted line after months of paperwork and now own Thistledown Farm. A rare move for the earl but he remembers Dad fondly and is also a fan of rural eco businesses, so is very impressed with Wylde Wool. Thank you, Chloe.

I get on well with Jonathan now after our shaky start. He's been a big support over the last few months. Turns out Jonathan Snr worked at the bank where Dad set up his life insurance – after a bit of digging the bank found their record of it. The payout, though not life-changing, was enough for me to buy my own second-hand little tractor and for Will to take on an extra farmhand so he could study for a degree in Agricultural Innovation. He started in September and loves it. He puts up with my bad jokes about joss sticks and pints of snakebite now he's a student, in return for me zipping over to help Jack and the new lass with the afternoon milking when Will's at college.

I had to stay at Thistlefold of course. I made that decision standing in a dusty barn back in December. Besides, all three heifers are in calf, due any day, I could hardly move them back to London with me.

Two more heifers and a young bull arrive next week from a farm over in Yorkshire. Will came with me to check them out but I did all the talking and got a good deal. He said afterwards it's sexy when I barter. Daft bugger.

I kept Penny and Nicola the Piggola, of course, as well as two more sows and a hog. The rest of the litter went to market though I've still not eaten bacon since the day they were born.

I'm also now the proud owner of twenty Sussex hens – plump and white with black speckled collars – and a very dashing if overly vocal cockerel. Good job I get on well with the neighbours. I'm contemplating eventually opening a small shop on my land selling my produce.

Every week I learn something new about farming and most days I sense Dad by my side looking out for me.

I am home now. I have family here and I have friends in the village. Beth and Alex are my besties, though Fay will forever be queen bee.

Oh and of course I have Will too. We are in love, though we joke that he should never dare ask me to choose between him and Penny, the real love of my life.

Mum, Will and I sit on the bench in comfortable silence and contemplate Dad's grave. The sky brightens, the sun casting a welcome warmth over the churchyard. I look up to the heavens and spot a faint rainbow appearing on the horizon and nod, my heart fit to burst. Will reaches into the bag and pulls out two mini bottles of prosecco for us and one of lemonade for Mum.

'A toast, to family and to you, Farmer Josie. You've done your dad proud.'

'Hear, hear,' says Mum.

'And,' I add as I look into Will's blue eyes that crinkle as he returns my smile, 'to love.'

We clink the bottles together and sip our drinks, not thinking of the past or even the future, just of the now.

Acknowledgements

This book wouldn't exist without help from a lot of excellent people:

Firstly my editor, Hannah Black, at Hodder. When the big fella with the beard (yes, Brian Blessed) was giving out patience, kindness and sparkling wit she was definitely at the very front of the queue. Hannah, thanks so much for not binning me off when I sulk and cry and sulk some more before realising you're right about everything and then doing what you gently suggested in the first place. For the next book I'm really hoping I can cut out the middle bit but I'm not optimistic. Many thanks also to Tom Atkins, Emma Knight, Vicky Palmer, Katy Aries and Al Oliver at Hodder.

Thanks to Antonia Hodgson, who came on board with some great guidance and suggestions and instead had to endure an excruciating Zoom with an insecure middle-aged woman who'd regressed to a scowling teen. Apologies. You too were right and I'm so grateful for your help.

Thank you to Mel Rockcliffe at YMU: agent, good friend and chief cheerleader over the past twenty-eight years. Love you, Mel. Plus Joe Hockley for his enthusiasm for work and not shouting when I'm late for meetings 'cos I've been riding my pony (not a euphemism).

Talking of ponies, thanks to Elaine Pearce, my riding coach; without her my horse Nelly would regularly have been getting fat in a field while I hunched over my laptop working on this book, so thank you for schooling Nelly, and also for my lessons: forty-five minutes where I escaped thinking about plots or pacing and instead concentrated on whether my shoulders were too tight.

Thank you to Nelly (look, they're my acknowledgements, I can thank a horse if I fancy) for being the best four-hoofed pal a gal could wish for and for helping me to take a breath and appreciate the skyline.

Thank you Emily Witt, one of my loveliest friends who rather handily is also a GP and gave great guidance on some of the medical issues touched on in the book.

For the cattle and farming advice, thank to Dumfries and Galloway community legend Richard Oxley, my *Love in the Countryside* pal and farmer.

Thank you to my lovely friend, the brilliant vet, television presenter and best-selling author James Greenwood for his veterinary expertise.

Huge thanks to chimney sweep extraordinaire Paul Clarke of Soot-busters for answering all my random sweeping questions and gifting me some great anecdotes about the extraordinary things found up chimneys!

A huge thank you to my friends who make me laugh and power me up with their love: my BFF Clare Hamilton and the remarkable Five Go French crew, Megan Carver, Eleanor Mark, Anna Richards and Emily Bernstein. Plus Annie Macmanus for always reading the proof immediately and being so ruddy encouraging. I'm grateful to have such awesome women in my corner. Love you all.

Megan actually gets two mentions, as she is the genius behind the award-winning Carver PR; she, along with Jacob, Lara and the rest of the team, works so hard to help me shout from the rooftops about my books. Thank you.

Thank you to Amanda Ross of Cactus TV, creator and queen of BBC Two's *Between the Covers*, for reigniting my love of reading by choosing such extraordinary books over the past seven (and counting) series.

Big-ups to my Radio 2 teatime team and the excellent listeners. When I occasionally arrive at the studio pale and subdued after a solitary morning wrestling with words, your hilarious input and funny tales never fail to put a whacking big smile on my face every weekday from 4 p.m. (subtle plug there).

Thanks to my Hereford farmer dad Len for inspiring the story (the farming childhood, not the traumatic bits luckily), and my mum Jackie for officially being a brilliant mum and proof-reader. Please note, my mum is very much NOT the inspiration for Sandra, thank gawd.

Love to my siblings Robert, Dorothy and Yvonne for always looking out for me, and special mention for David who is always in our hearts. I will for ever be the youngest of five.

I'd like to take this opportunity to reassure my husband Ben that currently I have no plans to divorce him and run off to take over a farm. The reason for this is that he's my soul mate and best friend and I love him very much. (Though maybe one day we'll move to a place with a paddock, babe... I'll keep on with that one.)

Thanks to my children for making me laugh every single day, for giving the best hugs and for understanding that I'm often busy. I love you so much and I'm so proud of you Lola, Isaac and Renee.